Balika 1

batika Badhu

Balika Badhu

A Representative Anthology of Bengali Short Stories

Translated
by
Monish Ranjan Chatterjee

Rupa & Co

Copyright © Monish Ranjan Chatterjee 2002

First in Rupa Paperback 2002
Fifth Impression 2011

Published by
Rupa Publications India Pvt. Ltd.
7/16, Ansari Road, Daryaganj,
New Delhi 110 002

Sales Centres:

Allahabad Bengaluru Chennai
Hyderabad Jaipur Kathmandu
Kolkata Mumbai

Typeset by
Mindways Design
1410 Chiranjiv Tower
43 Nehru Place
New Delhi 110 019

Printed in India by
Saurabh Printers Pvt. Ltd.
A-16 Sector-IV
Noida 201 301

In loving and respectful memory of:

Anima Mukherjee (Phoolpishi)
—tobu mone rekho

Shibapriya Mukherjee (Phoolpishemashai)
—passionately Bengali

Apurbanath Banerjee (Mejopishemashai)
—a bygone age of action and service

Pijush Kanti Sarkar (Pijush-da)
—the quest to find the *voice*

Haradhan Chakroborty (Mamadadu)
—simplicity, the noblest human virtue

And for:

Adrian Korpel
—scientist, scholar and renaissance man *par excellence*

Mamata Mukherjee (Didi)
—compassion true to her name

Sharmila Chatterjee (Boudi)
—a vibrant specimen of feminine energy

Nilima Bhattacharjee (Pishimani)
—ami kyamono koriya janabo amar juralo hriday

Contents

Translator's Preface

This project, which began with the desire to render into English a rather long tale by Bimal Kar about five years ago, eventually grew into a considerably more extended compilation of Bengali short stories by ten of the most well-known practitioners of that art since the heyday of Rabindranath Tagore. The collection is limited in many ways, not the least of which being that no woman writer has been included, and that it contains only a baker's dozen stories (if we count Bonophool's micro-stories collectively as one)—a number pitifully small considering the vast and prolific field of authors and stories a translator has at his or her disposal. I have attempted to explain my rationale for my intent and selections in the introductory essay.

Since beginning this project, I have sustained a number of personal losses, and what makes the completion of it particularly poignant for me is that the individuals who have left my world were almost unanimously supportive of my feeble efforts at upholding Bengal's contributions to the literary and cultural heritage of the world. My work continues, and my only solace is that I had come to know these kind people with extraordinary wisdom and humility, and that they had extended to me a generosity and affection that exceeded by far my capacity to reciprocate or demonstrate my worthiness.

For their support and encouragement, I must sincerely thank my friend and colleague Nikolaos Bourbakis, and another friend and mentor, Arindam Purkayastha—two individuals with unlimited optimism and uncommon goodness of heart. A special note of thanks is also due to a dear friend, Sandeep Mitra, whose enthusiastic and well-reasoned commitment to preserving and enhancing the history and culture of India is only matched by his genuine interest in all aspects of human civilization.

Finally, let me close this prologue by expressing the hope that my young son and daughter, growing up in a place separated by continents from the land of their parents' birth, may develop an active interest in the history, aspirations and achievements of India and Bengal, and attempt to bring those far-flung outposts of high civilization closer to the rest of the world—a world increasingly interconnected by commerce and communication, yet still so far apart, at times, in spirit and goodwill.

Introduction

Measured even by the standards of excellence achieved by Bengali literature in the past one hundred and fifty years, covering such diverse areas as poetry, fiction, drama, suspense, crime, *belles-lettres*, and historical and psychological novels, the short story as a literary genre stands apart in a class of its own. Several selected anthologies of short stories published in Bengali in the last two decades of the twentieth century emphasize two principal factors: firstly that the editors had to be virtually ruthless in limiting the collection, given the prodigious number of outstanding works in the pool from which the selections had to be made; and secondly that of all the components of Bengali literature, it is the short story which is truly and indisputably *world-class*. A two-volume anthology, entitled *Swa-Nirbachita Shreshtha Galpa* (Self-Selected Best Short Stories), edited by renowned authors Bibhutibhushan Mukhopadhyay and Samaresh Basu, and published by Model Publishing House, Calcutta, in 1987, attempted to cover one hundred years (with author's birth years in the range 1861-1960) of the short stories by bringing together a collection of, *self-selected best* short story contributed by each of one hundred and seventeen authors, including those widely acclaimed, as well as apparently less well-known. The anthology mentions that the selection was made with deference to *the noble tradition of the Bengali short story*, and to the creativity and variety represented by the collection. Another anthology, thematically compiled as the authors' *first acclaimed stories* (the title in Bengali was *Pratham Shara Jagano Galpa*), and edited by Ananda Bagchi, was published in 1989 by Pushpa Publishers, Calcutta. This anthology emphasizes the distinction between a *self-selected best story* collection, and a *first acclaimed stories* collection. While the former is picked out by the author alone, from the compendium of his or her works, reflecting individual taste or preference, the latter is based on viewing one's own work from the perspective of the wider readership, and finding a resonance within one's own mind. While such a collection may well be regarded as being driven by popular acceptance, and therefore become subject to reservations with regards to its literary merit, the anthology goes on to claim that *instant and spontaneous popularity* does have a measure of lasting value.

A slightly different class of selected short stories in Bengali, developed out of a tradition of *Sharadiya Special Issues* (published annually during the autumn *Durga Puja* festival in Bengal) of *Desh* and other literary magazines for well over fifty years, links the development of experimental and creative writing in Bengali with the proliferation of news and literary magazines. These two components have clearly been mutually supportive, and consequently short stories published in literary magazines have, within only a few decades, been accorded the same admiration otherwise reserved for classic works published by elite publishing houses.

During the 1970s, the National Book Trust of India took up a plan to publish short stories written in the constitutionally recognized regional languages of India, along with their translations in the other languages. This initiative resulted in a collection entitled *Ekushti Bangla Galpa* (Twenty One Bengali Short Stories), edited by Arun Kumar Mukhopadhyay, Professor of Bengali Language and Literature, University of Calcutta, and published by the Trust in 1977. Professor Mukhopadhyay has provided an excellent overview of the different periods, classifications and evolution of the Bengali short story. It turns out that the present collection of English translations, even if decidedly small in number and scope, does however contain samples from each of the key periods discussed by Professor Mukhopadhyay. The introduction presented here will draw generously from Professor Mukhopadhyay's commentary.

While selected anthologies in Bengali based on the works of a number of authors distributed over a certain period have started to appear more regularly in the last twenty-five years, it turns out that the history of collected or selected short stories by individual authors goes back a great deal further. Several of Rabindranath Tagore's short-story collections were published in the years 1895, 1912, 1916 and 1941, and his illustrious *Galpa Guchchha* (A Bouquet of Stories), was published posthumously in four parts in 1964. Likewise, collections of stories by Sarat Chandra Chattopadhyay were published as early as 1916.

By contrast, and with greater significance in relation to the present effort, English translations of Bengali short stories, taken as a whole, have been virtually non-existent. The same could in all likelihood be said of other works of Bengali literature, especially those of the last fifty years; however, that matter is beyond the scope of this discussion. With the exception of Rabindranath Tagore, Bibhuti Bhushan Bandyopadhyay, and a handful of others, few authors from Bengal have had their works competently represented, if at all, in English. Tagore was already known in English literary circles as a master story-teller as early as 1912, thanks to the efforts of painter William Rothenstein, *Modern Review* editor Ramananda Chattopadhyay, and others. Moreover, following the world-wide interest generated by his Nobel Prize in 1913 (which was won as the first *non-European* in the world to be so honoured), his short-stories, as much as his other works, began to be translated sporadically in many languages. With Bibhuti Bhushan, part of the impetus, no doubt, was generated by the runaway critical success of the film *Pather Panchali* by India's greatest director, Satyajit Ray. Thereafter, some of his writings appeared in translation under the auspices of UNESCO in the 1950s and '60s. More recently, a collection of Bibhuti Bhushan's short stories, translated by Phyllis Granoff, was published as part of the UNESCO Indian Series by Mosaic Press, Ontario, Canada, in 1984. The collection included the story *Puin Mancha*, which (as translated by the translator of this volume) is also included in the present anthology. Other writers who have received some attention include Mahasweta Devi (thanks in large part to the efforts of Gayatri Chakravarty Spivak in the United States), Satyajit Ray, and, to a much smaller extent, Premendra Mitra. The overwhelming absence of the best works of the greatest names in the post-Tagorean Bengali literature in the English language would readily explain why writers of Indian origin, writing in English *directly*, appear so much more successful in the international arena, and reach a much wider audience, compared with those writing in the regional vernacular within India. This leads us directly into the debate spurred by Salman Rushdie's famous (or infamous, depending on one's perspective) 1995 assertion that *"the best Indian writing in the past fifty years has been in English."* We shall return to this matter a little later.

According to Professor Mukhopadhyay, the first truly successful writer of the Bengali short story was, of course, Rabindranath Tagore. In his magical hands, the short story received its breath of life, and prospered in astonishing ways. His genius touched virtually every facet of the short story: romance, nature, social ills, philosophy, poetic subtlety, history, and humour. He made forays into each realm at will, and wrote almost uninterrupted for close to fifty years between 1890 through 1940.

Approximately contemporaneous with Tagore, we find Trailokyanath Mukhopadhyay, Prabhat Kumar Mukhopadhyay, Pramatha Choudhuri (who also wrote under the pseudonym Birbal), and, of course, the writer perhaps second only to Tagore in the areas of the psychological novel and the short story, Sarat Chandra Chattopadhyay (who also occasionally wrote under the pseudonyms Anupama Devi and Anila Devi). These gifted authors enriched the storehouse of Bengali short stories with a rich and varied harvest.

The period following Rabindranath and Sarat Chandra, which began approximately in the mid—to late 1920s, has represented well the evolution and experience of the Bengali psyche in the second half of the twentieth century. The period immediately following Rabindranath and Sarat Chandra is the well-known *Kallol* period. Chronologically, the period spans the years 1923 through 1939. Interestingly, the *Kallol* writers succeeded in pursuing their literary careers in relative peace and stability despite a worldwide economic recession and a growing opposition to English rule in India during that period. This period witnessed the emergence of acclaimed writers such as Tarashankar Bandyopadhyay, Achintya Kumar Sengupta, Premendra Mitra, Buddhadev Bose, Manish Ghatak (Yuvanashva), Prabodh Kumar Sanyal, and Bhabani Mukhopadhyay. In the pages of the literary magazines *Vichitra* and *Shanibarer Chithi* readers discovered other emerging high-impact writers such as Bibhuti Bhushan Bandyopadhyay, Manik Bandyopadhyay (the latter two, along with Tarashankar mentioned earlier, comprise the so-called Bandyopadhyay Triumvirate of Bengali literature), Annadashankar Ray, Bonophool, Bibhuti Bhushan Mukhopadhyay, Saradindu Bandopadhyay, Parimal Goswami, Premankur Atarthi, Sarojkumar Roychoudhury, Pramathanath Bishi, Ashapurna Devi, and others. The same period also produced accomplished writers of humour and comedy such as Parashuram (pseudonym of Rajshekhar Basu).

The generally prolific *Kallol* period was succeeded by an era (1939-1947) marked by the Second World War at the global level, and independence and partition of India at the domestic level. These roughly ten years represent a turning point in the history of Bengal and the Indian nation. These years were marred by a succession of mostly man-made disasters, including famines, air-raids, control and rationing of the food supply, military movements, an out-of-control black market, a decline in social lifestyles and values, economic crisis, degenerating moral and ethical values, communal riots, partition, and the relentless flow of refugees across the newly-created borders.

Those writers who had started their vocation during this period had developed an intimate awareness of the all-encompassing calamities of that age. The social environment of the age was filled with unrest and pent-up hostility. The result was a sharper edge to their perspectives, combined with a frayed temperament. The stories from this period are devoid of the *Kallolian* approach to romanticism, bohemian existence, and unrestricted love. The changes in Indian and Bengali society in this period were rapid and numerous. Established social norms were beginning to crumble, and were replaced by anomalous and aberrant behaviour patterns, people were afflicted with subtle psychological maladies, many were taking to deviant experimentation in search of newer thrills, many took unusual vows to face the challenges of life- such changes were unthinkable before the war. The Great War was also a great social earthquake. It shattered the ideas of civility, the protective shield of morality, the codes of honour inherent in familial bonds, and even the shadowy notions of compassion, devotion and religious reform. In the midst of the clang of falling icons, however, one can still discern the dreams of building a new society, and redoubled pledges to realize those dreams.

Authors whose works reflect the above changes include Subodh Ghosh, Satinath Bhaduri, Santosh Kumar Ghosh, Narayan Gangopadhyay, Narendranath Mitra, and Jyotirindra

Nandi. The list also includes some well-established *Kallol* figures, among whom Manik Bandyopadhyay, Achintya Kumar Sengupta, Bibhuti Bhushan Bandyopadhyay, Tarashankar Bandyopadhyay, Manoj Bose, Saroj Kumar Roychoudhury, Ashapurna Devi, Pramathanath Bishi, Parimal Goswami, Bonophool, Bani Roy, and Sushil Ghosh are especially noteworthy.

The post-*Kallol* decade was immediately followed by the blood-drenched independence, disfigured by partition. In its wake, there arrived waves of helpless, uprooted humanity—cross-border refugees further destabilized Indian society. Rising far above the words of hope and reconstruction delivered from the ramparts of the edifices of the newly independent state were the cries of the dispossessed and disinherited. In this disturbed and discontented age there appeared a new breed of storytellers—principal among these were Samaresh Basu, Bimal Kar, Ramapada Chowdhury, Syed Mujtaba Ali, Harinarayan Chattopadhyay, Pranatosh Ghatak, Sulekha Sanyal, Gour Kishore Ghosh, Mahasweta Devi, Kamal Kumar Majumdar and others. By all measures, the authors of this age are on the same wavelength as those immediately preceding them. The two groups are virtually indistinguishable. The majority of writers in the two groups were born in the years between 1916 through 1922. During the turbulent years in Calcutta and elsewhere in Bengal from the beginning of the Second World War, most of them had entered their youthful and psychologically most fertile years. Their active writing period spanned close to forty or more years, and during this time, they contributed to Bengali short stories with unabated vigour by chronicling the strange and curious changes in people's social and personal lives.

The second half of the twentieth century has witnessed another period of the Bengali short story. The authors representing this period were born approximately between 1930 and 1940. They are generally regarded as a new generation of writers, even though at the end of the century and millennium, many of these writers are approaching the age of sixty, and indeed younger writers are already appearing in the horizon. The new generation belonging to the above period includes Syed Mustafa Siraj, Mati Nandi, Sunil Gangopadhyay, Shyamal Gangopadhyay, Shirshendu Mukhopadhyay, Dibyendu Palit, Kabita Sinha, Shankar and others. These writers seem to have little in common with those from the preceding period. According to Professor Mukhopadhyay, these writers are viewed by the Great War and post-war writers as a new "blood-group." From the Great War and post-war generations' perspective, the new writers have no relationship or bonds with their predecessors. During their adolescence, the stable foundations of the joint family have started to crumble, and such concepts as devotion and veneration are to them nothing more than *parrot talk*. The relationship between men and women has changed fundamentally in that even though the sexual tensions and interactions are still much the same, these are not tempered or informed by any romantic notions or traditions borrowed from the past. They struggle to accommodate themselves in an alien world, and look for the means to alleviate a sense of complete isolation; therefore, they are in many ways neurotic and clueless. The Great War and post-war generations and the new generation appear to be islands separated by a gulf. The psychological and temperamental distance between the Great War and post-war writers and the new generation writers is far greater than that between the *Kallol* and the Great War and post-war writers. The *Kallolian* romanticism may have been absent in the Great War and post-war phase, but there was still a sense of joy in life, and reverence for traditional values. The new generation has none of these, and the distance is virtually insurmountable.

Moreover, the distance is not only one of temperament, it is also of language and style. It is not only one of viewpoints, but also of novel applications of the different components of life in the modern and technological age. These evolutions (or even revolutions) prove that the Bengali short story does not necessarily reach its ultimate perfection in Rabindranath alone. If anything, as an organic entity, it has repeatedly moved forward, negotiated sharp curves, persisted with experimentation, and never tired of examining life in fresh new ways. Echoing Professor Mukhopadhyay's words of regret as expressed in *Ekushti Bangla Galpa*, the translator of the present anthology also feels that any collection with limitations of space and selection criteria is guaranteed to leave many interested readers dissatisfied.

The initial impetus for the present collection came from the translator's desire to translate the inimitable storyteller Bimal Kar's *Balika Badhu*, in which the author's language and style, while quite original in many ways, may also be viewed as a bridge between Bankim Chandra Chattopadhyay's powerful classical prose, and Rabindranath Tagore's lyrical mastery. Having read the original as a teenager, as well as seen the film version of this tender tale about the life and times of young boys and girls growing up at the crossroads of tradition and modernity in a period of transition from colonialism to self-rule, this rather long tale made a lasting impression on the translator's mind. The story addresses several social issues pertinent to traditional Bengali and Indian society: arranged marriages and the marriage of adolescents, patriarchal value systems, the conflict between urban and rural lifestyles, the adaptability of immigrant communities in new environments, and others. The protagonist grows up under the stern stewardship of an idealistic father, himself much influenced by many nineteenth century reform movements in Bengal, led by individuals such as the legendary Vidyasagar Mahashay. Interestingly, the narrator's family had originally migrated from Rajasthan several generations earlier; over the years, their lives had become virtually inseparable from those of ordinary Bengali households. What is particularly appealing about this narrative is its tender yet keenly observant style- it explores the adolescent human mind, and in tracing the events surrounding the young characters growing up from uncertain roles as husbands and wives to life partnerships that mellow with the years, it also holds timeless glimpses of the human experience.

The two short stories that follow are by a master storyteller, sometimes considered second only to Rabindranath Tagore. Sarat Chandra Chattopadhyay needs virtually no introduction to anyone familiar with twentieth century Bengali literature. His vast collection of novels, short stories and essays have been read and deeply admired by arguably a larger number of Bengali readers (especially women) than have read the works of Rabindranath himself. He has been widely translated into almost every other language in India, and by all reckoning has been received with as much acclaim in each medium. As much as he was closely associated with the freedom movement in Bengal, Sarat Chandra identified deeply with the poor, the neglected, and the exploited. Women in practically every social category played a vital role in most of his works, and he portrayed their emotions, thoughts, vulnerabilities and longings with such sensitivity and understanding that his writing had a special appeal for housewives and other womenfolk within Bengal's homes. But Sarat Chandra's attention was by no means limited to women only. He frequently dwelt upon social injustice, incongruity, irony, and many stark and often shocking realities, in areas as diverse as religious faith, feudal land ownership and hired labour, poverty and starvation, and life within the lower and downtrodden classes. The two stories selected here deal with two extremely poor and ostracized communities: the *dulés* or palanquin-bearers in *Abhagir Swarga*, and the *tantis* or (in this case Muslim) weavers in *Mahesh*. In the first story, the wretched yet heart-rending and noble lives of a desperately poor *dulé* woman and her son are depicted against a graphic backdrop of deprivation versus affluence within the caste hierarchy. Sarat Chandra carries this contrast to the limit, it seems, by painting a stark picture of abundance and privation even in the finality of death, generally considered *the great leveller*. *Abhagi*, a creature of misfortune, does not have many aspirations—life holds little promise for any tangible improvement in her condition as a destitute with a child, rejected by her husband. She witnesses the grandeur and pomp accompanying the funeral rites of *Bamoon-Ma*, an elderly brahmin lady, and especially the red *alta* bordering her feet during her last journey. When she sees from a great distance behind the cortege the smoke rising from *Bamoon-Ma's* face when lit by the hand of her son, *Abhagi* wishes with all her heart that her own *Kangali* would offer her that fire when she would herself die. *No expectation whatsoever from life, but only the means to rise to the heavens as smoke from the flame offered by a son's hand.* Death is indeed her greatest romance in life. Yet this humblest of wishes, of course, is not to be granted by repressive and tyrannical society. In addition to highlighting the hypocrisy and cruelty inherent in power and authority, Sarat Chandra portrays a quintessential male chauvinism, which cuts across caste hierarchies, through the character of *Abhagi's* estranged husband, *Rasik Dulé*, who appears at her deathbed only to offer the poor woman the dust off his feet. The nobility of suffering womanhood depicted here, if dramatic, is nevertheless by no means unrealistic.

In *Mahesh*, Sarat Chandra explores with delicacy and deep empathy the privation and routine indignities suffered by another desperately poor community: the Muslim weavers. In this story, weaver Gaffoor lives in a shanty with two other beings he cares deeply about- his daughter Amina, and his pet ox, whom he fondly calls Mahesh. Pitted against a merciless and unscrupulous zamindar, and his hypocritical, scheming and unprincipled higher-caste retinue, Gaffoor has virtually little or nothing to feed himself or his daughter, much less the poor, emaciated beast. As is common in such grotesquely inequitable circumstances, Gaffoor's situation goes from bad to worse during a drought. His family of three is driven to starvation, insults, beatings, and further economic plunder. Driven to the brink of desperation, he even contemplates selling Mahesh to a butcher, only to change his mind at the last minute. In the end, when the village wells dry up, and Mahesh, starving and thirsty even more than his human companions, drinks from the pitcher of precious water fetched by Amina from a distant well, Gaffoor falls into an uncontrolled rage. He hits his dearest Mahesh so hard on the head with a ploughshare that the weakened animal dies.

The next story in the selection is by another legendary Bengali author, Bibhuti Bhushan Bandyopadhyay of *Pather Panchali* fame. Incidentally, it is important to mention here that Bibhuti Bhushan, together with Tarashankar and Manik Bandyopadhyay (who are also represented here), comprised what is known as the "tin Banrujje" or the "three Bandyopadhyays" of Bengali literature. These three writers have occupied a prominent place in twentieth century Bengali literature, with each having contributed major works to the literary archives. Bibhuti Bhushan, identifiable as a chronicler of simple village life in the rural areas of Bengal (in presenting which he skillfully portrays the virtues and vices of people in all walks of life in these communities), is also noted for his deeply insightful and sensitive observations of both nature and people. The story selected here, *Puin Mancha* (a translation of which previously appeared in the literary magazine *Sangbadik*, published from Long Island, New York, in 1995), brings out these characteristics of Bibhuti Bhushan's writing quite well. The young girl Khenti, who also happens to be the oldest of her parents' children, has only one observable vice—she has a sizable appetite. Now, in affluent homes, this would likely be considered perfectly healthy and normal. In fact, in her own home, her fondness for the fleshy *puin* plant, and other delicacies was well recognized, and her parents, despite their rather modest means, always attempted to satisfy her growing hunger. In describing the lives of Khenti and her family, the storyteller for the most part describes a tender and loving family, no matter that Khenti and her father occasionally incur her mother's wrath, such as following the yam-stealing episode. The tragedy central to the story is connected to the institution of marriage, according to which it is taboo to keep a daughter of marriageable age in her parents' home. Throughout traditional and typically rural society, this was quite common even until a significant part of the twentieth century. The resulting extreme social pressures, including covert and overt threats of ostracism and excommunication (as was brought to bear upon Khenti's father Sahayhari by the village elders), often forced unwilling parents, especially those with daughters for whom matches were difficult to come by, to marry the poor girls off to entirely unworthy prospects, including vastly older men, and even those gravely ill, mentally retarded or lunatic. Such a fate befell Khenti, and the tale of her tragically short life is only brightened, somewhat ironically, by the amazingly vigorous life, acquired against all odds by the *puin* vine she had planted prior to leaving her parents' home.

Saradindu Bandyopadhyay, whose work appears next in the selections, was another highly acclaimed and admired author. Although a "Bandyopadhyay" outside the "tin Banrujje" triumvirate, Saradindu nevertheless acquired an exalted status among Bengal's writers by virtue of his exceedingly original, daring and stylistically refreshing creations. Saradindu was neither a social commentator nor a messenger as such. He was an experimenter, and in many ways a modernist in terms of his themes and techniques. Even though the middle decades of the twentieth century produced several Bengali writers specializing in *detective* and *suspense* stories and novels, and Bengali super-sleuths and detectives such as Arindam Bose, Kiriti Roy, and several others earned considerable following among modern and forward-looking readers (incidentally, noted scholar Sukumar Sen in his introduction to the *Saradindu Omnibus, Ananda Publishers, 1970*, observes that the concept of the *super-sleuth* existed conceptually in India presumably even before it appeared in Western literature. To this end, he quotes several well-known folk idioms, including *"churi vidya bara vidya,"* i.e., stealing is a great art, and mentions that even in ancient times, expert thieves were trained to serve as policemen. Sen maintains that characters in many Indian children's stories may be seen as precursors of Sherlock Holmes' older brother Microft), the distinction of creating the first truly modern and versatile detective in Bengali fiction belongs to Saradindu Bandyopadhyay. His remarkable creation, the private detective Byomkesh Bakshi, was modelled no doubt after Sherlock Holmes; however, Byomkesh proved to be quintessentially Bengali in temperament and style. Saradindu's writing is characterized by a warm and what is referred to in Bengali as a *majlisi* or conversationalist style. The Byomkesh stories gripped the imagination of the Bengali readership during the 1960s and 70s—the present translator can still recall the suspense that surrounded the serialized publication of *Shajarur Kanta* (The Porcupine's Quill) in the literary magazine *Desh* in the late 1960s, when he was not quite a teenager. For this anthology, we have selected a short story, *Dehantar*, based on the occult. This story, like many others, brings out the great versatility of Saradindu as a writer. He had ventured into many different territories in his works, including suspense, crime, the occult, mythology, and, most of all, a number of historical intrigues. In *Dehantar*, Saradindu sets up the atmosphere for paranormal and psychic events by moving the principals to a hill station in the middle of the summer, where they encounter an attractive young widow being pursued madly by a young and infatuated bachelor. The story reaches its climax where first the persistent suitor's soul, and eventually his body appear to become possessed and transformed by the spirit of the widow's late, possessive husband, who was killed in an accident sometime earlier.

Another highly innovative author who was at the height of his creative powers from the 1950s through the '70s was Balaichand Mukhopadhyay, more widely recognized by his pseudonym, Bonophool. A doctor by profession, Bonophool was a keen observer of people from virtually every station in life—from the pauper and the destitute to the artist and the politician. His stories are rich and varied in content, and it is generally safe to assume that much of his material was gathered from direct life experiences. One of his stories, *Agnishwar*, which received wide acclaim as a film by the same name, is believed to have autobiographical overtones. Bonophool introduced a genre of ultra-short stories in Bengali (most of them between one-half to one page in length)—the current translator has defined these as *micro-stories*, and has selected six of them here. The beauty of these stories lies in the quirkiness of their message, which the author delivers with extreme brevity, while packing substantial punch. In order not to leave the reader with the impression that the micro-story was Bonophool's only *forte*, one of his more regular short stories, *Taj Mahal*, has also been included. Even though longer than the micro-stories, *Taj Mahal* illustrates Bonophool's imaginative use of atmosphere and theme, often leading up to climactic oddities and bizarre occurrences that leave the reader in a state of incredulity. With the peerless monument to love, the Taj, as the backdrop, Bonophool does not proceed to write another gushy story of love and romance. Instead, he introduces two shockingly pathetic destitute figures who, through the magic of Bonophool's pen, leave the reader at the end in complete bewilderment as to their identities.

Tarashankar and Manik Bandyopadhyay, whose works are represented next in this anthology, were the other two pillars of the Bandyopadhyay triumvirate mentioned earlier. These two authors, and especially the former (perhaps by virtue of a longer life), captured the imagination of the Bengali readership for several decades. Of the two, Tarashankar achieved a broader range in his writing career, and wrote novels and short stories with equal efficacy, many of which received great acclaim. His subjects were primarily based on the mores of rural life (as the selection in this anthology exemplifies), even though he frequently explored unusual vicissitudes such as mythology, folklore, and the occult. The short story *Tarini Majhi* portrays the life of a river boatman, who admires and almost dotes on his beautiful wife Sukhi. Tarini is a strong, even intimidating individual who, in addition to being a skilled boatman, has an uncanny ability to rescue hapless victims of the dreaded Mayurakshi river at full flood. The human limit of Tarini's devotion is tested to the extreme in this story, proving in the end that self-preservation is an instinct that is nearly impossible to overcome in all of nature, including the human. Manik Bandyopadhyay was only forty-eight at the time of his death. Yet, in a relatively short life, he wrote novels and stories that bear testimony to a writer with deep empathy for those in the lower strata of society. Manik was skeptical, even contemptuous of urban life, and all the trappings of capitalist exploitation and decadence in that environment. The story *Level Crossing*, selected here, examines the contrasts of rural and urban lives through the experience of a chauffeur who straddles both. The level crossing for trains is here a metaphor for *the great divide*, and the author deftly transports the reader between the two entirely different worlds on either side of the crossing. Ironically, even though Keshav has his roots in the relatively nurturing joint household in his village, and a caring young widow pursues him with genuine love, his heart is caught in a dilemma: loyalty towards, and responsibility for, his own family members (unsophisticated though they may be), on the one hand, and a dark attraction for the charms and comforts of city life, complete with the youthful infatuation of his employer's young daughter, on the other. At the end, the author demonstrates that Keshav maintains his village ties grudgingly, more as an unfair dictate of fate than out of any compelling allegiance towards the simple, plebian, and rustic lifestyle.

Subodh Ghosh, two of whose stories are featured in this collection, has been described in his *Collected Works* as a writer who literally *arrived*, *wrote*, and *conquered*. He began his writing career relatively late in life—more in response to a request from friends at a literary gathering to read a story of his own. This resulted in two stories that immediately earned him a lasting place in Bengali literature—coincidentally, these two stories, *Ajantrik* and *Fossil*, have been selected for the present anthology. Beginning with these, Subodh immediately gained widespread acceptance by readers, and placed himself in a position of inspiration for younger, aspiring authors. Ramapada Choudhury reminisced, "When we started to write, there were two avenues open before us—Tarashankar and Subodh Ghosh." Bimal Kar conceded, "His writing inspired us." Mahasweta Devi observed, "He opened a completely new vista in the realm of Bengali short stories." Subodh Ghosh is most noted for the remarkable freshness and vitality of his stories. They are characterized by an almost unmatched variety of themes—in story after story, plot after plot, he created relentless waves of intrigue. In *Ajantrik* (which the present translator first encountered during the screening of a retrospective of Ritwik Ghatak's films), Subodh portrays a fatally possessive, almost bizarre relationship between *man* and *machine*. Long before authors such as Stephen King (*Christine*) and others explored the subject, Subodh probed with extraordinary keenness the boundaries between human intelligence and consciousness, and that of the non-human or inanimate world. We must note, further, that in stories such as *Christine*, the machine actually *performs* acts of intelligence, thereby crossing the threshold between the purely psychic (where things happen within the human mind), and the fantastic (where strange events happen outside the human mind). In *Ajantrik*, however, the author carefully connects every nuance of the relationship back to the human partner and the workings of his mind. This approach makes the latter story more realistic, even as it explores the complex dimensions of the human psyche. *Fossil*, which depicts the machinery of oppression in a mining town- first, through the tyranny of a feudal lord who, rather anachronistically, rules his simple subjects with ruthless efficiency, and later, with the arrival of a team of European merchants (who collectively establish a so-called mining *Syndicate*), an equally cruel and despotic bureaucracy that sees the miners and other labourers as nothing more than potential tools for profit. Not surprisingly, then, that despite the apparent hostility between the Maharaja and the Syndicate, the two powerful rival groups band together in the end to eliminate their common rival, the union leader, and later, a group of vocal and unionized miners.

The 1986 *Selected Short Stories* of Narendranath Mitra in Bengali by Ananda Publishers, Calcutta, mentions that a French publication on contemporary India included one representative short story. The story was *Headmaster* by Narendranath Mitra. The Ananda volume goes on to suggest that while no doubt a curious development, the selection was by no means surprising, especially to those familiar with short stories of the world and "the world of Narendranath's short stories." Writer Abu Syed Ayub in a 1978 article in the literary magazine *Desh* ranked Narendranath's *Bikalpa* among the best short stories in the world. In a 1983 article by writer Santosh Kumar Ghosh, published in Ananda Bazaar Patrika, Narendranath is praised for his magical ability to present stories in the style of stories, yet maintain a delicate artistry as deftly as a dewdrop is held atop a blade of grass. For this natural talent, he is compared with the likes of O. Henry, Maupassant, and Tagore. In the present collection, we have selected Narendranath's *Ras*, a story later made into a feature film in Hindi by the name *Saudagar*. Interestingly, Narendranath, like several of his predecessors (Tagore, Sarat Chandra, Subodh Ghosh, among others) had the distinction of having several of his stories transferred to the film medium. Principal among these are *Mahanagar* by Satyajit Ray, *Headmaster* by Agragami, and *Palanka* by Rajen Tarafdar. In *Ras*, which revolves around a Muslim community of boatmen and sap collectors, Narendranath draws a sharp contrast between the sincerity and commitment shown by women in marital relationships, and the sometimes wavering, wandering and even devious response from men in return. Motalef, a handsome and skilled sap collector, has his eyes trained on Phoolbanu, a curvaceous and attractive young woman from the village. However, in order to garner her father's consent for his proposal of marriage, he needs to accumulate a large sum of money. To achieve his goal, he devises a sly and underhanded scheme. He proposes, and receives the hand of Mazu Khatun, an older and generally plain-looking widow, who has one great talent. *She knows better than anyone else how to turn sap into the best khejur gur (palm jaggery nuggets)*. Mazu Khatun's devoted, backbreaking labour, combined with Motalef's unmatched tapping skills produce the highest grade *gur* for the marketplace, and Motalef is rewarded with brisk sales. When he has collected the necessary funds, Motalef offers Mazu Khatun *talak* (an Islamic annulment of marriage), and immediately brings Phoolbanu home. In this manner, he has acquired both his object of sexual desire, as well as Mazu

Khatun's assets from her previous marriage. The fact that he subsequently suffers greatly from serious losses to his *ras* business at the hands of his beautiful but incompetent wife pales in comparison with the magnitude of his treachery towards the trusting and faithful widow.

The story *Ekti Shatrur Kahini* (of which the present translation was also published previously in *Sangbadik*) by Narayan Gangopadhyay rounds out the works by the ten authors selected for this anthology. Like Manik Bandyopadhyay before him, Narayan Gangopadhyay lived a tragically short life; yet, his literary contribution is by no means meagre. As with most of the writers selected here, Narayan also devoted a considerable part of his literary life writing for young readers. The present translator recalls from his youth the thrills and laughter that accompanied the reading of his many stories that chronicled the adventures of the *Char Murti* (The Gang of Four) whom he immortalized in his Tenida series. It was much later that this translator became familiar with the considerably more serious component of Narayan's works. As Professor Jagadish Bhattacharya notes in his 1949 (when Narayan was only 31) preface to *Narayan Gangopadhyayer Sreshtha Galpa* (The Best Short Stories of Narayan Gangopadhyay), first published by Prakash Bhavan, Calcutta, in 1954, "...(his) genius has already added a bright lustre to its signature upon the pages of time." Professor Bhattacharya goes on to maintain that Narayan's artistic world is filled with richness and variety defined by form, humour, reflection and anguish. From the violent hilltop forests of *Duars, Terai* and *Arakan* to the river deltas and the brackish coasts of lower Bengal, Narayan's vision has surveyed the entire panorama of human settlements and colonial interactions. His writing was shaped by the Great War and the Great Famine (the latter implying the infamous Bengal famine of 1943). Re-reading Professor Bhattacharya's extensive critique of 1949, it seems that this often greatly underrated author had acquired a significant degree of prominence in the world of letters at a surprisingly young age. The fact that in the remaining 21 years of his life he also explored areas of humour and light-hearted fiction only goes to show that Narayan was a writer with diverse talents who had not spent himself entirely in reaction to his early, stark experiences. In the domain of serious fiction, Narayan has created diverse and multi-hued characters: the devious coolie-recruiter Sadhu Sundarlal; the day-dreaming Rai-Bahadur of Manoharpukur Park who is obsessed with the bones of a sacrificed virgin; the mahajan and hoarder of Golapara Haat, Nishikanta; the modern-day Duhshasana (a reference to an infamous Kuru brother from the Mahabharata), textile merchant Devidas; and the transformed Christian missionary-turned-India-lover, Leipzig University Blue Hans, among many others. In *Ekti Shatrur Kahini*, Narayan explored the age-old quest to determine the friends and enemies of India. The old padre Donalds is shown as a failed missionary who is utterly dejected by the futility of his efforts to transform the "idolators" in the heathen land, India. In the latter years of his frustrating career among the tribals, his only companion (whom he despises with all his heart) is the former Donga Santal, who is transformed via conversion to Joseph Emmanuel, and who is relentless in his efforts to erase all traces of his Indian past. The little children of his enemy land, unfortunately, are his

Achilles' heel—they do not let him forget who he really is. In this environment there appeared one day the young German padre, Hans. His religious affiliation turned out to be no more than a clever disguise: in reality, he had fallen in love with India upon reading the works of Max Mueller. In virtually no time at all, he achieved what neither the missionary Donalds, nor the metamorphosed Santal Emmanuel could achieve in years: he won the heart of India. His victory was, of course, unforgivable to the missionaries. He was not supposed to love India, he was supposed to deliver her from the evil of idol worship. Then the war started in Europe. Germany became England's enemy, and by association, also the enemy of England's colonial crown-jewel, India. Hans' final act in the story graphically raises the eternal question: are *they* the friends of India, who perpetually treat her with contempt and condescension as the land of idolatry, and yet do not hesitate to worship Mother Kali when victory in the war becomes critical, or is *he* an enemy of India, who has embraced her by offering her, unconditionally, his heartfelt love? The war, Professor Bhattacharya concludes, is just a metaphor for the greater irony central to the story.

Returning momentarily to the matter of the so-called "*Best Indian Writing*," the present translator takes a view sharply different from that expressed by Salman Rushdie as mentioned earlier. Speaking strictly from the Indian context (although the conclusions, from this translator's perspective, apply just as well to established writers in other non-English languages), it is virtually needless to point out that languages (such as the many distinct languages of India) with long and evolving literary traditions almost always produce works that reflect the human experience and human genius at the highest level. To even imagine that there can be an objective, much less scientific, yardstick to judge what is the "best writing" across different languages and cultural experiences is extremely naive at best, and fraught with presumptive arrogance at worst. As an example of how meagre the process of literary migration from one language to another can be, and indeed how potentially misleading, let me cite Rabindranath Tagore's *Gitanjali* as an example. Any reader sufficiently fluent in Bengali will agree that even the inspired English translation by the great poet himself of the original *Gitanjali* poems does not, by any measure, do justice to the absolute beauty and perfection of his vernacular work. Yet, one must marvel at the fact that a fairly competent Western readership (including the likes of Yeats, Eliot, Pound, and a host of others whose credentials Mr. Rushdie can hardly dispute) gauged the greatness of the original work from the otherwise excellent, albeit significantly downgraded, English version. If a severely limited sample of his original Bengali work can, thankfully for Tagore, generate such unabashed enthusiasm in the minds and hearts of the greatest writers of the West—does this not at the very least indicate the immeasurable greatness that potentially exists in original vernacular writings that can only be tasted by developing a competent literary sensibility *in that language*? The fact that English has, through historic evolution and global adaptations, become the predominant language of our time, obviously lends to talented writers in that medium a range of advantages, such as access to a wider readership, sometimes at web-speed; immediate world-wide recognition (a phenomenon that began about a century ago); and, in many cases, far greater financial rewards. However, none of these parameters, and especially the dubious measure of international acclaim, necessarily elevate a work in English to the category of "best writing" in relation to works in other languages. To say so is to simply take an elitist position that places an unfair burden upon practitioners of vernacular literature, many of whom, in this translator's opinion, have achieved literary greatness that will outlive a great many award winners selected by the global imperial enterprise of the English language. Taking Bengali as a case in point, this translator considers it preposterous to believe that winning one or more awards recognized in Western literary circles, automatically elevates an Indian writer in English with a limited literary career above vernacular writers who have established a sustained body of work with a proven record of excellence. If, perchance, an argument is made that a vernacular writer is not *international* enough, or sufficiently in tune with the contemporary, globally interconnected world- such an argument can be refuted almost immediately by citing any number of examples to the contrary. This translator considers such relatively modern Bengali authors as Nabaneeta Dev Sen, Sunil Gangopadhyay, Bani Basu, Joy Goswami, Sanjib Chattopadhyay and others, not to mention the illustrious pre- and post-war writers discussed in these pages, to be perfectly worthy of being considered truly world-class, if indeed such a classification is based on unbiased and objective parameters. Furthermore, this translator postulates that such an objective classification may well yield unpleasant surprises for the pro-English establishment.

Finally, a few crucial words are in order with regards to

the specific selections presented in this collection. One of the most glaring shortcomings of this slender collection, without any doubt, is the absence of any woman writer in the group of ten represented here. As difficult as it has been to compile a representative collection from the vast galaxy of accomplished Bengali authors, male or female, this translator can only offer unqualified apologies that some of the great woman writers are not among those selected here. This was not by any means a conscious or deliberate decision. As it is, even among the male writers, several pre-eminent ones are not to be found here. Rabindranath Tagore is absent, as are Prabhat Kumar Mukhopadhyay, Pramatha Choudhuri, Rajshekhar Basu, Prabodh Kumar Sanyal, Nihar Ranjan Gupta, Achintya Kumar Sengupta, Harinarayan Chattopadhyay, Premendra Mitra, Premankur Atarthi, Samaresh Basu, Manoj Bose, Umaprasad Mukhopadhyay, and indeed so many others. This project began, as was mentioned before, with the initial impulse to translate *Balika Badhu*, and thereafter, stories were simply added to provide diversity and depth to the collection, representing a sample of writing from each period beginning with Sarat Chandra, and continuing with the *Kallol* age and thereafter. It speaks volumes for the magnitude of short story writing in Bengali that a true compendium rightfully deserves a series of well-crafted tomes. This translator regrets that he has been unable to include the fine works of Ashapurna Devi, Mahashweta Devi (who has thankfully been translated by very competent hands), Pratibha Basu, Nabaneeta Deb Sen, Bani Basu and other first-rate exemplars. A project of this nature is almost always ultimately an experiment, an inherently imperfect one. It is to be hoped that parallel efforts will add to, and further enrich this one, such that in the end a sizable body of Bengali short stories will become available to the English-speaking readership worldwide.

Monish R. Chatterjee
Binghamton, New York, 2001

Balika Badhu

The Adolescent Bride

A Fairy Tale of Youthful Love

PART 1

This anecdote is somewhat olden. Temporally it may be traced back about three *yugas*. Coins bearing King George V's head were then in circulation—it was the time of our youth. Of course, coins from that era are no longer legal tender; I suppose this old-fashioned rustic tale is likewise no longer *a la mode* in this day and age. Nevertheless, so many seasons later, I feel this great longing to narrate it here.

My father, Shashadhar Sinha Mahashay, who has since ascended to heaven, was a man with a rather curious disposition. Neither in style nor in acumen could he be equated with those around him. He was by nature unique, and by stature quite exceptional: six feet in height, and I estimate about four feet in circumference. His arms were long and powerful, and his spine was straight as an arrow. His complexion was golden like a fully ripened fruit of the *bel* tree. He considered it effeminate for men to fuss with grooming their hair, and, to lend credibility to his perception, he would never allow even the slightest tuft of hair to grow on his head. We had a family barber, whose job it was to shave my father's beard every morning, and to shave his head clean with *Sunrise* razor every Sunday. If necessary, he would wear a white turban on his head. Oddly enough, despite his utter disapproval of cranial hair, he sported a powerful mustache on his upper lip. He considered it an essential *purusha dharma* for a man to preserve his whiskers.

My father also wore the *upavita*—the sacred thread symbolizing high birth. We learnt from him that our forefathers were *Rajputs*. For a variety of reasons, my grandfather had left behind his kinfolk, his home, and his estate to migrate to Bengal. There, where the terrain had lost the moisture-laden, verdant and fertile climate characteristic of *Bardhaman* district to turn crimson and bone dry, where the barren fields stretched out without limits, interspersed with clumps of wild date palms and *palash* trees—my grandfather planted himself amongst the local *aghori, chattaraj, pankhi, sahana* and *majhi* tribes, and eventually became one of their own. Only a few of our ancestral customs and rituals survived within the household for a while- in time, these, too, were virtually obliterated. In our social activities, practices and modes of education, we soon became members of Bengali society. My mother was the daughter of a local estate manager. Perhaps because she was graceful of appearance and gentle of demeanor, she was called Lakshmi.

My parents had three children. I am the eldest; my sister

Chandra is about a year-and-a- half younger. Our youngest brother is six or seven years our junior. Father almost always addressed him by the name *Dharmaraj*. It was not that any special signs had appeared at the hour of his birth to signify our brother's future metamorphosis into a paragon of righteousness. At the instant of his arrival, Father was reading the eighteenth chapter of the *Mahabharata* in his room; a pair of distinctly martial cats was noisily defying one another to fight. Upon receiving news of the birth of his youngest son, Father closed his *Mahabharata*, and greeted his newborn with the appellation *Dharmaraj*.

I have mentioned that my father was a man with a curious disposition. He had no weakness about gods or demons; he would not partake of *prasad* consecrated at *pujas*, he would not offer any *anjali*—yet, he was sincere about his social duties and righteous actions. Reciting the *Surya-mantra* after his bath every day, and reading the *Mahabharata* and the *Bhagavadgita* every night were among his regular activities. He was a great admirer of the venerable Vidyasagar. As a rule, devotees tend to be emotional and zealous. It is not that Father did not possess a modicum of these two qualities. However, I suspect the real reason behind Father's particular attraction to a *mahapurusha* such as Vidyasagar Mahashay was the indomitable manliness of his character. Once, Father had a run-in with the local *thana* and police in attempting to carry out a widow re-marriage in some village. Later, he had opened a *pathshala* there in Vidyasagar's name, where the village boys and girls would nonchalantly munch on chick peas and puffed rice, and glibly rip up the pages of Vidyasagar Mahashay's *Varna Parichay* distributed free of cost to the school. I have even witnessed a few naked *Bauri* kids rollicking around the school yard, munching puffed rice. Sadly, that school is no more.

Grandfather had made our family prosperous before departing from *sansara*. Father gradually, but steadily increased the fortune over time. Farmland, abundant grains, homestead—these were already acquired; later, Father took up contractual projects at the coal mine. He would transport goods by lorries, and every once in a while auction off scrap metal. Once, he purchased an old boiler, and, installing it in the village, attempted to manufacture bricks using modern scientific methods. Unfortunately, in the end he only wasted money over the boiler project—the intended bricks never came off the assembly line. Presently, the junk boiler came to be covered with wild creepers and weeds, and frequented by venomous *gokhura* snakes. In the end, there remained no alternative but to have the boiler removed elsewhere by lorry.

When he was nearing old age, Father became obsessed by two whimsical ideas. For some inexplicable reason, he became convinced that early marriage was most beneficial for our society and way of life. He wrote a fifty-five page pamphlet on the subject, and, having it published at his own expense, began to distribute it. His second whim was to establish something like a new *Arya Samaj*. This latter whim did not last long- its only fruit was that, under the codes of that *Samaj*, we learned to use the more formal *sadhu bhasha* in our day-to-day conversation, apparently because it was considered a more civilized form of speech.

Father's first whim, on the other hand, has had a lasting effect in our lives. "All words, and no action"—Father was not such a person. To demonstrate first hand how useful and desirable early marriage could be, he married Chandra and me off the same month, only a few days apart. I was then a sixteen-year-old, Second Class student in the Ironworks High School about four miles from home. Chandra had just completed her fourteenth birthday. The early hints of a moustache had begun to appear on my upper lip, and Chandra had barely begun to get used to wearing a *sari*. She had also started to try out braids of various styles with her hair. Of course, I was supposed not to grow any hair on my head; however, my mother was greatly against my having my head shaved when both my parents were still very much alive. Therefore, there used to be a prickly mat of tiny hairs on top of my head, much like the ridiculous wig that adorns the head of a poor brahmin priest in a country opera. In effect, my hair was more a painful burden than an adornment. Chandra was draped in a *sari* like *kalabou* during her marriage ceremony. As for me, I had to wear a silken *piran* and *kurta* embroidered with gold threads, and a *pugree* on my head as befitting a *kshatriya*, Rajput groom. Thus attired, I had set out on my marriage mission. My father carried in his hand a sheathed sword, symbolic of our family's heritage.

In any event, my story revolves around the aftermath of this marriage. The brief introduction to my father was simply meant as a preface.

PART 2

My adolescent bride's name was Rajani. She had a pet name, *Chini*, which was the favoured 'sobriquet in her parents' home. In fact, the handkerchief verse which the bride's family had printed for our marriage, addressed Rajani as *Chini pata doi* (yogurt laced with sugar), lovingly penned by Nalini-didi. No doubt that the yogurt in question was laced with sugar, but poor me, I had to wait a long time for a taste of its sweetness.

At the time of her marriage, Rajani had completed fourteen years. It must be said that Father was greatly opposed to child-marriage, hence it was impossible for a young person to be married prior to completing his or her thirteenth year. It was his determination that childhood could be extended at most to thirteen years, after which one enters adolescence. Father had adhered to this principle in the case of his own daughter as well.

Being of similar age, the natural relationship between Chandra and Rajani had developed in time into one of deep friendship and love. In the company of daughter and daughter-in-law, even my father, the mighty and redoubtable Sinha Mahashay would forget his roar; my mother's face would be constantly beaming and aglow with a smile, and my little brother would be extra cautious about his *pentool*. Unfortunately, though, the sisters-in-law had few opportunities to be together. They would meet perhaps four times a year, during the religious and other festivities when Rajani would be summoned to her father-in-law's house, and Chandra to her father's.

Chandra's husband's name was Sarat. He was a city boy, slightly older than me in age. Like the rippling cheerfulness of autumn itself, my brother-in-law Sarat was full of laughter and fun. He was lanky and tall, and fair of complexion; his eyes gleamed with agility and intelligence. He was a matriculation student in a city school, and had a flair for mathematics. His elders had the desire that he be sent away to the Bankura Christian College, where he would live in a dormitory and study science.

Sarat was fortunate in more ways than one. His father was a bailiff at the court by profession; he lived in the city, studied in a city school, routinely got himself *six-anna* and *ten-anna* haircuts, had a wardrobe of designer clothes and shoes, and went to see the *bioscope* every now and then. Naturally, I would *have* to be a little jealous. Perhaps I was, too, but I envied him the most for a completely different reason. Sarat would have Chandra close to himself nine months out of the year, whereas I would not have Rajani even for three. Of course, the lucky Sarat eventually became a close friend to me, a friendship which stood me well in later years.

As I have mentioned before, I was married when I was sixteen, and in the Second Class. We were married in *Phalgun*, only a fortnight after Chandra's wedding. The matriculation curriculum in our time had nothing in it to enlighten young students about conjugal life. One does not gain the slightest knowledge about the institution of marriage from such charming English poems as *John Gilpin* and *The Pied Piper of Hamlin*, or any of the classic masterpieces by Shelley, Wordsworth or Keats about earth, sky, clouds and the birds. Moreover, most of the English prose was bland, and shorn of any luscious or romantic flavour. We did, however, like the Rajput stories as told by Todd Sahib a lot. In any case, I was not supposed to have read all of these by Second Class; therefore, we only had a few collections of Bengali poems and stories to assuage our romantic impulses and imagination.

I remember waking up very early on the day of my

marriage. The sky had turned fair and light very quickly that day. The *Phalgun* dewdrops on the empty fields and the blades of grass made the village paths and meadows appear soft and delicate. The birds had chattered energetically for a long time before flying away from their *mango*, *black plum*, and *shishu* tree shelters. As I took my ritual bath at sunrise, a sweet *kokila* of dawn sang a lovely melody perched upon a *neem* tree next to the family wellspring.

The marriage *lagna* was set for after dusk. The groom's party had set out in our rental lorry, with *dhurries* and sheets covering its floor. A bus had also been rented—the riders included some of Father's close associates, and, sitting on the nicely cushioned seat just behind the driver, Sarat and I, decked out as a groom. Father sat in the back of the bus. Along the way, the brisk afternoon winds of *Phalgun* began to blow. It was then that I had heaved a long sigh. At that, Sarat leaned over my side and whispered, "Haste not, haste not, lose not your heart, when Rajani arrives, your sadness shall depart...." I did not know then that Sarat was also a little bit into poetry.

The month was *Phalgun*, the moon was in its *shukla* phase, and the *lagna* was after dusk. As appropriate, presently my marriage ceremony was completed, following the invocation of *Agni* as witness, the *shubha drishti*, and *home* offering in the sacrificial fire. To be perfectly honest, I followed maybe one *anna* of the ceremony; the other fifteen *annas* were beyond my comprehension. I noticed more or less a repetition of those rituals, which had occurred during Chandra's marriage only weeks earlier. I respectfully followed whatever I was instructed to do. I had previously had a few mild bouts of malaria; fever always made my eyes turn red, and my hair to stiffen and stand erect like porcupine quills. My condition during the marriage ceremony closely paralleled that malady. During the *shubha drishti*, I had somehow glanced once with bloodshot eyes—I cannot recall what I had beheld, but the vision had reminded me of the goddess Saraswati's image in school, and, when garlanding my bride, I recall trying to be as humble as possible, as though I were offering *pushpanjali* to the goddess herself. I do not know how successful I had been. I did not see what Rajani had done when offering me her garland—I had closed my eyes. However, I have a strong suspicion that while slipping the garland over my head, she had grabbed my ears. Needless to say, Rajani flatly denies doing anything like that.

I finally had a good look at Rajani in the newlywed's hall. At the *basar*, there was a sizable assembly of revellers, both male and female; there were plenty of cushions and body pillows; sprays of rose water; a harmonium and associated musical instruments. Surrounded by girls and women of all ages and proportions, my fever gave way to a cold sweat. Fortunately, Sarat and a few other clowns had also joined in the festivities. He reassured me, and even gave clever answers to some of the girlish riddles and pranks. The commotion finally began to dissipate as the night grew longer. My groom's party began to disband and depart.

When it was a bit late, Nalini-didi came into the hall. She sang a few songs; there was much laughter and playful banter. I still remember parts of the refrains of one of Nalini-didi's songs:

> *"I've arrived, I've arrived, arrived this day my beloved*
> *With offerings of laughter, splendour and songs"…*

As she continued to glance at us suggestively and sing further:

*"May all the hopes, all the gladness and all the love of my
    heart
        Find their ultimate closure in you—"*

it was impossible for me to gauge the extent of the hopes, gladness or love that dwelt within the bosom of my newlywed bride. Anyhow, the jokes and capers began in the earnest after the singing was over. Finally, Nalini-didi asked me, "*Bhai*, now can you tell us just how sweet our *Chini* really is?"

I did not answer. Only my countenance grew red with embarrassment. Nalini-didi became insistent, while *Chini* and her playmates nonchalantly went on murmuring, laughing and playing ludo amongst themselves. Quite confused and tongue-tied, I simply muttered, "I don't know."

At that, Nalini-didi stood up laughing, entreated the other elders to do likewise, and, on her way out, approached me and whispered in my ears, "Steal a few peeks, see if she's like honey or sugar candy—Oh, mother! What kind of a boy *are* you, anyway?"

The elders left, but the youngsters remained. Youngsters such as girls the same age as Rajani, and a few sleeping babies. Two youthful wives also stayed behind, apparently to look after us. I must confess, this is when I gathered up enough courage to take a good look at my bride.

I have seen the many pieces of jewellery owned by my mother. Among them was a cloisonné butterfly. Rajani looked a lot like that butterfly. She was wrapped from head to foot in *sari*, blouse and gold ornaments; a variety of colourful and bright trinkets and decorations covered her small frame. Only now I could observe her countenance a little bit. She had a delicate, oval face, a sharp chin, a longish, flute-like nose, and a narrow forehead, much of which as well as her ears were concealed under her elaborate hairdo. Her eyes were dark as lampblack. Inside those long and paisley-shaped eyes, I could see the flighty and amused pupils darting left and right. Rajani had caught my attention; if her complexion were not slightly on the dark side, I would probably have liked her even better.

The little kids were already asleep; meanwhile, Rajani's girlfriends began to doze off as they played games of puzzles and limericks with me. I displayed uncanny incompetence at solving puzzles. Rajani conspired with her friends to befuddle me with the worst and most bizarre rhyming puzzles they could remember. She was having a great time conspiring against me. Eventually, her girlfriends all fell asleep, and the two married sentinels did likewise. Somewhere along the way, Rajani, too, took off her veil, and, curling up in a foetal position, fell asleep.

I, too, was yawning repeatedly. Outside the window, it was a full moon night. That silvery night appeared to be full of laughter before my eyes. Mesmerized by that laughter, presently I too drifted off to sleep.

PART 3

My father had not spared any expenses in ensuring a festive celebration of my marriage. The *shehnai* masters were there; the confectioners and cooks set up their large cooking fires, pots and woks; it was much like the arrangements for Chandra's marriage. In addition to sending invitations to the village households, Father had also invited my teachers from school. My teachers, though amused by the event of my marriage, were not particularly surprised. Such adolescent marriages were not uncommon in those days. A few of my classmates were present also—they whispered some such questions in my ear for which I had no answer. Consequently, they laughed amongst themselves, and thrashed me around a little. Privately, Sarat embraced me and gave me a few special instructions.

I beheld Rajani all over again in the flower-bedecked *phoolsajya* bedroom. Chandra held her brother's new bride by hand and walked her over to our honeymoon suite. I knew already that the two had become quite intimate in only the previous two days. Since her marriage, Chandra had developed a special sense of womanly dignity, and especially for her brother's marriage, she exerted her newly won rank and prestige in no uncertain terms.

When the two arrived, it was clear that some secret, private prank was brewing between them—even though there were no visible external signs, there were several implicit ones. Their attires indicated a conscious effort to make them appear grown-up; however, there was nothing grown-up about their bodies or demeanours. Even though their adolescence was yet to leave them, I must confess that they both were looking exquisitely beautiful that night (I have heard that an immature fruit is by nature sweeter and more tasty). Chandra said a few words in a hushed tone, showed us the *paan* and water on the round marble table, then left the room with a beaming smile. We heard the door being closed shut behind her after she exited the room.

It was springtime; however, our *phoolsajya* bed was not strewn excessively with flowers. There were a few blossoms plucked from the house garden, some buds of *bel*, and a couple of *bel* garlands. The bed was mildly fragrant. The sixteen year-old newlywed youth was gazing upon his bride, sometimes bashfully, sometimes perhaps with a touch of boldness.

Rajani looked truly beautiful. She was wearing a red and maroon striped *sari*, her blouse was slightly oversized, she had half a veil over her head, and her arms were draped in jewellery. Everything was a size or two too large for her, yet there was no deficiency in her bridal appearance.

After Chandra had left, Rajani stood for a while staring at the door. It seemed as though she was unmindful of whether I was there in the room or not. At this time, my heart, too, began to pound heavily, and it felt as though it were bouncing inside my chest.

Rajani walked to the door and closed the latch. Meanwhile, my ears were on fire, and my eyes felt gritty. Rajani's disposition seemed to be quite different. She leaned against the door, an ear pressed to it, an amused and excited smile on her face.

A Chinese table lamp lit up the room. The room was on the second floor. The eastern and southern windows were open; liquid moonbeams cascaded over the mango leaves outside; the sound of rustling leaves was in the breeze.

Even a short length of time seemed to be so long. I noticed, Rajani was quietly but unsuccessfully attempting to open the door latch. The latch in the room was a little tight, and could not be manipulated without applying a great deal of muscle power, or a mighty shove. Rajani made a few half-hearted attempts, then motioned me with her eyes to come over. I tiptoed slowly to where she stood. Rajani did not speak, but indicated with hand and facial signs that I must carefully and silently open the latch. I was about to ask her something, but Rajani immediately placed a finger over her lips to suggest that I keep quiet.

The latch was opened according to Rajani's wishes. She then suggested with her eyes that I stand aside. I did her bidding. No sooner had Rajani abruptly thrown the door open, than the figure of Sarat was seen planted at the threshold; Chandra was seen trying to run away—in her haste, she tripped and fell on the verandah with a loud crash.

There were peals and roars of laughter; other mysterious figures, hiding in nooks and crannies elsewhere, vanished in a flash.

Having been caught red-handed, Sarat mumbled like a petty thief, "I don't know a thing; they asked me to stand here."

Rajani stuck her tongue out, and said in a jeering voice, "Oh, sure, our unblemished *gangajal*.. !"

Presently, Grandma Moti came forward and said to Sarat, "Say, *Jamai*, go to bed now! Any idea how late it is—!"

Sarat followed her inside, docile as a pet.

This time, *I* closed the door shut. Rajani was still in a spell of laughter. She had obviously enjoyed the *let's catch a thief* game immensely.

Having regained some courage, I suddenly felt thirsty. I had myself a drink of water. Meanwhile, Rajani completely removed her veil. She had a good head of hair, no doubt, but still, it was not enough for the great big bun which adorned her top. Clearly, something quite clever went into the making of that bun, secured by a comb made of gold, and silver hairpins. She had fine shoulders, upon which the clasp of her beaded gold necklace could be seen glittering.

Walking over to the marble table, Rajani, too, poured herself a glass of water, which she promptly downed in a few quick gulps. Thereafter, she took out a couple of stuffed *paans* from her *paan* box, and, putting them in her mouth, began chewing contentedly. Before long, her lips became bright red with the *paan* juice. Obviously, the *paan* leaves were large in comparison with the size of Rajani's mouth. Some of the reddish *paan* juice trickled from the corners of her mouth to her chin; I watched those beads of *paan* juice on my bride's chin, spellbound and speechless.

Sitting on the bed, Rajani then loosened the *anchal* of her *sari*. Had she had her way, she would much rather free herself of that burden altogether. As she sat swinging her feet, she would stare at me one moment, then look away the next. Around her ankles, she had silver ankle bells; the more she swung her ankles, the more the silver balls inside the bells tinkled.

After staring at me a few times, suddenly Rajani began to giggle. Seeing her laugh, I too was infected and joined her in laughter. As though our first conversation was thus completed by exchanging laughs.

A sudden gust of wind had suddenly arisen. The open shutters of the windows began to rattle, and one closed with a loud bang. Outside, the branches of the mango tree crackled and rustled violently.

Rajani quickly stole a look outside the window, then withdrew her gaze. "What was that noise—?"

"The tree."

"What tree?"

"Mango."

"Sweet and tart?"

"Tart when young, sweet when ripe."

Rajani was not too pleased; casting a pall of doubt over her face, she said, "Oh, sure, and *you* should know—!"

A few moments of silence ensued. I went to re-open the window shutter which had closed in the gusts. Outside, the wind was still brisk, and the full moon was bright and silvery. The mango tree seemed to be bathing its leaves in the moonlight, and swaying its head in gladness.

When I returned to the bed, Rajani abruptly remembered something. Sticking her bright red tongue out full stretch, she muttered, "Uh-Oh!" Immediately, she jumped down from the bed to the floor. Perplexed, I stood up. Tinkling her ankle bells, Rajani came forward to face me, then instantly knelt down and did me a *pranam*. I stood frozen like an imbecile. Rajani stood up. She said, "Mother had asked me to offer my husband a *pennam*, *Didi* too. I had forgotten."

The word "husband" sounded very sweet in my ears; its sweetness penetrated to the core of my soul. Perhaps its euphoric quality caused me to close my eyes momentarily. But Rajani simply began to giggle loudly. Opening my eyes, I noticed Rajani covering her mouth with her *anchal*. I could not fathom from where she found the impetus to laugh; it appeared to me that perhaps my facial expression and my closed eyes had caused her some mirth. This hurt my feelings.

Then Rajani pointed me to the source of her amusement with her finger. I noticed a dab of vermilion smeared on a corner of the pleats of my *dhoti*. Clearly, it must have been smeared when Rajani was either bending over for the *pranam*, or when she was rising immediately after. I tried to dust it off hastily, but only succeeded in smearing it more—my *dhoti* became bright red, as did my hand. Rajani was tickled even more, and continued laughing. I may have felt a little embarrassed, but for some unknown reason, I could not also help feeling a thrill run down my spine.

When the laughing was over, Rajani walked over to the bed. Picking up a few flowers, she played "catch" for a while, the way girls play "catch" with *tamarind* seeds. She then tried decking her hair with some of the blossoms.

A pre-dawn crow cawed outside the window. Letting out a great big yawn, Rajani said, "The crows are cawing already. It's a bad sign when crows caw before dawn." She then muttered some *mantra* under her breath, apparently to dispel the effect of the inauspicious omen.

I said, "The crows caw sometimes when a full moon's out; they think it's daybreak."

Rajani was tempted to see the moonlit night, but she did not feel brave enough to walk towards the window. The large windows were open, the winds swirled and rustled through the branches of the mango tree, a complete hush had fallen everywhere, and the world all around had fallen asleep. Lacking the courage, Rajani looked towards the window several times, but did not step forward.

I gauged her feelings instantly, and walked over to stand by the window. Immediately, Rajani came forward to stand beside me.

There was a clump of *tamarind* trees just beyond the

boundary wall of our house, followed further in the distance by low bushes, pathways, fields, undulating terrain, and a distant railway track.

Inspired by the inexhaustible southern *Phalgun* breeze, and the enticing moonbeams, my adolescent bride became ecstatic. She exclaimed, "Look, such a yummy, *chum chum* full moon—!"

I started to laugh. "What on earth is a *chum chum* full moon?" I wanted to know.

Rajani was surprised. Good Lord, the man did not understand *chum chum* full moon! Dilating her lampblack eyes, she asked, "You don't know *chum chum*?"

"I know *chum chum*. It's something to eat."

My ignorance was obviously so vast that Rajani did not have the slightest interest to say another word about the subject. Making a crestfallen face, she said, "My gluttonous Lord…. Only knows sweets… !"

"I don't eat sweets or candies."

"Oh, sure you don't…. I just saw his Lordship wolf down so many with flourish."

"Where?"

"In our house, *your* house."

"That's because it's a wedding. Everyone said I should eat them."

Waving her head, Rajani repeated my last words in jest.

She then smiled slyly and said, "My poor *Narugopal*! Eats when told to, washes up when forbidden." With that, she puckered the corner of her mouth sarcastically in such a manner that all I could do was simply watch her, mesmerized.

Suddenly remembering something, Rajani said, "Have you had your ears boxed?"

"What?"

"Ears boxed!"

"Get lost!"

"Didn't Benudidi box your ears? I saw it right before my eyes."

"It's not *that* easy…"

"Oh, mother, what kind of a fellow *is* this!" Her eyes wide, Rajani raised her hand to her cheek, and said, "What happened to you on *bashi biye* morning?"

The event came back to my mind. One of Rajani's relatives did attempt to whisper some secrets into my ear, and in the process touched my ear with her hands and lips, without actually telling me *anything*. Now it was clear to me that the whole thing was part of a conspiracy. Trying to ignore the episode, I turned the pressure back on Rajani, "*You* were the one who boxed my ears."

"Oh, come on!"

"Yes you did. When exchanging garlands."

"Oh, mother, what a liar! Shame, shame—" Rajani almost died of embarrassment as she shook her head vigorously and said, "I could hardly reach! Such a *huge* head… ! And now to blame *me*…!"

Seeing both her fear and devotion, I started to laugh.

After a few meaningless exchanges, Rajani asked, "How far is your school from home?"

"Four miles."

"Do you walk?"

"Why should I? I have a bicycle."

"You are in Second Class?"

"Next year it's the First Class, then I sit for the matriculation examination."

"How many attempts before you pass the matriculation?"

"How *many*?"

"Madhu-dada passed it in his fourth attempt after failing three times."

"The heck he did... Only donkeys need three attempts to pass."

"Goodness gracious—how rude!"

I could not quite follow the reason for Rajani's reproach.

Rajani said, "You called an older person a donkey! Don't you have any sense of propriety?"

True, indeed. I bit my tongue. I said apologetically, "It just slipped out. I have a slippery tongue. *I* will pass in only one attempt, though."

"You'll go topsy-turvy," Rajani started to laugh.

Then Rajani yawned widely, and with her, I began to yawn as well. Yawning is terribly infectious.

"Do you know any stories?" Rajani rubbed her eyes with the back of her hand.

"Stories! What stories?"

"Who knows what? Not ghost stories, though. Or stories about *rakshasas* and demons." Rajani looked at me; she began to suspect that I was unable to follow whatever she was saying. Puckering her nose, she said, "What kind of a boy *is* this! And *he* has to marry—."

We came back to the bed and sat down. Moments later, resting her head on the pillow, Rajani lay down The great expanse of the *anchal* of her sari bothered her a great deal;

collecting some of it into a bundle, she set the heap aside. A little later, she abruptly asked, "Do you have a headache?"

"No, why should I?"

"I am supposed to ask. *Didi* had told me, ask your *bor* if he has a headache. If he says yes, gently massage his temples."

I started laughing; Rajani seemed a little embarrassed.

"Just listen to him laugh, weird—" Rajani said, puckering her lips.

"Shouldn't I laugh when I hear something funny!"

"Goblin!"

"Who, me?"

"Next to me." Then, remembering something, she looked me in the eye and said, "O.K., let's see you try this riddle:

His looks are dapper
Lordship, lightweight as you've ever felt—
Blows away if the wind is brisk
Drop him in water, and watch him melt."

I tried imagining who this air-blown, water-soluble, dapper looking lord could be. The "lord" in the riddle was causing most of the confusion. In the end, I did not disclose what I had surmised. Acting like I had puzzled over the riddle to a frustrating limit, I said in the end, "I don't know."

"Uh-oh, it's so simple- plain as water, you still can't crack it?"

"No, I give up- you tell me."

You'll pass *my foot!*" Convinced in her mind of my matriculation prospects, Rajani sighed, then went on, "O.K., let me give you a lead. The object is right here in this room." Having provided the lead, Rajani eagerly awaited my response.

"In *this* room—?" I pretended to survey the perimeter of the room.

"Very near—" Rajani abruptly stopped without finishing her sentence, as if she had almost given the game away.

I scratched my head. "Where?"

"So, must I tell you *everything*?"

"Near the window?"

"No."

"On the table?"

"No."

"Then where?"

"You can see it if you have eyes." Closing her lips shut, Rajani turned her gaze to the wooden beams in the ceiling.

I stared at Rajani's innocent and beautiful face with rapt admiration. In the middle of her forehead was a sandalwood mark of a *kadam* blossom; some of the tiny, sandalwood clove-tip marks had been washed away; lampblack mascara adorned her eyes; on her chin there was still a smear of red *paan* juice; on her neck was a pinkish mole like a pomegranate seed. The parting of her hair was very narrow; however, it was widely smeared with vermilion straight to the middle of her head. I must admit that my brother-in-law's instruction and advice now started to play notorious tunes in my ear.

Presently, I said to her, "I see it."

"What is it?" Withdrawing her gaze from the ceiling, Rajani looked at me.

"Shall I tell you?"

"Yes."

"*Chini*."

Rajani was quiet for an instant. Then, filling her entire face with a bashful, witty smile, she stuck out her tongue to taunt me, "Oh, sure, *Chini*. Well, what *Chini*, brown, country sugar, or white, refined sugar?"

"It's *my Chini*."

I hastily applied a crude version of the kissing technique Sarat had taught me. *Chini* alias Rajani did not make a sound at that moment. Thereafter, like a stolen glance, she gave me a kiss in return.

Like the *chum chum* full moon, I felt a *chum chum* thrill fill all my senses. Meanwhile, Rajani had covered her face with her bundled *anchal*.

PART 4

I woke up. In my sleepy stupor, I did not at first realize it; then it occurred to me that I was lying next to my brand new bride on a brand new bed. Feeling a special glow of romantic joy and the prestige of a grown-up, I opened my eyes. It was morning, but the day was not bright and clear yet. Crows had begun to assemble outside, and herald the advent of dawn with their cawing. I felt shivers in the chilly morning air. Turning my head to find her, I noticed Rajani's pillow was empty. Was she up already? Raising my head just slightly, I observed that my adolescent bride had turned around in bed like the hand of a clock. It was a huge bed, so she had no difficulty spinning in her sleep till her head was pointed at an angle towards my feet, while her feet were planted near my chest. Her knees folded in the foetal position, she was peacefully and comfortably asleep. Perhaps because of the early morning chill, she had wrapped her head and face with her *anchal*.

I was watching intently how small and delicate Rajani's *alta*—bordered feet were, and how thin and dainty were the sole of her feet. A faint, stale odour wafted into my nose-lowering my head, I realized it was the odour of a combination of fragrant *alta*, and the perfume sprayed over the bed sheets and Rajani's *sari*.

I became obsessed with the desire to awaken Rajani by tickling the sole of her feet. Deciding that tickling with bare fingers would not be sufficiently effective, I picked up a wilted flower, and began to tickle the sole of her feet.

Rajani's sleep was pretty sound. When the flower did not do the trick, I used my bare fingers to continue tickling her feet. Rajani responded by moving her legs aside—this added to my amusement, and I started to tickle even more energetically. Rajani began to curl up her legs and her body, and turn to her side. Finally, when goosebumps appeared in her hair follicles, she awoke and sat up with a shudder. The suddenness of awakening made her a little bewildered, somewhat flabbergasted, even a shade irritated. I was laughing. A few moments later, Rajani regained a bit of consciousness. Noticing the window, the four walls of the room, the bed, and her newly acquired sixteen-year-old husband she felt a little reassured. She brushed off the weight of sleepiness from her eyes by rubbing them with her hands, yawned, and quickly joined the palms of her hands to offer a *pranam* to the divine.

"Have you been tickling the bottom of my feet?" She spoke for the first time since waking up.

"Why, no!"

"Lying through a stale mouth!" Rajani shuddered.

"Why were *you* sleeping with your feet in my face?"

At first Rajani almost did not believe, then said, "Really!" Thereafter, noticing her orientation, and the state of the bed linens, she suddenly became very embarrassed and wrinkled her nose. "Uh-oh, shame, shame! I'll grow warts on my feet. Tell me, did my feet touch you?"

"No, not really." I shook my head, laughing. I cannot swear that my adolescent bride did not actually touch me with her feet in her sleep, yet I denied her having done such a thing out of generosity.

Rajani said, "My sleeping is really lousy. Mother, Auntie, Didi—they all chide me for it. They had warned me many times, sleep properly, lie down straight, don't touch your husband with your feet." As she said these words, she became crestfallen by her indiscretion. "Would you please lower your feet, let me do a *pennam*."

"Are you crazy... *pennam*!"

"No, you must, otherwise I'll be a sinner. Why did you touch my feet with your hands?"

Rajani stepped down from her bed, as though the burden of her sin was becoming heavier by the minute. I cannot lie, no matter how amusing this all was, I felt quite a sense of prestige from this unexpected acquisition of rank.

Outside, dawn was breaking as the darkness was receding rapidly. The corners of the room were becoming light. A bunch of crows was busy noisily flying back and forth between trees, while along the distant railroad tracks, an early mail train whistled by, delivering both a wake-up call and a vigorous shaking to the sleepy hamlet.

Rajani was getting impatient. Almost dragging my legs

towards herself, she did a quick *pranam*. She said, "Listen, I'll tell you something, promise me…"

"Promise what?"

"You won't tell anyone."

"Tell what?"

"Sure, as if he doesn't know," Rajani made a long face. "Don't tell anyone my feet had turned towards your head. It's not proper."

"What if I did?"

"You would!"

"No, I won't. Just like to know what would happen if I did."

Rajani stared at me in complete bewilderment, as if she simply could not fathom how such stark ignorance in me was even possible. She said, "People would call me impolite, they would deride my parents. They would say, they haven't taught me any manners. It's very unlucky to get a bad name in your father-in-law's home."

It was not difficult for me to appreciate that Rajani had come from her father's home with ample instructions regarding behaviour and expectations. I had noticed *my* mother similarly instruct Chandra soon after *her* marriage had been arranged. One day Chandra had pulled me aside and said, "Don't do this, don't do that, not this, not that—good heavens, if I must not do *anything*, then why marry in the first place? Is it *swasurbari* or a *pathshala*, can you tell me, Dada?"

Remembering that episode made me smile. A sense of duty to reassure Rajani came over me, so I told her, "No one will knock you."

"Oh, sure—so they told you!"

"I can see it. Mother has been doting on you."

"Father, too. Father tells me that I shall go to Ranigunj with you, and not return very soon."

There was nothing in the news to be thrilled about. In fact, even on this bright morning, it felt irritating like a thorn lodged in some corner of my mind. My face, too, became a shade long, and I said, "You go alone, I won't come."

"Yeah? Won't come, indeed! You *have* to, you know that. One goes as a couple to observe the *dhulo-pa*."

"I don't know pairs or oddities." I pretended complete ignorance as I shook my head and said, "You go live with your father, mother, aunt if you wish, what does it matter to me?"

"I am so thrilled about it!"

"You, *you, you... you* are a number one *selfish giant*."

"What?"

The words *selfish giant* had accidentally escaped my mouth. We had read the story *The Selfish Giant* soon after we had reached Second Class. We had been so enamoured and impressed by the story that in our regular conversations we used to use the expression *selfish giant* to connote the ultimate act of selfishness. It was a widely used expression amongst my friends. I had not imagined that Rajani would not be familiar with it. Even though she studied English, Bengali and Math at home, it seemed plausible that the expression would be outside the range of her vocabulary.

After waiting a moment, Rajani said pleadingly, "Please, tell me what you just called me."

Rising above a moment or two's hesitation, I finally decided to tell her. "You are a number one *selfish giant*."

I did not notice any resentment in Rajani over the

allegation of selfishness. It seemed she accepted the indictment without any resistance.

The room had meanwhile become quite bright and clear inside. The sun was still not fully out, but its radiance was already evident.

Rajani began tidying up her dishevelled raiment from the previous night. The pleats of her sari had just about disappeared; the edge of her *anchal* looked crumpled like a piece of rag; her hair was all tousled, with clusters of fine hair cascading over her temple; the redness of the vermilion had been smeared far and wide.

I told her, "You must not tell anyone in Ranigunj about me."

Rajani tugged at the bottom of the sari near her feet, then stood up straight. Looking at me, she then said without the slightest qualm, "Oh, sure—as if I wouldn't be embarrassed enough to talk about it."

The sound of soft knocking came from the door. Glancing at the door, Rajani said in a hushed voice, "It's *Thakurjhi*... please lie down as if you are asleep while I leave."

Opening the door to let in the morning light, Rajani left the room.

PART 5

The two days in the interim were like a couple gusts of wind, they were over no sooner than they arrived; I did not receive much by way of touch. But even in that short time my youthful heart had developed a substantial *maya* for Rajani. Realizing that her absence would not be particularly pleasant for me, I suppose I must have even let out a few sighs. But it did not seem Rajani shared my blues. The prospect of going back to her father's home made her so excited and restless that she hardly noticed my lack of enthusiasm.

As expected, on the appointed day, I accompanied Rajani for her trip back to her father's home. Manohar Kaka was with us. Father had arranged a motorcar for us; however, just before our trip, it developed a problem. There are many machines in life which do not repair easy; my devious instinct was hoping that the engine be busted for good. Rajani was up real early as she got busy for the journey. All the preparations for her journey were complete; yet, she was impatient and could hardly wait to leave. Sarat had informed me that she had been waiting eagerly by Chandra's window for the car to be fixed up. I don't mind admitting that I wished then that that selfish girl needed to be taught a lesson.

The day was wearing on. Just when Father was getting ready to abandon all hopes of the stalled car ever coming back to life, and arrange to send us off to Ranigunj by train instead, the lifeless culprit suddenly let out a frightening roar and announced regained life. With its canvas top, ramshackle body, and old-fashioned tires woven with cane, it was impossible to gauge the power of the mighty jalopy.

Poking my ribs with an air of frustration, Sarat said, "Dash it…!" Then, with a sly smile, he went on, "Your luck's bad!"

Father got into a dilemma—the way the motor car was acting, there was a definite possibility that it would malfunction somewhere on the way. If it should go dead on its tracks, what then. In such a situation, perhaps the train was safer.

I cannot tell what transpired between Father and Manohar

Kaka—we ended up travelling by car in the end. Mother wished us a safe journey; Father offered his blessings and instructed the chauffeur thoroughly. We understood that we would be travelling up to Asansol by car, then proceed to Ranigunj by train or taxi. If, perchance, the car chose not to give us any trouble, we might even go straight to Ranigunj. The journey began.

Manohar Kaka sat in front, and we in the back seat. Rajani may have been small in size, but this could not be said of the boxes and packages she had collected on her way from her home and back. In the car's trunk, there was room only for her huge steel box and a large sack. The rest of the luggage was scattered around our legs and around us. Rajani's suitcase, my suitcase, a bag of new clothes, a few pots of sweets. Father had also packed some fruits and vegetables from our garden for the in-laws. They were tied in a sack behind us. The box of jewellery was with Manohar Kaka.

On our way, the *Phalgun* sun became hot and oppressive. It was a country route, uneven and bumpy. Our car was prancing and swaggering like a drunken loon, trying, as it were, to impress the rough country path with its acrobatic skills. I was rather enjoying even the scary sounds emanating from its engine; Rajani, however, was not terribly thrilled.

Rajani was observing the charm of our village landscape, but did not appear to relish it much. *Palash* bushes, *shaluk* ponds, the ruins of Kartikpur's now discarded number two ravine, fields with edges hewed jagged by landslides, thickets of wild basil—we passed all of these one by one. Presently we crossed the railway bridge and reached the asphalt roadway. Finally, it seemed, the driver, too, was a little relieved.

Rajani's veil had slipped partially. There was at long last an expression of reassurance in her countenance.

After passing a farmer's *bazaar* near the coal township, we arrived before the gate of a railroad level crossing. The gate was closed, so the car had to be stopped. Suddenly, I noticed Satyanarayan approaching on a bicycle. Satya was my friend, we studied in the same class. Satya was going to school, a pile of books was stacked behind his bicycle.

We had been quiet until now, mainly on account of Manohar Kaka. By some unwritten law, we had both decided that it was unseemly for us to speak to each other in his presence. Seeing Satya, I was suddenly a little apprehensive. Satya was a smart-aleck, and a loudmouth. He had a thick voice, and screamed when he spoke. There was no doubt he would ride straight to the car if he were to spot me. There was no telling what that blabbermouth would blurt out if he were to see Rajani and me together like this. The oaf did not possess much common sense.

Satya was soon very near the car. I had no doubt the physical features of that jalopy would immediately draw his attention. I was so petrified by the prospect of that loudmouth seeing us and saying the most embarrassing things in jest, worse yet, spreading the most ghastly gossip amongst my friends in school, that I took hold of Rajani's hand and motioned her to lower her head. Rajani did not follow anything; she stared at me with bewildered eyes. The more I would hint at her to conceal herself, the more she would raise her head and look all around. Because of Manohar Kaka, I was unable to say a word. In frustration, I simply gave her a shove on the side with my elbow, and withdrew my gaze to the railway track. Rajani whispered a mild "ugh", and instantly gave me a shove in return.

Satya had seen me. A disarming, all-engulfing smile illuminated his face. He came forward.

Walking up to the door of the car, the rascal stared at us for a moment or two with his mouth open, his eyes round and bulging. An impish smile hovered around his lips.

"Wh-wh- where're you going?" Satya asked in a comical voice. He was a mild stutterer.

"Ranigunj."

"*Swa-swasurbari?*" Satya smiled quietly in a manner which suggested as though *swasurbari* were a platter of *rosogolla* in a confectioner's shop.

Forcing a smile, I tried to change the subject, "Are you off to school?"

"Yes, of course. Wha—what's it to you—having a swell time."

Just what the blathering dunce might say next before Manohar Kaka paralyzed me with fear, so I said hastily, "Hey, what is Pashupati Sir teaching in Math right now?"

"P-pr-pro-profit an-and loss." Satya had a real hard time saying the whole thing. It is unlikely, however, that this factor alone would cause his eyes and facial expression to become so bloodshot. I suspect he had become particularly embarrassed by his stuttering in this manner before a young girl he did not know.

Pretending not to have noticed his embarrassment, I said, "Guess what, I have missed quite a few classes. I'll have to report back to school as soon as I return."

"D-d-do that." Satya thought for a moment, then said, "Yyou have become an ex-exact model of *Kattick*. My, if he isn't *Lord Kattick!*"

At last, Manohar Kaka turned around and noticed Satya. I was warily counting the seconds. Surreptitiously, I pointed Manohar Kaka to him.

Satya took a quick look at Manohar Kaka, then said in a hushed voice, "*A sly fox met a hen*. Go on, get pampered at your *swa-swasurbari*. S-see you." Eyeing Rajani and me mischievously, Satya rang the bell of his bicycle.

The level crossing gate was being swung open, the engine of our car started, while Satya got on his bicycle. Fortunately, Manohar Kaka did not ask me anything.

As the car pulled forward, Rajani covered her mouth with her *anchal* to suppress her giggles. The reason for her amusement was beyond my comprehension. Even looking at her inquiringly did not elicit any response. Yet, not knowing why she was laughing like this made me rather ill-at-ease.

I asked her simply by eye contact, moving my lips without making any sound, "Why are you laughing?"

Sneaking a peek at Manohar Kaka, Rajani drew her veil over her face a little, then said something by moving her lips. I could not follow. I would persistently move my lips and ask her, "What—?" And she, too, would move her lips back in return.

Finally, she pulled my hand to her lap and started writing something on the palm with her delicate fingers. After she had written a few times, I realized that she had liked my newly acquired name *Lord Kattick* very much.

Sitting behind Manohar Kaka, the two of us thus spent our time finger-writing on each other's palms, and conversing by sign language and lip movement. These activities were interspersed with liberal doses of pinching, poking and pulling each other's fingers.

Soon, the car sped along the G.T. Road. The sun was now high, the air felt a little warm and moist, the fields were dry and barren; a few birds could be seen pecking desperately at seeds and grains scattered around the infertile fields.

Rajani was probably dozing off, so I gave her a nudge to awaken her, and prevent her from falling over. We arrived at Asansol.

Manohar Kaka had the car stopped near the marketplace. He was getting increasingly anxious for tobacco, *paan* and tea by now. Depositing the jewellery box in our care, he went off to alleviate his craving for tea. The chauffeur, too, followed suit.

Rajani removed her veil and said impatiently, "I'm thirsty-I'd like some water."

There was a *paan* shop ahead of us. I asked her, "Would you like a lemonade?"

"Sweet and sour water! It's got too much fizz..."

"Since when did lemonade have any fizz? You get that in a soda."

"Do you have any money?"

"Yes."

"O.K., I'll have some, then."

Leaving Rajani in the car, I went to the *paan* shop. She remained in the car, clutching the jewellery box. Being alone probably made her mildly apprehensive.

Rajani spilled lemonade over her neck and *sari*, made weird contortions of her face and burped a couple of times. Finally, she said, "My mouth feels funny. It's awful."

"Would you like a *paan*?"

Rajani immediately nodded her head eagerly, but thereafter became quite grave and complained, "But isn't *he* around- !" By *he* she meant Manohar Kaka.

Manohar Kaka and the chauffeur were still out, so who could possibly know if Rajani were to stuff a *paan* in her mouth! Moreover, it was quite unlikely that Manohar Kaka would notice anything if, sitting behind him, Rajani were to chew a *paan* behind her veil. I tried to explain this simple truth to her.

Rajani was pleased. She said, "Just hurry over and get one. But please, don't chew one yourself—you're on your way to *swasurbari*, remember." She had a rather grown-up manner to her sermonizing. I could not help laughing.

Seeing me leave, Rajani remembered something and said, "Could you have them put *that* in the *paan*—the thing which is icy cool, which tingles inside—" she made swishing sounds with her tongue as she spoke.

"Peppermint?"

"Yes—" Rajani nodded.

I bought two *paans* from the *paan* shop for Rajani. In one, I had peppermint put inside, while in the other, some *zarda*. I cannot tell why I had the mischievous notion to make Rajani chew *zarda*. Perhaps I had this desire to somehow get even with her.

Returning back to the car, I gave Rajani the peppermint *paan* and said, "Eat this one now. Eat the other when we reach Ranigunj."

Rajani stuffed the peppermint *paan* in her mouth and began chewing happily. As it turned out, she did not have to eat the *zarda paan* after all. I ended up revealing the secret to her for fear of a scandal of some kind.

My reception at my father-in-law's home was quite grand. There was conch-blowing, there were *ulu*-sounds and some family rituals—these were only the tip of the iceberg. The manner in which the elders as well as youngsters in Rajani's family set themselves to attend to me and my every comfort made me feel an unexpected sense of prestige about myself. Whether I was to walk, sit or stand, five different people would rush at me from five different directions to fulfill my wishes. What pleased me even more was the realization that I was receiving much greater attention than Rajani. The last several days, I had seen Rajani being indulged and attended to by a variety of people in my home—Father, Mother, Chandra— they had all forgotten their own son and brother, and become preoccupied with the daughter of another household. Finally, I was now witnessing this partiality being set right in Rajani's home.

Most of Rajani's relatives had already left after the marriage; only a few had stayed behind, among them, Nalini-didi, Chhoto-pishi, Mamima and others. Nalini-didi's husband Prabhat-dada was also there. Prabhat-dada had been much too busy taking care of outside affairs during the marriage, and had little time left to get to know me. He had been unable to attend the reception in my home, being down with the flu. This time, though, I became acquainted with him.

Prabhat-dada was quite an amusing person. It took him seven or eight attempts to get through the medical finals at Burdwan Medical School. Currently, he was employed at the same school following his successful graduation. He was a little plump—a bit excessively fair of complexion, a little short in stature. I suppose he was about twenty seven or eight. His home was in Burdwan, they had a number of businesses and were fairly affluent, therefore, his studying medicine was no more than merely fulfilling the wishes of elders.

Prabhat-dada was principally in charge of my care and upkeep in Rajani's home. Among other things, he kept me quite overwhelmed with a steady stream of stories.

Following the afternoon bath and repast, we returned to our designated room. A room on the first floor had been reserved for us. It was not too large, but was quite airy and open. The doors and windows had shutters. A pair of coconut palms leaned over the long and narrow verandah outside. The room had quite a bit of furniture. A bed, a glass cabinet, a mirror, a table and chair, pictures of deities, photographs and needlework. One piece of needlework drew my attention from the start—a green and red bird flying with wings unfurled, below which were written in uneven letters the words: Fly, fly birdie, tell him, that me he may never forget.

After we had entered our room, Prabhat-dada had closed the door and told us, "Go on, now, rest a little."

I did not sit on the bed, but stood by it. A pond filled with aquatic leaves could be seen at a distance through the open window to the west of the room. Shady trees lined a garden adjacent to the pond. The soft cooing of doves deepened the feeling of mid-afternoon lethargy.

Prabhat-dada took out a pack of cigarettes and a matchbox from his pocket. Sitting on the side of the bed, with his feet dangling, he happily lit a cigarette and said, "Would Chhota-babu like one?" With a broad, amused smile, he extended the pack of cigarettes in my direction.

My face turned red with embarrassment. I lowered my gaze.

Prabhat-dada observed, "You're nothing but a greenhorn *bemmhachari*...," and laughed in a deep voice. "You see, Chhota-babu, at your age I burned incense in my study room to smoke cigarettes."

Nalini-didi pushed the door open and walked in with a small tray of *paan*.

Prabhat-dada eagerly picked a *paan*. Nalini-didi held the silver tray before me and said, "Have one, *bhai*."

"Now, what's this! A brand new *jamai*, and *you* won't have a *paan*? C'mon, have one, O.K.? You should. *Chini* dressed this *paan*, please try one..."

"Try it, Chhota-babu..." Prabhat-dada interjected, "You must not push anything from your platter in your *swasurbari*." He then looked at his wife and smiled suggestively.

It was not that I did not crave a *paan* at the time, so I took one. Nalini-didi stood by, watching me.

As I chewed the *paan*, Nalini-didi asked, "How did she dress it?"

Embarrassed, I again looked down.

Prabhat-dada quipped jokingly, "Oh, she's dressed well, all right, spicy like yours..."

Nalini-didi knotted her brow and glared at Prabhat-dada reproachfully. "What a thing to say before a child!" She then looked at me and said, "Try not to associate with this man too much, *bhai*, he'll send you to the devil—."

Prabhat-dada retorted, "God only knows who is sending whom to the devil, Nalini. You know what, Chhota-babu, I got married right after entering medical school, it's seven years already—I've taken all this time to be a *lomfo* doctor simply because of your Nalini-didi. But I will tell you that history another day, when you are a little older."

In response, Nalini-didi cast another acerbic glance at her husband, flung a dressed *paan* at him, then stormed out of the room. Prabhat-dada began laughing hilariously.

Perhaps I did not entirely follow the youthful romance between Prabhat-dada and Nalini-didi; however, somewhere my senses instinctively revealed the sweetness of their relationship to me, and filled me with a sense of gladness.

During our afternoon respite, Prabhat-dada attempted to attract me to the city of Burdwan. He advised that I go there right after matriculation; the Raj College there was apparently quite renowned. That Bankura by comparison was hardly a city at all; that it was full of lepers; that the Christian College had far greater reputation than it really deserved. The prolonged comparisons between Bankura and Burdwan made me drowsy; presently, Prabhat-dada, too, drifted off to sleep.

I used to be able to recite the legendary *the wild are beautiful in the wilderness, the child in its mother's lap* fluently in my Bengali class. However, when I beheld Rajani back in Ranigunj, I was convinced that Sanjiv Chandra had quite forgotten to describe the beauty of a young bride returning to her parents' home. As beautiful as the wild is in the wilderness, a young married girl back in her parents' home is surely no less lovely a sight. As though each finds its own natural rhythm in the respective environment.

Once in Ranigunj, Rajani seemed to shed her bridal appearance overnight. The past several days she had to fulfill a role she was not particularly accustomed to, whether in the manner of her attire or her conduct. It seemed as if she was relieved of that burden as soon as she set foot in her father's home. Even though she did not appear before me directly, I could feel her presence within the house. I had an inkling that her female relatives were making fun of her, and she was actively poking fun at herself in return. When her girlfriends came along and surrounded her, I noticed how Rajani tied a knot with her *sari* around her waist, climbed a guava tree, and became engrossed talking to them. Her high voice, her shouts and screams, her boisterous running around reached my ears. However, not once did she actually appear before me.

Later that afternoon Prabhat-dada took me out for a tour of the town. When we had finished seeing the shops and the people, and were on our way back, Prabhat-dada bought some *zarda* for Nalini-didi. I had the desire to buy a bottle of peppermints for Rajani. Inventing some kind of an excuse, I took leave of Prabhat-dada and fulfilled my wish.

The evening passed wonderfully. It would not be any exaggeration to say that a *basar* was held all over again in my bedroom. The household elders peeked in briefly, then departed. Nalini-didi, a few ladies of comparable age, a group of Rajani's girlfriends, Madhu-da of the thrice-attempted matriculation fame, and a spurious youngster or two remained behind. Nalini-didi played the harmonium and sang,

> *Over yonder see the black bird*
> > *See the blackness of his wings,*
> *Folks call him a kokila*
> > *He appears when it's Spring.*

Prabhat-dada was an amateur magician, and the singing

was followed by various sleights of hand, and assorted jokes and pranks. In the middle of that fun-filled pageant, Prabhat-dada retrieved a coin from my nose, and a goose-egg from Rajani's lap. The laughter turned into a veritable riot. In the end, for his triumphant finale, he produced before that raucous audience the bottle of peppermint meant for Rajani from my pocket. The room exploded. I turned red with embarrassment and fixed my gaze to the floor; Rajani dashed out of the room.

At night, however, Rajani sat next to me, and, chewing a *paan* stuffed with the very same peppermint, observed, "You are nothing but a *kancha kala*."

I did not even try to figure out how Rajani could possibly have developed such a notion of me. I knew that the discovery of the peppermint bottle was at the bottom of all this. That blasted bottle was now in her hand; she had just finished smearing a dab of peppermint in her *paan* which she had then promptly dispatched to her mouth. I had no idea where she had learned to smear peppermint with a hairpin.

I said, "Prabhat-dada has four eyes."

Rajani was busy tossing and catching the peppermint bottle the same way she would play with tamarind seeds. Perhaps this was just another mannerism she had. Rajani said, "Serves you right—they all thought that you are insolent, that you are a *dempo* boy."

I became anxious and apprehensive whether the word may have migrated as far as my father-in-law's and Manohar Kaka's ears. I asked her, "Have they told mother?"

"She'll know soon enough."

"Manohar Kaka, *Swasur Mashay*?"

"I don't know all that."

I was a little irritated. It was all *because* of Rajani; none of this would have happened had she not been so greedy for a *paan*. To tell the truth, she was already becoming addicted to *paan* just like her older sister and others in her family. I admonished her, "What's with this *paan* addiction in a little girl! Your teeth will become tainted, they'll rot."

"It's common for wives and women to chew *paan*."

"Are *you* a wife, or a—" I showed her my thumb.

Rajani instantly stuck out her tongue and retorted, "And *you* too are not my husband but a *kancha kala*. He can't even hide a little bottle, yet has the gall to be a husband! And he studies in the *second class*—my goodness me..." Shaking her head, Rajani gesticulated in such a manner that I could not help laughing.

"And he laughs!" Rajani reproached me.

"Fine, I'll leave tomorrow, then I'll see how you..."

"They all go. What kind of *jamai* would live in his father-in-law's home?" Rajani quipped without batting an eyelid.

I suppose this hurt me deeply. Without another word, I lay down in bed.

It was night already. Rajani closed the shuttered verandah door as well, turned the light off and sat down bedside. She then gave me a shove and said, "I'll sleep near the wall. You move to the window."

"You sleep on this side; on my left..."

"No. *You* sleep on this side. You can see the coconut palm outside from here."

"There are spooks who live up there!"

Rajani said nothing, as if to say anything to confirm that notion was quite redundant. Instead, she started to pull my arms with all her might. Not having a choice, I changed my position and quietly lay down. Moments later, possibly out of the fear of evil, imaginary apparitions, Rajani turned towards me, and moved close against me. A fabulous peppermint flavour was emanating from her mouth.

The following morning passed. Then the preparations for my departure began. I took my bath, finished lunch, and was ready. My train was around two o'clock. We were supposed to return by train. Manohar Kaka was ready too. I had not seen Rajani since morning, even though I heard her movements within the house every now and then.

When it was almost time, Nalini-didi called, suggesting I visit the family shrine. I was headed for the interior of the house, when Rajani appeared out of nowhere and tugged at my shirt-sleeve. Gesturing with her eyes, she quickly scooted up the stairs nearby. There was no one about, so I followed the path up the stairs.

There was a small space under the attic, near the roof above the second floor. It was actually nothing but a wider landing along the staircase. Rajani was waiting there; she had no veil over her head.

She took a quick look at me, then said, "Be careful while in the railroad car. Don't get off the train when it stops at the stations. Do you understand—!"

Watching her deliver instructions like a guardian made me laugh till I almost died. I suppose one of the elders had instructed her to sermonize her husband in these terms before his departure, or perhaps she had observed that this kind of sermonizing was customary.

"Why do you laugh?"

"Where!"

"As if I don't have eyes... don't tell *Thakurjhi* anything when you reach home."

"Not tell her what?"

"Tell her nothing. Absolutely nothing about the peppermint."

I shook my head; no, I would not. I doubt if I would have said anything regardless of her prohibition, however.

Rajani thought for a moment or two, then said, "Make sure you attend school regularly, and study hard. *You* will be the loser if you slacken off." As she spoke, the tone of her voice and her expression changed. A kind of melancholy came over her innocent, cheerful face; her voluble lips suddenly became quiet and began to quiver.

I was summoned downstairs. Rajani hurriedly withdrew her right hand concealed in her *anchal* and placed a *paan* in the palm of my hand. She said, "Have it in the train." She then quickly went down the stairs.

Rajani had smeared peppermint in the *paan*.

PART 6

I now need to mention my father's *Kaishore Vivaha O Samajhita*. I was not supposed to be familiar with a book like that at that age. Sarat, though, had read a few pages. At the time of his daughter's marriage, Father had given his *Behai* a copy of *Kaishore Vivaha*; the implication was that his positions and ideas be followed *vis-a-vis* his daughter and son-in-law. Given the opportunity, Sarat managed to get his hands on the book, and, after reading a few pages, he had hidden it in some secret place. Following my marriage, Sarat had started to smile mysteriously. I had not paid much attention to it, however.

After I had returned from Ranigunj, Sarat and Chandra departed for their home. Father was not terribly keen about Chandra returning; however, her in-laws had indicated that they did not wish their daughter-in-law to be with her parents at this time. Therefore, Father had no choice but to agree. Before leaving, Sarat told me a few things about Father's book.

After they had left, I stole a copy of the book. Reading a few pages secretly, I began to realize why Sarat used to laugh about it like that. I do not have the slightest hesitation to state that even though there are several tragic and painful books in the world, those who happen to marry really young should definitely not read that book. It's agony goes right to the heart.

I shall not repeat here the vivid and detailed account Father had given of the dark abyss into which our society was sinking. Suffice it to say that, if we were to make each home an abode of happiness, if we wished that family life be beneficent and righteous, then it was essential to build up a healthy relationship between men and women. In other words, it was necessary to marry the young as adolescents. In marriage between adults, the heartstrings do not resonate as well, and the commodity called romance simply burns in the conflagration of youthful hormones, it does not glow quietly like a lamp. In Father's view, if marriage occurs during adolescence, the home becomes heavenly: the warmth of the heart, liveliness, love and compassion, romance, sense of duty, generosity, healthy mind and body—these all co-exist in such a household.

I was not exactly supposed to know much about family and society, good or evil at that age, hence I was unable to protest any of Father's views on the subject. Needless to say, I accepted the proposition that adolescent marriage was a great idea, and that society would profit much from it. However, I failed to see how Rajani and I could possibly build an affectionate relationship almost forty miles apart.

It was Father's belief that in adolescence, young boys and girls are mild in temperament, and on the verge of intellectual awakening. Their minds are then pure and vital; they possess a natural sense of reverence and generosity. Marriage at such an age builds a sweet relationship amongst the partners. The initial relationship is similar to that between brother and sister. They learn to be affectionate, they become friends, they pass through moments of civility and meanness—as readily as they exchange a few blows, they also embrace and comfort each other in times of sorrow. The intimate relationship which shall thus be fostered, will develop into genuine love in their youth, and their hearts will no longer become slave to the physical urges. And the merits that will accumulate in the storehouse of adolescence and youth, will together enable a comfortable passage through the gray years.

To add greater punch to his arguments, Father had judiciously incorporated examples from the lives of the great and noble men of Bengal. He had cited the adolescent marriages of Bankim, Navin and others. However, the author had failed to realize that one cannot cook rice by hanging the pot from the top branch of a tree, and lighting a fire on the ground. It was clear that there would be nothing more than a brother and sister relationship between Rajani and me for at least another three or four years. It was further clear that the modicum of contact we did have was due to nothing but the ceremonial customs of marriage. Therefore, I could not fathom how Rajani and I could build a sweet and loving relationship living so far apart.

A feeling of aversion pervaded my mind for a few days; every morning, afternoon and night I remembered Rajani again and again. After sunrise, I would sit down to study with my books and notes, and absent-mindedly listen to the crows cawing. It would seem to me then as though our house had suddenly become too empty. In school, I would sometimes stare vacantly out the window. Outside was a water tank, connected by rows of perforated pipes shooting fountains of water continuously. One could see a rainbow glistening over the streaming fountains—I would intently watch the rainbow for the longest time. At night, sitting by the light to study, I would scribble "Rajani" with a pencil on the back of my scratchpad, then erase it, then write again, and erase again. Around this time, our Bengali teacher Hem Babu had given us an assignment in class involving the contextual meaning of the phrase, "Is there not any contentment, is there not any bliss, is the world only with anguish filled..." Sitting in my study room at night, I had written an entire thesis on the anguish-filled world in a rush. It was no mean achievement for a sixteen year old youth to have acquired such deep and extensive knowledge about the agony of life on earth, perhaps it was beyond the reach of even Hem Babu. Having written the thesis on agony, I remember having wept for a while.

However, the childhood separation pangs did not last long, and soon the feeling of sadness passed. Summer had arrived, and morning school had begun. Riding a bicycle to school early in the morning kept the mind fresh and vigorous. The fields were peaceful and desolate, the morning air cool, the sky clear, the mango trees loaded with blossoms on the verge of fruition, *kaath champa* trees decked with flowers-riding past these bracing scenes, I would often think of Rajani. Immediately, though, I would realize that Rajani was now fast asleep. A feeling of envy would probably arise; I would not quite understand, and in the end I would find some peace of mind by branding her a descendent of *Kumbha Karna*.

I had little time to think about Rajani in the evenings. The game of football had already descended on our rustic village fields. After running around the field for two hours, I would return home at twilight, soaking in perspiration and quite weary. When I would sit down to study after a bath, my eyelids, heavy from sleepiness, would begin to close. I would try to memorize my lesson drowsily, until eventually Mother would shake me up and say, "What! Are you asleep? Come along, have your dinner."

Summer vacation arrived. Chandra was brought home. With her arrival, the house seemed fuller. Honestly, with Chandra in the house, my loneliness completely disappeared. Since it was impossible to have my little brother as a companion, I had ignored him in all grown-up activities. Chandra filled my need for companionship. In our spare time, we would play ludo and caroms, prepare and enjoy *amchur*, and secretly read the few novels Chandra had sneaked into the house in her suitcase.

Physically, Chandra appeared to have gained some weight. Moreover, her demeanour and language made her seem older than me. All my life, I had pulled her hair and tweaked her ears. Now, if I even touched her ear, she would take offense, and if I pulled her hair, she would complain, "God, that hurts! Look what you did—you pulled out a clump of my hair!" Even Mother would forbid me to bother or torment Chandra. She would warn me that Chandra was now a member of another family.

Around this time, one day Chandra became particularly chummy with me, then handed me a letter and a couple of rupees as bribe, and said, "Go to the post office and mail this."

The letter was contained in an envelope. It had Sarat's address written on it. I asked her, "Have you written to Sarat?" As though writing him was something improper.

Chandra replied, "You go mail it."

"What if Father finds out?"

"Let him. What does it matter?"

I did not know if it mattered. However, I assumed that in keeping with the regulations of adolescent marriage, such exchange of letters was also prohibited.

Within a few days, a letter arrived in my name. It was from Sarat. It *is* true that he had been writing me a letter or two of late, but these were postcards. This letter arrived in an envelope, whose colour , moreover, was pale blue. Almost as soon as the letter came into my hands, suddenly Chandra appeared, as if she had somehow received the news telepathically. Dragging me to a corner almost by force, she extended her palm in anticipation. "Give me the letter."

The letter was mine; I could not figure out how Chandra could have any rights to it. So I told her, "He's written it to me, it's mine."

"It's not yours, it's mine. Give it to me."

"Oh, sure, it's in *my* name, and it's *yours!*"

"It's mine. We had agreed that he would address it to you. Otherwise Father—"

I sort of followed the nature of the conspiracy, yet, not quite. As soon as I tore the envelope open, two or three colored sheets of perfumed paper emerged from within. They had my dear brother-in-law Sarat's handwriting on them. At the top, written in very ornate calligraphy were the words, *Priyatama Chandra.*

In the meantime, Chandra had sprung on me and snatched the sheets of paper from me. Only the empty envelope remained in my hand. Seizing the letter, Chandra quickly vanished.

Thanks to Chandra, I had started to read novels. Needless to say, the significance of the secret letter and the endearing address at the head of it was not lost on me. I felt a romantic thrill. It seemed incredibly sweet. A sigh built up inside my chest. Could *I* not write a letter to Rajani? Could Rajani not write me one?

Sarat and Chandra were quite clever. They had already planned the strategy to use me as a decoy for their correspondence, and thereby pull the wool over Father's eyes. But Rajani and I had no such pact. If I were to write her a letter, who knows what those in her family might say, how much they might laugh about it, what rumours they might spread! Would Rajani be brave enough to write me a letter? What if I were to receive a letter from her addressed to me, and Father were to find out? How would I hide the letter from Mother's eyes either?

After consulting Chandra, I eventually decided that I must write a letter. Chandra would seemingly write a letter to her brother's wife. No one would mind that. However, *I* would insert inside Chandra's envelope a letter with the words *Priyatama Rajani* at its head. I would not write all those embellishments like Sarat; Rajani would not read them, nor would she follow.

That night, after three different drafts, I wrote my *Priyatama Rajani* an epistle in large, bold letters. The following morning, the letter was enclosed in an envelope via Chandra, as planned. Later, I mailed it with my own hands at the post office. My heart was thumping all the while, whether out of joy or fear, it is hard to tell.

Three, four, five days went by waiting for a reply to my letter. Soon, a whole week passed. Correspondence between Sarat and Chandra usually did not involve this much delay. Did Rajani not receive my letter? Or, perhaps she has died of embarrassment before everyone because of it. I had the impression that Rajani was not particularly bashful. A fortnight was soon over, still no response. My impatience was turning into fear and anxiety. Then, one day Rajani's letters arrived in two different envelopes. One bore my name, written in amateurish English handwriting. Below my name was a line which read, *Class Nine, M.K.H. School.* Yet, below that there appeared our home address and post office. Who but Rajani would write something so laughable and stupid!

Upon opening the envelope, a lined sheet of paper emerged. On it was written in large script, *With a million pranams I humbly submit at your hallowed feet, I am well. How are you? Your letter has been read by Didi, by Pishimani. They've said, you're an obnoxious monkey. Please don't write me anything obscene again. Goodness, I am so ashamed.*

The letter-writing phase did not last long. Sarat and Chandra were alleviating their separation pain without any hassle, whereas we were unable to do so—whether or not this was proof of our incompetence, I felt frustrated anyhow. I was jealous of Chandra and Sarat. Once I thought of squealing on them. Only the thought of my sister's clouded face kept me from doing so.

The rainy season arrived. Clouds began to file in and out of the sky. When lightning flashed against the dense, dark backdrop of the rainclouds, trees and ferns began to quiver in delightful anticipation of impending rains. It was not unnatural that some days, under such circumstances, my mind would become despondent. Yet, I did not find the courage to write any more letters. At school, the football season was then on, and my mind would tend to lie there. After my classes, I would first go to the playing field, then ride my bicycle home, bruised and battered, drenched in the pouring rain. At night, I would use one hand to massage my aching limbs with hot soda lime and turmeric, while trying to read *The Gift of God* with the other. I would realize then that God in his infinite mercy has granted me a rather painful object of happiness. Perhaps then a deluge descends from the sky accompanied by thunderclaps, and my voice is drowned in the mesmerizing sounds of chirping crickets and croaking frogs. Then, sitting before the tremulous lamp, spellbound by the incessant, magical percussion of the rain, I would feel this great yearning for Rajani. Did not a downpour like this descend from this world-engulfing raincloud upon Rajani's *pitralaya*?

The day before the *Rathayatra*, Rajani arrived. Chandra had already brought me the good tidings in advance. Father had sent Manohar Kaka to bring Rajani over from Ranigunj, so he could take his daughter-in-law to the *Rath Carnival*.

I saw Rajani after sunset. She tiptoed into my study room with Chandra. What business was it to me that someone had come only for a day or two to see the *Rath Carnival*! With a solemn face I opened up my Bengali text and commenced reading aloud, *"Who resides within the temple? No one answered, only the melodious tinkling of jewellery wafted into the ears. Deciding that further vocal exertions would be wasteful, the traveller then…"*

Chandra interrupted me. Smiling, she said, "Put your book away; come, enjoy this—"

I looked. The delicious aroma of fresh, piping hot *begunis*, *phuluris* and *papad bhaja* was exciting both the olfactory tract and the taste buds. Chandra set the tray down before me. The two *nari-ratnas* already had their hands and mouths busy. Casting a quick glance at Rajani, I said with apparent disdain, "I won't eat. Let me study, don't bother me."

Chandra asked, "What are you reading?"

"Bengali."

"Isn't tomorow a holiday? Come on, eat while it's hot."

Deciding that further vocal exertions would be wasteful, I went back to my reading.

Instantly, a signal was probably exchanged between Chandra and Rajani; Chandra said, "Wait, Mother's making tea, let me go get it."

Even after Chandra had left, I remained steadfast in my resolve. After repeating *"Who resides in the temple?"* about five times, I stopped abruptly. Rajani was trying to poke me in the cheek with a hot *beguni*. I pushed her hand away. Rajani once again shoved her bangle, *sankha*, and *bala*-bedecked wrist under my nose.

"Don't fool around with me," I said, and pushed her hand away with a jerk.

Rajani doubled over with laughter. "Uh-oh, looks like he's upset!"

"Why are you here?"

"So what? I'm glad I'm here. Is this *your* house? Father's brought me here."

"So go to Father. Don't bother me."

"Oh, sure, such a studious boy! All you're doing is mumble *temple* over and over!"

"That's *my* business, what's it to you?"

"It's *kancha kala* to me." Rajani waved her thumb at me. She then said, "You have a belly full of anger."

"You are nobody to me."

"Really? Just because *you* say so!"

"I will marry again when I grow up."

"And *I* will turn into a *petni* and break your wife's neck."

"You *are* a *petni*..."

"Of course, *bhoots* usually have *petnis* for their wives."

Rajani was quite adept at talking. The fight did not intensify enough. I surrendered. Rajani stuffed my mouth with *begunis* and *phuluris*. Let *Tilottama* wait inside the temple; I am not interested right now.

Munching *papad*, Rajani spoke like a seasoned homebody, "I am worried to death thinking about you. Such downpours, frightening thunderclaps, I feel afraid—you go to school over open fields—who knows if... If you hear thunderclaps, pray to *Baaj Thakur*."

"Who is *Baaj Thakur*?"

"I don't know. Pishimani says *Baaj Thakur*."

"You are a liar number one."

"Liar number one, *me*?"

"You never think of me."

"Listen to this boy talk! *I* don't think—" Rajani seemed to speak to an unseen witness, "I can't even sleep, I'm so worried..."

The manner in which she said *"can't even sleep"* made me laugh. Rajani laughed too. She had imitated the speaking style of a true grown-up, such as her mother, aunt or older sister, and could not help laughing loudly.

The following day, Rajani and Chandra went to see the *Rath Carnival* six miles away with Father and Manohar Kaka. I did not join them. It was dark by the time they returned, the day-long drizzle had then turned into a torrential downpour. They were soaking wet and cold from the rain and stormy winds; Rajani was shivering violently. Sitting down to study, I prayed with all my heart that Rajani might catch the fever tonight; if she were to catch the fever, then certainly she could not dance her way back to Ranigunj in only a day or two.

After shedding her wet clothes and drying herself, Rajani came to see me. She appeared quite normal physically; only her hair seemed to be kind of wet. She walked over and sat next to me. Outside, the rain had not stopped yet, and the occasional rumbling of thunder could be heard.

I listened quietly as Rajani described the *Rath Carnival* a little bit. I had seen the *mela* many times; there was little reason to feel excited. Finally, Rajani plucked a photograph out of some secret place and placed it in my hand. She said, "I had a picture taken at the *mela*; *Thakurjhi* talked me into it."

I did not know they had photo stalls at the *Rath Carnival*. The freshly developed print was still sticky; there was more black than white in the photo. I asked, "Where's your ear?"

Rajani was puzzled. Confused, she immediately touched her ear with her hand.

"Darn, no—where's your ear in this picture?"

Hurriedly snatching the photo from my hand, Rajani eagerly scrutinized her picture. Her ear was indeed missing; the empty space looked kind of funny. Heartbroken, Rajani asked, "What will happen?"

"Give it to me."

"That's what *Thakurjhi* suggested. ...No, I guess not—there's no need for you to keep an earless photo. It'll turn you off every time you see it." Rajani put the picture out of my reach, then said ruefully, "As such I am *such* a sight to behold, and to top that, if you have to look at this earless *Taraka*, you will probably throw me out."

"It's not earless *Taraka*, it's *Surpanakha*..."

"Of course I know that, dear, you don't have to tell me."

"You said *Taraka*."

"I'm glad I did. We say such things."

Laughing at her sauciness, I grabbed a bunch of her wet hair and yanked. "Give me the photo, I'll have the ear fixed."

"How will you do that?"

"I'll say a *mantra*."

Hearing me mention *mantra*, and noticing the

mischievous smirk on my face, Rajani surveyed me with evident disbelief. She said, "Let it be, I'll keep my photo with me."

The next day, Rajani showed no sign of any fever or pain. I watched her happily run around, looking perfectly hale and hearty. For some reason, however, Father decided to keep her with us for a week. It was a mixed blessing for me. We could no longer meet in the bedroom; nevertheless, we did meet and talk to each other several times a day. Rajani had become quite a bit more talkative than before. She had also become much more mischievous. I had no doubt this had a lot to do with her association with Chandra.

Before she returned to her parents' home, Rajani took pity and presented me the photograph. She said, "I am giving you this because you were so eager to get it."

Seeing my prayer so generously rewarded, I gratefully planted a kiss on the lips of my benefactor. The benefactor accepted it and swiftly vanished out of sight.

PART 7

The monsoon ended. It was a while since Chandra had returned to her in-laws' home. Her mother-in-law was ill. I was alone in the house. My little brother would spend the entire day riding a tricycle and playing all kinds of girlish games by himself. He had practically no contact with me. Presently, the balmy season of autumn manifested itself. The *shiuli* bush in our courtyard had begun to bloom after dusk. The captivating fragrance of *shiuli* would make my mind restless. On my way to and from school, the sight of the green, furrowed paddy fields would soothe my eyes. The soft light of *Sarat* seemed to flood everything to the farthest horizon with warmth and joy. The sky was turning more sunny and blue with every passing day. Then, on the day when fresh hay was spread over the old platform and pedestal of the village *puja* house, the smell of *puja* in the air quite unsettled the mind. Rajani was expected to arrive around the time of the *puja*. I had heard as much through the grapevine.

Until now, there were only two things I would wish for prior to the *puja*, the *puja* holidays and the arrival of Mother Durga. I am not embarrassed to confess that this year it was Rajani's arrival which rose above all else in my mind. I had a calendar; I would check the date on it every morning, and, saying *twenty-eight more*, *twenty-seven more*, I would keep a close watch on that coveted day within my mind.

The *puja* arrived, Mother Durga arrived too, but Rajani did not. It seems Mother Durga took a rather severe revenge on me. I learned that Rajani's parents having requested that she be allowed to spend the days of the *puja* with them, Father had most generously granted their wish. Needless to say, his generosity had caused me great pain and exasperation.

I had received new clothes as *puja* gifts from both families. Chandra arrived as well, but for me the fun of the *puja* had just about evaporated. I was really upset with Rajani. She *must* have become hysterical and clamoured about staying with her parents, otherwise why would this happen? I felt my pride seriously hurt that my wife considered others closer to herself than her husband; I even felt terribly reluctant about ever seeing her face again.

Presently, *puja* was over as usual. On the twelfth day, Sarat

ived. He would stay for three or four days, then return to
pare for an important exam. He did not look the slightest
anxious, though. He had started taking snuff; apparently
helped stay up at night for his studies. I noticed that in
dition there was a more subtle purpose and a clandestine
nal associated with the snuff habit. The excessive
eezing would invariably cause Chandra to materialize from
newhere.

Witnessing the exorbitant intimacy between Sarat and
andra, their behaviour towards each other, their teasing and
wning around, their obvious love made my own heart feel
te barren and arid. I felt my own life to be so drab and
poverished compared to theirs, that Rajani seemed to me
be quite the unfit wife.

Sarat said, "You are what they call *Ram Chunder*, spending
e in *vanabasa* to fulfill your father's command.... Well my
r, for every rule there's a loophole. Where there's reason,
re's a way."

His words felt like salt over a wound.

On the day of *Kojagari Purnima*, Rajani arrived. Her father
t her, accompanied by a relative and an assortment of boxes,
dles and other paraphernalia. Sarat quipped, "Your *wife*,
rection, *sister wife* is here."

I did not bother replying.

Soon after her arrival, Rajani began offering Bijaya
nams with a flourish, even though she had already
pleted a round by mail. I knew that I, too, had the right
pranam from her. Mother would surely send her to me.
t so Rajani would not get any opportunity to offer me a
nam, and realize that I did not care for her a farthing; that

I was not waiting for her arrival like a destitute—I secret[ly]
slipped out of the house before she showed up.

But despite running out of the house, I had no peace [of]
mind. My heart was burning up from feelings of resentmen[t]
and hurt. The charming *Kartik* morning appeared empty [to]
me. The abundant *Kash* flowers swayed in the gentle breez[e,]
sending waves of whiteness over the fields. The pastel yello[w]
tips of the stalks of paddy whistled across vast stretches [of]
green rice fields in the brisk gusts of wind. The large leav[es]
of water lily on the surface of the lake sparkled in the war[m]
grains of sunlight. To me, however, all these exquisite sigh[ts]
appeared quite drab that morning.

I returned home late, deliberately letting the morning g[o]
by. Back home, it was the day for *Lakshmi Puja*. Mother w[as]
busy making all kinds of arrangements; Chandra and Raja[ni]
were following her around. Sarat was alone in his roo[m]
reading a novel. Seeing me, he smiled and said, "Where we[re]
you hiding? Your Rajani came around so many times, looki[ng]
for you. Poor thing, she looks so blue."

"I went to see someone," I replied rather nonchalantly, a[nd]
went in for my bath.

While taking my bath, however, I wondered if Sarat w[as]
merely putting me on, or if Rajani really did look for m[e.]

Chandra and Rajani were seen together when Sarat a[nd]
I sat down to eat. Mother was unable to wait on us becau[se]
she was too busy with the *puja* arrangements. Chandra h[ad]
taken over the role of the lady in charge of household functio[ns]
such as supervising meals; Rajani was helping her by keepi[ng]
drinking water, table salt, and the like handy. Presently, Raja[ni]
and I made eye contact; however, in her demeanour I did n[ot]

detect any sign of guilt or contrition. She did not approach me to offer a *pranam*, either.

During the meal, Sarat joked and kidded around a lot; Chandra joined him shamelessly, and even Rajani started using fairly piquant language in their company. Only I remained as poker faced as possible, did not eat properly, trying all the while to let the others know how upset I really was.

In the afternoon, Sarat was asleep. Lying on a cane mat in my bedroom, reflecting on this, that, and the other thing, I too had drifted off to sleep. Disturbed by a feeling of tremor caused by something, I stirred and moved in my sleep a few times, and eventually woke up. I noticed it was Rajani who was busy tickling me in my ears and nose with the rolled-up end of her *anchal*. When finally I awoke, she began smiling demurely.

I sat up, to be sure, but did not say a word.

Rajani began to gaze playfully at my face from various angles. She then said, *"When it's them, it's peachy and nice; when it's others, it's hell without disguise."*

Of the above, I followed nothing, and did not even try. I simply turned my face away. The window at the head of the bed was open, the shadows were lengthening outside, and, from the *neem* tree not far away, my little brother's swing could be seen swaying.

My silence was intolerable to Rajani. She suddenly grabbed my hand and gave it a tug. She said, "What's with all this irritation? Hey you, Mr. Deaf and Dumb! Do you hear, or not even that?"

I yanked my hand free in response. At this, Rajani sat dazed for a moment or two, then did something quite unexpected and weird. Pouncing on me, she scratched and slashed me all

over, pulled my hair, then began to cry hysterically. As s
cried, she told me a million things that I cannot even catalogu
Anger, hurt, insult, frustration—a combination of all the
emotions probably made her crazy. What a little girl!

From her words, I surmised that she had really wanted
come here for the *puja*, but her parents wanted her to be wi
them. How could she possibly ask them to send her off to h
husband! Doesn't one feel embarrassed?

My anger and hurt left me, and it felt like recovering fro
a fever. Attempting to assuage the burning from Rajan:
scratches, I said to her, "So, must you pull my hair out? Goug
chunks of flesh out like that!"

"I will scratch you even more. I'll even bite."

"What *are* you, a dog or a cat?"

"Dog, of course. Otherwise, who else would still follo
you after the way you behaved?"

"I had a lousy *puja* just because of you."

"Oh, dear! And *I*—?"

"Why, you had a swell time."

"Oh, some swell time for sure!" Rajani said in
dispassionate tone; then, remembering something, sh
continued, "It's O.K. for *your* family to have the daughte
spend *puja* at home, and for *me* to stay with *my* parents is suc
a grievous sin. *Thakurjhi* has told me she won't be comin
next year."

"And you?"

Rajani started saying something, then stopped abruptly
Her face solemn, she wiped her eyes with her *anchal* and said
"I'll think about that later."

Watching her grown-up attitude, I felt the desire to cares

her. Squeezing her cheek affectionately, I said, "You little *shakchunni*!"

Later, on that *Kojagari* full moon, we had a late night rendezvous. We had both sneaked out of the house when it was convenient and opportune to do so, and, standing behind the house in the silvery, moonlit night, chatted for a while. Meanwhile, Chandra had joined Sarat in my bedroom. The plan was that as soon as Sarat would whistle softly a few times, I would return to my bedroom and lie down beside Sarat, while Rajani would lie down beside Chandra. The idea, of course, was Sarat's.

Standing next to each other, while trying not to be seen in the bright moonlight, Rajani and I had talked about a variety of things. I do not see the need to recount them here. Standing beside the banana bush, intoxicated by the *Kojagari* light, Rajani said eventually, "Do you have any idea how often I cry secretly for you!"

"I cry too."

With those words, we looked at each other's eyes. It seemed as though we were once again exchanging *shubha-drishti*, this time wearing banana-leaf crowns. We both started laughing. Leaning against me, Rajani said, "You liar!"

PART 8

About two and a half years rolled by. There is little doubt time flows like the swift currents of a river. I had completed my matriculation examination. In the meantime, I had undergone a few changes, I daresay improvements. The outline of my moustache had become deeper; I had begun to get myself civilized haircuts; I had even turned into quite a snappy dresser. Father had not interfered with my grooming preferences. In fact, he was quite satisfied that I had studied hard and completed the examination. Bhuvan Babu, my private tutor, assured my father that he need not worry about my chances of passing the examination. I had no anxiety about my prospects either.

I was already dreaming about studying at the Bankura College. Sarat was a student there. My mind had been strongly inclined towards college studies ever since Sarat told me stories about college life. I had even heard that Father had plans to send me to college. Of course, following my matriculation examination, Prabhat Dada also wrote me an enticing letter exhorting me to go to Burdwan for my studies. He wrote, "*Chhota Babu*, if you choose Burdwan, I will take care of all your needs. Tell you what, I may even bring Chini over for a month or two. Your academic progress is guaranteed to double under such circumstances." Even though I was in a quandary regarding the choice between Bankura and Burdwan, I also knew that ultimately there was little I could do about it. Everything would happen according to Father's wishes.

After the matriculation examination, I had all the time in the world. There was not the slightest care to burden my mind, which felt light as a feather. I spent a few days sleeping to my heart's content. After that, I went to fetch Chandra from her father-in-law's home. Father sent me.

How things change with time right before one's eyes! The extent to which Chandra had changed in the last two or three years had never been more vividly apparent to me than this time. I can barely describe the physical grace and beauty which have descended upon Chandra with age. It is as though a leaf has turned sleek and supple following the nourishing monsoon showers. The girlish flightiness in her restless spirit had given way to a joyous and self-assured maturity. She no longer speaks quite like she did before, her voice has become a little heavier, and her eyelids have taken on a droopy charm. Seeing Chandra, a feeling of gladness filled my mind.

Again and again, I kept thinking about Rajani. I had last seen her during the previous *puja*, and we had not met since. Already, Rajani's sweet sixteen comeliness had caught my eyes. She had grown a little taller, and proportionately rounder. Her complexion, too, had seemed a shade or two lighter than before. I wondered how much she must have changed in these six or seven months.

I felt a desire to write her a letter. Yet, I could not write it.

My father-in-law had a bit of the travel bug. I had seen few others with such a passion for the *tirthas*. He would set off on his pilgrimages at the drop of a hat, gladly leaving his *compounder* in charge of his dispensary. He was a simple man, and had little to worry about financially. I had heard that my *swasur mahashay* had left for Hardwar with his wife and daughters. Of course, Father knew the actual facts, but I could not possibly ask him.

Chandra retrieved the news for me. She informed me that Rajani and her family were scheduled to return shortly, and that they would visit us afterwards.

Chandra said, "It's boom time for you."

"Why?"

"Rajani may come and stay here this time."

"Who said so?"

"Mother was saying so."

"Come on, this is not *your swasur-bari* that they'll keep their *bou* here."

"This time they will, *you'll* see. But then, what difference will it be to you? You won't be here, but Rajani will—" Chandra smiled cryptically, then, feigning a sigh, she said, "What does it matter to the crow if the *bel* ripens?"

She was right, yet, feeling quite elated by the news of Rajani's impending arrival, I complained, "How come you're calling her Rajani—shouldn't you say *Boudi* instead?"

Chandra smiled again, and said, "So, aren't *you* really into it!"

My mind was in a state of pure exhilaration. Laughing heartily, I responded, "You're into it no less."

Suddenly a little embarrassed, Chandra withdrew out of sight.

Chaitra arrived on the heels of *Phalgun*. Then *Chaitra*, too, was almost over. My holidays passed wandering about, sleeping, and reading novels and stories. Father had an extensive collection of the classics, from Bankim and Navin to Prabhat Kumar. He also subscribed to several literary magazines. These used to be strictly out of bounds for me, but not any more. They became my staples; once in a while, I would also borrow books from friends. My fellow students, too, suffered from the same affliction; all they did was eat, sleep, chat and read novels.

Presently, I received news that Rajani and her family had returned from their trip. Ever since, I waited for her arrival like the legendary *chataka*.

It was after noon on that day. I was not home. I was at

the school playing field, watching a football match. It was a warm and humid day; everything was strangely still as evening drew near. The ominous signs of a *kalvaisakhi* storm appeared across the sky. I was hurrying home, but the *kalvaisakhi* descended upon the fields on my way. The skies grew dark, then the darkness became solid and hard as black marble. Brisk winds began to blow, and it became increasingly harder to ride the bicycle. I pedaled with all my might. Close to home, I noticed that the *kalvaisakhi* had struck the terrified fields and trees with a vengeance.

The storm arrogantly wreaked destruction for a long time. It rained copiously, and, mixed with the intensity of the rain, the roar of the storm reverberated from the corners of the vast fields. Soon, a dense, black, rain-drenched night covered everything, and it felt as though we were stranded in some desolate island.

Chandra came in and said, "You have a bit of bad news."

Bad news! Was it the examination? That was impossible! "What is it?"

"Rajani isn't coming."

My hopes of the past several days shattered, I instantly felt an emptiness which made me quite numb inside. An intense impulse of grudge and antipathy towards Rajani arose in my mind. An irrepressible urge to cry was welling up my chest.

I do not know if Chandra had noticed my expression and was trying to be sympathetic; at any rate, she said, "You have some good news too."

Was Chandra pulling my leg! Irritated, I was about to tell her something when she interrupted me. She said, "Rajani cannot come. Her father broke his leg; he is confined to his bed. He has requested that you visit them. You are to spend a few days there."

Now, my father-in-law went out on a trip covering remote and difficult terrain of every description, and nothing happened to his legs; yet, just after returning home, when it was time to send his daughter away, he managed to break his leg—this *had* to be a machination of my cruel and evil fate. It is quite likely that in my grief I must have viewed my father-in-law's broken leg as nothing but a mutation of my own broken heart.

Per my father's instructions, I went to my father-in-law's home to spend a few days. On my way, I told myself that one must not bear any grudge against someone in trouble. Besides, was it Rajani's fault that her father broke his leg! It was just my own bad luck. In fact, what if I were not given even this chance to visit Rajani before leaving for Bankura? To tell the truth, my mind turned to mush thinking about the plight of others, and my heart danced in anticipation of the two or three days I was to spend with Rajani.

It had been a long time since my last visit to Ranigunj. This time, Nalini Didi was not there; after the pilgrimage, she had returned to Burdwan. Only Rajani remained anchored in Ranigunj indefinitely.

Rajani came in after dark. The room was lit by the light of a table lamp. Closing the door, Rajani approached me. There was a pleasant and joyous smile on her face.

"Hey, mister, how *are* you?" She walked over to my bedside. With her left hand, she lowered her veil to her shoulder. As usual, she had a *paan* in her mouth.

One quick glance at Rajani revealed to me that my *balika*

badhu had just metamorphosed into a young woman. Her voluminous hair gathered in a bun, her swan-like neck, the expressiveness of her eyes and face, her graceful arms, and indeed her entire body had acquired a whole new measure of delicacy and beauty. It seemed as though I had never before noticed or understood just how beautiful Rajani really was. I gazed at her with unwavering attention and admiration.

Sensing my overwhelmed condition, Rajani felt amused. She said, "What are you staring at? Can't recognize your own wife?"

"Really! You've changed *so* much!"

"You too."

"How quickly girls change—! Even Chandra…"

"Of course, *Thakurjhi* is going to have a baby."

"Who told you?"

"*Thakurjhi* has written to me."

For some unknown reason, the breezy currents of my thought drifted to a mysterious realm and began to hover in the dark.

"Would you please stand up?"

"Why?"

"Let me see if I have grown past your shoulders or not!"

I stood up. Rajani came forward to measure her height against me, but suddenly she bent over and did a *pranam*. I was unable to stop her. After the *pranam*, she stood up and said, "One should offer *pranams* after completing a pilgrimage; after all, you *are* an elder to me!" Laughing heartily, she proceeded to check her height. She had indeed surpassed my shoulders and come up to level with my cheeks.

I sat down. Rajani asked, "I heard you are going to pass

in one try?" She then started gazing at me mischievously.

"A gentleman's word is good as gold." I began laughing, too.

"Then you will go to Bankura for your studies?"

"Father has asked me to."

"Girls study there too—grown-up girls. *Thakurjhi's* told me. You cannot mix with the girls."

"What if I did?"

"Oh, yeah!... Then what about me!"

Rajani said it in such a manner as though she seriously worried about what would happen to her. I cannot express the thrill I felt noticing her innocent foolishness. Laughing, I promised her, "No, I won't mix with them."

"Remember, you've touched me and made this promise."

"Yes, I have."

It seemed Rajani was at a loss for words momentarily to express her gratefulness to me. She then wrote the word "Rajani" on my chest with her finger, and said, "There, and no one else." With that, she quietly placed her head upon my chest.

The night wore on as we talked. Rajani and I were lying next to each other; the table-lamp was still burning, but trembling every now and then. There were stormy gusts outside. It was raining intermittently.

Suddenly, Rajani remembered something and said, "I have now learned how to sleep properly. I will not point my feet towards you again."

"So what if you do?"

"Why?'

"*Dehi padapallavamudarang...*"

"What is that? What does it mean?"

When I told her, Rajani pulled herself away from my feet and said with a mild rebuke, "Oh, come on!"

PART 9

What Chandra had said in jest was in fact true; a crow like me had no cause for mirth just because the *bel* fruit had ripened. Indeed, a little reflection would reveal just how unlucky I really was. There was a song by Dwijendralal I had heard somewhere, "Oh why did he appear before me, dear, would be so much better if he had not—" I must have understood then the fullest significance of those words. Rajani's appearance turned out to be like a flash of lightning— no sooner than it had revealed itself, it hid behind the clouds. After a few days in Ranigunj, I returned home, and passed the entire month of *Vaishakh* listening to the cooing of doves in the afternoon, and counting the stars in the sky at night. Around the middle of *Jaishtha*, rather dejectedly I had to leave at last for Bankura.

The few days I spent with Rajani back in my father-in-law's home made the whole world appear exceedingly sweet to me. It was an entirely new experience for me.

Of course, I had also noticed the changes which had taken place in Rajani's personality. Maybe her restless spirit had not been subdued as much as Chandra's, maybe her movements and utterances did not reflect quite the same degree of intimacy, joy and self-assuredness. Nevertheless, Rajani was no longer the naive and foolish young girl she used to be. The restlessness of her manner had been replaced by a sense of purpose and determination, and flashes of lightning had begun to accumulate in her glance. Observing Rajani's conscious efforts, through her actions and demeanor, to reveal her exalted status as a housewife, I could not help laughing heartily. Before leaving her, I had confessed that no matter how amusing her conceptions regarding marital life were earlier, they had now improved considerably.

As for myself, I can claim with some confidence that I now had a clearer and deeper perception of the feelings which were fuzzy and only partially comprehensible in my youthful years. That keener sense of perception sent waves of tremor and thrill up and down my spine observing Rajani in her resplendent glory. If I were to express our condition at that time in the language of poetry, I would perhaps liken myself to a flighty and restless breeze, agitated by the impulses of youth, and Rajani to a bloom, newly-blossomed and laden with heavenly fragrance. Fate, however, had not written for us any ballads of spring; separation came between us once again. Rajani remained with her parents, and I went to Bankura.

Father personally accompanied me to Bankura, and had me admitted into college. As per the arrangements made earlier by Sarat, I was supposed to live in a hostel on campus. Father approved of the hostel itself; however, the manner and lifestyle of the residents left a negative impression on him.

I need to mention something in this context. My father was slightly displeased with his son-in-law and his family. The reason for his displeasure, of course, was that the precepts outlined in Father's *Kaishore Vivaha O Samajhita* had been grossly neglected in that household. If those precepts were observed, Sarat would not be faced with the prospect of fatherhood at this time. If that auspicious event were to occur a year or two later, Father would have experienced absolute happiness.

Father was displeased with Sarat for another reason. Sarat's personality, style and manners were quite unlike anything Father wished to see in his son-in-law. Sarat was much too modern and *avant-garde* in his comportment, fashion sense and hair-style; Father considered these decadent and effeminate. The lack of manliness in his son-in-law was painful to him; however, it is also true that privately he admired Sarat's brilliance, intelligence and extroverted nature.

Therefore, suffice it to say that in their style, fashion or manners the young students Father met in the hostel were no different from Sarat, and this observation led him to conclude that the unhealthy winds of change had reached the youth of even small, suburban towns such as Bankura, corrupted their minds with crass materialism, and rendered their characters soft and pliable. I cannot tell how deeply this abject degeneration of the nation's youth hurt him, but I suppose he must have felt gravely concerned about the future of his son and son-in-law.

As planned, and with Sarat's efforts, I found accommodation in Sarat's room. Father went home. Thence, he wrote us a long letter filled with sundry instructions. The essential truth contained in the letter was that both good and evil co-exist in this world, and especially in this day and age, evil was more plentiful; under these circumstances, he who could conquer all weakness and attraction towards the evil, and hold his attention and faith upon the good, would ultimately develop strength of character. And he who did not possess strength of character, could do nothing but harm to society and the world. Therefore, Father primarily cautioned us against falling into the company of the evil and the unscrupulous, and succumbing to the temptations of luxury and comfort. He instructed us to build our characters in every possible dimension.

Reading the letter from beginning to end, Sarat observed dejectedly, "My Swasur Mahashay is too old model... go on, frame it and hang it on your wall; make sure you read it once every morning." Thereafter, he picked up his favorite flute from a corner of the study table and sat down on his bed with it.

Since coming to college, Sarat was practicing playing the flute. As bad luck would have it, Father had walked into his room, and, observing the flute upon his study table, become speechless with shock. Moments later, gesturing with his eyes in the direction of the flute, he had asked in a sombre voice, "Who plays that?"

The colour had drained from my brother Sarat's face. Scratching his head, his mouth dry, he eventually replied, "Sir, I do."

"They give you flute lessons in college?"

Sarat did not comprehend the sarcasm implicit in the above remark; he was in no condition to do so. He fell quiet. Then, suddenly, he had a brainwave. Sounding apologetic, he said in a defensive tone, "Yes, Sir, it's sound.... we are studying sound in physics. ...I was playing the flute the other day to test its resonance..."

With a reproachful glare, Father instructed his son-in-law not to tell lies.

Sarat almost shrank from embarrassment. ...It was the very same flute which he was playing now.

Father's sermon-filled letter remained in its place, while Sarat continued playing the flute. I sat by the window staring outside.

Clouds heaped up across the sky. The monsoon had arrived. The earthy scent of the monsoon breeze made my mind listless and homesick. I had received news that Rajani had arrived at her father-in-law's home.

Sarat tried playing the vague and flawed melody of a song on his flute for a short while, then abandoned his musical exertions. He then asked, "Would you like to go to the cinema?"

Just then my mind was preoccupied with the vision of Rajani braiding her hair in the evening—perhaps at this late twilight hour Chandra and Rajani were braiding each other's hair and, watching the accumulating rainclouds, perhaps thinking of us.

"Well, would you like to go?" Sarat repeated.

"Where?"

"The cinema. ...What are you thinking about? Is it Rajani?"

"Didn't you say you would take me to the bookstore to buy those two books?"

"Of course—we'll buy the books *and* see a film—we'll do both."

I said hesitantly, "But, do you suppose seeing a film every day—!"

"You're *really* like father, like son—!... Now, come along. There's no need for you to go crazy about building character; it will develop on its own."

Whether we call it addiction, or whether we call it a fatal attraction, it always takes time to be hooked on to something. In the beginning, one becomes curious simply out of watching others, one feels a desire, even eagerness; but every new habit is replete with hazards. At first, it does not often agree with one's constitution; one has to gradually tune into it. But in the end, the addictive power of the habit assumes control by arousing one's passions.

No matter how much the lure of studying in college fascinated me, once in Bankura, I felt low and despondent most of the time. Since childhood, I had grown up surrounded by my parents and siblings; suddenly leaving that intimate homely environment and being in an entirely strange place did not make me happy. I had a rather minor addiction, perhaps it was a weakness: prior to my bath, my mother would gently massage oil into my scalp. Ever since childhood, and well into adulthood, I was unable to kick this addiction; neither did my mother ever deny me that indulgence. In the hostel, while applying perfumed oil to my hair prior to my bath as per Sarat's suggestion, I would feel the air freeze and collect like a hard lump inside my throat. Lest Sarat suspect something from my facial expression, I would quickly dash off towards the bathroom. For my father, my little brother, even Chandra, whose absence I should have become accustomed to by then, I would feel sad and downcast. Not to mention the never-ending misery I felt not having Rajani around.

There was not the slightest similarity between the quiet serenity of my home and the atmosphere of this boys' hostel. The sudden demise of my lifelong, tender relationship with the familiar and soothing natural surroundings of our village made my mind feel limp and lifeless. I was a simple village boy—the iron factory school I attended was quite rustic and lustreless, part brick and concrete, part mud and thatch. The school teachers, likewise, were very simple and unpretentious village folk. The intimacy between the students, teachers and the various school buildings ran very deep; at the college in Bankura, I did not experience the slightest trace of it. Being a missionary college, it was constructed with appropriate splendour—great edifices, imposing mansions, pervasive solemnity, and urban style. These only served to overwhelm a newcomer such as myself.

The eagerly anticipated college experience, therefore, felt a lot like the experiments of an adolescent with such taboo activities as smoking or drinking to me. My inexperience caused me exasperation and suffocation at every step.

Soon, however, the rush and stimulation of the new experience intensified. All that had initially seemed bereft of any charm gradually turned into sources of great pleasure.

The academic grind went into full gear, I developed friendships with fellow students, and even became acclimatized to life in the hostel. My homesickness was largely mitigated. I started tasting the romance and excitement, the freedom and joy of college life.

I must confess that it was Sarat who helped me get over the inferiority complex stemming from my rustic upbringing and schooling. From somewhere within my manner of wearing the *dhoti*, my hairstyle, and the agrarian cuts of my shirts, a refined colonial youth began to be excavated. My speech, too, had started to sound a whole lot smarter.

There was one matter that Sarat had warned me about,

however. He said, "There are a few ultra-rowdies, I call them the *"out signals"*—make sure you don't get involved with them."

Giving me a list of those *ultra-rowdies*, and an outline of each, Sarat forewarned, "They are regular *Don Juans*, they drool at the very sight of a girl—watch out!"

Sarat had simply fulfilled his duty as a relative and a friend, but he need not have. No interaction ever occurred between those *dangerous* boys and me anyway. I had always had a fear of such things. I could not tolerate any vulgarity or indecency. Those ultra-rowdies were crude, lascivious and obscene.

Rajani had been apprehensive that if I came into contact with grown-up college girls, I might simply lose my mind. I shall not hide the truth, I had confessed rather innocently and frankly to Rajani in a letter—I had written that I did not think of anyone but her, that I had the desire for no other face but her.

Only the good Lord knew how true my confession was. In reality, there was only a minuscule number of girls in our class. They would always file in right behind the professor at the beginning of every class, then disperse rapidly as soon as class was over. The clowns of the class called them *the damsels of the opera*. It is not that a few words of jest and tomfoolery were not exchanged about them, but no one ever said anything distasteful. Nor was there any kind of romantic involvement. There was no opportunity either. Regrettably, our class had not a single truly beautiful and attractive female student; moreover, being from rather simple and ordinary households, and therefore decidedly conservative and introverted, our female classmates would pretty much keep themselves within their limited confines. Needless to say, I had not exaggerated in the least in my letter to Rajani—there really was no plausible reason for me to contemplate any other face beside her own.

Of course, Sarat would remark that repeating Rajani's name night and day in my head had made my entire world Rajani-intoxicated. He had even written a couplet about me and sent it to Rajani. It was proof, if not of his poetic talent, then definitely of his sense of humor. I still remember that couplet after all these years; brother Sarat wrote:

*The day seems slow, my heart all aglow, I implore you, my
    dearest—*
*When the day is done, grant me the vision, of my Rajani
    fairest.*

To the above, Rajani, too, had not hesitated to respond in kind. She wrote back,

*When night does fall, creatures big and small, slip into
    slumber's den—*
*Nandai Sarat, Nanadini Chandra, each in the other find
    heavenly bliss then.*

Even the prankster Sarat had admitted that her response was quite apt.

I have forgotten to mention that Sarat and I employed a trick which enabled us to correspond with Rajani and Chandra. Direct correspondence with our wives was proscribed; we had great reservation about father either approving of or sanctioning such exchanges. Not that there was any verbal prohibition; however, according to the laws he had set down in his *Early Marriage and Social Welfare*, writing of romantic letters before attaining the age and maturity appropriate for conjugal life was forbidden. The foolhardy Sarat with his indulgence had adversely influenced the rest of us. For one thing, there was no doubt that by acquiring the status of a father-to-be in a hurry he had already seriously violated a law. On top of that, if we were to commit another transgression, it was unlikely that we would find any clemency. In my father's eyes, we were still not old enough for leading a full-blown married life. Hence, we *had* to devise a scheme.

Before my arrival in Bankura, the letters Sarat would write me home could hardly be described as *my* letters. The letters contained within the envelopes bearing my name on the outside were actually Chandra's. Prior to coming to Bankura, I had finalized a conspiracy with Chandra along similar lines. It was decided that Chandra would advise Rajani about our plan when she would come home. According to the plan, I would address all letters sent from Bankura to Chandra (except, of course, letters written to my father). This left the impression that the letters were from a brother to his beloved sister. In reality, the letter inside the envelope would be either from Sarat to Chandra, or from me to Rajani. We used a special sign to distinguish the intended recipient of a particular letter. An inconspicuous slanted cross in a corner on the back of the envelope would make the letter Rajani's; otherwise, it would be Chandra's. The reverse arrangement similarly had Chandra addressing letters to me. No doubt, there were some inconveniences involved when two young couples had only one channel of communication available to them. After all, the impulse to write a tender epistle cannot be expected to follow any scheduled or prescribed pattern. Yet, I observed that whenever, moved to ecstasy by the rains, the fragrance of new *kadamba* blossoms, or the lingering memories of an especially sweet dream from the night before, I had felt the desire to write a love note, it invariably turned out that it was Sarat's turn to write one. And he was not big–hearted enough to give up his turn for my sake. And neither was I.

Of course, my ever-vigilant sister sometimes made major blunders—failing to use the correct sign code, she caused me great embarrassment. Thinking it to be Rajani's letter, I would open it only to discover Chandra's letter to Sarat. Before realizing my mistake, I would end up reading several *private* lines and later feel quite contrite. The thought that such a forgetful young woman was about to become a mother on whom a little baby would be entirely dependent would cause me great anxiety.

The *puja* holidays had arrived. The rainy season was busy wrapping up its activities for the year. The skies appeared freshly washed, wet and clean, but not quite autumn blue nor radiating golden sunlight yet. As the fragrance of the impending *puja* intensified in the *Sarat* breezes, I began to feel increasingly homesick. One day around this time I received the news that Chandra had been blessed with a boy-child. My informant, naturally, was Rajani.

News of a momentous event such as this rendered Sarat completely speechless, dumb and out of his wits for a while. When he had safely withstood the initial impact of the incredible, almost unbelievable event, he regained his natural self and jumped up in the air out of sheer delight. Completely messing up his own bed as well as mine, he then executed a few somersaults and tumbles, tossed his pillow across the room, and started to laugh and scream hysterically. Finally, when he had recovered his sense of propriety, he stood before me, and, raising his hands, declared, "Now I am a Father...!"

I would rather not recount Sarat's behavior the rest of that night. If my grown-up father were to witness the decidedly immature antics of the brand new father, I am convinced he would not condone such lighthearted buffoonery and caricature of something as grave as fatherhood. All in all, suffice it to say that Sarat was as amused by the event as he was filled with thrill and ecstasy.

At some point, my brother Sarat had also wept a little. I do not know why. I did not understand if they were tears of joy or some inexpressible emotion.

PART 10

I returned home for the *Durga puja* holidays. Sarat did not come with me. It was planned that he would visit us during the *Lakshmi puja* which followed within a few days after the *Durga puja*.

There was much to see at home that was new or different. Chandra's little boy, Chandra herself, Rajani—all sights to behold. When I saw Chandra's son for the first time, something made me laugh heartily. I suddenly remembered some old events. One day as a little girl Chandra had massaged some oil on her little clay doll and left it out to soak in some warm winter sunshine. Out of nowhere, I had shown up with some water and proceeded to give the doll a bath. Not unexpectedly, sometime later, the doll's head had melted and turned into a soft lump of clay. Chandra had wailed and shrieked longer and louder that day than any bereaved mother could ever hope to match. Incensed by her hysteria, I had placed a curse upon my sister akin to the fabled *Durvasa* to the effect that if she were to bear any child, it would be born with two heads. I have no idea why I had cursed her in such a strange fashion; perhaps there might have been a subconscious hope that if the baby had two heads, at least one would survive if the other were to either blow up or melt when soaked in water. Remembering that curse now, I laughed heartily. Chandra's son did really amuse me much. He had Sarat's complexion and almost his appearance; however, he seemed to have inherited Chandra's weeping, snivelling temperament. The greatest surprise for me was to discover Chandra in such a gentle and deeply affectionate state of motherhood—it seemed as though her entire attention was focused exclusively on her child. Moreover, she seemed to be a great deal more competent handling the baby than I would have ever imagined. Rajani, too, was effortlessly rocking and cradling that tiny little infant. Lightly tapping on its cheeks, making strange faces, and reciting all kinds of rhymes to him, she displayed such excessive fervour that I felt quite alarmed. I did not regard Rajani as particularly cautious. Smiling, I advised Chandra, "Don't let everyone handle him at will. They may leave him with a broken arm or leg."

Rajani was nearby; as soon as the words reached her ears, she turned her face around, and, knotting her brow, made an expression which implied, *Oh, is that so!*

Chandra, too, quipped jokingly, "Do you think your wife is still a little girl?"

It was quite unnecessary for Chandra to remind me that my wife was no longer an immature young girl. In fact, it seemed she had undergone some fundamental personality changes compared to only a few months earlier. In reality, since her marriage, the few times she had been to our home, and virtually flown away by daybreak every time—her comings and goings were little more than pleasure trips. She would seem no more than a guest of this household. She would be received and attended to like a guest; Rajani, too, would bring a few moments' worth of joy and pleasure, and then depart. Now, she was no longer a guest, she was a bonafide member of our ménage. She was busy finding her niche and strengthening her relationships within this environment. Naturally, in her activities and disposition, one could observe reflections of her new-found rights. It could be, though, that in the affairs of the household she was far more of a vocal than an active participant. Sarat had told me once that a certain Sanskrit epic described a peacock's plumage and a woman's voice as their greatest adornments.

I had taken the night train from Bankura via Adra and Asansol to reach home. I was covered profusely with coal dust and grime by the end of the trip. By the time I had bathed, scrubbed myself clean, and finished my meal, the late *Ashwin* afternoon suddenly turned rather dark and dismal. Noticing the fading light, I looked at the sky—dense clouds were gathering overhead. The winds were high—peering out the window, I noticed waves of green sweeping over the paddy fields to the distant horizon, carrying upon their crests, sometimes patches of sunlight, sometimes shadows. The hissing of the winds was ceaseless, the white tassels of the *kash* bushes swayed in the brisk gusts, and every now and then the sweet sound of the *doyel* floated in. Feeling the intimacy of these with my being as I stood by the window, the memories of my childhood gathered over my eyes like a dreamy reverie.

I do not know when I had fallen asleep in my bed; when the sleeplessness of the previous night had taken the full measure of its dues from the languorous afternoon, I opened my eyes and observed that the room was dark. As soon as I walked over to the window, the overcast cloud-laden monsoon outside appeared before my eyes against the backdrop of the darkness of my room. Perhaps crazy *Ashwin's* long, melancholy face was not about to change until another day.

The rains, though imminent, would not come. I dusted off my bicycle and carried it outside; I must go visit my friends. My mother, of course, had advised me against going out. However, I had decided that I would rather get drenched riding out to see my friends' than stay home per my mother's advice. I would have no peace of mind until I had shared with my village friends the stories, the ecstasies and the adventures of my college days. Among my friends, too, a few had been away studying at Hetampur, Burdwan and other colleges. I was eager to hear their stories as well.

As I was rolling my bicycle over the courtyard, I ran into Rajani. Noticing me, she stopped, stole a quick glance at her surroundings, then, shrugging her shoulders in a strange, wavy motion, whispered, "Ugh, what a fine outfit, indeed! The crumple-rumple *Babu*. Go on, get your *dhoti* all ripped up."

I enjoyed Rajani's tart and ripe manner of rebuke so much that I began to laugh. I replied, "It's an old *dhoti*... a gift from my *swasurbari*."

Rajani was probably quite surprised by my spirited response, and was gazing at me intently; flashing a naughty smile at her, I suddenly rang my bicycle bell. At this, Rajani apprehensively looked all around her, then, sticking her tongue out at me in her characteristic manner, hastily ran into the house.

It was well past dusk when I returned. After a quick shower, the clouds had dispersed, and the wind was quite high. The trees, grasses and meadows had all been soaked; the air was loaded with moisture. It was the *Holy Panchami*; the festive drumbeats from the village *chandimandaps* could be heard rolling in the airwaves. I had been singing a song I had learnt from Sarat with abandon all along my way home. I cannot recall exactly where some of its refrain was led drifting on the wayward wind, but the rest of it left me greatly moved and inspired. Even as I stood under the *shiuli* tree in our garden, I was unable to stop myself from humming its captivating tune. Suddenly, it occurred to me that I was home. The humming stopped abruptly. I noticed the lighted interior of my father's study on the outer edge of our house. I did not know if my unrestrained musical exultation had reached his ears or not. I felt a little panic-stricken. Nevertheless, the few droplets of water on my head and torso, the traces of sticky mud on my feet, the moistness of the *Sarat* air, and the divine fragrance of *shiuli* seemed to bring me back to my very own world after a long interlude.

Later that night, I was in bed reading a volume of *Bankim's* collected works. I finished several pages, yet the one I waited eagerly for did not arrive. Every now and then I would glance at the doorway, or listen eagerly—yet not even the hint of the footsteps of the one whose arrival I awaited expectantly could be heard. Staring at the window made it seem as though the night was dissipating rapidly.

At last, Rajani appeared. Hearing her footsteps, I immediately turned over in bed and buried myself in the *Bankim* volume with rapt attention like the most dedicated of students.

Rajani walked in. I did not raise my head, but still could tell that she closed the door.

Rajani walked up to the bed and stood close by the side of my head. Despite being fully aware of her presence, I turned a page and continued reading.

Rajani stood there a moment or two, perhaps planning her strategy. Suddenly, I noticed the light of the table lamp become dimmer and dimmer. Finally, I raised my head. Rajani was holding the knob which moved the wick in and out of the oil in the lamp. She was gradually but steadily lowering the wick.

"Oh, it's *you!*" I played quite the innocent.

Tilting her head to one side in a playful manner, Rajani said, "Oh, yes, *Mister*, it *is* me—."

It is impossible to describe in words the charm contained in Rajani's expression and manner of speech. I was about to tell her something, when suddenly I remembered something else. I told her, "Please turn the wick a little higher."

"Why?"

"Do it. I'll show you something interesting."

Rajani extended the flame of the lamp.

"Now sit here."

"What?"

"Darn it—just sit down…"

Rajani sat down in a corner of the bed by the side of my head. I extended the book to her. "Please read over here."

"What should I read!... What book *is* this?"

"It's *Indira*.... Read over here. Aloud."

"Oh... quite the *professor*...!" Rajani leaned close to me; I pointed to her the top of the sixteenth chapter.

Rajani lowered her eyes and read quietly. After waiting a little, I gave her an expectant nudge, controlling the urge to laugh, of course. "Read loudly, please."

Pushing the book back towards me, Rajani looked up. "Oh, sure, as if *I* am *her*. As if I have nothing better to do than pester you. *You* go read that stuff."

Pulling the book to me, I started reading aloud: *"Every technique the Maker has made available to womankind to make men burn and agonize inside and out, I employed each one to badger my husband around the clock. I am but a woman—how can I possibly come out and say such a thing? Had I not known how to light a fire...."*

Rajani suddenly turned the wick down enough inside the lamp on the table to almost put it out. To tease or perhaps provoke me, she said, *"Shall I*—well, *shall I* turn the light off! .... Let's see what kind of fire gets started..."

So what was so wrong about Indira confessing to badgering her husband around the clock, I could not quite comprehend; I shut the book.

Rajani now slowly raised the flame of the lamp back up. She said, "You've become a real smart aleck ever since joining college."

I could not entirely deny that college life had made me a bit of a show-off. There was no reason to protest Rajani's allegation, either. I could have objected to Rajani's emphasis on the word *real*, but I chose not to. I simply replied, "And have *you* become a real greenhorn?"

In response, Rajani pulled my hair a little bit. After a moment's silence, she said, "Please get up a little."

Even if I felt no need to stand, I did sit up on the bed. Rajani insisted, "How come you're still sitting, please stand up on the floor."

"But why?"

"Look how you've crumpled the bedsheets; let me straighten out the bed."

The naughty smile on her face was enough for me to figure out Rajani's real intentions. I told her, "*So you may move about in the branches, but I move among the leaves.*"

Rajani tried to look innocent, as if she suspected nothing.

"It won't happen this time." I folded my legs together.

"What won't?"

"*Pennam.*"

Rajani started laughing. Then, turning serious, she said, "It *has* to… Oh, what a shame, how can one not do what must be done?" Then, contorting her face, she said spiritedly, "After all, it's a husband, someone to pester and badger." She took my hand and began tugging.

Therefore, I got off the bed and stood up. Rajani offered me her *pranam*. I was laughing the whole time.

Rajani inquired, "So why do you laugh?"

"Because I gave you my *ashirvad*!"

"Oh, sure, *ashirvad*, indeed!… So, what *ashirvad* did my Lordship bestow on me?"

"I bestowed it privately. I can't tell you."

"I know."

"What?'

"That I die, and you marry again."

"Good Lord! What *are* you!"

"Of course! Isn't that what you had wanted at first?"

"No, never. Don't fool around with me."

"You liar! Didn't you tell me, you would leave me and marry again when you grow up?" Rajani reprimanded me with her eyes, shook her head and demanded my acquiescence to the truth of her statement.

I remembered making such a resolution once. But I had not wished that Rajani should die. Amazing memory, indeed— Rajani still remembered the event! I replied, "So when did I say such a thing, Sir? When was it? Did you not also say that you would turn into a *petni* and break my wife's neck?"

"Of course I will." Rajani had not changed her mind about this matter.

We both laughed.

We stopped laughing eventually. Rajani was straightening out the bed with great care. There was a great deal of fastidiousness about her adornments tonight. She wore a few heirloom pieces of jewellery, filigreed scorpion gold chain around her ankle, a finely designed gold hairpin held her hair in a bun. Her hairstyle was especially exquisite. To top it all off, she wore a sky-blue *sari*.

After she had made the bed wrinkle-free, and fluffed up the pillows, Rajani went to the head of the bed. "Would you like some water?"

"No, thanks."

She picked up a *paan* from the *paan* case and came close to me. "Please open your mouth—"

"*Paan*, this late at night!"

"Have it, dear, have it, it's from your *bou's* hand—." It was not merely her jesting which rang in Rajani's seductive voice, but also her newly acquired, housewife-like maturity and command.

She stuffed the *paan* in my mouth; I started to chew.

Rajani withdrew, then delicately drank a little water before putting a *paan* in her own mouth.

I felt a rather mysterious taste sensation inside my mouth—it was something familiar yet new. The more the *paan* juices would wrap the taste around my tongue, the more it would seem to me that it was not something unknown to me. Presently, the inside of my mouth felt very cool; I caught the scent. Peppermint. It was Rajani's good old peppermint.

I was watching Rajani closely. She had not appeared quite like this even a few months earlier. If there were any trace of imperfection in her physique then, it had all been fulfilled today, as though the clay goddess had completed her immaculate perfection.

Approaching the bed, Rajani suddenly caught sight of my transfixed, admiring gaze, and perhaps froze for a moment. Her eyes met mine, and, as if catching herself watching my stare, she became a little nonplussed. She said almost apologetically, "*Thakurjhi* insisted that I dress up." Then, smiling bashfully, she sat down on the side of the bed. Immediately thereafter, she looked up, "She's made me a real clown, hasn't she?"

"You've become even prettier."

"Sure...go on, flatter me..."

"No, really. Most beautiful!"

"Won't you sleep!"

I slowly walked to the bed and sat down.

Rajani lovingly and gently brushed aside the hair from around my temples and said, "Your lips get very red."

"They do if I chew *paan*."

"Of course. And because your wife loves you *so much*, isn't it?" Laughing, Rajani buried her face in my shoulder.

"And how sweet and fragrant your mouth becomes–because your husband loves you *so much*, right?"

Rajani, it seemed, could not bear some unknown, intense bashfulness any longer. She hastily turned the flame of the lamp off. A sudden gust of darkness blew in and whisked us away from the rest of the world.

Feeling the touch of Rajani's hands, her body, her aroma, and her closeness in the dark, I realized at some point that my once adolescent bride had arrived today decked in the burgeoning blossoms of youth. In the pristine, peerless splendour of her youthfulness, my heart found its deepest fulfillment.

Kissing my wife, I whispered softly, "Rajani!"

Rajani remained silent for a moment, then said despondently, "When will you finish your studies at college?"

"Four… another four years."

"They sure teach a *lot*!" Rajani was not too thrilled about this *long* course of study.

"The time will pass, you'll see."

"It doesn't, dearest, it *doesn't*––."

"I feel that too." I confessed, and heaved a sigh. In that darkness, the four years looming before us seemed immeasurably long. Even though I felt quite dejected inside, I was careful not to express my feelings. Trying instead to console Rajani, I said to her, "We get five months' vacation each year—I'll spend them at home, of course. After that, permanently here, *by your side*."

Rajani was silent. She turned to face me. With a voice laden with the fragrance of peppermint, she said softly, "From now on, I will stay here."

PART 11

R ajani is with me to this day. For forty long and wonderful years she has stayed with me, and me alone. We are no longer young newlyweds; we are now an elderly couple. My hair has turned gray, my body is beginning to break down. The parting of Rajani's hair has become broader with the gradual erosion from years of applying vermilion. Her hair has streaks of white in it; her body has become heavier with age; her vision has weakened, and she now wears glasses.

With the passage of the years, my life is nearing its end. Through happy days and gloomy ones, so many of those years passed in the company of this Rajani. My father passed away a long time ago, and so did my mother. My little brother, too, has advanced in years, and established himself well. He lives here with his wife, son and daughter, working as a surveyor at the colliery. Not that he really needed a job; but then, a man cannot pass his days without some kind of steady work, hence he chose to work as a surveyor. My daughter is married; my son has completed studying medicine and works at the hospital. My venerable father had arranged an adolescent marriage for Chandra and me; I could not be as daring. These are different times. Chandra and brother Sarat did not approve of any such notion, either. Nevertheless, I married my daughter off at eighteen. I arranged my son's marriage, too, but only recently. Our children had arrived somewhat late.

The sleeping arrangements in my bedroom have only been modified slightly. I sleep alone in the large, king-size bed; Rajani sleeps nearby in a smaller, twin-size one. I have asked her many times, "Do you worry about leaving me alone in the bedroom?" My middle-aged Rajani does not respond.

Old age comes packaged with all kinds of minor or not-so-minor ailments. Some nights I cannot sleep at all, other nights I suffer from asthma attacks, and yet other nights I feel as though my chest is being compressed in a vice. Driven by such afflictions, if I happen to sit up on bed, or make any kind of Oohs and Aahs, Rajani instantly leaves her bed to check me out. I do not quite know how she is awakened from her sleep every time. Once alerted, a protracted regimen of treatments and care begins. I cannot understand how Rajani turned into such a light sleeper.

Full moon nights still appear outside the bedroom window; however, the old mango tree no longer makes rustling sounds, and the moonlight no longer glimmers on its leaves. Its top is now bereft of leaves entirely; somehow, some day, the old tree had died. Once in a while, if I awaken in the middle of the night, I quietly and carefully sit up on the bed. I sit there watching the moonlight, and reflect on that once-living mango tree, and on my own life. Some nights I stare at the far away fields. Even though my eyesight is failing, I can still discern the outline of the old familiar shapes—fields, meadows and shrubs in the moonlight. The world outside seems much more vast and limitless.

Gazing at the moonlit world with all its emptiness and fullness in the middle of the night, my feelings sometimes become blurred and fuzzy. I suppose on clearer nights, the distant stars look down at this humble dwelling of mine and wonder how it is that I found my peace with so little.

These days I often feel as if the surreal eyes of that boundless world outside watch me with pity and disdain. I realize I must go to them some day, that my entire existence shall not measure up to even the tiniest speck of dirt in the all-pervading and sweeping emptiness of the Universe. I shall simply disappear without a trace....

Then I turn my sight back inside the room; I notice my once adolescent *Chini,* now middle aged, still by my side, sleeping contentedly without the slightest care. I feel that even though our room *is* rather small and cramped, what I have received right here is not all that negligible. What it is exactly that I have received, I can feel only in my heart—I cannot express it in words.

That infinite sky outside my window, the vast galaxies scattered in its most distant corners, the blissful moonlight, the far-reaching woodlands teeming with animals and plants—some day these will drag me scornfully out of this insignificant room, and snuff out my very existence in a twinkling. But they shall never understand that it is beyond the capacity of their universal emptiness to fill the corners of my heart with special gifts. Yet, in this very negligible corner of the world, my adolescent bride filled my whole life to the fullest with those very gifts beyond the reach of that vast world outside.

I offer my *pranams* to my dearly departed father with the utmost gratitude. By his grace, this life has been filled with immeasurable treasures.

Abhagir Swarga

Abhagi's Heaven

SARAT CHANDRA CHATTOPADHYAY

1

The venerable wife of *Thakurdas Mukhujje* died of a seven-day-old fever at a ripe old age. Old *Mukhopadhyay Mahashay* had made a fortune in the paddy trade. His four sons, three daughters, numerous grandchildren, sons-in-law, neighbours and servants gathered around the departed—it seemed like a spectacular festival. The entire village rushed in to witness the impressive funeral procession. The daughters, weeping bitterly, painted scarlet borders of *alta* around their mother's feet, and smeared bright red vermilion on the parting of her hair. The daughters-in-law applied cool sandalwood paste to her forehead, draped her lifeless body in expensive silk and brocade, and lovingly wiped the dust off her feet with their *anchals*. In the torrential plenitude of flowers, fragrances, garlands, and the general commotion, it did not appear as though this was an occasion of mourning—it was as if the mistress of a great household was only making another magnificent journey to her husband's home, fifty years later. Old *Mukhopadhyay* silently bade goodbye to his lifelong partner, wiped away a few private tears, then proceeded to console his distraught daughters and daughters-in-law. Presently, with resounding chants of *Hari* filling the airwaves of dawn, a vast retinue of mourners accompanied the departed in her last journey. Unbeknown to most, another creature joined the procession at a distance. She had picked a few eggplants from the yard in front of her shack, and was headed for the market; seeing the spectacle, she almost froze on her track. She forgot about the market, the eggplants remained tied in her *anchal*—wiping a profusion of tears, she arrived at the cremation *ghat* at the far end of the great procession.

The cremation *ghat* was at the edge of the village, by the bank of the *Garuda* river. Stacks of firewood logs, sandalwood chips, *ghee*, honey, incense and ceremonial fragrances had already been assembled at the site. Poor *Kangali's* mother was a low caste—being the daughter of a *Dule*, she dared not get too close. Keeping a safe distance, she stood on a termite mound, and proceeded to observe the cremation ceremony with rapt attention. When the corpse was installed upon the ample and deep pyre, the sight of the scarlet feet soothed the core of her heart, she felt an impulse to rush in and gather a drop of *alta* to smear on her own head. When the son touched his mother's countenance with the torch, and profound chants of *Hari* reverberated in the morning air, the tears welled out of her eyes in irrepressible torrents. She said repeatedly in her heart, "My fortunate and blessed Mother, I know you are on your way to Heaven—please grant me this one wish—may I, too, receive the fire from my *Kangali's* hand the same as you." The flame from a son's hand on the last journey! It's no ordinary thing! This ascent to Heaven, this leaving behind a prospering, glowing family, a household brimming with husband, sons, daughters, grandchildren, maids and servants, and scores of relatives—witnessing it made her heart swell with thrills, as though she simply could not adequately measure the scope and extent of such fabulous fortune. The blue smoke from the freshly lit pyre was rising to the sky in spirals—*Kangali's* mother vividly perceived the outline of a small chariot within the spiraling smoke. Countless pictures were painted as decorations on its sides; on its crest were clusters of vines and tendrils. Seated inside the chariot was someone whose face could not be seen; however, she had the vermilion mark on the parting of her hair, and the soles of her feet were doused in *alta*. As she looked skyward at the wondrous sight, tears flowed incessantly from *Kangali's* mother's eyes. Suddenly, a fourteen—or fifteen-year-old boy began to tug at her *anchal*, and pleadingly said to her, "You are just standing here, Ma, aren't you going to go home and cook the rice?"

The mother started, then, looking at her son, replied, "I'll cook it later, dear!" Eagerly pointing her finger skyward, she told her son, "Look, look over there, dear—the *Bamoon-Ma* is going to Heaven in a chariot!"

Quite astonished, the son asked, "Where?" Then, staring in the direction pointed by his mother for a short while, he said, "Are you crazy! That's just smoke!" Irritated, he then complained, "It's past midday, don't I get hungry?" Then immediately, noticing the tears in his mother's eyes, he said, "The mistress of the *Bamoon* household has died, but why do *you* cry so bitterly, Ma?"

Suddenly, *Kangali's* mother became aware of the situation. She felt a little embarrassed that she was shedding tears thus for someone else's dead at the cremation *ghat*. In fact, lest her tears bring any kind of misfortune upon her son, she quickly wiped her eyes, and, forcing on a smile, said to him, "Why on earth should I be crying, dear!—It's nothing but the smoke in my eyes!"

"Huh—*nothing but smoke in my eyes*! You *were* crying!"

The mother did not protest any more. Holding her son's hand, she waded into the river, then, bathing herself and her son, she returned home. She was unable to witness the conclusion of the cremation at the *ghat*.

2

At the time when a newborn child is named by its parents, the Lord of Destiny does not merely laugh at the parents' foolishness in making a poor selection, and let the matter rest; in fact, most often he delivers his protest in no uncertain terms. Thereafter, the child is haunted by the ill-chosen name and subjected to unmitigated ridicule for the rest of its life. *Kangali's* mother's life history was short; however, for some mysterious reason, her short, destitute life had been spared the ridicule of Destiny. Her mother died immediately after her birth; her father, out of anger, named her *Abhagi*. She had no mother, her father spent all day fishing in the river—to the child *Abhagi*, day or night had little distinction. It is a matter of great bewilderment, therefore, how the tiny and utterly neglected *Abhagi* survived in this world to become *Kangali's* mother. The man she was married to had the name *Rashik*

Bagh; unfortunately for *Abhagi*, the *Bagh* had a *Baghini* on the side—one fine morning he left the village for good with the woman. Poor *Abhagi* was left in the village with her luckless, infant child *Kangali*.

That *Kangali* has grown up to be a young lad of fifteen today. He has only just begun to learn how to work with wicker—*Abhagi* nurtures the hope that if they can fight their misfortune and penury for another year or so, their days of hardship shall be over. How excruciating that hardship—no one would ever know but for the one who gave it to them.

Kangali washed himself at the pond and returned home to find his mother putting away the remnants of his meal in a clay container. Surprised, he asked her, "Why did you not eat, Ma?"

"It's been a long day, dear—I am not hungry any more."

The son did not believe her excuse; he said, "Oh sure, *not hungry any more*, come on, let me see your *hanri*!"

Kangali's mother had deceived him in this manner many times in the past. Therefore, he was adamant about checking his mother's pot of rice. This time, however, he found there was indeed enough rice there to feed one more person. Satisfied, *Kangali* beamed and happily sat down on his mother's lap. This was not something children his age did as a rule; *Kangali*, however, was too sickly since his infancy, and had not had the opportunity to leave the safety of his mother's lap to play with other children. He had to fulfill all his childhood play in that shelter. Putting one arm around her neck, *Kangali* affectionately placed his cheek against his mother's, then immediately exclaimed, "Ma, your body feels hot—why on earth did you stand out there in the fiery sun to watch the corpse being burned? And then why did you bathe right after that? That corpse-burning—"

The mother hastily covered her son's mouth, and said, "Shame, son—one does not say *corpse-burning*, it's sinful. The *Sati-Lakshmi* mistress went to Heaven in a chariot."

Doubtful, the son replied, "That's the one thing you keep repeating, Ma! Does anyone ever go to Heaven in a chariot?"

The mother said, "But I saw with my own eyes, *Kangali*, the *Bamoon-Ma* sitting inside the chariot. Everyone else, too, saw her dainty feet smeared in *alta*, dear!"

"They all did?"

"They all did."

Kangali buried his face in his mother's bosom, and wondered. He was accustomed to trusting his mother; he had been taught from his childhood to do so. Now, if that same Ma was telling him that everyone had seen such a fantastic thing with wide open eyes, then there was no longer any reason to disbelieve it. A little later, he said softly, "Then you too, Ma, will go to Heaven, right? The other day Bindi's mother was telling Rakhal's aunt, "There's not another woman in the *Dulé* community as *Sati-Lakshmi* as *Kangla's* mother."

His mother remained silent; *Kangali* continued in the same soft tone, "When *Baba* left you, so many pleaded with you to marry again. But you only said, "No." You said, "If my *Kangali* lives, all my sorrow will be over—why should I marry again?" Well, Ma, where would I be if you had married again? I would probably have died of hunger a long time ago."

His mother held him tightly to her bosom. It *was* true, many had indeed advised her that way back then; when she refused to accept their suggestion, they had teased and tormented her mercilessly. Remembering those times, tears began to roll down *Abhagi's* face. The son wiped her tears with his hand, and gently asked, "Shall I spread the *kantha* for you, Ma, would you like to sleep?"

The mother did not respond. *Kangali* quietly spread out the mat and the *kantha*, then plucked the small pillow from the *mancha*, and, holding his mother by her hand, helped her lie down on the bed. His mother then said, "*Kangali*, there is no need for you to go to work today."

Kangali was positively thrilled to hear the proposition; however, he said, "Then they will not give me the two pice for food, Ma!"

"Let them not—come, let me tell you fairy tales."

He did not need any further tempting; immediately lying down next to his mother, he said excitedly, "Then tell me about the prince, the gendarme's son, and the flying horse—"

Abhagi began with the stories of the prince, the gendarme's son and the flying horse. These were stories she had heard from others and told others so many times. Moments later, however, she began spinning a yarn entirely her own—it no longer had the prince or the gendarme's son in it. As her fever climbed higher and higher, and the fiery blood began to circulate faster through her brain, she wove deliriously intricate, fantastic and novel fairy tales. Fearful, mesmerized and thrilled beyond measure, *Kangali* embraced his mother desperately, and buried his face in her bosom as if wishing to lose himself entirely within her.

The daylight faded outside, the sun sank over the distant horizon, the deep darkness of night soon swallowed everything in sight. Yet, no one lit the evening lamp inside the home, no one rose to perform a householder's final task of the day—within that impenetrable darkness, only the delirious murmur of the mother went on pouring honey inside her speechless son's eager ears. It was the tale of the cremation *ghat* and the grand procession. The chariot, the scarlet feet, the ascension into Heaven. How the grieving husband offered the dust off his feet for the last time and bade his tearful farewell, how the sons carried their departed mother amid chants of *Hari*, and then, to cap it all off, the warmth of the funeral fire from a son's own hands! That was no ordinary fire, *Kangali*, that was *Hari* himself! Its spiraling smoke rising to the sky was no ordinary smoke, dear, it was the chariot from Heaven! *My Kangalicharan*, my dearest, sweetest *Baba*!

"Why, Ma?"

"If I could get that fire from *your* hands, dear, I too would go to Heaven like *Bamoon-Ma*."

Kangali barely whispered, "Shh—no, you must not say it."

Perhaps the mother did not even hear his words; her breath heavy and fiery from the fever, she went on, "Then no one could despise me like a low-caste any more—no one could keep me far like a destitute. Of course! Funeral fire from a son's own hands—the chariot *has* to descend for me."

Placing his terrified face next to his mother's, the son said with a broken voice, "Don't say that, Ma, please don't say that—I feel terribly afraid."

The mother continued, "And look, *Kangali*, would you be a sweetheart and get your father to come here just once—plead that he offer me the dust off his feet before sending me away, just like the *Bamoon* Master. And the same scarlet feet smeared with *alta*, the same deep vermilion mark in the parting of my hair—but who would give me those? *You* would, wouldn't you, my sweet *Kangali*? You are my son, my daughter, my everything!" She then gripped her son and held him tightly to her bosom.

3

The final scene in the drama of *Abhagi's* life was about to be acted out. It was not particularly long, in fact rather short. It is doubtful if the drama had extended beyond thirty summers; the end, too, turned out to be brief and unspectacular. The *kaviraj* did not live in the village; he lived in a different one. *Kangali* wept and pleaded, prostrated and clung to his feet; finally, he pawned a brass pitcher and offered him a rupee coin. The *kaviraj* did not come; he only gave *Kangali* four pills. What an elaborate prescription for their administration! Mortar, honey, dried ginger pulp, the juice from basil leaves—*Kangali's* mother became irritated and complained, "Why did you not ask me before running out to pawn the pitcher, dear?" Extending her hand, she took the pills, and, touching them reverentially to her forehead, she threw them into the cooking fire and said, "If I should get better, it will be by itself—no *Bagdi* or *Dulé* was ever cured by medicines."

Two or three days passed in this manner. The neighbors stopped by to see her; they recommended whatever home remedies they kı best. The extract of a stag's antlers rubbed on a grindstone ι _ mixed with water; knotted *cowrie* shells,

fired, ground up, mixed with honey and licked by the patient—
they suggested a variety of such sure-fire cures and went on
their way. The child *Kangali* became anxious and overwhelmed
by the situation; hence, his mother pulled him near and said
comfortingly, "Even the *Kobrej's* pills did me no good, dear,
and now I must follow *their* quack prescriptions? I will become
well by myself."

Kangali wept and said, "But you did not take the pills, Ma,
you threw them in the fire. Does anyone get well just like that?"

"I *will* get well just like that. Instead, why don't you cook
yourself some rice and potatoes, and let me watch you eat."

For the first time in his life, the novice *Kangali* proceeded
to cook rice. He could neither drain the cooked rice, nor even
ladle it out properly. He had a terrible time lighting the
cooking fire—the fuel became wet and began to smoke badly;
the cooked rice splattered everywhere when he tried draining
the pot. The mother's eyes became filled with tears watching
him. She tried to rise once, but could not keep her head up,
and immediately fell back on the *kantha*. When he had finished
eating, she called him near and began to instruct him about
how to and how not to do things; however, her feeble voice
soon became inaudible; only drops of tears fell uninterrupted
from her eyes.

Ishwar, the village barber, knew how to read pulse. The
following morning, he checked her pulse, put on a grim
expression right before her, sighed dolefully, and finally shook
his head and went out. *Kangali's* mother understood the
meaning of it, but she was not the slightest bit afraid. When
all the visitors had left, she said to her son, "Would you go
ask *him* to come just once, dear?"

"Ask whom, Ma?"

"*Him*, dear—who has moved to the other village"

Kangali understood and asked, "You mean *Father?*"

Abhagi fell silent.

Kangali asked again, "Why would he come, Ma?"

Abhagi herself had strong reservations; nevertheless, she whispered softly, "Go tell him, Ma wishes only to have the dust off your feet."

When *Kangali* immediately proceeded to go out on the assignment, she held his hand and suggested, "Make sure you weep and plead with him, dear, tell him Ma is on her way."

Pausing momentarily, she continued, "On your way back, get a little *alta* from the barber's wife, *Kangali*. You have to just tell her my name. She loves me very much."

There were many who loved her. Ever since she came down with the fever, he had heard these requests from her so many times that, crying bitterly, he then went out on his way.

4

When *Rashik Dulé* arrived the next day, *Abhagi* was barely conscious. The shadow of death had fallen across her face; its task complete, her gaze had left the realm of *sansara*, and migrated to some unknown, ethereal world. Sobbing, *Kangali* pleaded, "My sweet Ma, Father's here!—Won't you take the dust off his feet?"

Perhaps the mother understood, perhaps not; perhaps her deepest, most cherished wish shook a region of her subconscious mind into a misty sense of awareness. The unconscious, dying woman extended her inert arm beyond the edge of her bed, and opened the palm of her hand.

Rashik stood by, dazed and listless. That the dust off *his* feet could be of any value in this world, that someone could actually *ask* for it, then too from her deathbed, was beyond his imagination. *Bindi's* aunt, who stood next to him, said, "Go on, dear, let her touch your feet and receive the dust."

Rashik came forward. The wife whom he had never offered his love during her lifetime, never provided any support or care, whose welfare he had never inquired about—now, at the time of her death, having to offer nothing more than the dust off his feet to her, he began to weep.

Rakhal's mother said, "Why did such a *Sati-Lakshmi* choose to be born in a *Dulé* home, and not in the home of a *Brahmin* or a *Kayet*? Now, please help her find her peace and salvation, dear. She gave up her ghost almost out of the desire to receive the funeral flame from *Kangali's* hand."

I do not know what the deity presiding over *Abhagi's abhagya* thought of the above; however, the words pierced the adolescent *Kangali's* heart like the point of an arrow.

Somehow, the rest of that day passed by, and the night as well, but *Kangali's* mother could no longer wait for the dawn to come. Now, who knows if there *are* actually any chariots in Heaven for such low-caste souls, or whether they are required to walk on their own feet in the dark—however that may be, it was clear that she had left the world of mortals before the night was over.

There was a *bel* tree on the yard in front of the shack; borrowing an ax from a neighbor, *Rashik* had barely struck at its trunk once, when, out of nowhere, the zamindar's sentry suddenly rushed in and slapped him hard on the face. Snatching the ax from *Rashik's* hand, he yelled, "You scoundrel, do you suppose this is your damned father's tree that you have started to cut it down?"

Stunned, *Rashik* began to massage his jowl, while *Kangali*, on the verge of tears, asked, "But, *Darwanji*, this tree was planted by my mother with her own hands. Why did you beat my father for nothing?"

The Hindustani *darwan* hurled an unutterable, abusive epithet at him, too, and was about to strike him, when he suddenly realized that the young boy had touched his dead mother not long ago. Fearing unholy contamination, he instantly recoiled. A large crowd had gathered because of the din; no one, however, came forward to refute the charge that it was improper for *Rashik* to try to cut down a tree without permission. Instead, many among the throng started to fall at the *darwan's* feet and implore him to grant the poor man his wish. After all, they explained, *Kangali's* mother had held the hands of anyone who had come to visit her, and expressed her one last wish.

The sentry was not to be easily persuaded; gesticulating with his hands and face, he told the villagers that he would have none of their tricks.

The zamindar did not live in the village; he had a *katchhari* there, and the *gomasta* Adhar Roy was its manager. While the villagers were busy pleading with the intransigent Hindustani, *Kangali* made a mad dash and arrived right at the *katchhari* house. He had heard that sentries and guards often took bribes; he was convinced that if only he could bring such extreme tyranny and torture directly to the master's attention, he would not be deprived of justice. Alas, the poor greenhorn! He did not know the true nature of the zamindar of Bengal or his cohorts. The young child, rendered motherless only hours earlier, had rushed up the *katchhari* stairs in his state of shock and bewilderment. At that very moment, Adhar Roy had completed his *ahnik* rituals and a light snack, and emerged outside—surprised and greatly irritated, he asked, "Who are *you*, now?"

"I am *Kangali*. *Darwanji* has beaten my father."

"Serves him right. I bet the son of a bitch did not pay his taxes?"

Kangali replied, "No, Sir, my father was cutting a tree— my mother just died—" and with that he could no longer control his tears.

Such inauspicious crying and wailing in the morning vexed Adhar terribly. The urchin had touched a corpse—who knows if he might have touched anything here! Scolding the child, he admonished, "So if your mother died, go stand downstairs. Ahoy, is anyone there—wipe this spot with some *gobarjal*! What caste *are* you, boy?"

Frightened by the harsh rebuke, *Kangali* immediately ran down the stairs to the yard and said, "We are *Dulé*, Sir."

Adhar scoffed, "*Dule!* Now why in Heaven's name would one need firewood logs for a *Dule* corpse?"

Kangali replied, "But Ma asked me to offer her the funeral fire! Why don't you ask everyone, *Babumashay*, Ma told everybody, everybody heard!" Recalling his mother's pleas from her very final hours, all her entreaties and parting wishes, he felt as though his voice would burst from the explosive surge of tears and overwhelming grief.

Adhar grimly said, "If you are *so* eager to cremate your mother, go get five rupees for the tree. Can you?"

Kangali knew that was impossible. With his own eyes he

had seen Bindi's aunt take his brass rice platter to the pawnbroker's so she could get a rupee to buy his ritual cloak. "No," he shook his head.

Contorting his face viciously, Adhar snapped, "Well, if you can't, just go bury your mother by the riverbank. How dare your *Baap* go after someone else's tree with an axe! The rogue, the thief, the scoundrel!"

Kangali informed him, "But the tree's in our own yard, *Babumashay*! It was planted by my Ma with her own hands."

"*Planted by her own hands!* Say, Pandey—smack the goon across the back and kick him the hell out of here!"

Pandey came forward, struck the grieving child across the back, and uttered unspeakably filthy epithets which only a zamindar's employees are capable of.

Kangali stood up, brushed off the dirt, then slowly went out. Why he got beaten up, what exactly was his offense, the poor child simply could not understand. The unprovoked brutality inflicted on the defenseless child did not perturb the *gomasta* in the slightest. If he had the slightest trace or hint of a conscience, he would surely not be hired to do this job. When *Kangali* was out of sight, he said to a subordinate, "Say, Paresh, go find out if this *Dulé* tramp is delinquent on taxes or not. Make sure you confiscate anything valuable—he may try to run."

Only a day remained before the *Shraddh* ceremony at the *Mukhujje* house. The plans and arrangements were commensurate with the honor due to the departed matriarch. Old *Thakurdas* was busy supervising the activities himself; suddenly, *Kangali* appeared before him and said, "*Thakurmashay*, my Ma's died."

"Who *are* you? What do you want?"

"I am *Kangali*. Ma asked me to offer her funeral fire."

"So go do it."

The story of the incident at the *katchhari* had already passed on far and wide by word of mouth. Someone said, "I believe he wants a tree."—He then proceeded to describe the incident.

Surprised and irritated, Mukhujje said, "Just listen to their fancy! Here we are, a major event only two days away! Now, run along, boy, run along. There's nothing here, there's nothing here." With that, he simply went elsewhere.

The *Bhattacharya Mahashay* was sitting nearby writing up an itemized list of ritual materials; he said, "Whoever cremated the dead among you *Dulés*, eh? Go on, stick a rag flame in her mouth and bury her by the riverbank."

Mukhopadhyay's eldest son was busily passing by; listening to the discussion, he observed, "Did you see, *Bhattacharya Mahashay*—now they *all* want to be *Bamoons* and *Kayets*." With those words of wisdom, he hastily went back to work.

Kangali did not plead any more. Within the past two hours, he felt he had grown into an old man much experienced in the ways of this world. Slowly, and without another word, he went back to his departed mother.

After a hole was dug by the riverbank, *Abhagi* was laid to rest in it. Rakhal's mother lit a slender stack of hay, and helped *Kangali* hold it in his hand, touch his mother's face with it, and throw it aside. Thereafter, together the mourners piled mud over the dead woman until there was no trace left of her.

Afterwards, everybody else was busy with all manner of

work—only *Kangali* sat transfixed and motionless watching the faint curls of smoke rising from the burning hay and ascending in the direction of the sky.

Mahesh

SARAT CHANDRA CHATTOPADHYAY

1

The village was called Kashipur. A rather small hamlet, its *zamindar* even smaller—yet so absolute was his sovereignty that his subjects dared not pip or squeal a word in complaint.

The *puja* ceremony to celebrate the birthday of the *zamindar's* youngest son had just been conducted. Shortly after noon, his *puja* over, Tarkaratna was on his way home. *Vaishakh* was almost nearing its end, yet there was not even the hint of any cloud anywhere. Only streams of molten fire seemed to pour down relentlessly upon the drought-stricken plains.

The vast terrain in front of him, burnt to cinders by the merciless heat wave, was cracked and bone-dry as far as the eyes could see. From the million fissures on the parched landscape, it was as though the very life-blood of mother earth was going up in smoke. Staring at the serpentine ascent of the spirals of air, rising like shooting tongues of flame, made one's head swim; it made one feel inebriated.

At one edge of the parched terrain, next to the pathway, was the home of Ghaffoor the weaver. Its boundary wall had crumbled to the dust, thereby making the courtyard within merge with the pathway without. Any claim to honor, reticence or privacy on the part of the inner sanctum of the house had long since been surrendered to the mercy of the passersby as a declaration of peace.

Planting himself under the shade of a *pitali* tree by the side of the pathway, Tarkaratna bellowed, "I say, ahoy Gofra—I say, are you home or what?"

The weaver's ten-year-old daughter answered from the doorway, "Why do you call Baba? Baba is down with fever."

"Fever, indeed! Go call that bastard. The scoundrel! The *mlechha!*"

Disturbed by the great commotion, Ghaffoor Mian emerged from his room shivering with high fever, and stood outside. There was an old *babla* tree next to the collapsed boundary wall; tied to one of its branches stood a bull. Pointing towards it, Tarkaratna bellowed, "Now what do you think is going on? Don't you know this is a Hindu village, that it has a brahmin *zamindar*?" The blood had rushed to his face as much from rage as the searing heat; therefore, it was not entirely unreasonable that harsh and caustic words should emanate from his mouth. However, unable to decipher their cause, Ghaffoor only stared vacantly at the priest.

Tarkaratna elaborated, "I noticed it tied to the tree on my way to the *zamindar's* house earlier today. Now, on my way back, I see it is still tied as before. Now, you ought to know that if that bull should die, the *zamindar* will bury you alive for committing *go-hatya*. He is no ordinary brahmin, I warn you!"

"What am I to do, *Babathakur*, I am quite helpless. I've had this fever for several days now. If I try carrying him out to the field by his leash so he may graze a little, I black out and drop."

"Then why not just release him—let him go graze on his own."

"Where would I release him, *Babathakur*, the farmers haven't completely winnowed their paddy yet. The stubbled ridges are burning up from the heat, there isn't a shred of hay in sight. Who knows if the poor animal won't begin to forage in someone's grain bin or someone else's haystack? How am I going to release him, then, *Babathakur*?"

Softening a little, Tarkaratna said, "Well, if you cannot release him, then why not tie him somewhere cool, and throw a stack or two of fodder for him to chew on? Didn't your girl cook rice? Why not mix the scum with water so he can lap it up?"

Ghaffoor was quiet. Staring helplessly at Tarkaratna, all he could manage by way of a response was a long and dispirited sigh.

Tarkaratna went on, "Why, then, you don't even have that, or what? What did you do with your share of hay from the harvest? What else—I guess you sold every last thread to feed yourself, right? So, doesn't one leave even a small bundle for the poor bull? You infernal butcher!"

This malicious and ruthless accusation rendered Ghaffoor speechless. After a moment or two, he said slowly, "I'd received a *kahan* or so worth of hay this time, but the Master impounded all of it as payment against his due from last year. I cried, fell at his feet, said to him, *Babumashai*, you are my

Lord, my *Hakim*, where would I run from your territory, I pray to you, please leave me at least ten *pawns* of fodder. I have no thatch on my roof—my little girl and I have no more than a room for shelter; even so, we will use *taal* leaves to plug the holes, and somehow survive the rains. But, kind Master, my poor Mahesh will starve to death without his fodder."

Tarkaratna said with a smile, "Well, well! So the pampered beast even has a name—*Mahesh*, eh? Well, if *that* isn't downright amusing!"

The derision did not reach Ghaffoor's ears; he continued, "But the *Hakim* showed no mercy. He left about two-months' worth of paddy for us, but the entire bundle of hay was impounded for the *zamindar's* loft. My Mahesh did not get a thread of it." As he spoke, his voice began to choke from the rush of tears. Tarkaratna was not moved, however; he said, "Some kind of a fellow you are—you owed him, and you won't give him back? So, must the *zamindar* feed you out of his own pantry? You all live in *Rama's Kingdom*—but then, being illiterate low castes, you know no better than to vilify him."

Embarrassed, Ghaffoor replied, "Why would I vilify him, *Babathakur*, we don't speak ill of him. But, tell me, how would I possibly repay him? I get to cultivate no more than four *bighas* on rent; we have had a drought two years in a row— the paddy dried and burnt out in the furrows. My little girl and I don't get enough to eat at mealtime. Take a look inside— I spend the nights crouching in a corner with my girl to avoid getting drenched by the monsoon downpours—I can't even stretch my legs to rest comfortably. Just look at Mahesh—the poor beast, you can count his ribs; —I beg you, *Thakurmashai*, lend me a *kahan* or two, let me feed the poor creature properly a day or two,—" and, as he spoke, he abruptly sat down on the floor by the brahmin's feet. Instantly, recoiling a few feet, Tarkaratna said sternly, "Damn you, have you no sense? Were you going to touch me or something? Good grief!"

"Why, no, *Babathakur*, why would I touch you, I won't. But please, please lend me two *kahans* worth of hay this time. You have four huge stacks—I saw with my own eyes the other day— you wouldn't even notice any difference. I don't mind much if *we* starve to death—but that poor beast, he's mute and helpless. He can't say a word—only stares as the tears roll down his eyes."

Tarkaratna inquired, "If you want it on loan, pray, how on earth are you going to repay?"

Encouraged, Ghaffoor said eagerly, "I *will* repay you any way I can, *Babathakur*, I won't deceive you."

Mimicking Ghaffoor's eager pledge, Tarkaratna said with a sneer, "*I won't deceive you! I will repay you any way I can!* Indeed! My *Rasik Nagar*! Now, move, move, get out of my way. It's getting late, I must go home now." With that, he smiled curtly and had barely taken a step or two, when suddenly he retreated fearfully and said in a huff, "O my good Lord! That beast's coming after me waving his horns—is he out to gore me to death or what?"

Ghaffoor stood up. The priest had a sack of wet rice and fruits in his hand; pointing to it, he said, "He caught scent of it—just wishes to eat a handful—"

"Wishes to eat! Of course! Like *chasha*, like *balad*. Can't afford any hay, but now greedy for rice and fruit! Now go on, move him out of my way and tie him up. What menacing horns—I bet he'll kill someone one of these days." With that, carefully bypassing the bull, Tarkaratna made a hasty departure.

Ghaffoor turned his attention away from the retreating brahmin and quietly stared at Mahesh. His deep, dark eyes were filled with hunger and pain. Ghaffoor said to him, "He wouldn't give you any, would he? They have so much, yet they won't ever share. Well, let them not —" his voice began to choke, and teardrops started to fall from his eyes. Approaching him, he began to tenderly stroke his neck, head and back as he whispered to him, "Mahesh, dearest, you are my son, you have looked after us for eight years and grown old, and yet I can't feed you properly—but, dear, you must know how much I love you."

In response, Mahesh merely extended his neck and closed his eyes contentedly. Wiping off his tears on the back of the bull, Ghaffoor whispered again, "The *zamindar* confiscated the food from your mouth, then sold off the small pasture by the burning ghat for money—tell me, dear, how should I protect you in an evil year like this? If I set you free, you will surely raid someone else's haystack or banana tree—what am I to *do* with you! You no longer have any strength, no one wants you any more—they suggest I sell you off at the cattle fair,—" as he spoke, the very idea of such an act brought the tears back to his eyes, from whence they issued forth once again. Wiping the tears with his hand, Ghaffoor looked furtively around a little; he then went quietly to the back of the shack, and, retrieving a clump of withered and faded fodder, placed it before Mahesh and said in a hushed tone, "Now, go on, dear, eat it quickly, or else who knows—"

"*Baba!*"

"What is it, Ma?"

"Come eat your rice—" Amina said, as she emerged from

the room and stood by the doorway. Staring at the scene for a moment, she said, "So you have ripped off a bit of thatch from the wall to feed Mahesh again, have you, *Baba*?"

This was just what Ghaffoor had been afraid of; embarrassed, he mumbled, "It's rotten old thatch, Ma, was falling off on its own—"

"Didn't I just hear you from the inside, *Baba*, tearing it off the wall?"

"Well, no dear, I wasn't quite *tearing* it—"

"But, *Baba*, the wall is sure to collapse—"

Ghaffoor did not say anything. After all, who knew better than him that he had nothing left but this one room, and that, at this rate, even this would not survive another monsoon? Yet, how many days could they possibly last even at this grievous cost?

Amina reminded her father, "Wash your hands, *Baba*, and come eat your rice—I've served it already."

Ghaffoor said to her, "Could you give me the starch, Ma—let me feed it to him before I eat."

"There's no starch left today, *Baba*, it dried in the pot."

"There isn't *any*?" Ghaffoor fell silent. That in these trying times one cannot afford to waste the smallest resource, even this ten-year old girl had understood as much. Washing his hands, Ghaffoor went inside the room. Serving her father's rice and spinach on a brass platter, the little girl had taken a small portion for herself on a saucer made of clay. Watching the arrangement for a moment, Ghaffoor at length said slowly, "Amina, I am getting the chills, Ma—is it right for me to eat any rice with this fever?"

Concerned, Amina said, "But didn't you say then that you were hungry?"

"*Then*? Maybe *then* I didn't have the fever, Ma."

"Then why don't I save it, *Baba*—you can eat it later."

"But, Amina, my fever will only get worse if I eat cold rice."

Amina asked, "What then?"

After thinking for the longest time, or so it seemed, Ghaffoor came up with the perfect solution. He said, "I say, Ma, why don't you go give Mahesh the rice instead. Won't you be able to cook me a bit of fresh rice later in the night, Amina?" In response, Amina raised her head and stared at her father's face for a while. Thereafter, lowering it again, she nodded and said, "Yes, *Baba*, I will."

Ghaffoor's face turned red. The small game of deception that was just played out between father and daughter, perhaps no one except these two, and the One dwelling in ethereal space, witnessed it.

2

About five or six days later one afternoon, an ailing Ghaffoor sat on his front porch, his expression solemn and fretful. His Mahesh had not returned home since the previous day. Ghaffoor was himself terribly weak, hence Amina alone had been running around since the morning looking for Mahesh. When the daylight was beginning to fade, she returned at last and said, "Have you heard, *Baba*, Manik Ghosh and his family have seized and deposited our Mahesh at the *Thana*."

Ghaffoor replied, "Now come on, it can't be, my little *Pagli*!"

"Yes, *Baba*, it *is* true. Their servant said to me, go tell your father he should retrieve him from the pound in Daryapur."

"What had he done?"

"He entered their garden and ruined a lot of plants and trees, *Baba*."

Ghaffoor, thunderstruck by the news, simply sat down, paralyzed by the shock. He had imagined a variety of calamities that could befall Mahesh, but this one was not one of them. He was as inoffensive as he was poor, hence he had little reason to worry that any of his neighbors could harm him so grievously. And especially Manik Ghosh. His devotion to cows and brahmins was well known across the length and breadth of this region.

The daughter reminded him, "The day is about to be over, *Baba*, won't you go get Mahesh back?"

Ghaffoor replied, "No."

"But *they* said the police would sell him off at the *go-hata* if he is not retrieved within three days!"

"Let them."

Amina did not know exactly *what* this *go-hata* was, but she had certainly noticed many times before how perturbed it would make her father to even hear of such a place in connection with Mahesh. Yet, inexplicably, this time he did not say another word as he slowly walked out.

When the night was dark, Ghaffoor secretly arrived at Bansi's pawnshop and said, "*Khuro*, I must have a rupee,—" and with that, he placed his brass platter in front of the broker's cushion. Now, Bansi was well aware of the value and weight of this particular object. At least five times in the past two years or so he had held it as pawn in exchange for a rupee. Therefore, without the slightest hesitation, he gave Ghaffoor the rupee he had requested.

The next day, Mahesh was seen again in his usual place. The same shade of the *babla* tree, the same leash, tether, empty feeding pot, and the eager stare of dark, hungry eyes. An old *Mussalman* was giving him a razor-sharp scrutiny. Not too far away, Ghaffoor Mian sat quietly in a corner with his hands around his knees. His examination over, the old man took out a ten-rupee bank note from a knot in the corner of his shawl, and, smoothing it repeatedly with his fingers, offered it to Ghaffoor, saying, "Fine, I won't ask for any change—you can have the whole thing."

Ghaffoor extended his hand and took the money, but continued to sit quietly. When the two helpers who had accompanied the old man started to unleash the bull, however, Ghaffoor suddenly stood up and growled, "Don't you dare touch his leash, I am warning you-you'll be in *big* trouble if you do."

The men were startled by the unexpected intervention. Quite astonished, the old man asked, "But why?"

Quite enraged, Ghaffoor replied, "What do you mean, *why*? It's *my* bull, and I won't sell him—that's all there is to it." He angrily tossed the bank note in the dust.

They reminded him, "But didn't you take an advance yesterday?"

"Fine, here's your damned advance." He extracted two one-rupee coins from a pouch in his loincloth and flung them on the dust disdainfully. Realizing that an unpleasant dispute was imminent, the old man smiled and said calmly, "You want to start a row for a couple more rupees, right? Well, fellas, go ahead and give his daughter two rupees to buy treats. Well, is *that* OK?"

"No."

"Do you realize no one would give you a half-rupee more?"

Ghaffoor shook his head vigorously and repeated, "No."

The old man became quite irritated; he said, "What do you mean, no? After all, only the skin might fetch some money— what else *is* there?"

"*Towba*! *Towba*!" A terrible expletive escaped Ghaffoor's mouth as he instantly rushed into his room, whence, screaming wildly, he began to threaten that unless the three men left the village immediately, he would call the *zamindar's* guards to whip the living daylight out of them.

Fearing unnecessary trouble, the men departed. Soon thereafter, however, Ghaffoor received the summons from the *zamindar's* front office. Ghaffoor realized that news of the event had reached his Master's ears.

Within the front office, a large crowd of mixed social standing had gathered. Shibubabu, the *zamindar*, stared at him with fiery eyes and said, "Now, Gofra, I can't imagine what is the best punishment for you. Do you have the slightest idea just where it is you live?"

Folding his palms, Ghaffoor replied, "I do. We don't get enough to eat, yet, I would not have refused any penalty you might have imposed on us today."

This surprised the assembly. They all knew this man as stubborn and ill-tempered. Such a man, to their utter astonishment, seemed on the verge of tears as he pleaded with the *zamindar*, "I will never do such a thing again, Master!" With those words, he boxed his ears with his own hands, and then, rubbing his nose from one end to the other of the office compound, he stood up.

"Fine, that's enough. Now go away, and never think of doing it again." Shibubabu's voice had a touch of kindness.

A chill ran down the spine of everyone who heard about the incident. No one had the slightest doubt that only the *karmic* merits of the Master and his iron-fisted, righteous rule had prevented a grievous sin from occurring. Tarkaratna, who was present, elaborated on the scriptural significance of the word *Go*, and thereafter helped awaken the supine wisdom of his listeners by elucidating precisely why such barbaric infidels should never be allowed to get anywhere near the precincts of the village.

Ghaffoor did not say a word. Accepting the great burden of insults and reprimand as proper retribution for his transgression, he returned home with a lightened heart. Collecting some starch from a neighbour's home, he fed Mahesh, and, running his hands gently over his head and horns, proceeded to whisper many a sweet nothing into his ear.

3

Soon *Jaishtha* was almost over. One could never conceive, even remotely, that the terrible visage of *Rudra*, revealed only in a fleeting glimpse at the end of *Vaishakh*, could turn into something so sinister, so brutal, without looking up at the sky today. In it, there was not even the hint of any mercy. That its appearance could someday undergo the slightest change, that someday, this sky could return loaded with cool and soothing rainclouds, was today quite unthinkable. It seemed as though the fire that rained from every corner of space overhead had no limit or end to it—it would not cease until everything within its sight had burned to cinders.

On such a blistering day, Ghaffoor returned home a little after noon. As such, he was not accustomed to working as a manual laborer; moreover, he had recovered from fever barely four or five days ago, and was physically as weak as he was weary. Yet, he had ventured out looking for a job today. Despite his efforts, however, his only reward was the scorching heat wave that blew over his head. Almost blacked out from hunger, thirst and fatigue, he called from the yard, "Amina, dear, is the rice ready?"

The little girl slowly emerged from the room and, holding on to a bamboo stake, stood quietly.

Hearing no response, Ghaffoor raised his voice, "Well, is it *ready*? What did you say—it's *not*? May I know why?"

"We have no rice, *Baba*!"

"No rice? Then why didn't you tell me in the morning?"

"I told you last night."

Imitating her voice scornfully, Ghaffoor said, "*I told you last night*! Indeed! Does one remember such a thing in the morning?" His wrath suddenly doubled at the harshness of his own voice. Contorting his face even further, he shouted, "How *could* we have any rice left? So what if sick old *Baba* went unfed, his grown up daughter has to stuff her face four or five times a day. From now on, I will lock up the rice every time I step out of the house. Now, go on, give me a pitcher of water—I'm dying of thirst. Or say we have no water either!"

Amina continued staring at the ground without a word. After waiting a moment or two, when Ghaffoor realized they did not even have any water to drink, he could not control himself any longer. Swiftly walking to her, he slapped her hard across the face and said, "Disgusting *blackface*, what the hell do you do all day? So many die every day, why don't *you*?"

The little girl said nothing; wiping her eyes, she quietly picked up the empty clay pitcher and set out in the fiery sun. When she was out of sight, however, Ghaffoor suddenly felt an arrow piercing deep inside his heart. Only he knew what all he had to do to bring his little motherless girl up from her infancy. He realized that his gentle, affectionate and dutiful daughter had done nothing wrong. Until the last grains from the field were used up, they never had enough to eat two square meals a day. Some days they ate once, some days they did not eat at all. For either of them to eat five or six times a day was both impossible and hideously untrue. He also knew very well why they had no drinking water. The ponds in the village had all gone dry. The village folk had no access to the little water left in the *zamindar's* private pool. In some places, water would rise through holes dug in the dry bottoms of the ponds, forming meager puddles. A great crowd would gather immediately, pushing and shoving for a share of the precious supply. For Amina it was double jeopardy: the crowds were by far too big for her; moreover, being a Muslim, she would not be allowed to get anywhere near the water. After hours of waiting at a distance, if perchance someone would be moved by her earnest pleas to pour a bit of water into her vessel, she would bring home that hard-earned bit. Ghaffoor knew all this. Perhaps there was no water left today, perhaps the pushing and grabbing had been a little too intense for anyone to pay attention to the little girl—deciding that something along these lines must definitely have happened, Ghaffoor's eyes filled with tears. While he was ruminating thus, suddenly one of the *zamindar's* sentries, built like a big bully, walked up to the house and planted himself in the middle of the yard. "Hey Gofra, are you home?" he bellowed.

"Yes, I am. Why?" Ghaffoor's voice sounded bitter.

"*Babumashai* has summoned you, now come along."

Ghaffoor answered, "I haven't eaten yet, I'll go later."

This was too impertinent for the sentry. Hurling a grotesque epithet at Ghaffoor, he said, "*Babu* has commanded that you receive lashes from the sole of a shoe all the way from here to the *zamindar's* office."

Ghaffoor lost his common sense a second time. Hurling a nasty epithet himself, he said defiantly, "No one is a slave under the laws of Her Majesty the Empress. I pay my taxes; *I won't go.*"

Unfortunately, for the weak to marshal such powerful authority to support his defiance is not only futile, it's downright dangerous. Fortunately, his feeble voice did not possess enough energy to reach the mighty ears of the tyrant— had it done so, the consequence could be fatal for Ghaffoor. As it was, it is needless to describe in detail the fate that befell him soon after he had spoken the last words. Suffice it to say that when he returned from the *zamindar's* office about two hours later, and went into his room to lie down without a word, his face and eyes appeared badly swollen. Apparently, the primary reason behind this severe punishment was Mahesh. After Ghaffoor had left the house that morning in search of a job, Mahesh had broken his leash, and, invading the *zamindar's* garden, munched on a variety of flowering plants and plundered trays of paddy drying in the sun. In the end, when the *Babu's* youngest daughter had attempted to catch him, he had knocked her over and escaped. Apparently, this was not the first time such a thing had happened— Ghaffoor had been spared in the past only because he was poor. Quite likely, if he had pleaded for mercy and groveled at the Master's feet, the *zamindar* would once again have forgiven him. Instead, the fact that he had the audacity to assert that as a tax-paying member of the community, he was nobody's slave—this was far in excess of any affront on the part of a subject that Shiv Charan Babu, being the *zamindar*, could tolerate. Surprisingly, the severe retribution, both verbal and physical, that he received at the *zamindar's* office in consequence did not elicit a single word of protest from him. Quietly enduring the flogging and humiliation, he returned home and lay down without a word. He forgot hunger or thirst, yet it seemed as though a fire as furious as the midday sky outside was burning inside his heart. He did not know how much time had elapsed in this manner; suddenly, the shrill sound of his daughter wailing made him spring up and rush outside. There, he found Amina lying on the ground, and water spilling out of her broken pitcher. Standing next to the pitcher, Mahesh was greedily lapping up the water with the rapidity of an arid desert. In an instant, Ghaffoor went completely out of his mind. Grabbing the plow share he had set aside for sharpening the previous day squarely in his hands, he struck Mahesh upon his lowered head with all his might.

Mahesh attempted to raise his head but once, then his

starved, emaciated body crumpled to the ground. A few drops of tear fell from his eyes, and a drop or two of blood trickled out of his ears. His entire body went through a few rapid convulsions; thereafter, stretching his fore and hind legs as far as possible, Mahesh took a last, agonizing gasp of breath and died.

Letting out a pitiful wail, Amina said, "What have you done, *Baba*, our Mahesh is *dead*!"

Ghaffoor did not stir; he did not say a word in response. Staring transfixed at another glassy-eyed pair of deep, dark eyes, he sat motionless and frozen like a stone sculpture.

About two hours later, hearing the news, cobblers from the edge of the village arrived, and, securing Mahesh with bamboo poles, proceeded to drag his carcass to the dump. Observing the knives with shiny blades in their hands, Ghaffoor shuddered in horror and closed his eyes, yet he did not say a word.

His neighbours said to him later that the *zamindar* had instructed him to consult the priest Tarkaratna for the necessary arrangements. Speculation was rife that perhaps this time Ghaffoor would have to sell his home in order to meet the expenses for the *prachittir*.

Ghaffoor did not respond to any of the above. Planting his head between of his knees, he continued to sit motionless and still.

When the night was deep, Ghaffoor awakened his daughter and said, "Amina, dear, come let's go—"

The poor girl had fallen asleep on the veranda; wiping her eyes, she sat up and said, "Where, *Baba*?"

Ghaffoor said, "To work at Phoolbere's jute mill."

The girl stared at him in disbelief. In the past, no matter how great his hardship, her father had never agreed to work there—it was an immoral place, women had no honor or dignity there—she had heard these things many times.

Ghaffoor urged, "Don't delay, Ma, we have a long way to walk."

Amina was preparing to bring the water jug and her father's brass platter along, but Ghaffoor forbade her, saying, "Let those be, Ma—they will be needed for my Mahesh's *prachittir*."

In the deep, dark night, holding his daughter's hand, he went out. He had no kinfolk in this village, therefore there was no one to inform or send word about his departure. Crossing the front yard, when he reached the bottom of the *babla* tree, he suddenly froze on his track and burst into uncontrollable tears. Looking at the black, starlit sky, he said, "Allah! Punish me as much as you want, but know that my Mahesh died of thirst. No one left even the flimsiest pasture for him to graze. He who deprived him of the green grass from *your* meadows and the cool water from *your* ponds, Allah, I beg you, do not ever forgive his transgression."

Puin Mancha
The Vine On the Bamboo Trellis

BIBHUTI BHUSHAN BANDYOPADHYAY

Stepping on the courtyard, Sahayhari Chatujje said to his wife, "Would you give me a large bowl, or a jug, or anything? Tarak Khuro has felled a palm, let me go get some nice syrup."

Annapurna, his wife, was sitting casually by the threshold of her kitchen. It was a winter morning, and she was massaging on er hair and scalp the precious traces of oil she extracted from the sides of a piece of broomstick she inserted inside a bottle of coconut oil. Seeing her husband, she merely drew the edge of her sari a little. As for bringing out a bowl or jug, she neither exhibited the slightest interest, nor elicited virtually any response.

Sahayhari moved closer and asked, "Now what's the matter, did you not hear me? Why don't you please give me a bowl? Ah—now where on earth did Khenti and the rest go? Are you not going to touch anything because you're oiling your hair?"

Putting away the bottle of oil, Annapurna stared at her husband for a while. Then, with a very calm voice she asked,

"Would you please tell me exactly what you think you are up to?"

The excessive chill in his wife's voice scared Sahayhari—knowing this to be the stillness of the sky before the onset of the storm, he waited desperately for its arrival. Almost apologetically, he stammered, "Well.. why... what again...."

Her voice even quieter, Annapurna said sternly, "Look, I'm telling you, please don't joke around. If you must act the innocent, do it some other time. Do you really not know anything, or care not to find out? Can you tell me how someone with a full-grown daughter possibly whiles away the whole day drinking syrup and fishing? Have you any idea what rumors are spreading in the village?"

Puzzled, Sahayhari asked, "Why—what rumours?"

"Go ask the Chowdhuries, what rumours. One cannot afford to live in a decent society associating with the *Bagdis* and *Dules* night and day. To live in the society, one must follow its rules."

Astonished, Sahayhari was about to say something, when his wife continued in the same tone of voice, "Oh dear, oh dear, they will make us *pariahs*—they discussed it at the Chowdhury Chandimandap yesterday. No one will touch our water again. The poor girl was not married off even after the *ashirvad*—they say she is an *uchchhuggu* girl—now no one in the village will invite you to conduct any ceremony—this is just great! Now just go celebrate—spend all your time hobnobbing in the *Dulé* and *Bagdi* homes!"

Attempting to pooh-pooh the allegations away, Sahayhari said, "Is *that* all! And *I* was beginning to wonder what's going on. *Pariah*! Well, they have all made *pariahs* out of us, and now it is Kalimoy Thakur's turn! *Sure!*"

This time Annapurna flared up like eggplant in hot oil, "And why not? Do you think it takes much to make you a *pariah*? Who do you think you are—any bigwig of the society, or any VIP? Has no status, no means, no power to do *anything*—so what's so impossible that the Chowdhuries will make you a *pariah*?—Besides, it *is* true, the girl is now fully grown." Then, lowering her voice, she said, "She just turned *fifteen*—so what if we go around telling people she is younger, don't people have eyes?"... Suddenly raising her voice once again, she went on, "No attempt to marry her, no enterprise! Must *I* go hunt for a groom?"

Realizing that as long as he remained near her, there was a zero likelihood that his wife's tone would ever soften, Sahayhari quickly grabbed a brass bowl and began walking towards the back door. However, seeing something near the doorway, he suddenly stopped and said with delight, "What is all this? Khenti-ma, where did you get all this from? Oh, well, indeed! It's..."

A girl of about fourteen or fifteen walked in, followed by two younger ones. In her arm she carried a stack of *puin* vine, its stalks thick and yellow, the yellow indicating that some neighbors must have uprooted their overgrown and overripe *puin* vine to clear their courtyard; the girl had fondly gathered their trash for all she was worth. Of the two younger girls, one was empty-handed, the other carried some stuff wrapped inside two or three ripe *puin* leaves.

The older girl was rather tall and plump, her hair was dark and dishevelled—blowing in the wind, her face was quite large, her eyes were very expressive and peaceful. The stack of thin glass bangles on her wrist was secured by a safety pin bought at two paise a dozen. A search for the pin's age would take us to prehistoric times. This older girl must be the one called Khenti, for she quickly turned around and, taking the stuff wrapped in *puin* leaves from her younger subordinate's hand, opened it, and said, "It's shrimp, Father. I got it from Gaya the old woman by the street side. She wouldn't give it to me at first—said your father owes me two paise from the day before. So I tell her, please give it to me, Gaya *Pishi*—my father won't run away with your two paise. And Ray *Kaka* from the river bank gave me this *puin* vine, said take it, it's nice and thick...."

From the kitchen foyer, Annapurna screamed in an extremely acrid tone, "Oh sure, *take it*, indeed! What manna from heaven they've given you! A bunch of ripe old *puin* stalks, dry as wood, they would have thrown it out in a day or two... *take it*, and our darling girl brings in their wild weeds—that's just wonderful, they didn't have to take the trouble to cut down the bush. All the stone headed morons come to lean on my shoulders... stupid grown-up girl, how many times have I asked you not to step outside the house? Do you have no shame loitering around the neighbourhoods? Would have been the mother of four, if married? Have no sense of propriety when it comes to food, huh?... Where can I get some greens, where some eggplants; the other one roams about, where to find some syrup, some junk and crap... throw it out, I say... throw it out!"

Staring quietly at her mother, the frightened girl let go of her grasp; the bundle of *puin* vine fell to the ground. Annapurna continued angrily, "Go, Radhi, go dump that trash by the backyard pond... if I *ever* see you leaving the house again, watch if I break your leg or not..."

The bundle had fallen to the ground. Like a mechanical toy, the younger girl picked up the stalks and started to walk towards the backyard pond. But she was much too small, and could not grasp the large bundle, so that most of the stalks dangled around her as she dragged them along. Sahayhari's children were very much afraid of their mother.

Half apologetically, Sahayhari attempted to defend the older girl, "So she's brought it to eat, she's only a child... must you really... why don't you..."

Still dragging the bundle of *puin* vine, the younger girl Radhi stopped and turned to look at her mother. Annapurna looked at her and said, "No, just take it away, she need not eat it—why should a woman have such a long tongue! Going out to some other neighborhood to beg for some overripe *puin* vine! Go, go right now... throw it in the wild dump..."

Sahayhari turned to look at his oldest daughter, and noticed her two eyes had filled with water. He felt very sorry for her. But, no matter how fond the girl was of *puin* vine, he could not muster the courage to accost his wife over it at this time of the day—quietly he walked out the back door.

As she sat cooking, Annapurna recalled the pleading look on her oldest daughter's face. She remembered, the day before the last *arandhan*, when *puin* greens were being cooked in her kitchen, Khenti had requested her playfully, "Mother, *half* of these are for me alone, the other half are for the rest of you..."

There was no one home, so she herself got up and gathered the few stalks which lay scattered by the backyard and the back door. The rest were lying in a filthy heap by the stagnant pond, too filthy to retrieve. She secretly cooked the stalks with the little shrimps her daughter had so eagerly collected.

Seeing the *puin chachchari* on her platter at lunch time, Khenti's expressive eyes were filled with surprise and joy as she looked nervously at her mother. After making a round or two about the kitchen, Annapurna returned to find that the *puin* greens had disappeared from Khenti's platter without a trace. She knew well how addicted this daughter was to *puin* greens, so she asked her, "Well, Khenti dear, would you like some more *chachchari*?" Khenti at once nodded her head in delightful affirmation. Thinking of something, Annapurna's eyes filled with tears. In an effort to suppress them, she looked up and began plucking dried red chillies from a cane basket stuck to the underside of the tin roof.

That afternoon, Sahayhari was called to the *Chandi Mandap* of Kalimoy. After a brief, premeditated introduction, Kalimoy said in an agitated tone, "Those days are no more, brother. Why, take our Kesto Mukhujje... made such a racket about not marrying his daughter unless the match was worthy, and of high character. Well, in the end he barely managed to save face by practically begging and handing her to Hari's son. Now, what's worthy about *them*? Goodness, they are degenerate *kshotriyas* for six or seven generations running!" Then, lowering his voice, he said, "Is anything left of society's ability to impose its laws and regulations? It's vanishing rapidly. In fact, why do I even go far, think of your own thirteen year-old daughter right here..."

Sahayhari tried to interrupt him, "She'll be thirteen this *Sravan*..."

"Ah, ha, thirteen or sixteen, what difference does it make? What's the difference, thirteen or sixteen? Now, whether it's thirteen, or sixteen, or even fifty, we have nothing to do with that—that's something for you to account for. But the point is, the *ashirvad* of the groom was already over—pray, why on earth did *you* suddenly turn so stubbornly knotty? She is, after all, almost like an *uchchhugge* girl. If the *ashirvad* is done, it's the same as if the marriage is done—only the ritual of walking seven times in a circle was left incomplete, right?... Now, don't you imagine that you will live in the society and get away with doing these things right before our eyes. If you wish to preserve the honor of the Brahmins in the society, arrange for her marriage... a groom is a groom, is there no groom except a prince? You're a poor man, obviously can't offer much, that's why I made the match with Srimanta Majumdar's son. So what if he is illiterate is someone completely unworthy unless he is a judge or a magistrate? They have a house, a garden, a pond, I am told they have even harvested some *aman* paddy from their small plot this year—now, isn't that a royal estate? What do the two brothers lack?..."

The fact is, it was Kalimoy who had made the connection with the above-mentioned son of Srimanta Majumdar from Manigan. Now, as for why Kalimoy took the trouble to arrange the marriage of Sahayhari's daughter with Majumdar's son, some maintain that Kalimoy apparently owes Majumdar a lot of money, including a large amount of unpaid interest, and that a court summons will be issued soon, and so forth. These rumours are not only preposterous, but in all likelihood without any basis. They must be fibs concocted by wicked minds. In any event, a few days after the groom's party had left following the *ashirvad* ceremony, Sahayhari found out that some months earlier, as a result of some scandalous act in his village, the groom had been thoroughly beaten up by the relatives of a married *kumbhakar* woman, and consequently was bedridden for a while. Not willing to give his daughter unto such a groom, Sahayhari had called off the match.

About two days later. Sahayhari was leisurely smoking his *hookah* as he savored the little bit of soft morning sunlight seeping through the leaves of the grapefruit tree in the yard, when his eldest daughter Khenti walked in and whispered to him surreptitiously, "Father, don't you want to go? Mother's gone to the *ghat*..."

For some reason, Sahayhari first glanced at the path to the *ghat* near the house. Then, lowering his voice, he said, "Go, quickly get the shovel." Thereafter, he began taking vigorous puffs at his *hookah* pipe, and cast a second, nervous look at the rear path to the *ghat*. Presently, Khenti returned desperately grasping an incredibly heavy iron shovel, after which father and daughter slithered out the front door. Together, the two presented the impression as though they were out to burglurize someone's home.

Annapurna was making preparations to light the cooking fire after she had changed following her bath, when the young girl Durga of the Mukhujje house came in and said, "Auntie, Mother asked me to tell you, she will not touch anything, would you please come by and prepare our *nabanna* rice, and put out *Itu's* clay pots?"

Along the way to the Mukhujje house in another neighborhood, one comes across a dense thicket of *Sheora*, *Vanbhant*, *Rangchita*, *Vanchalta* and other trees to the left of the path. The strong odor of some wild vines and creepers was permeating the winter morning air. A long-tailed, yellow *lajjhola* bird was hopping from one branch to another of an *amra* tree.

Durga pointed at the bird and said, "Auntie, look, look at that bird!" As she turned her head to spot the bird, Annapurna noticed something else. From somewhere in the dense thicket, a thup, thup sound was emanating for some time, as if someone was digging for something, but as soon as Durga spoke, the sound suddenly stopped. Annapurna stood there frozen for a while, then resumed walking. After they had gone some distance, the thup, thup sound started again.

It was a while before Annapurna finished her work and returned. Returning, she noticed Khenti sitting in the sun on the courtyard with a bowl of oil, letting her hair down. Looking sternly at her, she asked, "How come you haven't gone for your bath yet, where were you all this time?"

Khenti hurriedly replied, "I'll go right away, Mother. I'll be back in no time."

Shortly after Khenti had left for her bath, Sahayhari appeared, enthusiastically carrying a large wild yam on his shoulder. Running into his wife, he immediately proceeded to produce an alibi, telling her, "Moysha the Chowkidar from over there tells me often, Master, you used to come visit us every now and then when your father was alive, but not any more; well, I have grown a large yam against the fence, why don't you..."

Annapurna stared coldly at her husband and said, "May I know what you were doing in the Barojpota bush a little while ago?"

Stunned, Sahayhari replied, "Me? No... when?... Never, just now I was..." His manner indicated as if he had just fallen from the sky.

Continuing her cold stare, Annapurna said, "So you *will*

steal, nothing can change you, but now that you are past three quarters of your life, please stop lying like this. I know everything. You thought the damned spoiler had gone to the ghat... well, Durga's mother called me, so I was off to their neighborhood, when I hear this thup, thup noise coming from the Barojpota bush. I knew right away; the noise stopped when we made a sound, then started again when we went farther ahead. So maybe *you* don't care for your present or after life—go ahead and steal or even rob, but why spoil the girl's future by dragging her into your mischief?"

Sahayhari made some futile efforts to prove the impossibility of his presence in Barojpota at the alleged time, but in the face of his wife's stare, he could not find the right words or arguments, and even what he managed to say sounded quite garbled.

Half an hour later, finishing her bath, Khenti returned. She stole a quick glance at the large yam lying on the yard, then started to put her wet clothes out to dry with great concentration.

Annapurna called out to her, "Khenti, come on here and listen."

Hearing her mother's call, Khenti turned pale. When she hesitantly came near her mother, she asked, "The two of you went out and dug up this yam, right?"

Khenti looked at her mother a little, then at the yam on the ground, then back at her mother, and immediately also stole a quick glance at the bamboo thicket in front of the house. Beads of sweat appeared on her forehead, but not a single word escaped from her lips.

Annapurna now hardened her tone, "Why aren't you

saying anything? Have you, or have you not brought this yam?"

A distressed Khenti was already staring at her mother's face; she replied, "Yes."

Annapurna at once exploded in anger, "You wicked waif, wait till I break a hunk of wood on your back today! Slinking off to steal a yam from the Barojpota bush! Full-grown girl, long fit to be married, goes into the dense, elephant-grass bush, where tigers hide during the day, and digs up someone's yam? If the Gosains had sent in their chowkidars and had you arrested? Which father-in-law of yours would come to bail you out? If I have it, I will eat it, if I don't, I won't. But steal from someone else? Oh, Mother, what will I do with this girl?"

One evening about two or three days later, her hands caked with mud, Khenti came in and said, "Mother, Mother, come and look..."

Annapurna went out and saw that, upon the small plot of land next to the broken boundary wall, which had become overgrown with pebbles and wild, thorny weeds, Khenti was most enthusiastically making arrangements to start a full-scale vegetable garden with her little sister as assistant. As the forerunner of the many anticipated fruits and roots which were due to appear, a rickety and rather frail-looking *puin* plant stood dangling against a dry, bamboo trellis serving as a scaffold, suspended from a piece of cloth, much like a convict hanging from the gallows. The rest of the fruits and roots obviously existed only inside the oldest girl's head, they were yet to see the light of day.

Annapurna started laughing, and said, "You crazy, foolish girl, does one plant a *puin* sapling in this season? You should plant it in the rainy season. At this time, won't it die without water?"

Khenti replied, "Why, I will water it every day."

Annapurna said, "Well, maybe it *will* live. It *does* get pretty dewy early in the morning nowadays."

It was a harsh winter. Arising in the morning, Sahayhari noticed his two younger daughters, wrapped up in quilts, standing under the jackfruit tree on the courtyard in the hope of catching some sunlight. Then, shivering in the cold, Khenti appeared with some cowdung she collected from the Mukhujje house in a broken cane basket. Sahayhari said to her, "Mother Khenti, what is the problem that you don't put on your flannel dress in the morning? Don't you see how cold it is?"

"OK, Father, I will put it on now—but where is the cold, it's hardly..."

"Yes, Mother, put it on, put it on right away—you know you could catch something nasty." As Sahayhari departed, he thought to himself, had he not looked at his daughter for a long time? Had Khenti's countenance really become so graceful?

The history of the dress went as follows. Many years have gone by since Sahayhari purchased the dress in question, made of black flannel, for two and a half rupees from the *Raas Mela* at Haripur. It had been ripped, patched and mended several times, and since Khenti's body had started to develop during the previous year, the dress had become too small for her. Sahayhari had little information regarding such intimate family matters. Moreover, Annapurna, too, did not know anthing about the current condition of the dress—it used to be stored inside Khenti's own broken trunk.

It was the *sankranti* of the month of *Pous*. After the sunset, Annapurna sat mixing together rice flour, wheat flour and molasses in a large brass bowl, periodically dipping her hand in a small bowl of oil. Alongside her, Khenti was busy grating coconut, and collecting the fine grated powder on a banana leaf tucked under the grater. Annapurna had at first refused to accept Khenti's help, on account of her "unclean" habits, such as sitting in all kinds of places, loitering around in jungles, and wearing unholy clothes. In the end, when Khenti had really pleaded with her, she assigned her to this task, but only after she had thoroughly washed herself, and put on fresh clothes.

When the mixture was ready, Annapurna was getting ready to place a pan on the fire, when her youngest daughter Radhi suddenly extended her right hand and, cupping it, said, "Mother, may I have *just* a little bit of *that*?"

Annapurna took a dollop of the mixture from the large bowl and, inscribing a special symbol on it with the five digits of her hand, placed it upon Radhi's extended hand. Her middle daughter, Punti, thereupon wiped her right hand quickly in her *sari* and extended her palm also with the words, "Mother, me too..."

As she sat grating coconut in a freshly-washed *sari*, Khenti could not help watching the scene wistfully every now and then. Afraid to ask for some too, lest Mother should scold her about it being quite the wrong time, she did not speak.

But Annapurna herself said, "Khenti, dear, would you pass me the coconut half-shell, let me set a little aside for you too." Khenti instantly grabbed the half-shell without the hole, and presented it to her mother, who poured an extra generous portion of the mixture into it.

The middle sister Punti said, "At Jathaima's they've bought a lot of milk—Rangadidi was making *kheer*. They'll make different varieties."

Khenti looked up and said, "Are they making more for supper? I thought they'd invited Suresh Uncle and Tinu's father for the Brahmin's feast. They've already made *payesh*, *jhol-puli*, *moog-tokti* and other sweets for supper.

Punti asked, "Mother, is it true you can't make *patisapta* without *kheer*? Khendi was saying, "What's *patisapta* without *kheer* stuffing?" I told her, "Why, *my* mother makes it with caramelized grated coconut, what does *that* taste like?"

Annapurna dipped a severed eggplant top in oil and, lacing the inside of the pan with the oil, searched for a satisfactory answer in her head.

Khenti said, "That's just the way Khendi talks. As if Khendi's mother is *some pithe* cook! Is making *pithe* as easy as stuffing the dough with *kheer* and frying it in *ghee*? The other day didn't I go to their house when their son-in-law was visiting? So, Auntie gave me two *patisaptas* to eat—my, they had a funny, smoky smell... does *pithe* ever smell smoky? *Patisapta* tastes yucky with *kheer* stuffing!"

Presenting her opinion almost recklessly, Khenti looked at her mother and asked, "Mother, may I have a bit of grated coconut?"

Annapurna told her, "OK, but don't eat here—you'll drop crumbs or something. Go over there."

Khenti took a fistful in the coconut half-shell and, moving over some distance, began to eat. If one's countenance be the mirror of one's mind, then there could not be the slightest doubt watching Khenti's face that she was in a very high state of bliss.

About an hour later Annapurna said, "All right, you all! Sit down with your banana leaves, let me serve you hot and steaming. Khenti, there's some leftover rice from lunch soaking in water, go get it."

It was clear from Khenti's expression that she did not like her mother's proposition much. Punti said, "Mother, let Bardi eat *pithes* only. She loves them. Let the rice be left for tomorrow—we'll eat it then."

After she had eaten a few, Punti did not want to eat any more. She was not terribly fond of sweets. When everyone else had finished eating, Khenti was still going strong. She usually ate quietly, and said very little. Annapurna noticed that she had eaten at least eighteen or nineteen *pithes*. She asked her, "Khenti, would you like more?" Busy eating, Khenti nodded her head. Annapurna gave her a few more. Her eyes and face seemed a bit bright and shiny. With smiling eyes, she looked at her mother and said, "They taste wonderful, Mother. It's the way you whisk the batter till it becomes frothy, *that* does the trick!" She then resumed eating.

As she started to put away the ladle, spatula and cooking stove, Annapurna tenderly gazed at her quiet, inoffensive daughter who was slightly addicted to food. She thought to herself, "This Khenti of mine will bring great contentment to whichever family she goes to. She's so good-natured, you scold her about work, beat her, swear at her, she doesn't say one word. No one ever heard her raise her voice..."

Through the mediation of one of Sahayhari's distant relatives, Khenti was married off around the beginning of *Vaishakh*. Even though it was his second time, the groom could definitely not be much over forty. Still, Annapurna was at first very reluctant about this match, but the groom's family was well off, had a house in the city, apparently made some money in the quicklime and brick business. It was not easy finding such a groom!

The groom being a bit older, Annapurna was hesitant at first to come out before him, but later, lest Khenti's feelings be hurt, she took Khenti's well-rounded hand and placed it in the groom's during the *baran* ceremony for the groom. Her voice became choked with tears, and she could not say anything.

Leaving the house, the *palki* bearers once lowered the *palki* on the ground under the *amlaki* tree in order to properly re-load it. Annapurna noticed that the *anchal* of Khenti's inexpensive *cheli*, reddish like beach sand, was rolling among the bunches of blue *mehendi* flowers hanging low by the fence. Thinking about this disorganized, utterly innocent, and a little overly food-addicted girl of hers, her heart began to pitch and roll with misgivings about sending her off to another home full of strangers. Would *they* know or understand Khenti like her?

Her eyes overflowing with tears, Khenti had consoled her mother when going away, "Mother, make sure you bring me back in *Asharh* itself—send Father—it's *only* two months."

Old *Than-didi* from another neighborhood said, "Why would your Father go to your home, dear? Let the grandson arrive first, then he will."

Khenti's face turned red with embarrassment. Spreading a hint of a smile over her large, tear-filled eyes, she said stubbornly, "Why, of course he will go! I'll see how he doesn't."

Picking up the *aamsattva* put out to dry in the afternoon sun of *Phalgun* and *Chaitra* on a scaffold in the courtyard, Annapurna's mind would pine and agonize—her greedy, tactless daughter was no longer around, that she would appear from nowhere and, extending a shameless hand, implore her, "Mother, may I ask something? Would you tear a bit of that corner..."

More than a year passed. It was *Asharh* again. The monsoon was in full force. Sitting on the floor outside his room, Sahayhari was talking to his neighbour Vishnu Sarkar. Preparing the hookah pipe, Sahayhari said, "You may take it for granted, Dada, it's bound to happen. How can those like us expect anything better?"

Vishnu Sarkar was squatting on a palm-leaf mat, appearing to be kneading dough for bread from a distance. Clearing his voice, he said, "No, not everything... besides, I shall pay cash for everything. Well, then, what exactly had happened to your daughter?"

Sahayhari inhaled a few drags of his pipe, coughed, and said, "Pox, I heard. You know what it came to? They would simply not send her home. I still owed two hundred and fifty rupees on the dowry, so they said, pay it up, then take your girl home."

"Absolute low-lives!"

"Then I told them, look, I will pay it by installments. I figured the *Puja tattva* alone would be no less than thirty rupees. They began a variety of insulting rumours and diatribes against my girl... that she behaved like a savage from a rustic home, ate like someone raised impoversihed and famine-stricken, much more. In *Pous*, I went to see her—couldn't stay away from her, you know."

Sahayhari paused, and began to smoke silently for a few minutes. Neither of them spoke for a while.

A little later, Vishnu Sarkar said, "Then?"

"When her mother started to cry and complain excessively, I went to see her in *Pous*. *What* they had done to her! The mother-in-law spoke loudly so I would hear, "This is what happens when you tie family bonds with no-good, rustic paupers! Like daughter, like father! So he comes to visit his daughter in *Pous, empty-handed*!" Then, looking at Vishnu Sarkar, he said, "Now, whether we are rustic or aristocratic, you know very well, Sarkar Uncle. After all, in the *Nilkuthi* period, tigers and cows drank together from the same *ghat* in the name of Parameshwar Chatujje—so may be *now* I have fallen in dire straits... " Recalling his lost aristocracy, Sahayhari elicited a dry, unemotional Ha, Ha in dispirited amusement.

Vishnu Sarkar made a muffled sound of acquiescence, and nodded his head a couple of times.

"Then, in *Phalgun* she had the pox. Such low-lives—as soon as the pox blisters appeared, took her to this distantly-related sister of mine who lives in Tala—found out about her once when they'd gone to the Kalighat temple for *puja*. Dumped her there. Not one word to me, no contact, nothing. My sister's family gave me the news. So I went there..."

"You didn't see her again?"

"No. Such low-lives—they removed all her jewellery from her body even as she fell sick, and sent her off to Tala. ... Anyhow, let's go now, it's getting late. So, what lure did you settle for? We can't lure ants with puffed rice, you know."

A few months had gone by. It was time once again for the *Pous* celebrations. This year, the winter was so severe near the end of *Pous*—they had not seen a winter this severe in their lives.

In the evening, Annapurna sat in her kitchen, mixing rice powder for *saruchakli pithes*. Punti and Radhi were warming themselves by the fire.

Radhi said, "You must add a little more water, Mother— why did you make it so thick?"

Punti said, "Mother, shouldn't you add a little salt in it? Oh, look, Mother, Radhi's wrap is dangling by the fire. It will catch fire any moment..."

Annapurna admonished Radhi, "Move away from the fire, Mother—can't you get warm without sitting right against the flames? Move over here."

The batter was ready—Annapurna set up the pan, poured the batter, and covered it with a cane basket. Presently, warmed by the mild heat, the *pithes* swelled up like *topors*.

Punti said, "Give me the first one, Mother, I'll go leave it for *Shanra Shashthi* over by the corner."

Annapurna told her, "Don't go alone, take Radhi with you."

It was a bright, full moon. The silvery moonbeams were trapped on the dense bunches of white flowers of the *telakutcha* vine, which had wrapped itself on top of the *shanra* bush in the back of the house.

When Punti and Radhi opened their back door, making a rustling sound and trampling the dry leaves, a fox dashed off into the dense bush. Startled, Punti quickly threw the *pithe* on top of the *shanra* bush with all her might. Then, terrified by the strange quietness of the bamboo thicket around her, the child hastily retreated back to the house, and shut the back door.

When they had returned, Annapurna asked, "Did you offer the *pithe*?"

Punti replied, "Yes, Mother—I threw it where you had picked up the lime plant last year."

Then, many hours passed by that night. When the *pithes* were almost entirely done, it was pretty late. In the bright moonlit night, a woodpecker was busy making a constant tuk-tuk-tuk sound in the woods behind the house. Gradually, even that sound was becoming dull. As she started to tear up banana leaves for their supper, Punti suddenly said absentmindedly, "Didi loved *pithes so much*..."

All three sat speechless for a while; then, somehow, their gazes fell together upon a corner of the courtyard, and froze. There, carrying the memory of the deepest cravings of the greedy young girl upon its leaves and veins, the *puin* vine she had so lovingly planted with her own hands had proliferated across the length and breadth of the scaffold. Nourished by the rain water and the dews of *Kartik*, the tender young shoots had run out of room on the scaffold. They swayed in lush cascades over its sides... sleek, supple, filled with the richness and grace of young life.

Tarini Majhi
Tarini the Boatman

TARASHANKAR BANDYOPADHYAY

Tarini the boatman walked with a stoop. Being exceptionally tall, he had learned the hard way to stoop before entering through doorways, walking beneath low-hanging tree branches, and standing erect under the ceilings of tin shacks. He had literally learned from hard knocks. Yet, when he rowed his boat in the river, he would sit ramrod straight. Standing tall atop his *donga*, which was simply the hollowed-out trunk of a *taal* tree, he would deftly maneuver a long bamboo pole until he had delivered his passengers to the other shore.

It was the month of *Asharh*. Hordes of passengers, returning from the *ambubachi* pilgrimage, had set up a veritable *haat* at the Ganutia *ghat* by the shore of the Mayurakshi. Each passenger, weary from days of great labor, was eager to be among the first to be ferried across.

Presently, puffing on his tobacco pipe, Tarini thundered, "No more, my good ladies, no more. That holy dip in the Ganga has made you all extra heavy with *punya*. Be careful, now."

An old woman quickly pleaded with him, "Just one more person, son, this little boy here." Someone elsewhere was heard calling out, "Ahoy, Sabi, come on in, dear, come on in. Stop giggling with those crooked teeth."

Sabi, a.k.a. Savitri, was a young girl. She was far too busy giggling and laughing it up with a bunch of other girls from her village. She answered back, "You carry on. The rest of us will take the next ferry."

Tarini insisted, "No, you better come aboard now. The boat is guaranteed to sink if the whole lot of you get in." Sabi, being quite garrulous, immediately retorted, "If it must sink, it will definitely do so with all these old hags in there, Majhi. Each of them has bathed ten or twenty times in the Ganga. And *we*, no more than just once."

Folding his palms, Tarini replied melodramatically, "Well, my venerable Ma, *one* bath is *all* it took for you all to carry those tidal waves back ashore." The entire boatload of passengers broke out in laughter. Bamboo pole in hand, the boatman took one leap and planted himself at the head of the *donga*. His assistant Kalachand was meanwhile busy collecting the fares. "Is there anyone who hasn't paid to cross over? Please check to make sure, one last time, I tell you." Kalachand thundered, then, pushing the boat off the shore, hopped right in. Pushing the shallow river bottom with his pole, Tarini said, "Say *Hari Hari*, one and all, say *Haribol*." The passengers replied in one voice—"*Haribol*." The sound of the collective chant reverberated from and within the deep forests on both banks. Below, the swift Mayurakshi with its vicious currents cooed ominously to herself in an inaudible undertone. Tarini suddenly laughed and suggested, "You might as well pray to me—after all, *I* am the one carrying you across."

An old woman said, "Of course, *Baba*! Who else would deliver but *Tarini*, tell me who?"

Lifting his pole up with a quick jerk, Tarini screamed in exasperation, "Say, Kele, you dud—grip your oars *tight*—now, whose grains do *you* feed on, pal? Can't you feel the deadly pull?"

Indeed, the vicious current *was* Mayurakshi's most-feared attribute. Of twelve months, she is generally dry as a desert for seven or eight—nothing but a sandy shoreline extending a mile to a mile and a half in width with barely any visible sign of water anywhere. Yet, at the very onset of the monsoon, she undergoes an incredible metamorphosis—turning into a veritable demoness. Overflowing both banks in deep murky currents of water up to five miles wide, she rushes to the sea in a maniacal frenzy of destruction. Then there is the so-called *horpa* flood, an absolutely killer tidal wave cresting at over twenty feet high, which wipes out homes, farms, village after village without discrimination or mercy in no time at all. Of course, such floods rarely happen—the last one came in about twenty years earlier.

The sun had intensified overhead. A male passenger unfurled an umbrella.

Tarini cautioned him, "Do not open up a sail now, *Thakur*. It can blow *you* away."

The man closed his umbrella. Suddenly, from further upstream, there arose a great commotion—a terrifying sound of mortal fear.

The passengers in the *donga* became very restless and

alarmed. Quietly manoeuvering his pole, Tarini reassured them, "Now, now, calm down, you all! Nothing's happened to you. A dinghy has gone under near the *Olkura ghat*. Now, my old lady, why do you tremble so? Here, *Thakur*, please hold the old lady. What's there to fear? We are almost near the *ghat* now."

Indeed, the river crossing was almost complete.

Tarini shouted, "Say, *Kele*!"

"What is it?"

His eyes focused upon the river, Tarini said, "Come hold this pole for me."

Kalachand stood up. Handing him the steering pole, Tarini said, "Look, there, *there*, look—there, now, just went under." As he spoke, he suddenly plunged right into the violent river with the vicious currents. A few old women on the *donga* cried out, "Oh, good God, *Baba* Tarini, what will happen to us, *Baba*?"

Kalachand shouted in reprimand, "Now, look—the old hags are calling him from behind. I'm telling you, you will all die, just die. I'm telling you."

Within the murky waters, something white was going under every now and then, only to float up again after some distance. Tarini was swimming hastily and swiftly against the currents towards the object. His rapid movements seemed almost effortless. Presently he was almost upon the object itself. Just then, it again went under, and with it went Tarini. After some anxious moments, he was observed emerging from under the waters, something black held in his grip. Changing directions slightly, he then let himself be propelled by the currents.

The crowd on both shores watched Tarini with rapt attention and curiosity. Presently, from one coast there arose the high-pitched cry, "*Haribol.*"

From the other coast, there arose the scream, "Is he up? Is he up?"

Meanwhile, Kalachand steered the *donga* vigorously towards the shore.

Tarini was lucky. The drowning person turned out to be a married woman from a prosperous local family. No *donga* had capsized near the *olkura ghat*. The poor young woman had a long veil covering her face, and, when trying to shift herself by holding on to the edge of the *donga*, she had caused the accident. She had missed the edge altogether, and tumbled overboard. Fortunately, even though she had swallowed some water, it was nothing critical, and she regained her consciousness with minimal paramedical assistance.

She was quite young—no more than thirteen or fourteen. She was also quite attractive, and was wearing quite a bit of jewellery—hoop earrings, tasseled nose ring, thin bracelets, and a neckchain. A short time later, when her husband and father-in-law arrived, she was still quite exhausted and was breathing heavily.

Tarini offered the father-in-law a *pranam*, and said, "*Pennam*, Ghosh *Mashai.*"

The girl quickly drew the veil over her face.

Tarini said, "Don't block the air out, *Ma*, now breathe, *breathe*. Like they say, should a bashful young one cower, danger redoubles its power."

Ghosh Mahashay asked, "What would you like, Tarini, tell me."

Tarini only managed to scratch his head to no avail—he could not figure out what reward he could possibly claim. At length, he only managed to blurt out, "Money for a jug of beer—eight *annas*."

The girl Sabi, who was standing among the crowd, observed, "Oh, better that I die! Can't you ask for something more *expensive*, for heaven's sake?"

Suddenly brought to his senses, Tarini kept his head bowed, smiled shyly, and said, "May be a tasseled nose ring, Ghosh *Mashai*."

It was Sabi once again who spoke. "So, *baba* Tarini, does *bouma* swing her nose a lot when she talks?" She was imitating an inquisitive elder.

The ferry *ghat* suddenly reverberated with the sound as the gathered throng burst out in laughter.

The young girl had not unveiled her face. Only her delicate and fair hand emerged from within—upon the rosy palm of her hand, a golden nose ring glittered brightly in the sunlight.

Ghosh Mahashay said, "I promise you a *dhoti* and a *chadar* at the time of *Dashara*—you understand, Tarini? And for now, here, keep these five rupees."

Gratefully offering his *pranam*, Tarini suggested, "Sir, could you make it a *sari* instead of the *chadar*?"

Smiling, Ghosh Mahashay reassured him, "Of course, that will be so, that will be so."

Never one to give up, Sabi quipped, "I'd like to see this wife of yours, Tarini."

Tarini told her, "She's really dark and ugly, Ma."

That night Tarini came home after drinking up to his gills. His legs were very wobbly, and he repeatedly missed his steps. Presently, quite frustrated, he complained to Kalachand, "Who do you suppose dug all these canals on our street, huh, Kele? Nothing but *nullah*, just *nullah*, just this one, this one, this—"

Kalachand was just as drunk; he merely said, "Hum."

Tarini went on, "Tanks—they all turn into tanks—we can swim home. Goddamn—there is no *khal*, no *nullah*—they are a-l-l the same."

Even as he waddled unsteadily along, he waved his hands in the air as though he were swimming home.

Home was at the edge of the village. Holding a lamp in her hand, Sukhi, his wife, stood at the doorway.

Tarini began singing a ditty, "Now, *that's* a new import into the country, that tasseled nose ring—"

Sukhi came forward and took him by his hand. "That's enough, now come inside. Your rice has gone cold and brittle."

Pulling his hand away, and tying his *dhoti* more securely, Tarini said, "But first I have to put this ring on your nose. Now—where is that *loth*—where is that *shala loth*?"

Sukhi scolded him, "One of these days you will eat me alive trying to do this kind of thing. I am telling you, I will just hang myself this time."

Tarini stared at her, rather bewildered. "Why, now, what have I done?"

Sukhi continued, "Such a swollen monstrous river, and you—"

The stormy, dark and rain-drenched night became fretful as Tarini broke into a sonorous laughter. Presently, he stopped his guffaws, and said, "Since when did mother's bosom become a place to fear? You tell me dear, am I right, or what? The rice we get to eat is provided by *that* Mayurakshi. Answer me, go on, answer me!"

Without wasting another word, Sukhi went inside to get his dinner ready.

Tarini called after her, "Sukhi, hey Sukhi, my dearest, listen to me!"

Sukhi did not answer. Tarini stood up with a tipsy swagger, and headed towards the interior. Getting a hold of Sukhi from behind, he said to her, "Come, you have to go with me right away."

Sukhi said, "Let go, let go of my *sari*."

"You *have* to go. Absolutely, a thousand times—three hundred times." Tarini insisted.

Prying her *sari* free from his grasp, Sukhi said, "All right, I will go, but let go of my *sari* first." Delighted, Tarini set her free. Sukhi left the room with his platter of rice.

Tarini went on, "Come, I will carry you on my back and plunge in at the *Gonoot ghat*, then come up at *Panchthoopi ghat*.

Sukhi said, "Fine I will go as you say, but finish your rice first."

As he tried leaving the room, Tarini struck his forehead against the door-frame; thereafter, his bravado became somewhat subdued.

As he ate, he started again, "So, did I not rescue a pair of cows that time? Can't you recall I made fifteen rupees-five under twenty, then? And didn't that scoundrel Madan Gope cheat me in the deal? Then, how do you suppose you got the gilded *sankha* for your pretty wrists—tell me, which rich *nana* of yours gave you those?"

Sukhi was passing *amani* through a strainer inside—the cool liquid was a good antidote for intoxication and hangovers. Tarini continued, "Scoundrel Madna—you cheated me, right? Fine. At least Sukhi has her gilded *sankha*—so what if *I* got nothing. I hope the bastard falls into the Mayurakshi flood one of these days—I will shove him in for a few gulps before I pull him out. That should teach him."

Placing the bowl of *amani* before him, Sukhi began to undo the knot of his money pouch. Inside, she found the nose ring and three one-rupee bills.

Sukhi asked him, "Where are the other two rupees?"

Tarini said, "That Kele, I gave him the money—go on, have it, I said."

Sukhi did not argue the point, it was not in her nature. Tarini rambled on, "That one time, when you were quite sick—well, the mail wouldn't cross the raging river; even the Police *Sahib* stood by the bank, anxious and fretful. Finally, Tarini here to the rescue—the reward paid for your bead earrings. So, go on, go to the riverbank, call the river, Come up, come up, you treacherous river! I'm telling you, it will, it will.

Sukhi said, "Wait, let me get the mirror and put on the *loth*." Delighted, Tarini finally fell silent. Holding the mirror before her, Sukhi proceeded to wear the nose ring. He stared at her intently, and pretty much forgot about eating. When the ring had been properly worn, he eagerly picked up the lantern to scrutinize the result. "Where, let me see, let me see!"

A smile of contentment arose on Sukhi's face; she had a light olive complexion—her face suddenly turned red.

Tarini had lied to the young lady Sabi. Sukhi was slender, Sukhi was graceful, Sukhi had a light olive complexion. Tarini's happiness was without any limit because of Sukhi.

Even if he had spoken while drunk, Tarini had not lied. It was indeed Mayurakshi that provided Tarini with his food and clothing. At the *Dushara* festival, Tarini would religiously offer worship to the river. This time, in the year 1342, Tarini was busy following the *puja* rituals as usual. He had put on a new *dhoti*, while Sukhi too had put on a new *sari*—gifts from Ghosh Mahashay as promised. The dry, sandy womb of Mayurakshi sparkled in the high summer sun. The rains had still not descended. Kesto Das of Bhogpur stepped onto the dry riverbed near the *ghat*. Surveying the scene, and glancing up at the sky, he said, "Now, Tarini, make sure you offer good worship to the river goddess, let the floods come—how else would there be any planting or harvest?"

Mayurakshi's alluvial soil was capable of sprouting grains of pure gold.

Smiling, Tarini said, "So that's what it is. You know what people say, Das—they say Tarini offers *puja* for the floods. After all, the blessings of Lakshmi in this area are all bestowed by the grace of the river goddess. Now, Kele—hold on, hold on, the goat is ready to flee."

The sacrificial goat was quite unwilling to stand around on the scorching, sandy riverbed.

The *puja* ceremonies went smoothly. Quite drunk, Tarini sat by the riverbank as he spoke to Kalachand, "Gurgle, gurgle—swirl in, flood waters, rush in, come take it all in ten days."

Kalachand told him, "I tell you, you will not capture what floats to you this time—this time, *I* will catch it—I tell you now."

Laughing wildly, Tarini said, "When the giant whirlpool catches him, it will take just three gulps—boog, boog, boog—that's it, Kalachand's finished."

Deeply inflamed, Kalachand asked, "What did you say, you scoundrel?"

Tarini had stood up for a showdown, but then Sukhi fell between and offered them a compromise to end the feud. "At low floods, when the water is up to that *pakur* tree over there, *devar* will take the catch; at high floods past the *pakur* tree, the catch will be yours."

Taking the dust off Sukhi's feet, Kalachand wept in delight and said, "Who but a *bou* would say this?"

The next day they began repairing the *donga* in preparation for the ferry season. Hammer and drill in hand, working from dawn to dusk, the two soon made the *donga* almost good as new.

However, pummeled by the heatwave, the *donga* developed cracks before long. The entire month of *Asharh* went by, but the floods did not come. In fact, even the dream of a flood was far-fetched, since the little moisture generated was not enough to even cover the sandy riverbed. The rainfall was minuscule—the few isolated drizzles only helped generate a muted, collective moan of despair from the heartland. It was as though the entire region wept in anticipation of the calamity ahead. Perhaps the fleeting, elusive touch of moisture was a messenger of the propagating misfortune that had already visited some distant precinct. Tarini could not go on much longer without ferrying people at full flood. Right now, all he did was carry the bicycles of government employees on his shoulders across the dry riverbed, and with the few *paisas* thus earned, buy himself cheap liquor. These government workers were having a field day right now—they arrived in droves to investigate if indeed the countryside was in dire straits, and if the people needed help. Their arrival would bring an added bonus—vast quantities of discarded cigarette butts.

The flood finally came early in *Sravan*. Tarini breathed a sigh of relief. The first day of the flood, he jumped off a tall cliff into the river, and made the floodwater more agitated and boisterous than it already was.

Unfortunately, though, the flood waters receded dramatically after only three days, and the river became barely knee high. The *donga*, tied to a tree, was swaying gently in the waves. Tarini and Kalachand sat in the *donga*, waiting for an occasional householder to stop by and request passage— someone who would not wade across. When such a client would show up, Tarini and his assistant would push the *donga* with the passenger across the shallow river.

It was getting dark. Tarini said, "Now, say, what do you think is going on, Kele?"

Visibly worried, Kalachand answered, "Yes, what indeed!"

Tarini went on, "I have never seen anything quite like this."

Kalachand again answered, "Yes, indeed!"

Glancing at the sky, Tarini said, "Look at the sky, Kele— it's clear blue. There is not even the hint of a westerly."

Kalachand replied again, "Yes, indeed!"

Suddenly infuriated, Tarini slapped Kalachand hard across

the face, and said, "Yes, indeed! Yes, indeed—as if that's what I am asking him to say. Yes indeed! Yes, indeed!"

Quite dumbfounded, Kalachand could only stare at Tarini's face. Unable to bear the stare, Tarini turned his face away and sat quietly. Sometime later, he abruptly became animated, sat upright, and said, "The wind is shifting, isn't that right, Kele, isn't that the westerly blowing?" As he spoke, he jumped up and, grabbing a fistful of dust, began to pour it in the air. The wind, however, was very weak—it was not at all clear if it was a westerly. Not to be dissuaded, Tarini said, "Sure enough, *pochi* is packing a little punch now. Come on Kele, let's go get drunk. I have a couple of *annas* with me today. I stole them from the knot in Sukhi's sari."

The affectionate invitation delighted Kalachand greatly. Joining Tarini as they walked towards the liquor store, he said, "Your wife has money, Dada. You will surely get your daily rice when you go home. It's us who are doomed."

Tarini answered, "Sukhi is really good, you know, Kele, *really* good. Without her, my lowly fate would be worse than a *dome's*. That time, at my brother's marriage ceremony—"

Interrupting him, Kalachand said eagerly, "Wait, Dada, wait. There's a *taal* over there on the ground—let me go pick it up."

He ran down the slope of the embankment to retrieve the precious fruit.

A group of people sat huddled under a tree at the edge of the village; Tarini asked them, "Where are you all going to, where are you all from?"

One of them answered, "We are from Birchandrapur, brother, and we are on our way to Barddhaman to work as day labourers."

Kalachand asked, "Has there been any flood in Baddhaman?"

"No, there was no flood—they have a canal there."

Soon there was great panic and lamentation throughout the land. It seemed as though the demon of famine was merely hibernating under the soil, waiting for the opportunity to strike. Now, with the parched earth opening up through cracks and fissures, it found an easy way out from the depths, and revealed itself in all its malevolent dimensions. Householders sealed off their pantries. Day labors contended with starvation. People started to flee the afflicted areas *en masse*.

One day, Tarini arrived at the *ghat* to discover that Kalachand was not there. Three hours passed, still no sign of Kalachand. Concerned, Tarini walked over to Kalachand's home and called, "Say, Kele!"

No one answered. Entering, Tarini found no one anywhere—the emptiness was frightening. He found the neighbor's house likewise empty and abandoned. At the adjacent farmer's community, he heard that everybody from Kalachand's neighbourhood had left their village the previous night.

Habu, the village chief, said, "I pleaded with them, Tarini, don't go, please, don't all of you go. They wouldn't listen, kept saying they would go begging at the doors of the rich folk."

Tarini felt something churning inside. Looking back at the deserted village, he heaved a long and hollow sigh.

Habu went on, "Now, is there *any* rich folk left anywhere in this accursed land? There's nothing at any level. To top that, the so-called rich have another problem. Even if they are starving, they can't admit as such. The other day, in that village—what do they call it—yes, Palashdanga—well, this high class Palashdanga gentleman just hanged himself. Couldn't stand the starvation."

Tarini shuddered.

The next day, a grotesque scene unfolded at the *ghat*. An old woman's corpse was lying near the embankment. It was partially devoured by dogs and jackals. Tarini recognized her; the unfortunate woman was the old mother of a cobbler's household. The preceding afternoon, they were all praying that the immobilized old woman should die and relieve them. They had taken shelter at the *ghat* on her account. During the night, they had simply abandoned her right there at the *ghat* and run away.

Tarini did not wait there any longer. Going straight back home, he told Sukhi, "Go on, Sukhi, wrap a few clothes and your ornaments around your waist. We won't hang around here any more—we'll move to the city. At least find something to do, and something to eat, right?"

As she began packing, he noticed that Sukhi had no ornament except the *sankhas* on her wrist. Shocked, Tarini as her, "Where's the rest?"

With a weak smile, Sukhi replied, "How do you suppose we managed *this* long?"

In the end Tarini, too, left the village. Three days later, having walked to the edge of the village, they had taken shelter for the night. At dinner, they were assuaging their hunger with the pulp of two ripe *taal* fruits. Suddenly, Tarini stood up and walked to an open spot. Presently, he said, "Come, Sukhi, give me a *gamchha*." Dangling the *gamchha* before him, he stared at it for the longest time. When Sukhi awoke early in the morning, she noticed he was sitting exactly in the same spot, wide awake. Perplexed, she asked him, "Didn't you sleep?"

Smiling, Tarini replied, "No, dear, I couldn't sleep."

Sukhi began reproaching him, "Now, what do you think I should do if you fall sick or something? Why on earth does such a person even venture out of his own home—oh, shame, shame, shame."

With delight in his voice, Tarini said, "Sukhi, have you seen, have you?"

"What ghost and spook must I see now, pray?"

"Look, the ants are carrying their eggs up to higher ground. It means the rains are coming." He told her.

Sukhi observed, indeed thousands of ants were transporting little white eggs in perfect file up the wall of their dilapidated shelter.

She said, "Well, you and your absurd ideas—"

Tarini assured her, "They know instinctively, dear—the lower levels will flood when the torrents arrive. Have you also noticed the wind picking up? It's straight from the west."

Looking up at the sky, Sukhi said, "But the sky is so clear—it's glistening."

Tarini was looking elsewhere; he said, "How long does it take for the clouds to arrive? Look, the crow is collecting twigs—it will repair its damaged nest. Let's spend another night here, Sukhi, and not go any further. Let's see which way the clouds drift."

A boatman's forecast is rarely erroneous; towards the afternoon, the sky filled with dark clouds, and the winds from the west began to pick up.

Tarini said, "Get up, Sukhi, we must return."

Sukhi asked, "At *this* odd hour?"

Tarini assured her, "What are you afraid of—I'll be with you. Just put this wrap over your head—the mild drizzles are quite harmful."

"And how about you—are *you* made of stone or something?" Sukhi complained.

Tarini laughed. "Now, dear, *my* body is a product of water—it begins to dry up in the sun, and plumps up when soaked. Give me the bundle, let's go."

The clouds were becoming more dense. With the brisk winds, a fast torrent would fall briefly, then stop. A short while later, the winds would pick up again, and the downpour resume.

The distance that they had traveled in three days when leaving their village, it now took them only two to return. When they reached home at dusk, Tarini said, "Wait, I will quick go check out the *ghat*." Presently he returned, and said with obvious mirth, "The river's full from shore to shore, Sukhi!"

At sunrise, Tarini got up, and immediately began making preparations to go to the *ghat*. The sky was filled with ominous clouds, there were tempestuous winds, and the rain fell in torrents.

Around noon he returned and announced, "I am off to the blacksmith's—be back later."

Anxious, Sukhi asked him, "Then eat your lunch before you go."

Looking quite worried, Tarini replied, "No, I can't now. A large nail has fallen off the *donga*. Otherwise—had the flood been milder, I might have; but right now the river's like a raging beast—come, I'll show you."

He wouldn't stop until he had shown her the sight. Standing atop the high slope next to the Pals' pond, Sukhi observed Mayurakshi's full, frightful visage. She appeared without any limit or shoreline; swirls of foam rode the crests of her vicious, crimson currents at lightning speed. Tarini remarked, "Have you heard the hissing sound, Sukhi—the flood will get worse. You go home now—I am off to the blacksmith's. Or else, I won't be able to deliver the mail tomorrow."

Quite disgruntled, Sukhi complained, "But, in *this* storm and rain—"

Tarini paid no attention to her. Single-mindedly he stepped out into the rainstorm.

When he returned, it had already turned dark. He was walking briskly. Suddenly, he thought he heard a soft drumbeat—doog, doog. Yes, indeed, it *was* a doog, doog. He knew what that ominous sound foretold—it meant imminent danger. When that sound would arise from villages bordering the river, it meant that a flood was on its way.

Mayurakshi flowed on one side of Tarini's village; on the other flowed a small tributary. To enter the village, one had to cross a small bamboo bridge over the tributary. Walking along the roadway, Tarini could still see no sign of the bridge. Then did he lose his way? After sometime, when in the darkness he regained his bearings, he realized that the bridge entrance lay at least a hundred acres further down. He also realized that he was right at the edge of the rising flood. Within seconds, the water reached his ankles. He tried to listen, but all he heard was the sound of the hissing winds and the vicious currents, and a deep, gurgling roar. Suddenly, he felt his whole body getting covered by a swarm of insects. The hapless, wingless insects were trying to flee the flood.

Tarini jumped into the water.

Swimming vigorously, he crossed the field of water and entered his village. What he saw was shocking. The flood had entered the village. Everywhere, the water was at least waist deep. Stranded villagers stood in the water, and in terrified voices called one another. Petrified dogs, cattle, goats and sheep moaned and bleated hideously. Yet, surpassing all the mortifying sounds were the frightful roar of Mayurakshi, the sadistic cackle of the wind, and the incessant, relentless din of the deluge. It all resembled the ear-splitting screams and guffaws of a band of vicious robbers that drown out the piteous cries of a terrorized family.

In the pitched darkness, virtually nothing could be discerned. Tarini abruptly stepped on something in the water—it felt like some poor creature. Lifting it with his hands, he found it to be a little goat kid—it had drowned already. Casting it away, he walked to his house, and called, "Sukhi—say, Sukhi!"

A voice answered him from within; with amazing calm and self-assurance, Sukhi said, "I am here inside the room."

Entering the room, Tarini found the interior courtyard about waist-deep in water. Holding a bamboo pole in her hand, Sukhi stood vigil upon the raised portico that was about knee deep in water.

Holding her hand, Tarini tugged her in his direction and

said, "Come on out, for heaven's sake! Is this any time to be inside the house—you could get buried under falling debris!"

Sukhi replied, "I was waiting for you. Where would you find me otherwise, tell me, pray?"

Stepping outside, Tarini asked, "What should we do now, Sukhi?"

Sukhi answered, "Let's wait right here. Let whatever happens to everybody else happen to us."

Tarini went on, "What if the flood gets much worse, Sukhi? Can't you hear the groaning and hissing?"

Sukhi replied, "How much worse can it get? If it got any worse, what would be left of the land? Would God Almighty allow His great creation to be destroyed thus?"

Tarini tried hard to accept these words of assurance, but could not.

Suddenly, the flood waters around their feet became very agitated, and there was the sound of something crashing. Tarini remarked, "That was *our* house going down, Sukhi. No more, let's go now. It's past my waist now—must be up to your chest, my dear."

A piteous wail rended the night air—it was not known from where it arose, or to whom it belonged, but a woman's voice cried out, "Help, O please help, someone, my little *khoka* has fallen from my arms! O my poor *khoka*, *khoka* dear!"

Tarini said, "Sukhi, stay right here; answer back when I call you."

He vanished in the darkness. Only his voice could be heard—"Who is it? Where? Whose son fell in, answer me, where are you?"

Someone answered, "O, here, over here."

Tarini called again, "Ahoy!"

The exchange of voice signals continued for a short while, then stopped. After that, Tarini called, "Sukhi!"

Sukhi replied, "Yes!"

Following her voice, Tarini approached her and said, "Hold on to my waist, Sukhi, the signs are not good."

Sukhi did not protest. Grabbing the *dhoti* around Tarini's waist, she asked, "Whose boy was it? Did you find him?"

Tarini answered, "Yes, I did. It was Bhupte Bhalla's son."

They were walking in the water with the utmost care. It seemed the water was rising continuously. Presently, Tarini said, "Ride on my back, Sukhi. Now where in the Devil's name did we just end up, Sukhi, ee, ee..."

Before he could finish, they both fell into deep water. Moments later, Tarini floated back up and said, "Hold the *dhoti* around my waist, and stay afloat, Sukhi."

By then they were being dragged along by the swift currents. It was an impenetrable darkness; the wind was hissing by their ears, and its sound was compounded by the crashing and gurgling of Mayurakshi's murderous flood. The shafts of rain were hitting their faces like arrows as they were carried away like chaff in the wind. They lost all possible measure of how long they had been carried thus—it could be days or months—they had no reference whatsoever. Tarini began to feel that his strength was failing. At times, the currents and waves of the river were suffocating him. Then, suddenly, it seemed that Sukhi's grasp had changed. She began to feel much heavier. Tarini called her, "Sukhi, Sukhi?"

Sukhi's answer was garbled and guttural like that of an incoherent lunatic.

"Have no fear, I am—"

Instantly, Tarini realized that they were being sucked into bottomless depths—they were caught in a vicious whirlpool. With all the strength he could muster, he tried to push the water away. Presently, he felt that they had risen above the surface. However, he knew that there was danger ahead—they would sink again. He tried to bypass the trough in the swirling eddy. But what was this—Sukhi was gripping him like the coils of a python! He called out, "Sukhi—Sukhi!"

As they continued being sucked into the vortex, Sukhi's grip tightened, and Tarini felt his body going numb. As he struggled for air, he felt his heart was virtually ready to burst. He tried to wrench himself free from Sukhi's mortal grasp, but she only tightened her grip further. Air—oh, oh, some air! In extreme agony, Tarini started grabbing the water with his fists for a hold. His hands fell upon Sukhi's throat. With both hands, he clamped down hard on her throat with all his might. It was a vicious, insane, vice-like hold. As though he had concentrated every last ounce of his strength in his fists. Before long, the enormous weight that was pulling him down like a rock into the deadly depths fell off, and set him free. Instantly, he floated back to the surface. Ah–ah–he took in several gulps of air and prayed piteously for land and the light of day.

Dehantar
The Transmutation

SARADINDU BANDYOPADHYAY

Barada declared, "Those who do not believe in apparitions should not be persuaded by any kind of coercion to change their views. I for one never try to do so. Except for that one occasion—"

The searing high summer was already here in full force. *Mahakavi* Kalidasa has said, the sun at this time is unbearable, and the moon highly desirable. The sun's intensity does not require any verification; however, in order to test first hand the desirability of the moon this time of the year, a few of us club members had assembled after sunset on the sprawling lawn outside the clubhouse, lounging upon a *dhurrie*. A nice and plump moon had already climbed above the trees in the eastern sky; we could see each other's face without any difficulty. Several of our fellow members had already relieved themselves of any vestments above the waistline.

The club orderly had been instructed to prepare chilled *bhang* shakes for everyone. No matter how desirable the moon might be, an ice-cold beverage would no doubt bring faster relief from the blistering heat. We all waited thirstily for the drinks to arrive.

Under these circumstances, when Barada made the pronouncement, "Those who do not believe in apparitions—" etc., we became decidedly alarmed. That this rather pointed declaration would soon lead to an expansive story, no one had the slightest doubt. Moonlit summer nights are not the perfect setting for ghost stories; for them, what you need is a frigid winter evening or a rain-drenched monsoon night. But, regardless of the weather, now that Barada had broached the subject, there was going to be no escape.

Fortunately, the beverages arrived just at this moment. Each of us gladly picked a glass from the tray. Taking a small sip of the cool drink, Prithvi remarked, "Ah, yes. If only the whole world were to turn cool like this drink by some magical *mantra*—"

Barada retorted, "What is your conception of *the whole world*? There are places right here in India where it is snowing at this very moment. Last year around this time, I went vacationing in the mountains—I found really cold weather—"

I asked him, "Mountains? Which ones?"

Barada replied, "Assume they were the ranges in Mussoorie or Nainital. I won't tell you exactly where, but let's say it was not a place for tourists or amateur sightseers. My older brother-in-law has been transferred there; I went to spend a month there at his invitation. While I was there, something happened—"

Amulya asked skeptically, "So maybe something happened, but why are you embarrassed to tell us the name of those mountains?"

Barada replied, "I am not embarrassed. Actually, the characters in the story I am about to tell you are all alive, so

I must conceal a few details. Indeed, such weird things happen sometimes. Anyway, let me tell you the story."

Those who reside at hill stations tend to become somewhat westernized. The men usually wear trousers and suits. The women, though, still wear *saris* as a rule; however, their conduct and manners are not exactly what we may describe as native. Men and women dining together at a table; drinking a peg or two of whiskey or port after dinner—these have become part of the social etiquette. They cannot really be blamed, though—it is better to follow the accepted rules of arctic lifestyles.

Having received my *shyalak's* invitation, I arrived there. Within only a few days, I gained quite a few muscular pounds. My *shyalak* is a serious carnivore; we engaged in a veritable feast comprised of mutton and poultry every day. To top that, there were regular treks over the hills. Naturally, we were haunted by almost hourly pangs of hunger. It was without question a most wonderful place; great climate, even greater scenic beauty.

I made several new friendships. There were about ten or twelve Bengali families in the area, all extremely sociable and delighted to entertain new guests. I met a young fellow named Pramatha Roy. About twenty-five, soft-spoken and very handsome. He worked as a high government official; even though he was thoroughly modern in his outlook, he was not exactly a chauvinist. He would stop by almost daily on his way back from a tennis game. He was single and lived alone; he would stop to chat with us, drink a cup or two of tea or a cocktail, then return home shortly after sunset.

One day, during our usual conversation, my *shyalak* brought up the matter of *pretayoni*. He observed, "Now,

Pramatha, young men like you do not believe in ghosts and spooks. Let me assure you, though, our Barada here is a seasoned specialist on phantoms. If ever you need to learn about their kind, just consult him."

Pramatha began to laugh. He remarked, "An educated man like you actually *believes* in such fantasies?"

Even though he spoke them lightheartedly, the words stung. I replied, "Educated people often believe in a lot of things which the uneducated find too embarrassing to admit."

"Such as?"

"Such as Freudian psychoanalysis or Pavlovian behaviorism."

Pramatha started laughing. He was an intelligent young man, and therefore chose not to argue adamantly. The matter of ghosts was laid to rest for that night.

Two weeks passed since my arrival at the hill station. The comforts were incomparable, and I was putting on weight. No worries, no sweat, no bedbugs; days and nights were passing almost unnoticed simply eating, sleeping, and sightseeing. Such pleasant times do not come by often in one's lifetime, and when they do, they are generally short-lived.

One day, Pramatha invited us to tea. My *shyalak* and I arrived at his place at the appointed time. We thought there were no other guests invited beside us; upon arrival, however, we found ourselves in the company of a young woman. I had not seen her before. She was tall, slim and quite attractive. She had a melancholy expression; her attire and makeup were not flashy, but did reflect care and attention. From her appearance, she seemed to be about twenty or twenty-one. Perhaps a year or two older.

My *shyalak* eagerly greeted her, saying, "Hello, Mrs. Das, what rare and good fortune to find *you* here! I had not expected to see you—"

The woman smiled and returned his *namaskar*. "I was in the city for my weekly shopping. Ran into Pramatha Babu on my way; he brought me here."

Pramatha introduced the young lady to me. From their gestures I gathered she was a widow. About three miles outside the city there was a high cliff named Har-Jata—nestled within its crevices was a small habitat with hardly ten or twelve bungalows. Mrs. Das lived there. The route from Har-Jata to the city was quite treacherous; with the exception of a valley in between, it was craggy and precipitous. Those who lived there came to the city every so often to do the necessary shopping.

Lighthearted conversation was accompanied by rounds of tea and cakes. I noticed that Mrs. Das was modern, yet quite reticent and controlled. There was something attractive about her, something magnetic; however, one could not get too close to her. It was the easiest thing for her to flirt with and tease young men, yet no man would dare to be flirtatious or brassy with her. Her charming youthfulness was also her shield.

I observed Pramatha's demeanor too. I had never before fathomed that there could be a romantic complexity to his life, but now I noticed he was caught in the vortex of a romantic whirlpool. The needle of a compass is normally quite steady and stationary, yet it goes into convulsive paroxysms when brought near a magnet. Pramatha was in precisely such a state. His every word, every gesture, even his body language made it amply clear that he was head over heels in love with this woman. He did not have the slightest power to conceal his true feelings even for the sake of public decorum.

Yet, the fact remained that Mrs. Das was a widow; no matter how modern and progressive, she was still a Hindu widow.

I became quite agitated inside. This curious romance which had sprouted in the chilly mountain air, where was it destined to culminate?

When tea was over, Mrs. Das stood up; she would have to return to Har-Jata while there was still daylight. Warmly inviting all three of us with her gesture, she said, "Why don't you come to Har-Jata one of these days? It's a bit desolate, but quite lovely, I assure you. You won't find such exquisite sunrise anywhere else in the world. Please come."

We thanked her for her invitation. She left. After sitting a little longer, we too got up to leave. Observing Pramatha's valiant efforts at being a gracious host despite his obvious absent-mindedness, we decided that we must not aggravate him any further.

On the way back, I asked my *shyalak*, "Well, what do you suppose is going on? Is there an inside story here?"

Shyalak looked at me, smiled, and said, "You noticed too, I see. I had heard rumours before; saw it with my own eyes today. Pramatha has gone crazy about marrying Savitri."

"So her name is Savitri? Well, what does *she* say?"

"As far as I have heard, she does not want to."

"But why not? Is it Hindu conservatism, or something else?"

"That I cannot say for sure. It may be part conservatism, part her love for her dead husband."

I inquired, "How long has he been dead?"

Shyalak answered, "About two years, I believe. He was a high-ranking engineer with the railways; one day accidentally fell on the tracks and was run over."

"Did you know him?"

"Only a little. He was powerful, influential, about thirty-five. Had been married to Savitri for barely a year."

"Why does Mrs. Das live in Har-Jata?"

"The house belonged to Das, so Savitri inherited it. Since Das died while on duty, his widow receives a monthly allowance from the railway. That's her only income."

"What's your impression of her as a person?"

"Excellent; you don't often see a nicer girl. Lives alone at such a young age, yet no one has ever said anything slanderous about her."

"What are your views about widow-remarriage?"

"In cases such as this, it is highly desirable. It is utterly meaningless to waste one's entire life looking back at the past. One might pause to think if there were any issues. But then, it seems unlikely that Savitri will marry again."

About ten days passed since this event. Pramatha did not show up. He was probably avoiding us because we had gauged the state of his mind.

Soon it was time for me to leave paradise. I was slowly getting ready for my departure, when one day Pramatha came to visit. After a few matter-of-fact words, he said, "Mrs. Das has written a letter inviting us to visit Har-Jata and witness its legendary sunrise. Would you like to come?"

I had no objections whatsoever. My *shyalak*, however, had some reservations about such a trip; he said, "To see the sunrise, we must either spend the night before in Har-Jata, or start from here at two in the morning. Is either option feasible?"

Pramatha extracted a letter from his pocket and said, "Please read her letter; I don't think there should be any problem."

The letter went as follows—

With a warm Namaskar, Pramatha Babu, it seems you and your guests from the other day considered my invitation nothing more than an act of politeness. My invitation, I assure you, was quite genuine. So why don't you come? Stay the night at my place, and watch the sunrise at dawn. You won't have any discomfort; there's room enough in my home for three guests.

Let me know when you plan to visit. On the other hand, if you decide to come over without notice, I shall be even more pleased. Hope you are well. Sincerely, Savitri Das.

Upon reading the above, my *shyalak* had no further objections. Quite encouraged, Pramatha proposed, "Today is Saturday, why don't we go there today? If we start at five, I am sure we'll get there before sunset."

Accordingly, we were soon on our way.

The Har-Jata peak is visible from the valley. Indeed, the name Har-Jata is perfect for such a glorious summit. It is as though the locks upon the meditating Mahadeva's head have ascended to the sky in spirals; the white bungalows in their folds appear to be *datura* blossoms. It's a spectacular sight. The passage leading to the bungalows, however, is anything but wonderful. It took us two-and-a-half hours to climb the three miles up to the bungalow where Mrs. Das lived.

When we arrived there, daylight had almost faded; upon Har-Jata, Shiva's matted coils were still bathed in the deep crimson of sunset. Mrs. Das was relaxing upon an easy-chair in the front verandah of the bungalow; seeing us, she stood up and received us with great warmth and flurry. Her genuine pleasure in seeing us was very gratifying.

It is said that sometimes misfortune is preceded by a long, tell-tale shadow. Surprisingly, we did not have the slightest notion of the impending misfortune that day. The ochre mountain light that evening had only presaged divine grace and benediction. It was impossible for anyone to imagine there could be anything calamitous in store. I believe even Pramatha had no premonition or inkling.

Mrs. Das took us inside. After freshening up, we gathered in the drawing room for tea. There was no man-servant in the house; two mountain girls lived there at night, and did the housework and cooking.

Electricity had still not arrived in Har-Jata. We sat in the drawing room drinking tea in the soft glow of a kerosene lamp. Mrs. Das and her maids waited upon us with great care.

An enlarged photograph hung upon the drawing room wall. I could not see it clearly from far in that dim light. When I had finished my tea, I walked over to the picture. No doubt, this was the untimely deceased Mr. Das. I took a close look. He was not exactly handsome, but there was a kind of firmness to his expression. His wide chin had a cleft in it, and his gaze was a little stern. There was a smile in the corner of his mouth much like the kind one wears when being photographed; it did not, however, conceal the power of his personality.

I was comparing the face in the photograph with

Pramatha's soft, boyish face in my mind, when I heard a whisper, "My husband."

Mrs. Das had quietly joined me next to the picture. Then Pramatha, too, joined us. Mrs. Das stared at the photograph for a while, then abruptly turned her gaze on Pramatha. Her expression seemed quite tranquil; one cannot necessarily read someone's mind from the facial expression alone. Somehow it seemed to me that, like me, she too compared Pramatha's face with that in the picture.

We returned back to our seats.

It is not easy to read a woman's mind, especially that of a woman like Mrs. Das. The poet has said, *The mind of a woman is a treasure won only after a thousand years of sadhana.* I began to wonder, it *is* true she had turned down Pramatha's marriage proposal, but did she not have the slightest love for or weakness about him? That she had invited a total stranger like me to her home today, was this merely social etiquette, or was it an excuse to fulfill a surreptitious desire to bring a special someone close to herself?

It is unnecessary to describe Pramatha's condition. He was much like I had seen the other day. A compass needle drawn to a magnet, he was completely oblivious of everything else around him.

The night grew deeper. An ice cold wind blew in from the north and began to swirl and hiss overhead.

It naturally took a while for dinner to be ready. By the time we finished dinner it was around eleven. Mrs. Das said, "You should go to bed now. We must be up before three-thirty, otherwise we'll miss much of the beauty and charm associated with the sunrise."

We became concerned; what were our chances of waking up before three-thirty, given this late hour? Yet, awaken we must, otherwise the entire journey would be for nothing. I asked, "Do you have an alarm clock?"

Mrs. Das replied, "No. But don't worry, I will awaken you at the right time."

My *shyalak* observed, "But what is the guarantee that *you* will wake up?"

Mrs. Das smiled a little, and said, "I'm not going to sleep; I'll spend these few hours reading. I am quite used to this."

We stared at her, perhaps a little puzzled. Our hostess would stay awake all night while we would sleep?

Suddenly Pramatha walked up to her and said, "In that case, I too will stay awake. Why don't the two of you go to sleep?"

I could not acquiesce to this proposal. We two older gents will go to sleep, while these two young lovebirds would spend the night awake together?

My *shyalak* resolved the dilemma. He suggested, "Then why don't we all spend the night awake? I for one don't sleep well in a new place; as it is, I will probably do nothing but stare at the ceiling."

I added, "My condition is likewise."

Mrs. Das protested a little, but we paid no attention. We all thereafter made ourselves comfortable in the drawing room. Mrs. Das stretched out on a recliner; relaxing on the sofa, my *shyalak* lit a cigar; I began to feel quite cozy in an overstuffed chair. Only Pramatha started to pace up and down the floor, quite restlessly, sometimes nervously fiddling with this and that, and sometimes pushing the wick of the oil lamp higher or lower.

Mrs. Das' quiet gaze followed his every move.

The clock struck twelve. It was midnight.

My *shyalak* sat up; smothering the cigar butt on the ash tray, he suddenly asked, "Now, Mrs. Das, since you live alone in this house, don't you feel afraid?"

Mrs. Das raised her eyebrows slightly and said, "Afraid? Afraid of what?"

The cold wintry wind was howling viciously over the top of the roof. Suppressing a yawn, I said, "Well, say it's the fear of ghosts."

Pramatha was standing before the photograph of Mr. Das on the wall, staring at it disinterestedly. Suddenly he turned around, and walked over to us. His voice laced with scorn, he said, "Fear of *ghosts*? What on earth is that? Are there such things as ghosts? Our Barada Babu is just plain superstitious."

I asked Mrs. Das, "Is that what *you* think, too?"

After a brief silence, she replied, "I believe in reincarnation. But *ghosts*—well, I really don't know—"

Pramatha almost shouted emphatically, "*Bhoots* do not exist. Doesn't matter how you interpret the word *bhoot*, it cannot *be*. There can only be the present and the future, but never the past. Isn't that sufficient?"

I looked at his face; it had become quite flushed. Pramatha was by nature quiet and gentle; I had never seen him so excited and perturbed. It seemed as if he was simply bursting to tell Savitri something, but was unable to do so with us around.

My *shyalak*, too, must have surmised something similar; he said, "If the present and the future exist, then the past must necessarily exist also. Each of us has a past life—*that's bhoot*. You too have a *bhoot*, Pramatha, it's not easy to shake it off. The difference between us and the dead is that the dead are entirely in the past; we have a bit of the present and the future left."

Pramatha did not follow the pun in my *shyalak's* play on the word *bhoot*. He was quite adamant by then. Waving his hand, he said, "I don't care much for that kind of abstraction. Do you have any proof that there remains a spirit after death has occurred?"

Smiling, my *shyalak* replied, "I cannot prove anything. Barada here is much better informed about *pretayoni*. Ask *him* that question."

I observed, "Look, Pramatha Babu, he who sleeps while awake cannot be awakened from slumber. Likewise, if you have convinced yourself that you will not change your opinion or belief, then no one can ever make a believer out of you. However, I can only tell you that many brilliant, scientific-minded men believed in *pretayoni*—for instance, William Crook, Oliver Lodge, Conan Doyle—"

Clenching his jaws, Pramatha said, "But *I* don't. If you can prove anything, do so, but don't try to hoodwink me by parading a bunch of Western names. It won't work."

I was a little annoyed. I said, "Fine. To believe or not is your choice. But is there any harm in trying? Come, Mrs. Das, let's conduct a planchette."

Alarmed, she saked, "Planchette? Are you going to call a spirit?"

I said, "I do not see any other way to convince Pramatha Babu. Of course, if it scares you, we should rather not."

She said, "No, I am not scared." Stealing a quick glance at Pramatha, she continued, "Go ahead, do it. If nothing else, it would help us pass the time. What would you need?"

I said, "Not much, just a three-legged table will do."

Fortunately, there was just such a table in the room. I then briefly explained the planchette procedure to everyone. Thereafter, dimming the light of the lamp, the four of us sat ourselves around the table.

My *shyalak* asked, "Well, whose spirit shall we call?"

I replied, "Could be anyone. However, it must be someone we all know. At least we all must know what that person looked like in life."

Not far from where we sat, the photograph of Mr. Das was hanging on the wall. Pramatha sat with his back to the photo, while Mrs. Das sat facing it. Mrs. Das glanced at the photo, and our eyes followed hers. In the semi-darkness, the photo was quite obscure, except for the face, which was quite distinct.

Withdrawing her gaze from the picture, Mrs. Das looked at me imploringly. Recognizing the suggestiveness in her expression, I said, "Fine, why don't we call him. Even though I have never seen him, the photo will do. Now, each of you must close your eyes and concentrate all your thoughts on him."

Intertwining fingers with those of the neighbors, we placed our hands on the table. We then closed our eyes and began contemplating on the departed spirit of Mr. Das.

When the *pretayoni* descends upon the planchette table, it begins to shake. It feels as though life has been instilled in the dead wood—it pulsates with awareness. We sat for about ten minutes, but the table did not vibrate; it did not show any sign of life. I then opened my eyes and looked at the others.

One glance at Pramatha confirmed that a spirit had

descended—not inside the table, but within a person. This does happen sometimes. His head was slumped over his chest, and his lips were trembling. His facial expression had undergone a transformation.

I inquired of the spirit, "Is there someone here?"

Pramatha slowly raised his head, then, opening his eyes, fixed his blood-shot gaze upon Mrs. Das.

Mrs. Das was staring at Pramatha hypnotically. Suddenly, Pramatha thundered in a loud and invidious voice, "Savitri!"

His voice had changed completely. Mrs. Das became thunderstruck; her eyes became dilated, and her lips parted. Screaming "What! It's you, *you!*", she fainted and fell to the floor.

What happened after that is almost indescribable. Pramatha jumped up, foaming at the mouth. I tried holding him, but it was beyond my ability to restrain him. He was possessed by a demonic power. Flinging me aside with one swift buffet, he pounced upon Savitri's limp body on the floor, and, shaking her violently with both hands, roared, "You think you will marry again? I won't let you—I won't, I won't—you are *mine*—"

Imagine, these were words emanating from *Pramatha's* mouth! We were not, however, in any position to speculate about this fantastic phenomenon. My *shyalak* and I together wrenched Pramatha away from Savitri. Meanwhile, awakened by the great commotion, the two mountain girls had rushed in. They lifted Savitri up and placed her upon the couch. We, meanwhile, dragged Pramatha towards the bathroom; depositing him on the floor, we began to pour buckets of water over his head, screaming, "Go away, please go away—"

"No I won't—I won't let Savitri marry again—" Pramatha growled between clenched teeth. We continued pouring water, until eventually his voice became weak and incoherent, and he stopped flailing his arms and legs.

About half-an-hour later, we carried him, stretcher-style, and gently laid him down on a bed. He no longer had that demonic strength, but still went on murmuring, "I won't— I won't—"

Leaving my *shyalak* in attendance by his bedside, I went back to the drawing room. Mrs. Das had regained consciousness. Seeing me, she began to wail in a terrified voice, "What happened, Barada Babu, what just happened?"

When the deepest secrets of a woman's heart become exposed, her fear and shame know no bounds, and tears are her only shield. I sat next to Mrs. Das and attempted to appease her in whatever way possible. I then instructed the maids to prepare a strong cup of tea for her.

Naturally, our plan to watch the sunrise from the top of the hills was suspended. Caring for the two afflicted, we lost track of time, and soon it was seven in the morning.

Presently, Mrs. Das gathered herself together. Pramatha, however, fell asleep and showed no signs of waking up. We did not dare awaken him, thinking he might resume his crazy behavior from the night before. Meanwhile the day was wearing on. We needed to return to the valley while there was daylight; otherwise, we might face a lot of hassle going back down the treacherous mountain.

When it was one o'clock, and Pramatha was still fast asleep, we became worried. Fortunately, there was an old doctor who lived in Har-Jata; we called him. He gave Pramatha a careful check-up, and said, "It's nothing serious, he has a congestion in his chest. However, he must not leave his bed the rest of today."

Greatly perturbed, we looked pleadingly at Mrs. Das. She had completely regained her composure by now. Witnessing our anxiety, she said, "Let Pramatha Babu stay here today. If the two of you absolutely, positively *must* return, then—"

Quite embarrassed, my *shyalak* said, "You must understand, it really is essential for us to return. However, if our leaving should cause you any inconvenience or discomfort—"

Mrs. Das replied, "Please don't worry about that."

The doctor heard the exchange; he suggested, "What's there to worry? I live quite nearby; if necessary, I can spend the night at Savitri-Ma's house, or perhaps my wife can. You may go back."

The old doctor was a compassionate man; he did not pry unnecessarily for any details. Relieved, we prepared to leave. There was no reason to worry about Pramatha; he was sure to return to normal as soon he would wake up.

On our way out, Mrs. Das said to us privately, "It is better if the incident from last night is not discussed any further."

We reassured her, "Please don't worry about it."

Then we descended from Har-Jata.

The next day, we heard that Pramatha had also returned. He did not, however, come to see us.

Meanwhile, my holidays were winding down; I would have to leave in a day or two. So I thought, well, let me go see him myself. Perhaps he was feeling a little reluctant to see us after that incident.

The next morning, after my usual stroll, I went to his house. The main entrance was closed. When I knocked, Pramatha immediately opened the door. There seemed to have occurred a subtle change in his appearance. He looked at me almost maliciously, then slammed the door on my face.

That was the last time I saw him. The next day, I left the hill station.

Having narrated thus far, Barada paused. The moon, meanwhile, had risen quite high in the sky. Whether it was because of the *bhang* in the drink, or the story Barada had just narrated, it suddenly felt very chilly.

Prithvi asked, "Does your story end here, or is there an epilogue?"

Lighting a cigarette, Barada said, "There is a short one. About a month later, I received a letter from my *shyalak*. He reported something rather unexpected: Savitri and Pramatha had registered a civil marriage. I was under the impression that, after what had happened up on the hill, it was impossible for them to marry each other. I had even ascribed Pramatha's rude behaviour on the day of my departure to his sense of failure caused by his inability to win the woman he loved. Now I realized, I was entirely wrong.

My *shyalak* reported something else, even stranger. In this short period of time, Pramatha's appearance has apparently changed significantly. Everyone seems to think he is gradually beginning to look like the deceased Mr. Das, Savitri's first husband. In fact, a cleft has appeared in the middle of his chin—"

Taking a long drag at his cigarette, Barada said, "So far, I have narrated the story simply and linearly, without any personal interpretations or theories. Now perhaps *you* should analyze and interpret, what exactly happened here! Is it possible that the departed Mr. Das' spirit has somehow ejected Pramatha's soul from his body, and installed itself there. Is it possible that it has done so to re-marry his widow? Or else— well, what else could it be?"

No one had any explanation. After a pause, Barada said almost to himself, "If that's what really happened, then whatever happened to Pramatha's spirit? Where did *it* go?"

Suddenly, there was a shrill, high-pitched squeal overhead. Startled, we all instantly looked up at the sky. A bat-like, shadowy creature was flying over the moon—spreading its triangular wings, it gradually vanished into the distance.

Our bodies filled with prickly gooseflesh as we stared collectively at the eerie sight.

Chokh Gyalo
The Lost Eyes

By normal standards perhaps she was not pretty. Not that I considered her particularly beautiful myself—yet I loved her. There was something in her eyes which I cannot explain. I had never seen eyes so dreamy and ethereal in my life. She also had gained notoriety as a tomboy and a flirt.

That graceless and restless Mini had stolen my heart. Her eyes had enchanted me.

I remember embracing her privately one day and telling her, "I feel like stealing your eyes and keeping them with me."

"But why?"

"They drive me crazy. I love them the most."

I loved her so intensely—but I did not get to keep her.

Someone completely unknown, a total stranger, came along one day and, with the accompaniment of much music and festivity took her away.

It hurt deep inside my soul.

Perhaps I would have overcome that anguish some day, were it not for something truly heart-rending which occurred soon afterward.

When Mini returned to her parents' for the first time, I noticed both her eyes had gone blind. It came to be known that she had accidentally splashed some medicine into her eyes thinking it was rose water.

One day we had a clandestine rendezvous.

I said to her, "You lost those precious eyes to carelessness."

And she replied, "If you have not understood why they were lost, then perhaps it's best that you never know."

Parul Prasanga
About Parul

BONOPHOOL

"Must she *earn* a living like you to feed herself?"

"May be not earn a living; but still, to steal milk and fish regularly—"

"I shall feed her *my* portions."

"That you do already—but she steals still. If she does it every day—"

"You really know how to exaggerate. She steals *every* day?—"

"Whatever it is—I shall not feed precious fish and milk to the cat. My money is not so cheap."

With those words, an irate Binode threw a slipper in the direction of the accused feline. With a frisky leap, Meni the cat evaded the projectile and slipped out of the room. His wife Parulbala, too, immediately drew her *anchal* over her eyes and went out. Binode sat glumly for a while. But how long could he possibly remain glum? Finally, he stood up. Coming out, he noticed Parulbala stretched out on a mat on the floor of the verandah on the west side; it was obvious she was upset and hurt.

Attempting to lighten up the atmosphere, Binode smiled a little and said, "You really *are* being childish! Am I *really* going to chase your cat away?"

Parul was silent.

Binode continued, "OK, let's go feed your cat fish and milk, then."

Parul—"Sure, and she is waiting for *you* to feed her fish and milk! If you must throw her out, could you not have waited until daylight?"

"All right, I'll go find her—where can she possibly go?" Binode walked out with a lantern.

He searched here and there, around the streets and lanes, under the *jamun* tree, and a dozen other places, but did not see any trace of Meni. Finally, he gave up, and, coming inside the house, found Parul still lying in the same position. —"Well, I couldn't see her outside. She'll be back. Come on, let's go have dinner."

"Fine, let me serve you then; I am not hungry tonight."

"Are you going on a hunger strike or something?"

Entering the kitchen, the sight that Parul saw may be described like this: the cauldron of milk was empty; all the pieces of fried fish had vanished; the bowl of *dal* was turned upside down.

Observing the unsightly scene, Parul became quite embarrassed.

Binode decided it was unsafe to discuss this matter any further; he quietly sat down to eat whatever was retrievable.

Parulbala had her dinner also.

Later, going into their bedroom, they found Meni comfortably curled up on the bed, fast asleep.

Ek Phonta Jal
A Lone Teardrop

BONOPHOOL

I knew *zamindar* Shyam Babu of Ramganj was whimsical. But even *I* would never have guessed that his whim could be so positively weird. The other day, fairly early in the morning, I received a printed invitation from him. He had invited the whole family to his departed mother's *shraddh* feast. The letter struck me as rather strange. I wondered how it was that Shyam Babu's mother was taken ill, yet I did not hear a thing. I happen to be the resident doctor in this precinct.

Be that as it may, if he had invited us, then we would have to go. So we went. Arriving there, we found Shyam Babu, a ceremonial scarf around his neck, receiving his guests. A dark shadow of grief clouded his countenance. When he saw me, he greeted me warmly, saying, "Come on in, *Daktar Babu*, it is such a privilege!" After a few words, I asked him, "So, what happened to your mother?"

Looking a little puzzled, Shyam Babu replied, "Oh, well, I see! You haven't heard, have you! My mother passed away when I was a little boy—I don't even remember her. *This* was my other mother—a true mother to me."

His voice began to tremble.

I said, "How is that? Who was she?"

He said, "She was my cow *Mangala*—my mother died when I was a child; since then it was that cow who fed me her milk and helped me grow up. My body and soul have been nourished by her milk. That sweet mother left me after all these years, *Daktar Babu!*"

He started to cry bitterly.

My bewilderment knew no limits.

Sarthakata
Fulfillment

BONOPHOOL

I look back at my life, and it fills me with sadness. As if the life I had left behind me was nothing more than a melancholy dream. The memories of my life are today just that—memories. Sometimes I wonder where that life had gone. That beautiful, enchanting, elegant life.

Once I possessed beauty, fragrance, sweetness. In those mellow days of my youth, many a honey-crazy hornet would sing sweet nothings in my ears, serenade me with flattery and hymns of devotion.

This sky, this breeze, this light—how dearly I once loved these! Once I would be possessed by their charms—but where is that craziness today—that easy indulgence—that sweet, addictive thrill of falling in love! Where are they today?

Today I am ripe and old, full of experience. The pliable feelings of my youth have now hardened into rocks.

I get the feeling again and again today, that my past will never again return—but then—how about the future? What is it going to be like—who knows! This ripe old age, filled with experience garnered at the cost of my joy-filled past—what does it lead to? What is its fulfillment?

A ripe old fruit, hanging from the branch of a tree, was ruminating thus. Suddenly, a gust of wind dislodged it from the branch and it fell to the ground. A bird picked the fruit up with its beak, flew to a branch, and happily began to gorge itself on its flesh.

Nudi O Taalgaachh
The Pebble and the Taal Tree

BONOPHOOL

A vast terrain. Standing tall right in the middle of it is a *taal* tree. No one knows how long it's been there. There is no other tree nearby. Everywhere around it, as far as the eyes can see, there's an infinite stretch of land, reaching to the farthest horizon.

Lying on the ground directly below the *taal* is a small pebble. No one knows how long *it's* been there. Tender blades of grass surround the pebble. As far as the pebble can recall, it has seen nothing but these blades of grass. They emerge in the rainy months, then dry and wither away when summer arrives. When the rains return, they awaken once more, and lovingly caress the pebble. This is all the pebble has seen for as long as it can remember. Grasses grow out of the soil, then dry up, then grow again.

Then suddenly one day it became aware of the *taal*.

What was this strange, dark and tall object? It's risen straight up towards the sky. The pebble remembers, the *taal* has been exactly the same way forever. Straight, powerful, skyward.

"Do you hear me?"

The *taal* did not answer.

"Do you hear me?"

No response.

The pebble, though small, was quite stubborn. After repeated calls, it finally caught the *taal's* attention.

"Who's that? What do you want to say?"

"I am here at your feet, a tiny pebble, Sir. Who are *you*?"

"I am a *taal* tree."

"Oh, I see."

Even though it has been lying below the *taal* all these years, it still had never heard its name. The pebble was intrigued. The *taal* had risen to such a great height! Suddenly, it felt perhaps the *taal's* experience would be a little different. After a pause, it asked:

"Well, Sir, what do you see every day from that great height?"

"The sun rises from one end of the sky, then sets in the other."

"And then?"

"It rises again."

Pukure

In the Pond

BONOPHOOL

Scallop: I suspect there's something wrong inside.

Clam: Of course something is wrong; why would anyone leave one's own society otherwise?

Algae: When I first noticed that he was extroverted and drawn to the world of light out there, I knew there would be trouble.

Chuno: You should have disciplined him early. After all, you are our leader.

Punti: It's debatable whether *he* or *Kelp* is our leader. Anyway, it *is* true he should have regulated him. After all, *he* was his guardian.

Algae: I regulated him as well as I could, brothers. I coaxed, cajoled, even admonished. But you know, brothers, I cannot be too tough; I am not made of stone, after all.

Clam: Thank God for that! If you were made of stone, would any of us have survived? You don't have to turn into stone; we're only asking that you tighten your control a little.

Nyata:	Nothing can be done now.
Scallop:	But something *must* be done. I am convinced there's something terribly wrong inside.
Larva:	I know what's wrong. I am moving upwards every day. I know what's wrong.
Algae:	What is it?
Larva:	He has made friends with some good-for-nothing flies. They hover and buzz around him constantly—
Clam:	Is that so! I sometimes feel he must have gone crazy. He keeps looking up. Sometimes sways—
Chuno:	These are bad omens.
Punti:	We shall not tolerate such behavior. If Algae cannot take any corrective action, we shall go to Kelp. We cannot allow such licentiousness. *(To Clam)* It's not what you think. He is not crazy at all. It's only a put-on, a sham—

Nyata did not say a word, only smiled a little.

Second Larva:	(whispering) I have heard, though, that he has fallen for a woman.
Scallop:	Now, now, just listen to this!
Clam:	Is that so!
Second Larva:	(whispering) Oh, yeah, her name is Light.
Scallop:	See, I said there must be something wrong.
Pond Water:	I haven't said anything so far. I was just listening. None of you knows anything. Now listen to the real thing. He has neither gone crazy, nor is he smitten. He is neither a lunatic,

nor a lover; actually he is simply a traitor. He is involved in a conspiracy. Do you know whom with? The Sun! The Sun who is drying me up every passing second—

Everyone was stunned by news so terrible.

Chuno: So what shall we do?
Punti: What else but protest? We must agitate; there is nothing that cannot be settled by agitation. Soon the little rebel will learn his lesson—
All Together: Fine, let's agitate, then.

A variety of demonstrations and rallies began immediately.

Algae became entangled in the profusion of mud and slime kicked up by the turbulence.

The exquisite *Lotus*, object of the concerted protestations just described, however, continued to be in full bloom, bright and resplendent as ever.

Taj Mahal

BONOPHOOL

The first time I visited Agra, it was to see the Taj Mahal. I still remember the great surprise I felt at that first sight. The train had not reached the station at Agra as yet, when a fellow passenger said excitedly, "There, we can see the Taj Mahal." Eagerly I stuck my neck out the window.

"There it is—"

Looking at the Taj from a distance in broad daylight, I was honestly quite disappointed. It looked no grander than a whitewashed mosque—so *this* is the Taj! Yet, I stared at it, transfixed, for the longest time. After all, this was still the *Taj*! This was Shah Jahan's immortal memorial for his beloved Queen. On slow afternoons, imprisoned in his own Agra Fort, the aging Emperor would gaze at that peerless building from the terrace verandah. This was Mumtaz's building. The *Badshah* Alamgir was not such a heartless brute, after all. He fulfilled his father's last wish. I could see it now. A grand cortege was proceeding towards the great building—the Emperor Shah Jahan was on his way to a rendezvous with his beloved. He could no longer remain apart from her—slowly the casket descended down into the earth—his final resting place had been prepared next to that of Mumtaz, inside the

Taj itself. There used to be another tomb—may be it is still there, next to the Taj—the tomb of Dara Shikoh.

The Taj, looking like an ordinary whitewashed mosque, soon vanished from sight.

The day after the full moon. The moon had not risen yet. There was a hint of *jyotsna*, the molten silver glitter of the full moon, in the eastern sky. That night, after sunset, I went to see the Taj for the second time. I remember well the feelings from that second sight. No sooner than I had entered the grounds past the gate, I heard a soft, ethereal whisper. It did not come from the trimmed evergreen hedges—it seemed to come from the distant past; it was not really a whisper—it was more like a repressed wail. That dense heap of liquid, translucent silhouette in the distance, was *that* the Taj Mahal? I proceeded slowly. Gradually the main dome, the minarets and the overall form of the mausoleum started to become discernible. The pure whiteness of the building, too, became increasingly apparent to the consciousness. Then, suddenly, the entire edifice revealed itself—suddenly the majesty of the magical memorial was manifested in full glory. The moon came up. It seemed as though Shah Jahan's Empress Mumtaz herself, wrapped in a dreamy shawl made of moonbeams, came forward to receive me in all her gracious majesty. Utterly mesmerized, I could only stare spellbound and speechless.

Many years have since passed.

Stories about contractors making money by exploiting the Taj; hotel owners earning a fortune by the Taj's grace; street vendors making a living selling *hookah* pipes and replicas of the dream memorial made out of cheap soap stone; *tonga* drivers cheating innocent tourists by charging outrageous fares—all these have become quite old. I have since seen the Taj many more times—in the dark, in the full moon, at dawn, at twilight—in each of the four seasons—many times, in myriad forms. So often, in fact, that it no longer strikes my eyes, sometimes I do not even notice it—not even while passing right next to it. I now pass the Taj regularly on my way to work. Currently I am a doctor in a charitable clinic near Agra. I am no longer spellbound by the Taj. One day, though—but then, well—let me tell you from the beginning.

One day, following my "Outdoor" session, I was going downstairs from the verandah, when an old *Mussalman* entered through the gate. He had an enormous basket tied to his back. The poor man's spine had become bent from the weight of the basket. I thought the basket must contain some sweet confections or something. When he put the basket down, however, I noticed that it contained, not sweet confections, not candied fruit—but a woman who had her face veiled behind a *burqa*. The old man had the appearance of a *baul*—dressed in a robe, sporting a long, flowing white beard. Coming forward, he saluted me, and informed me in chaste Urdu that he had brought along his *Begum* to have her checked by me. He was rather poor. He did not have the means to visit me at home—he could not afford the fee. If I would do him the *meherbani*-

Approaching the woman, I detected a highly putrid odor. Taking her inside the hospital, and removing the *burqa* (despite her strong protestations), I realized it was a case of *cancrum oris*. Half of her face had rotted away. The right cheek had disappeared, and in its place, a row of teeth was exposed hideously. The foul odour made it impossible to even stand alongside. Such a patient cannot be treated by regular transportation, piggy-back style. There was no space left in my "Indoor" section at the time. Therefore, I recommended that she be kept in the hospital verandah. Ultimately, though, she could not even be left there. The stench was unbearable. Other patients started to protest. The *compounder*, the dresser, not even the janitor would go near her. The old man, though, was completely unperturbed. He stayed with her night and day, tending after her. Ultimately, on account of the highly vocal protests, she *had* to be removed from the verandah. There was a large tree next to the hospital. We asked them to take shelter under the tree. And that was where they remained. The old man would regularly carry medicines and supplies from the hospital back to his *Begum*. Every now and then, I would go and give her injections. It went on in this manner for a while.

One day, a severe downpour started. I was returning from a call, when I observed that the old man was standing under the tree, getting soaked. He had tied two knots to the tree with two ends of a sheet; he held the other two ends with his own hands. I turned the car around. An ordinary sheet cannot possibly keep out the pouring rain. The *Begum*, I noticed, was wet from head to feet. Her body shook uncontrollably. There was a grotesque smile on her face—the half of it that was there. She was burning up with fever.

I told them, "Let's get you back to the verandah." Suddenly, the old man asked, "Is there any chance she will survive, *Huzoor*?"

I had to tell him the truth, "No."

The old man stood there quietly. I returned back to work.

The next day, I found the space under the tree empty. There was no one there.

It was several days after that. I was again returning from a call; as I passed a field, I saw the old man again. He was sitting on the ground, doing something with his hands. The noonday sun was blazing hot. What on earth could he be doing? Had he become hampered by his dying *Begum* in the middle of the field? I went forward. I noticed the old man was plastering a bunch of broken bricks with mud.

"What is going on here, Miyan Saheb?"

The old man stood up respectfully and curtsied.

"I am building my *Begum's* tomb, *Huzoor*."

"*Tomb*?"

"Yes, *Huzoor*."

I fell silent. After a few disquieting moments of silence, I finally asked him, "Where do you live?"

"I go around Agra begging, my Lord."

"I don't recall seeing you before. What's your name?"

"Fakir Shah Jahan, *Huzoor*."

I just stood there without a word.

Level Crossing

MANIK BANDYOPADHYAY

The car was badly damaged in the accident. Bhupen, his daughter Lalana and their driver Keshav were very lucky to have narrowly escaped with their lives. For a while afterwards, they all sat stunned and speechless.

Lalana shook violently.

Wiping his glasses and face with a handkerchief, Bhupen eventually asked, "Now, what on earth just happened, Keshav? You are not a novice driver, then how did this happen?"

Keshav answered, "Perhaps *that* is the reason why we are all alive now."

It really was not Keshav's fault at all. The accident was not because of any negligence or irresponsibility of his part. Otherwise, would he have to nerve to speak with such boldness after causing such a major damage to the car?

Swallowing, Lalana asked, "What happened?"

"The steering gave out all of a sudden."

"Is that so? I see."

"You always complain when I drive slow. Had I been driving any faster, today all three of us would be badly injured, if not dead. Something told me the car was ripe for some malfunction. Damn rotten old jalopy—"

Lalana was sarcastic as she reproached her father. "So go ahead and trust Salil Babu. Could a friend's son cheat you?"

Bhupen sounded regretful. "Truly, we just cannot believe in people anymore. A smart, educated boy from an honourable family—"

There was no use griping about what had happened. Bhupen was out on an important assignment, he would *have* to get to his destination on time. Lalana was out to see a movie; she was supposed to have been dropped off at the cinema house. Of course, seeing a movie would not qualify as important work.

Lalana suggested, "You go ahead and take a taxi, Baba. I will go home. We'll find transportation."

When Bhupen had left, she said, "Then you have saved our lives today, right?"

"Well, to save myself first."

Lalana could have easily had Keshav find her a taxi and gone home. However, she simply sat in the damaged car and went on talking to him. Initially, Keshav used to feel quite uncomfortable answering prying questions about himself and his family. It would irritate him, even make him angry.

Gradually, though, he realized it was not Lalana's fault. He was himself responsible for having crated this sense of curiosity within her. So maybe she was the modern and smart daughter of affluent parents; maybe she was proficient in her studies as well as in music; maybe she had the capacity to hold the attention of a cultivated gathering—nevertheless, there is no denying that she too had a responsive heart.

Therefore, it was entirely possible that a natural curiosity about the home-life of their hired chauffeur would arise in her heart.

After completing his duties at the end of almost every day, Keshav would return back to his battered old village home in the suburb.

Bhupen's large, newly painted modern house stood in the posh and prosperous part of the city. The driver's room next to garage, though small, was nevertheless shiny and clean. Each year, the house was white-washed and re-painted—this operation included the driver's room.

Bosepara was a long way from the train station. The ancient house he lived in had plaster falling off, with the bricks exposed and the walls crumbling due to corrosive calcium deposits. The rooms were like little pigeon-holes; there was poor circulation through the tiny, tar-coated windows. The house was stuffed inside with loads of broken and worthless junk.

Instead of returning to spend his nights in that uninviting setting, Keshav could easily stay in his room in the city; as a bonus, he would also receive his supper for free.

Supper was a most attractive prospect—a nutritious meal at the home of a wealthy employer would be a welcome respite from the usual fare at home of petite shrimp and greens. Yet, it was obvious that Keshav preferred his own home to the tidy accommodation and finer meal at his employer's house.

Unless it turned out to be terribly late, he could always avail of trams and buses to get to the train station. Beyond the level crossing adjoining the train station, however, no motorized transportation was available.

He would have to walk about a mile from the train station to get to Bosepara. The village did have cement houses, old and new; it did have electricity. It also had a stocked general store, a laundry, and a hair-cutting salon. But these amenities were relatively minor. The more dominant features of the village included the old, rundown houses, bushes and bamboo thickets, insect-infested ponds and water holes, filthy shanties and open drains.

There were a few garden-houses, though. Some home-owners had lovingly planted flowering shrubs in the small tracts adjoining their houses; however, the overpowering stench of the neighbourhood generally smothered the fragrance of the blossoms.

Then there were the mosquitoes and flies. Both wielded great power over the community.

Yet, Keshav *had* to return each night!

On special nights when it got really late, and no conveyance was available, he would simply walk all the way.

The train station was about half a mile from Lalana's home.

He would have to be back at work early each morning. He had the task of driving Animesh's seventy-three-year-old mother to the Ganges *ghat* each morning.

Keshav was a bachelor.

Therefore, for Keshav to return home every night, leaving behind the room in the beautiful house within the affluent locale, and the fine meals he was entitled to, could be for no other reason but to go back among his dear ones and sleep for the night.

Did this make any sense at all?

The dear ones were coarse and simple country folk. Even though he was himself a virtual outsider in this world of mother, aunts, brothers, sisters, in-laws, nephews and nieces, they were still his kin.

After the arrangements had been made to tow the damaged car to the garage, Lalana proposed, "Why don't we go to the movie? Now that the car is no longer there, we might as well forget the distinction between the car-owner's daughter and his driver."

It was clear that this was not just an impulsive statement from her. All the while that she was talking to him, asking him probing questions, she was toying with the proposition in her head. Somewhat cagily, Keshav said, "Now that I have the day off, I was thinking of going home."

Lalana was not hurt, she did not get upset, she only stared at him out of surprise.

She said, "I will go to your place one of these days to find out what it is you have there. What it is that makes you so eager to go home. Can you not go after the movie?"

"I hate movies."

"That's because you go to bad movies. My friends urge me often to go with them—have you ever seen me go to the cheap movies?"

With a sullen expression, Keshav sighed and said, "Would you believe me if I tell you the truth? I don't feel well, my head hurts badly."

Lalana turned pale.

"Are you sick or something? You don't look like it—"

"I am not sick. The doctor has examined me thoroughly, he hasn't found anything wrong. What plagues me is really quite strange. It isn't exactly a headache, it isn't like my head swims—it's like something is clamping down on the inside. You know how I feel right now? I feel like running away somewhere."

Disheartened, Lalana told him, "Well, go home, then."

Keshav stood and thought for a while.

Suddenly, he brightened up and said, "Fine, let's go see a movie. Let me see if that relieves my discomfort. Let me try to conquer this ailment rather than keep pampering it."

"If you really don't feel well—"

"Well, let me see what happens."

They went to the movie hall.

After bravely making it till the intermission, Keshav said, "That's it, I can't hang around any longer."

Lalana replied, "Let it be. I want to go home also—don't feel like seeing the rest of it. By the way, you don't have to come back tomorrow."

She then said, "I will take a taxi home—you can come along with me."

It was past sunset when they reached Lalana's home. As he got off the taxi in front of Bhupen's well-lit mansion, Keshav asked again, "Are you sure I don't need to come in tomorrow?"

Lalana replied, "What for? This time, we have to carefully look for a new car ourselves before buying one. Father will probably not have any time until day after tomorrow.

Lalana spoke in a manner suggesting that like Keshav, she too felt a pressure within.

Keshav took the tram to the station. As soon as he would walk past the level crossing beyond the station, the city outskirts would take on a completely different look.

The railway tracks separated the bright and shiny high rises and massive mansions of the big city from the dark, dingy and decaying countryside. One side marked the limits of the city corporation, the other that of the local municipality.

A brisk but heavy rain had fallen in the afternoon. The rural roads were covered with slimy mud and runny cowdung. The many potholes were filled with murky slush.

Despite these conditions, the crowds were unbelievable!

And they were not only the street dwellers, either half-naked or clad in tatters and rags. Well groomed *babus*, suited *sahibs*, and ladies in stylish *saris* were all there, walking the same filthy road, shopping at the roadside stores. Further down was the cinema. A show was on, the hall was likely filled to capacity, yet a crowd consisting of men and women of all ages had assembled outside.

These were queued in advance for the next show.

He ran into a familiar person who asked, "Kind of early tonight?"

Keshav answered, "I got an early leave."

The acquaintance, weary from a day at the office, observed caustically, "You sure have a cushy job! Ride in someone else's motor car, eat fabulous meals, then lie on a cot and snore comfortably all night."

Keshav only contorted his face in response.

"You should see for yourself—try to do my work! *Babu's* order, *Go Fast*. So now you drive like a maniac, run over people, get beaten to pulp and thrown in jail. *Some cushy!*"

As he walked further, the street lights became dimmer, the shops began to be sparse, the number of worn out houses and hovels began to increase. From the uneven main road, made of beaten bricks, narrow brick alleys snaked into congested neighborhoods. The open bazaar in Bagchipara was completely deserted. A morning bazaar gathered at this location every day.

At the Bosepara crossing, a low-power electric lightbulb burned faintly atop the faded and battered old lamppost. As if this was only to demonstrate to the riffraff from the shallow pond and bamboo thicket neighbourhoods that simply having a lightbulb does not a glittery esplanade make!

But, this too is an electric light; stare at it, then light your hurricane lanterns at home and be happy.

Light your evening lamps with adulterated oil, dipped in wicks made from torn rags. That light is calm, it is soft and gentle. The electric lamp, by comparison, is merely a glass toy. Keshav stopped momentarily. It now seemed to him he had left Lalana's shiny city way behind, on the far side of the level crossing. The blinding glare of city lights, the glamorous sights, the gleaming cars and the milling crowds—these all seemed to have been wiped off his mind.

He too must believe in this charade, then—this running away from the hustle and bustle of city life in search of the mythical peace and calm. Why else would he return to this dark, dank, stinky hellhole infested with stagnant mudpools, instead of spending time with an eager Lalana, or at least staying long enough for the movie to end?

The light in Sarat's general store glowed quite brightly. Keshav walked over to get himself two-paise worth of snuff.

Handing him the snuff, Sarat also gave him a brown paper bag, saying, "Would you please deliver this *gur* home? I'll tell you, those kids sure have the stomach for sweets!"

There was a quiet, almost vacant look in the elderly Sarat's expression. He didn't seem to have any excitement or zest left in life. He taught Bengali at the local school, and ran this store—outside of these, his life had become quite barren and uneventful.

Walking past Sarat's store, Keshav walked south towards the Bosepara lane. The houses in this area were arranged in dense clumps. Ten houses all packed close to each other, then an expanse of a small tract, a pond, a garden and some bushes—this was the general pattern.

Only the bigger houses and some of the new ones occasionally stood apart, separate from the clusters.

The night was not that late back in the city. Bosepara, on the other hand, had turned out the lights, and, if not fast asleep, it had at least become very quiet and desolate. There were few people about. Upon some front landings, there were small *addas* in progress. From within a few homes one could hear little children reciting mathematical tables or other school work, while the radio could be heard playing inside yet others.

The newly whitewashed one-story house next to the giant *banyan* tree seemed rather mysterious in the interplay of light and shadows. The two thatched huts next to it made the mystery even deeper. One could see light within, hear the sound of voices inside, and smell the odours of cooking spices wafting out of the kitchen. Yet, much like the wide open sky which is manifest yet enigmatic; like the motionless *banyan*, alive yet eerily reminiscent of death in the airless *Vaishakh* night—likewise, the shaded innocence of the small house, like a cloudy nebula, seemed to stir the senses with feelings of the unknown.

Inside the house, there was a small yard. Outside, on one side, there was a fenced garden. There were three trellises, supporting vines of long-neck gourd, bitter gourd and pumpkin. There were also a few blossoming hibiscus plants.

The cooking took place at some distance inside one of the thatched huts. One could go straight to the kitchen without entering the main building.

Maya had set the curried vegetables to cook over the clay fire, and was busy applying medication to Sarat's son Ganesh's prickly heat. Noticing Keshav, a strangely tranquil and sweet smile appeared on her face.

Keshav said, "Sarat-da sent some *gur*."

Putting away the bag of *gur*, Maya kissed Ganesh on the chin and said, "Now go do your studies, precious. You don't have to stand guard any longer."

The main building was nearby; one could always hear the voices of people. However, Maya always felt afraid to be alone in the hut at night, cooking. She needed someone to be with her.

On this side of the hut, there was no other house—only trees, bushes, and a pond. On the other side was Keshav's house.

Keshav teased her, "It's barely dark, and you are *so* scared?"

Maya replied, "And why not? Such a dense bush—good thing Ganesh was here, even then I felt the creeps."

A year ago, this room would be lit by an oil-lamp. Now, an electric lamp planted on a *sal* stump illuminated it.

Maya said, "You look worn out. Did they really overwork you?"

"No, I slept all afternoon."

"Then?"

"There was an accident. We were lucky to escape unhurt."

In the strange glow of the lamp, Maya's pale and ashen expression was not discernible. Only her still gaze and open mouth suggested the extent of her dismay at the news.

It was hard to tell if Maya was beautiful. However, upon her olive-complexioned face surrounded by waves of dense black hair there was an uncanny grace. The simple handloom *sari* further enhanced her appearance.

Smiling, Keshav asked, "What's the matter?"

Maya swallowed.

Keeping her voice down, she said, "Now, look. There's Kali coming over. I can't even talk freely for a moment or two."

Sarat's daughter Kali was eleven—even at this age, she had already graduated from adolescent frocks to *saris*. The *anchal* of her striped *sari* overflowed on the floor, as she came in swinging her long braids. Casting a suspicious glance at Keshav, she pleaded with Maya like a child, "Mashi, doesn't one get hungry, doesn't one get sleepy? How much longer are you going to cook?"

Maya snapped at her, "Did you think I am not done cooking? I am about to take the vegetable curry off the fire. Now you run along and tell everyone to set up the places. Make sure you get the lantern."

As soon as Kali disappeared into the main house to call her siblings, Maya walked up to Keshav and said, "My heart's still pounding. You *must* quit this job. My heart won't stop racing until I hear the details of everything that happened. Do this—change your clothes, then walk over to the house and tell everyone the story. Then I too will get to hear it. That snoopy Kali just saw us—if we talk too long, *Didi* will really take it out on me."

Keshav had taken the garden route to the kitchen; this time, he returned through the main house.

Inside the building, Sarat's oldest son Ranjan was in the verandah, reading. He noticed Keshav and asked, "Say, Keshav-da, which way did you come in?"

Keshav answered, "Sarat-da gave me a bag of *gur*—I just dropped it off to Maya in the ktichen."

From her room, Abala asked him, "Is that you, Keshav? Aren't you going to sit for a while?"

Abala was paralyzed. For three years now, she was confined to her bed night and day. This was the reason why she needed her sister Maya to come live with her—to take care of her half-a-dozen offspring.

Keshav said, "I was almost killed in an accident today. I'll go change and come back to tell you about it."

There were quite a few people living in Keshav's house. His widowed mother, three brothers, two sisters, a second sister-in-law, her two children, a paternal aunt and her son.

It had several tiny cubbyholes that served as living spaces. Even though Keshav had a whole room to himself, generally there was no real dearth of rooms in the house. It was clear, though, that once his third brother Pranav and his cousin Bhola were married, a space crunch would be inevitable.

His *pishi* was eager enough that she would marry her son off overnight, if she had her way. Only fear of Keshav prevented that. Just what kind of reasoning did *he* exhibit, though? So what if Bhola was without work—surely a young man would find work sooner or later—be it a regular job, or that of a street vendor, or a menial porter. May be he would get to live on fine fare within a fine brick home, or dine on rice and greens in a hovel—*that* was for fate to decide, not Keshav.

But, if he went too far past his youth, was not the main purpose or the joy of marriage rendered quite meaningless? Even if short-lived, *this* was really the age for it, the age for its delights.

After all, was not human life much too fragile?

Quite possibly because he had himself missed the boat, Keshav was so indifferent about anyone else's prospects.

A few of the residents had ordered items from the city. Bimala asked, "How come you came home empty-handed? Didn't you get the floormat?"

Keshav said, "No. Here I was, about to be killed in an accident—"

"Oh, good lord! What are you saying? Oh, *Dinabandhu!*"

Everyone else who had lined up to complain that their shopping request had not been honored suddenly fell silent.

After briefly describing the incident, Keshav picked up fresh clothes, and went to the pond for a bath. He was in no hurry. A half-dozen kids had just sat down to supper—Maya would be unable to stop by and listen to the story of his near-fatal accident until they were finished.

When he eventually walked back to Sarat's house after waiting a long while, he found that Sarat had already closed shop and returned home.

Sarat said, "I heard you had an accident? Well, you sure got us terribly concerned."

They spread out a mat for him.

Abala said from within, "Speak a little loudly, Keshav. Now, you all be totally quiet."

Keshav narrated the story; cradling Sarat's four-year-old son in her lap, Maya listened intently.

In the dim light of the lantern, her face appeared ashen; a soft squeal of alarm escaped from her mouth.

When he was finished, Abala said, "Well, at least thank your good fortune!"

Maya remarked, "Why do the kind of work that can injure your arms and legs, or even kill you!"

"How would I feed myself without work?"

"Is there no other work in the world?"

"I am doing work I know best how to do. Should people stop driving cars simply because accidents happen?"

There was so much empathy and support both in his own home and in this friends' home. Yet, somehow, Keshav felt an increasing emptiness. Everything seemed bleak and tasteless.

On his way back home, the bleakness and fatigue felt even heavier. Bosepara was now completely desolate; the residents had withdrawn themselves from the world. Why had he eagerly hurried back here? Life was so quiet, so barren here. He knew he would not get any sleep under the burden of this weariness—he would simply pass the uneventful night listening to the crickets outside.

After supper, Keshav went to his room. Except for the light in his room, all other lights in the rest of his house, as well as those in Sarat's went out at around the same time.

It is possible that some lights were still on in other houses, but they were surely on for other reasons. Who else would keep a light turned on simply because of the need to read something spurred by the inability to sleep?

Suddenly, Keshav was startled to hear Maya's hushed voice coming in from the window facing the bushes outside.

"Can you hear me? Please listen to me."

"Maya, is that you?

"Turn off the light."

Turning it off, Keshav walked to the window and asked, "Did you really walk alone *this* late at night right through the jungle?"

"What could I do? You will leave for work right at dawn, won't you?"

"I have the day off tomorrow. Weren't you afraid?"

"Yes, of course. But I managed to cancel the smaller fear with the bigger one—and here I am."

Keshav thought a little, then said, "Will you come in, or should I come out?"

Maya said, "Whatever you say."

"Well, then, I'll be out. There's no telling who might see from some room or the other. If they see me, they'll think I am off to the *ghat*."

Keshav opened the back door and went out. Walking some distance away, they stood in the deep shadow under a tamarind tree.

"What is it, Maya?"

"I couldn't help it. I was feeling suffocated. Promise me you will give up this job."

Maya was weeping as she spoke.

Keshav sighed and said reassuringly, "Why are you getting so worked up? The car has been repaired; moreover, I have the day off tomorrow."

Maya stopped sobbing and said, "O, I see!"

Then she continued with an anxious voice, "Seems you are upset I came?"

"Are you crazy? You just surprised me, that's all. Come, let me walk you back."

In the faint light of the dawn, Keshav had just bathed in the pond and was drying himself, when Maya walked over with a drinking glass and said, "Drink this up, quick."

There was more than a quarter *seer* of milk in the glass.

"What on earth is this?"

"This is from the cow who recently delivered. You must drink some fresh milk every day."

Keshav said, "I understand that, but what will they tell you back at the house when they notice the shortage?"

Laughing, Maya said, "So you think they care to keep watch? Moreover, it is *I* who must milk that cow. Drink up, someone might see you."

Therefore, Keshav *had* to sip the milk. Newly calved, the milk was rather thin. But it was not that. It was Maya's excessively eager attention that made it taste even more insipid to Keshav.

"Why are you bathing this early?"

"I'll go to the city."

"Isn't it your day off?"

"It's for something else."

This was bogus. Keshav had no work to do.

He was feeling very anxious to go back to the city. He felt a tremendous pressure inside, a pressure that was prompting him to rush past the level crossing like a madman and head for the city. He would be unable to take a single breath until he had heard the noisy bustle of the city workday, or sat in his tidy little room next to the garage surrounded by the garden and lawn, listening to the lilting voice of the young maiden floating in from within the mansion.

But he also knew, no sooner than the day was over, he would be just as crazy to return to this dark and dismal Bosepara. The two worlds on either side of the level crossing would continue to alternately pull him in, and push him back out.

Fossil

SUBODH GHOSH

Anjangarh is a native estate, precisely sixty-eight and one half square miles in area. It *is* a native estate nevertheless; a tiger cub, after all, *is* a tiger. There is a Maharaja; there are the necessary troops, a commandant, a treasury and assorted offices. The Maharaja has over twenty honorific appellations to his name. He is the *Tribhuvanapati*; he is also the *Narapala*, the *Dharmapala* and the *Aratidamana*. About four generations ago, convicts would be routinely impaled on the *shula* here in accordance with strict scriptural guidelines. It is no longer possible. Nowadays, convicts are merely stripped naked and forced to run from a colony of bees.

The old fortress no longer has any beauty or grace left in its appearance; its stone facade, however, is still entirely intact. A rusty old cannon sits like the crumbly skeleton of a wild elephant on each side of the main gateway to the fortress. Inside their barrels flocks of pigeons happily nest, lay eggs and raise their young; under their shades weary dogs rest their bones. Within, there are endless displays of swords and *pugrees* in room after room; stashed against the walls of those rooms like dry cowdung cakes are shields of iron and copper. The rooms still serve as offices.

There is a *sachiv* and a *serestadar*. One finds a strange mix of both Kshatriya and Mughal nomenclature in the royal offices. As though the Maharaja conducts his administration using the combined talents of bureaucrats from two eras and two different races. Irked by the quirky and bizarre kind of tyranny exercised by such an administration, at least half the subjects have moved to faraway Mauritius to serve as *coolies* in sugar factories.

Anjangarh is a sixty-eight and one half square mile parcel of land covered by clumps of *Ghoraneem* and *Phanimanasa*, a craggy, pebble-strewn terrain, and bare hills with virtually no vegetation. The local *Kurmis* and *Bhils* fetch water in sacks made of buffalo hide from secret reservoirs tucked away on the sides of hills at least four miles away. They use the precious water to irrigate their fields and grow corn, barley and maize.

Every year a clash develops between the *tehsil* department of the estate and the *Bhil* and *Kurmi* subjects. The farmers refuse to donate any grain to the royal granary; in the end, though, they *have* to part with half their harvest. The Maharaja has a well-groomed polo team. The royal stables are ever alive with the neighing of well over a hundred of the finest breed of Wellers from Sydney. The Maharaja is deeply devoted to these divine beasts. Obviously, they cannot be fed ordinary chaff and oil cakes from the mills. They *have* to have corn, barley and maize.

Hence the *Tehsildar* has to call in the troops. Sparks of *Kshatriya* valor fly furiously from the lances and sticks of the Rajput aces. Within an hour all protestations cease, all rebellions are quashed.

The vanquished *Bhils* ultimately forfeit even their

legendary forbearance, and move *en masse* to neighboring states and big cities in search of jobs at recruitment camps for *dhangars*. Some move to New Delhi, and some to Calcutta or Shillong with wives and babies. The migrants never return.

The ones who refuse to move no matter what are the *Kurmis*. Seven generations of their forbears have lived in this region. Here they have lived surrounded by the cool clumps of earth beneath the shades of *Ghoraneem* and bushes of *Kalmegh* and *Anantamul* saplings. Here, where the earth has the fragrance of *Salsa*. They are connected to this earth, as it were, by an invisible umbilical cord. Shamelessly they keep on farming despite countless beatings and futile uprisings. Like the changing seasons, their nights and days revolve around this tri-state cycle of existence. Nothing has the power to break the cycle and release them from its grip.

Kindness and rule of law have not vanished entirely from Anjangarh, however. Every Sunday a vast congregation of the destitute converges on the great courtyard in front of the fortress. From the royal *durbar* they dole out *chinre* and *gur*. On the day of *sankranti*, the Maharaja comes out in a grand procession, riding an elephant regally decked and decorated with *alpana*, and offers his blessings to the subjects. On the monarch's birthdays, *Ramlila* music is performed on the fortress courtyard; the subjects receive invitations. The excessive *Kshatriya* fervour, however, usually mars these festivities with the unrestrained application of the *lathi* in all matters. Where there is a crowd, and where the crowd chants words of victory, there *will* be a *lathi-charge*, and there *will* be a few fractured skulls. The *chinre*, the royal blessings, and the *Ramlila* are all served with a generous helping of the *lathi*. The subjects, curiously enough, seem to relish this kind of entertainment, perhaps by force of habit.

No doubt, the power of the *lathi*cracy was proving quite effective in the administration of the estate, especially in such critical areas as revenue collection, forced foreclosures and acquisitions; however, it was still not nearly enough for adequate regal upkeep. After all, there were the obligatory purses of the royal guests, and the hefty expenses incurred in maintaining the polo team. In the end, the royal arm had to reach inside the family vault for the gold and silver stash accumulated by the forefathers. And sure enough, the vault was soon beginning to be depleted.

At this juncture, when Anjangarh was in the grip of great uncertainty, a legal advisor with expertise in English law arrived at the *durbar* as the new *law agent*. It was our own Mukherjee. Mukherjee was broad-chested, athletic, and particularly skilled in both the game of polo and the running of the estate. Presently he became the indispensable right-hand of the Maharaja. Before long, Mukherjee was a *de facto* Chief Secretary, while the role of the real office holder with that title became little more than that of a rubber-stamp.

Our Mukherjee is an idealist. The concept of *democracy*, learned in his school days, continues to run through every strand of his thought processes. Despite his relative youth, he is extremely cool-headed. He believes strongly that one with noble courage can never lose, and he who does good can come to no harm.

Mukherjee applied every ounce of his genius to the upliftment of the estate. The denizens of Anjangarh, old and young, soon came to know their *Agent Sahib* as exceedingly tough on the one hand, while at the same time exceptionally friendly and empathetic. The people simultaneously feared and adored him. The scourge of *lathi*cracy was eliminated by his order. Every department underwent an exhaustive audit. A new survey of the holdings of the estate was conducted, as well as a new census. To top it all, even the two rusty old cannons at the entrance to the fortress were polished to a mirror finish.

It was the *law agent* Mukherjee who one day discovered the subterranean treasures of Anjangarh. Hiring a team of geologists from Calcutta, he conducted an underground survey of the region which revealed that in the folds of the granite interior were abundant reserves of mica and asbestos. Inviting merchants from Calcutta, he leased out vast stretches of the rocky terrain for mining operations. The millions of rupees generated as revenue soon revived Anjangarh back to prosperity and vigor.

Today, a sprawling palace constructed in the Gwalior style can be seen next to the fortress. Within, one finds lavish appointments made from the finest marble, mosaic, and Venetian glass. The royal garage is chock-full of luxurious sedans and limousines imported from Germany. The royal stables are alive with the frisky acrobatics of Irish ponies. A gigantic new electric power plant loudly proclaims Anjangarh's new-found life night and day.

Truly a tidal wave of vitality has swept over Anjangarh. The merchants have collectively established a mining syndicate. Wide, asphalt roads have appeared near the mining area, along with barracks for the *coolies*, tube wells, spacious bungalows, a club, landscaped flower beds, and even a *gymkhana*. The *Kurmis* have rushed in droves to occupy the barracks. They now earn wages in cash, sacrifice chickens to their gods, drink *hanria* with reckless abandon, and every night enliven the mining area with the considerable din of their *madals* and *dholaks*.

The Maharaja has more plans—two new polo grounds have to be constructed; the palace gardens must be expanded by adding twenty-two *bighas* of land. For the royal band, he wishes to hire, preferably, an Italian bandmaster.

Spreading out Anjangarh's map on the table before him, Mukherjee contemplates his irrigation scheme. Ten parallel canals running north to south. Interspersed between the canals, mighty dams complete with concrete pylons and sluice-gates. With the help of clever engineering design, the powerful flow of the Anjana river must be diverted to the stony, arid fields of Anjangarh—like veins transporting blood. Each *Kurmi* subject must be given a complimentary *bigha* of land, leased tax-free for the first five years. One *aush*, one *aman*, and at least one *ravi* crop per year. Three harvests a year. The northern parcels will be apportioned entirely to a nursery, potato and tobacco, while the southern will be given to sugarcane, wheat and barley. Then—

Well, then gradually a bank, a tannery and a paper mill. The royal treasury is not that impoverished any more. This is the most auspicious hour. Like the masterly strokes of an artist, he will change the very mien of Anjangarh one plan at a time. He will prove that the administration of a state is not merely *lathi*cracy—it too is an art.

As for a school—well, to that the Maharaja responded with an unequivocal *Kabhi Nahi*. Mukherjee stood up; we'll see. Maybe he can prevail upon the Maharaja with reason and some persuasion.

Vigorously wringing his stupendous beard, the Maharaja dangled two pieces of paper in front of Mukherjee—Take a look.

The first letter: *Almighty Durbar, and Lord of the Durbar, our Maharaja! You are the father of your subjects. That you give to us so generously is why we get to eat. Therefore, grant that the Tehsildar does not harass us at the time of this year's maize or corn harvest. We pledge to pay our taxes in cash. That which is legally due to the government, we shall pay and ask for a receipt. Signed on behalf of the devoted servants of the Durbar, Dulal Mahato.*

The second letter: *The Maharaja's gendarmes have arrested four Kurmi coolies from our mines and beaten their wives with lathis. We consider these actions beyond the Maharaja's legal authority, and demand that the Maharaja ensure proper restitution without further delay. Sincerely, Gibson (Chairman of the Syndicate).*

"Can you believe the *chutzpah* of these bastards, Mukherjee?" The Maharaja inquired.

"Incredible, indeed!"

Thumping his fist upon the table, the *Aratidamana* bellowed grotesquely, "The heads! Bring me the heads of the sons of bitches, throw them before me. Let me sit here and watch. Let me watch for two days and two nights."

Mukherjee placates the obviously irate Maharaja, "Do not worry. Let me find out what is really going on from the inside."

Old Dulal Mahato had returned from Mauritius after many years. To enjoy his remaining years, he had returned with cash savings of seven rupees, and a chestful of asthma. Since his return, it seems that a new level of excitement has gripped the

Kurmi community, as though their lives have entered a new phase.

The *Kurmis* have learned from Dulal the value of earning wages in cash. Load the ten-*seer* luggage of a Babu from Faizabad into his train compartment and—*voila*! You have just made yourself a full *anna* on the spot!

Dulal has told them—"My brothers—believe me when I say that this old man has been cheated in return for my trust as many times as I have gray hair on my head. From now on, we trust no one. All wages must be paid in cash. You will receive your money in one hand, and only then offer your *salaam* with the other."

Dulal conducts negotiations with the *Sahibs* of the syndicate regularly. The rate of pay for the *coolies*, designated weekly pay days, earned leaves, pensions and medical care—on all such issues, he has represented the *Kurmis* and wangled concrete and substantial pledges from the management. The syndicate, in turn, also coddles Dulal all the time—Dulal, come on over. If you wish, we will put up twenty dozen barracks overnight and admit every last *Kurmi* under your command.

Dulal replies, "Well, we'll see about that. For now, I would like to request that each *coolie* be granted a free quota of coal and kerosene."

"Very well, it will be done"—the syndicate *Sahibs* assure him.

At Dulal's invitation, one day a large crowd of *Kurmis* gathered at the *Ghoraneem* bush. Taking his *pugree* off the top of his almost entirely gray-haired head, Dulal stood up to speak: We have established our *mandal* today. Now think about what we need to do. Find out who our friends are, and who the foes. We must no longer live with fear. Those who attempt to drive knives into our bellies or our honour, we shall not forgive under *any* circumstances.

Like a broken conch shell, Dulal's long dormant larynx quivers in excitement as he calls out, "My brothers, from this day, this Mahato's life is for the *mandal*, and the *mandal's* life is for..."

The vast *Kurmi* throng raises a thousand *lathis* in the air and replies, "For Mahato!"

Amid the booming sounds of *dhaks* and *dholaks*, they even unfurled a pennant. Thereafter, they all went home.

No matter how secretly the event was organized and conducted, nothing could be concealed from Mukherjee. He knew instinctively that clouds of precisely this nature carried thunderbolts within. Something *had* to be done before it was too late. The Maharaja, however, must know absolutely nothing about this *under any circumstances*. Otherwise, it would be very nearly impossible to control such vain rulers blinded as they are by feudal pride and tormented by an honour complex. It may even result in an unnecessary and futile bloodbath. Instead, maybe he should himself try to conduct a civil fight for a round or two.

One day the royal informants informed the Maharaja. "The *Kurmis* did not report for labor duty at either the polo grounds or the royal gardens. They say—it is a sin to work without pay; to do so would be unpropitious for the kingdom."

Mukherjee was summoned. Dulal Mahato, too, was subpoenaed. Prostrating before the Maharaja with folded palms, Dulal Mahato stood up, trembling like a lamb.

"Are *you* the one behind all this wickedness?" The Maharaja wanted to know.

"I am nothing but the dust underneath my Lord's boots."

"Shut up."

"As you wish, my Lord."

"Silence!" Thundered the Maharaja. Dulal became stiff as a wooden puppet.

The Maharaja said, "You must abjure your relationship with the *vilaiti* merchants. No *Kurmi* will be allowed to work as *coolies* in the mines without my express consent."

"As you wish, my Lord. I shall convey your orders to my brothers."

"Go now."

Dulal curtsied and went out. The next order was for Mukherjee—"Put the syndicate on notice that they may not hire any of my *Kurmi* subjects as a *coolie* without my recommendation."

Soon the responses arrived from the appropriate sources. There was a letter signed by Dulal Mahato—"Since we earn wages in cash, and cannot survive without those wages, we *have to* obey the mining *Sahibs*. We hope that the *Durbar* will not interfere in this matter.... Our new temple will be inaugurated next month. We request that His Majesty grant one thousand rupees to be released from the royal treasury for this purpose. Also, may we have permission to use logs and kindling from the forest without any taxes during the next winter."

The syndicate also sent a letter in response to the notice—"We are willing to enter into a new pact with the Maharaja. But not now. We shall do so when the current agreement expires—ninety nine years from today."

"What do you think, Mukherjee? Seems I have no choice but to call the police commissioner. May I ask, are you going to stop daydreaming about your canals and start worrying about my honor now, well?"

The Maharaja spoke the words softly, no doubt, but it was clear from his expression that a murderous rage was coiled within him like a hundred-hooded serpent, struggling to be free.

With utmost humility, Mukherjee requested, "May the *Sarkar* not be too perturbed. Give me a little time, I will put everything back in order."

Mukherjee knows well the power and inspiration behind Dulal's audacity. The devious instigation by the syndicate is the engine that has powered the *Kurmi* uprising and the associated brouhaha. Unless this malicious bond is severed, it is going to bring great turmoil, even calamity to the kingdom. But what can be done about it?

Mukherjee stood before Dulal Mahato's hut. Hastily, Dulal emerged from within and offered Mukherjee a stool to sit on. Taking the *pugree* off his head and placing it near Mukherjee's feet, Dulal sat on the floor. Mukherjee patiently explained events to him one by one. With hurt in his voice, Mukherjee pleads—"What *are* you doing, Mahato! You are like the children of the *Durbar*, so sometimes the son makes a mistake, sometimes the father. But that does not mean one dishonors one's home by inviting outsiders in. Maybe the syndicate is feeding you well today, but remember, once its work is done, it will not so much as look at any of you another day. Remember, it is *this Durbar* that will rescue you on that inevitable day with a handful of *chinre*."

Placing his hands on Mukherjee's feet, Dulal said, "I swear, *Agent Baba*, we will keep your word. The Maharaja is like a father to us, we are prepared to give our lives for him. But, we hope our appeal will be granted a little bit quickly by the Durbar."

Without waiting for another question or answer, a frustrated Mukherjee departs from Dulal's shack—well, the disease was already there for a long time, now it's clear that delirium is setting in.

Mukherjee had to skip his bath, lunch and even a change of clothes today. Driving nonstop, he arrived at the syndicate office.

"Now look, Mr. Gibson, we plead with you to kindly not interfere with the relationship between the king and his subjects. You will be granted any facility you need for your projects simply by appealing to the Durbar."

Gibson replies, "Mr. Mukherjee, we are not money-grabbers, we have a mission. We have always fought on behalf of the downtrodden and the persecuted. If necessary, we will continue to fight."

"You have enticed all the *Kurmi* subjects to turn into *coolies*. Tell me, how can the state's agriculture survive under such conditions?"

Mukherjee impulsively confesses the true cause of his gripe.

"May be the agriculture will not survive, but can you deny that your treasury is not being depleted as much?" There is ridicule in Gibson's voice.

"Think about cooperation instead of confrontation, Mr. Gibson. Before you hire your *coolies*, simply obtain permission from the Durbar, that's all. It would please the Maharaja, and I am sure do *you* a lot of good also."

"Sorry, Mr. Mukherjee." With a sly smile, Gibson lights a cigar.

In extreme exasperation, Mukherjee's earlobes turn red. Angrily pushing his chair away, he stands up, and immediately storms out of the office.

McKenna comes in and asks, "What's the matter, Gibson?"

"Mukherjee, that monkey of an administrator, I really let him have it straight. Didn't agree to *any* of his terms."

"You did the right thing. You must have heard about his irrigation scheme, right? We must demolish that scheme before it's too late—otherwise we will run into a serious labor shortage. The project is right now in the middle of a major growth spurt—we need to be extra careful."

"Don't worry. We've got Mahato, our very own tamed cat, on our side. We will use him to disrupt their designs."

After exchanging a few laughs, McKenna says, "Well, Mahato has been waiting outside. Go ahead and call him in, and get on with your plan."

Mahato had been sitting near the back door of the syndicate office. Escorting him to a private room within the office building, Gibson says, "Here you are—the application is ready. Everything is written here. Sign it, and we will mail it to Delhi by today's post."

Mahato signs. Patting him on the back, McKenna ushers him out, saying, "*Daro mat*, Mahato, we are with you. If they evict you from your land and homes, our *dhaoras* will always remain open for you and your people—*daro mat*."

Sitting in his office, Mukherjee speculates and fantasizes.

He doesn't feel like writing a word. He cannot think of one word of hope or assurance to offer to the Maharaja. He probably can no longer drive someone else's chariot. The reins must now be handed back to the charioteer. On the other hand, it seems as though all these people suffer from a common malady—a dried-up brain. Driven by their own half-witted fantasy, they seem hell-bent on self-destruction. Or, could it be that he had himself miscalculated somewhere?

The Maharaja summons him to his inner sanctum.

The police commissioner and the chief secretary are seen sitting there with grim faces. The Maharaja walks around the couch, greatly agitated. He explodes as soon as Mukherjee enters.

"Go on, take it—I will spit on the *gaddi* and leave. *You* sit on it and run the state."

Stupefied, Mukherjee glances at the chief secretary, who hands him a letter. It is a note from the political agent. — *Many complaints have been lodged against the internal affairs of the state. Newer and more serious allegations are coming in every day. I hope the Durbar will be able to put things in order before I have to intervene.*

The commissioner frowns and remarks, "Agent Sahib—your reconciliation policy is responsible for all this."

Echoing the commissioner's allegation, the Maharaja screams, "Absolutely, it's absolutely true. I know everything, Mukherjee. I am not blind."

"Know everything? What are you saying, *Sarkar*?"

"Stop it—I *do* know. Or else, how could the *banias* who earn their wages selling the rocks and ores of *my* territory have such gall? Who encourages them?"

Gasping for his breath, the Maharaja abruptly collapses on the couch. A royal orderly anxiously begins fanning him back to normal. Meanwhile, the chief secretary, the commissioner, and Mukherjee sit speechlessly, staring in different directions.

Presently, the Maharaja cleared his throat and continued, "*Foujdar Sahib*, this time *you* must restore my honour."

The chief secretary said, "That's right, you must teach the *Kurmis* a lesson, *Foujdar Sahib*, while I implicate the syndicate in a civil suit. I am sure we will find many loopholes advantageous to us in the contract."

The Maharaja quickly glanced at Mukherjee, then turned his head away. Mukherjee, however, caught a glimpse of the Maharaja's tear-filled eyes.

A lion in tears. Even Mukherjee, by nature more like a rabbit, could gauge just how much internal anguish and inflammation was at play here. Indeed, he had never observed the matter from this angle before. It was his mistake. Walking up to the Maharaja he quietly submitted his final plea. "It was my mistake, *Sarkar*. Please permit me to leave now. If ever you should call me again, I will surely return to you."

In a flash, the Maharaja softened noticeably, and said, "No, Mukherjee, what *are* you saying! Where on earth will you go? True, people have said a lot of things, but I do not believe them. However, the policy must change; we *have* to be sterner. I cannot let myself be kicked around by a bunch of toads any longer, Mukherjee."

A languid emptiness, like the lifeless clouds of winter, had numbed every joint in Mukherjee's limbs. He stopped going to his office. Only in the evenings, putting on his riding breeches and piling a couple dozen mallets on his caddy's shoulders, he would go to the polo club. There, he would play full gallop, like a furious and unstoppable hurricane, until the very end. He would hit under-the-neck shots indiscriminately to his left and right. Mallet after mallet would split and scatter in the air from his relentless onslaught. Drenched with the spray from his foaming mouth and free-flowing perspiration, the flannels on his midnight black Weller's sinuous legs would swell up like balloons. Obsessed about scoring, Mukherjee would, however, continue to charge like a maniac. The startled rival team could only retreat into a slow, defensive trot. Even after the match would be over, Mukherjee would continue circling the polo field at lightning fast canter. Occasionally he would stand upright on his stirrups, eyes closed, as if to fill his lungs with gulps of the speeding air.

The day's games over, the Maharaja would complain, "You are playing way too rough, Mukherjee."

That day, as usual, the sun sank behind the hills in Anjangarh just before dusk. The Maharaja, regally attired, was getting ready to go to the polo field. Just then, a messenger brought him the news—pit number fourteen at the mines had collapsed, and the landslide triggered by the collapse had not abated. Ninety male and female *Kurmi coolies* were buried in the pit.

"That's great!" Massaging his beard, the Maharaja let out a grotesquely triumphant scream. "Call the Chief Secretary, I mean our old *Dewan Sahib*, call him immediately! I must now trample the bloated syndicate's vanity in the dirt."

The chief secretary arrived, but he had an expression no more lively than that of a dead *katla* fish. He said, "Bad news!"

"What bad news?"

"The *Kurmis* were logging without a permit. The forest ranger challenged them. The *Kurmis* then beat up the ranger and the guards and drove them out."

"And then?" The Maharaja's jaws tightened.

"Then the police commissioner went in, and ordered the troopers to open fire. It would have been better if blanks were used. Instead, they used *Mungeri* rifles and heavy-duty slugs. Twenty two dead, over fifty wounded. The corpses are still scattered inside the *Ghoraneem* bush."

The Maharaja, quite bewildered, stared blankly for a while. The political agent's note dangled before his eyes like the dazzling, needle-sharp tip of a spear.

"Has the news broken everywhere?"

"I know that the syndicate has heard." The chief secretary replied.

The Maharaja called Mukherjee. "This is the situation, Mukherjee. It's time for you to show your Bengali ingenuity— find us a way out."

After thinking about it for a brief moment, Mukherjee advised the Maharaja, "Please do not delay. Arrest Mahato before you do anything else."

About fifty troopers armed with spears and *lathis* rushed towards Dulal's hut under the cover of night.

Mukherjee said, "I do not feel well, *Sarkar*—I feel kind of nauseous. Please let me go home now."

Pit number fourteen has collapsed. The merchants are very nervous. The ceiling over the third seam was improperly timbered, hence the accident. Mingled with the rocks and debris kicked up by the collapsing pit is a pitiful, intermittent wail—a muffled boom, boom, boom. The quartz pillars have disintegrated under the pressure like exploding firecrackers. Already, the mouth of the pit has been secured with a barbed wire fence.

Groups of *coolies* were rushing in from neighbouring barracks. However, they have been turned back about halfway by the sentries posted near the accident site. "Go back to work; nothing has happened, no one has been injured or killed."

Huddled in the dark some distance away, the merchants are discussing strategies in low voices. Gibson suggests, "There is no way to fill up the pit with dirt—it will continue sinking for two more days. Instead, we must burn the attendance register and prepare a new one with at least a hundred fewer names in it."

McKenna observes, "What good will that do? This must have reached the Maharaja's ear by now. Moreover, how are we going to convince that Mahato chap? By morning tomorrow the city papers will receive the news, and scandal will spew out of the press for days after that. An "inquiry committee" will follow—who knows, a Gandhi-ite scoundrel might even be among its members. Just imagine!"

That night, the lights were not lit inside the clubhouse. Instead, a hundred dazzling electric chandeliers lit up inside a grand hall within the palace. Once more, Mukherjee received a call.

An absolutely unimaginable sight. The Maharaja, the chief secretary and the police commissioner were all there, as were Gibson, McKenna, Moore and Patterson. The vast mahogany table in the middle of the hall was loaded with decanters and glasses.

The Maharaja was unusually gracious as he greeted

Mukherjee. "Mahato has been captured, Mukherjee. Good thing you offered your plan while there was still time."

Gibson nodded in agreement. "Exactly—your plan has saved us from having to deal with a clumsy nuisance. I must say both sides gathered here have been extremely lucky."

Then the police commissioner whispered into Mukherjee's ear the decision and plan of action agreed to earlier by those present at this meeting. Listening to him quietly, Mukherjee became stupefied by what he heard, and the blood drained out of his face. All he managed to do was bury his face in the palms of his hands.

Patting him on the back, Gibson tried to rally him around. "You have to be tough in matters like this, Mukherjee, you must not be nervous."

In the middle of the night, under the cover of darkness, there was once again a gathering of cars and people near pit number fourteen. Guards unloaded Dulal Mahato's corpse, wrapped in blankets, from inside the police commissioner's car. Then, a truckload of corpses arrived from the *Ghoraneem* bush. Carrying the bodies to the cavernous mouth of the collapsing pit, the guards proceeded to assuage its hungry belly.

Mukherjee's eyes were glistening from the mild intoxication of champagne and cigar smoke. As he reclined himself on top of the trunk of his car, he was pondering something else. He was pondering something that occurred perhaps many, many years later.

One hundred thousand years later, in a museum somewhere here on earth, a team of archaeological experts was gazing intently upon a collection of fossils. Half-beastlike, small-brained with suicidal tendencies, these were the fossilized skeletons of their sub-human forefathers. Scattered among the fossils were crude and awkward instruments, such as hammers, drills and picks, made of iron. Perhaps they conclude that on some fateful day in the distant past, an unfortunate group of humans must have become buried inside a quartz and granite cavern during an unexpected geological cataclysm. They gaze at an array of white fossils, inside which not even a trace remains of the bright red blood streaming out of the corpses today.

Ajantrik
The Human and the Android: A Dark Empathy

SUBODH GHOSH

Bimal's stubbornness is perhaps as immutable as his old taxicab's longevity. It is a clunky old Ford, built like a prehistoric beast, bearing palpable, grotesque marks of penury all over its ramshackle body. Other than someone faced with an extreme emergency or who has never before seen a motor car, no one will go anywhere near it.

It looks utterly dilapidated; however, when called upon to get a job done, Bimal's taxi is an amazing performer. Tasks that daunt much larger and stronger automobiles, it can accomplish almost effortlessly. On stormy, tempestuous nights, when every other taxi in this impassable terrain of mica mines will flatly refuse to venture out along the forbidding, pothole-infested tracks twisting through dense forests, only Bimal's ancient jalopy comes forward without a trace of fear. Thus, when all the others have turned down his pleas, and every other option has been exhausted, only then does a would-be rider come to Bimal out of sheer desperation.

At the taxi-stand, parked conspicuously among rows of shiny new models, Bimal's old Ford dozes all day, like *Jatayu* burdened by a hundred ailments. It is a true eyesore if ever there was one. It has a hood with multiple dents and patched-up holes; a broken rear-view mirror; a banged-up trunk; curtains covered with layers of soot, and tires full of cracks and punctures fixed with putty—altogether quite a sight to see. When you set foot inside, the floor squeals pathetically like a stray dog that has been accidentally stepped on. The seats are covered with layers of grease and oil—no well-groomed gentleman would risk sitting on them, no matter how sincerely the owner might plead with him to do so. It takes an incredible amount of effort to get the doors to shut, and, once shut, even more difficult to open again. Once seated, the passenger is greeted in the head and face by Bimal's *gamchha*, his oily wrap, and a couple of his undershirts hanging from the ceiling of the cab.

As soon it hears the ear-splitting roar of Bimal's taxi at a distance, each and every rickshaw instantly dashes for the nearest shoulder of the road. Even otherwise reckless cyclists are sufficiently terrified that they avoid passing Bimal's menacing taxi at all costs. Late at night, every now and then, one may see a bellowing, one-eyed monster barreling down the road towards the observer. The observer must understand that it is Bimal's taxi *sans* a headlight. Adding to all its other terrifying and repulsive features is a wobbly body with joints so loose that it might at any moment disintegrate into a hundred pieces.

Of all the moving objects on the road, it is Bimal's taxi that will kick up the most dust, enrage the largest number of water buffaloes, and create the greatest bedlam. Yet, no one dares complain to Bimal about any of these things. If the unwary or unwise were to do so, he would be rebuffed instantly and resoundingly— "So, the venerable gent *never* does a dirty deed, never screams, never dashes, huh? I suppose it is *my taxi* alone which is to blame for all these faults, huh?"

What variety of ridicule and epithets has this taxi not endured—*buddha ghora*, *khonra hans*, *kana bhains*. However, from Bimal it has received yet another endearing name— *Jagaddal*. This is the name by which Bimal calls it—this mechanical beast, companion of the past fifteen grueling, crazy working years of his life, his servant, his friend, his bread-winner.

It is reasonable to be skeptical—so, *maybe* Bimal calls it by that name, but does he ever get any response? This may be quite difficult for outsiders to comprehend. However, Bimal can read *Jagaddal's* every whim, every desire, every grudge in an instant.

"You are *really* thirsty, isn't that right, *Jagaddal*? That's why you are panting so much—quite out of breath, aren't you? Just wait, dear, just wait." Parking *Jagaddal* under the shade of a large banyan tree, Bimal fetches a cool pail of water from a nearby well, and pours it lovingly into the radiator. *Jagaddal* gulps down four or five pails, making happy, gurgling sounds, then becomes quiet at last, and starts moving again.

Bimal is both the owner and the operator of this amazing taxi. For fifteen straight years they have been together.

In a corner of the taxi-stand, poor old *Jagaddal*, carrying the full burden of old age and its associated ailments, waits for a passenger. Reclining comfortably upon the gray hood of his sleek, newer-model cab, which stands next to *Jagaddal*, Pyara Singh asks Bimal sarcastically, "Why go on like this, Bimal Babu? You should really give your old lady her pension now."

"Oh, sure, and then keep me a glossy new whore, just like you, right?" Bimal immediately retorts. Pyara Singh decides it is quite unnecessary to say another word; after all, if he were to say anything more, it would only provoke Bimal further— he had an uncontrolled, almost primitive kind of rage.

It is *Kartik Purnima*, and a large fair twelve miles away is drawing scores of people from neighbouring villages. At the site of the fair there is a temple containing the sacred image of the deity *Narasimha*. The taxi-stand is crowded with passengers. Soon, all the other taxis load up and depart in a hurry. Finally, the stand is empty except for decrepit old *Jagaddal*, left behind, gasping. Who in their right mind would come to something so prehistoric in appearance, clad in such ancient, outmoded gear?

"*What*, Bimal Babu, you haven't found a *single* rider?" Govinda expresses his sympathy.

"No."

"What then?"

"What indeed! I will get even after dark. I will take double overloads, come what may. I too am a machine—hum, actually, the Bengali Club was right about that." Bimal smiles surreptitiously.

That in fact *Jagaddal* is more like a human, the Bengali Club cannot comprehend this—this is Bimal's principal regret. In this age of cut-throat competition, thrown in with a crowd of vultures, it is after all this decrepit old *Jagaddal* who provides him with two or more rupees at the end of each day. In turn, how little petroleum he consumes! Runs twenty two miles straight per gallon. As if *Jagaddal* truly empathizes with Bimal's desperate penury.

Jagaddal hurtles towards Ranchi with the unbridled pace of an Arabian racehorse. Blessed his stamina, his sprinting ability, his capacity for overload. Bimal holds on to the vibrating steering wheel with his two hands and his chest. He feels the vim and vigour of *Jagaddal's* enlivened spirit. The icy wind of *Magh* slices the skin like blades of steel. Bimal pulls the comforter over his ears and head; he isn't getting any younger—these days, he catches nasty colds rather easily.

An undulating *ghat* appears ahead. So many times *Jagaddal* has growled his way up this steep, long and winding gradient like a furious leopard. This time, too, Bimal pushes down on the accelerator with utmost confidence at the bottom of the gradient. Lunging forward about fifty yards, *Jagaddal* suddenly begins to moan, eliciting a loud, clanging sound. As though a few ribs in his chest have been dislocated. Bimal listens to the moaning intently. No, there is no mistake— *Jagaddal* has a broken piston.

A few days later, a bearing melts unexpectedly in the middle of a trip, causing him to lose a large contract. After that, a new symptom manifests itself just about every day. One problem gets fixed, only to have a new one replace it. One day it is a broken fanbelt, the next day the carburetor malfunctions, and the day after that the spark plugs go dead.

Perhaps Bimal's rock-steady confidence in his machine is

finally shaken a little. He appears uncharacteristically morose several days in a row. He runs frantically from one place to another. *Jagaddal's* legendary punctuality has also been compromised—he misses his attendance at the taxi stand every now and then. Bimal's heart races with anxiety. Will *Jagaddal* really retire after all?

"No, *Jagaddal*, no, I am still here for you. Have no fear, I will definitely nurse you back to health." Bimal, the expert motor mechanic, gives his word of honour.

From the auto suppliers in Calcutta, Bimal orders only genuine replacement parts for *Jagaddal*. New battery, distributor, axle, piston—everything. He spends freely—when necessary, he even telegrams orders in overnight. The repair proceeds all night long—hammering, banging, drilling, changing parts, adding fluids. *Jagaddal's* fallen sick—Bimal has gone insane. Soon he runs out of money—sells his watch, his utensils, and finally even his bed.

He has lost everything—well, so be it. His dearest friend of fifteen years, his *Jagaddal*, will be very happy this time, and recover. Quite a lot has been done, thank God. Now, with only a new hood and a new paint and varnish job he should really look sharp. Bimal's fantasy smiles happily inside his mind.

In the middle of the night, just before locking *Jagaddal* up inside the garage, Bimal raises his lantern for one more look. Happiness oozes out of his eyes at the sight. How well *Jagaddal* wears his new look! A few tireless nights of caring has indeed turned him around—he looks sinuous and powerful. Ready to contend with the rest of the crowd at the wink of an eye. Washing his hands and face, Bimal lies down. He's worked much too hard the last few days. Yet, he feels so contented—

Jagaddal has recuperated; when he will arrive at the stand tomorrow blaring the brand new horns of a rejuvenated *Jagaddal*, how amazed they will all be, and how jealous!

Suddenly, Bimal wakes up with a start. The night is almost over, yet there is an impenetrable darkness. Bimal sits up in a hurry—could *Jagaddal* be soaking in the downpour? The tin roof above the garage is old and badly banged up, it must have a hundred cracks and holes. If any water gets into the engine, heaven help him! Moreover, leaking rainwater will ruin the shiny new coat of paint *Jagaddal* has just received.

Lighting his kerosene lamp, Bimal enters the garage and almost immediately screams—"O god, no! O god, no!" Streams of rainwater are flowing from the holes in the roof directly into the engine. Rushing back to his bedroom, Bimal returns with his waterproof, blanket, bedsheet and *dhurrie*.

Wiping dry *Jagaddal's* wet hood, Bimal covers it with the blanket, then covers the blanket with the waterproof. Wrapping the rest of the car snug with the *dhurrie* and the bedsheet, he climbs inside and curls up comfortably upon the soft new upholstery. Utterly exhausted, he soon falls fast asleep.

This is the history of the following day. An eager crowd gathers at the stand, as if the impossible has happened. An admiring throng stands and ogles the magnificent evidence of Bimal's genius as an auto-mechanic. Bimal, too, grins a few times in return. It is not, however, a transparent smile—it is touched by a tinge of uneasiness.

But why? A nagging suspicion makes Bimal very uncomfortable. *Jagaddal* is running, it is true—but where is his irrepressible agility, his bold and boisterous roar, his impala-like swiftness of motion?

Far from the city, next to an empty field, Bimal gives *Jagaddal* a thorough scrutiny.

"Let's go, *Jagaddal*, old buddy! Let's see you spread your wings like a *pakshi-raj*, come-on, come-on!" Bimal presses the accelerator. But no, it's just no use—*Jagaddal* is too frail and infirm.

Bimal frantically changes gears—first, second, third, back and forth. Then he gets really mad—"I say, move! Move, or I will kick your guts out."

Jagaddal wheezes and gasps as he hobbles along like a rickety old man.

"Goddamn iron-brain, deadbeat zombie, illiterate and pampered bastard!" —livid with anger, Bimal actually kicks the clutch hard, twice.

Bimal's rage intensifies—it is his characteristically wild and uncontrolled rage. He is determined to wrest a final answer from the iron-beast today. Does *Jagaddal* wish to stay or does he want to leave? He has been coddled long enough, no more.

Anger has probably driven him to insanity. Bimal heaves seven or eight massive boulders right up to the car. His *khaki* shirt becomes soaked with perspiration from his exertions. One by one, he loads the great boulders inside his taxi. Now, *this* is a load if ever there was one. *Jagaddal* must transport this load today. Let's see if *Jagaddal* is still up to it, or if he has lost it forever.

"Let's go." *Jagaddal* begins to move. As he moves, every joint inside him begins to moan and groan in agony. He is a total invalid—he will never again carry such a load.

Now Bimal knows for sure. *Jagaddal* is in the vice-like grip of *Yama*. There is no doubt about it. Even *Jagaddal's* strong liver has finally started to rot. It's the call from beyond the grave—nothing can save him now—darkness will soon swallow the dwindling daylight. Bimal's very last *cowrie* was not enough to save his *Jagaddal*.

"Me and me alone, now left to go"—a weary Bimal whispers to himself. "But my days too are numbered. My hair's beginning to turn gray, bluish veins criss-cross my skin like leeches. The day is not far when, like *Jagaddal*, I too will become a limp and pitiful invalid."

Lighting a *bidi*, Bimal quietly gazes at *Jagaddal*. A disturbing void desperately thrashes about inside his mind. "Seems like *Jagaddal* is going to go first. Then it will be my turn. Fine, you go ahead, *Jagaddal*, I let you go without any grudge. You have fed me, clothed me long enough—how much longer can you do that? Don't worry about me, go on—whatever will happen, will happen." Something then happens that had never happened before. Two warm droplets of tear appear in the corners of Bimal's steely cold eyes.

Upon his return, Bimal parks *Jagaddal* under the *bel* tree outside his garage, and steps out. Without looking back, he walks to inner courtyard and sits down with a couple of bottles of distilled *mahua*.

He barely takes a sip, when a voice calls out to him, "Bimal Babu, are you home?" It is Govinda.

Govinda walks in, along with a Marwari gentleman.

"Adaav, Babuji."

"Adaav; so, which car are you the agent of?" Bimal asks. Govinda introduces the visitor and says, "He is not an automobile agent. He has traveled here from Calcutta to buy scrap iron. You have piles of broken axles, rims and other junk, right? Why don't you dispose of them for a fair price?"

For a few moments, Bimal stares blankly at both his visitors. The apparition of inviolable destiny stands hungry before him, extending its begging bowl. It will not be satiated with the ordinary, it must receive the best. Bimal understands.

"Yes, I have scrap iron, lots of it. What is your offer?"

"Fourteen *annas* a *maund*, Babuji." The Marwari replies eagerly. "—The war has started, this is a golden opportunity— sell *everything* you have, Babuji."

"Yes, I *will* give you everything. My car, too. It has become quite useless."

Stunned, Govinda asks, "Good heavens, what are you saying, Babuji?"

After a long sleep, Bimal feels sobre. It still is night— hence, finishing the contents of the second bottle, Bimal lies down again.

Dawn arrives. Bimal has been waking up fitfully all night long. Of all the sounds of the world outside, only one drowns out the rest. It crashes near Bimal's ears: *Cling, Clang, Boom, Boom*. The Marwari's hired hands have arrived early, and have already started to dismantle Bimal's car, piece by piece.

Grief and intoxication. *Jagaddal's* ribs are coming apart, one by one. Bimal's consciousness, too, is swirling down into a bottomless abyss of silence every now and then, only to feel light and airy and float back up again. In between this interminable bobbing and sinking, he hears a relentless *Cling, Clang, Boom, Boom*, as though a team of undertakers is frantically digging a grave for the dead and disemboweled *Jagaddal. Cling, Clang, Boom, Boom*—like the reverberations of a thousand hatchets and shovels.

Ras
Sap

NARENDRANATH MITRA

Around the middle of Kartik, Motalef began tapping the Chowdhurys' *khejur* groves. Then, in less than fifteen days, he came home with Mazu Khatun, widow of his neighbor Razek Mridha, after a hasty *nikah*. The neighbors were befuddled. Not that this was Motalef's first marriage. His first wife had died about a year ago. Then, too, he was a strapping young man of twenty-five or twenty-six. On the other hand, Mazu Khatun was not exactly a young doe—she would be right around thirty. On the plus side, she was not burdened with underage children. She had married her only daughter off to the Sheikhs of Kathikhali. So she was unencumbered, true, but what on earth did she actually *have*, that any able-bodied young man would even be interested? As if Razek Mridha had left behind safes stacked with gold and jewels, or fields laden with bountiful crops for Mazu Khatun to inherit! All she had was a *katha* or so tract of land, her share of Razek's estate, and a ramshackle thatch hut. So much for her inheritence; well, then was there anything particularly angelic about her looks? Other than the robust and tight body of a matronly and quarrelsome woman, what physical charm did Mazu Khatun possess to win the attention of men?

The wives of the Sikdar and Kazi households laughed about the whole matter. "She's cast a spell, the witch! She's sprayed stardust in his eyes," they jeered.

Sakina, the youngest daughter-in-law of the Munshis, observed, "Good for her, if she did. And why not? Men like him deserve to get magic dust sprayed in their eyes. *Khoda* did not give him eyelashes—haven't you seen him stare, that lecher? I'll tell you, she's done a lot of good, if she has done it."

She was not entirely wrong—Motalef *did* have a sly stare. He stared only at pretty faces. His eyes were constantly wandering in search of pretty faces. Until now, he had tried to find a beautiful young girl whom he would bring home as his wife. But in the matter of dowry, he had always fallen short. A household with a young and nubile girl invariably demanded no less than five—or seven-score *takas*. Personally, Motalef had liked Phoolbanu the most. Phoolbanu, the daughter of Elem Sheikh of Charkanda. She was about seventeen or eighteen. The sap of youthful sensuality rippled down her body from head to toe, and she possessed an impetuous mind that matched her restless, blooming body. Of course, Phoolbanu was really second-hand, she had gone around once already. Complaining that he did not feed or clothe her properly, and often beat her up, she finally managed to get the *talak* from Ghafoor Sikdar of Koidubi. Truly, though, it was because she did not like Ghafoor, who was old and ugly. So she had purposely started the quarrels and fights with him for no particular reason. That she was now second-hand, having been with Ghafoor, had not diminished her in the slightest, though. If anything, her physical lustre and charm had only increased, and waves of sensuality flowed in torrents through her mind. Motalef had seen Phoolbanu at the river *ghat* in Charkanda one day. He knew immediately that he, too, had drawn her attention. His own physical charms were not inconsiderable, after all. A deep blue *lungi* would particularly highlight his fair complexion and slim figure; moreover, who else in this neighbourhood could boast such a wavy and curly head of hair parted at an angle? Motalef gauged right away that Phoolbanu had signaled to him her approval. After some inquiring and searching, he had finally arrived at Elem Sheikh's home. Unfortunately, though, Elem did not pay him much attention. He said he had learned his lesson well the first time around. He would never again give his daughter to anyone without a thorough investigation. It was clear to Motalef what Elem really wanted was money. He intended to make up in both principal and interest every last *taka* he had spent in gaining the *talak* for his daughter. He was determined to turn that loss around. Motalef found out that Elem expected not one or two scores of rupees, but as much as five! He would not settle for anything less. Now, where would Motalef get money like that?

Motalef had returned from his failed mission with a long face. Within the dilapidated shed surrounded by wild and overgrown clumps of *ash-sheora* and *chokh-udan*, he saw Phoolbanu once again. She was heading for the *ghat* to fetch water, carrying her clay jar seductively poised against her hip in the manner of village women. Motalef realized immediately that there was something deliberate about her sudden need to fetch water.

Glancing left and right, Phoolbanu smiled. "What, *Mian*, are you going away mad?"

"And why shouldn't I? Didn't you hear what a money-grabbing leech your *Ba-jaan* is!"

" 'Course I've heard. So what if he asked for money? You want to get something from him that you like, and not pay for it?" Phoolbanu replied.

Motalef was even more sarcastic. "Well, well, it seems *Ba-jaan* is not the real money-grabber—it's his beloved *Maiya*. Why don't you stuff yourself in a basket and go get sold in the bazaar."

Watching Motalef get so upset, Phoolbanu started to laugh. "Why just a basket, I will go sit on a balance. You will pile fistfuls of gold and jewels on the balance. Then I will *really* know a man's power; the size of his fist." Motalef was hastily departing. Phoolbanu called him from behind, "*Sondar Mian*, why are you so cross? Now, listen, listen."

Looking back, Motalef asked, "What's there to hear?"

Glancing left and right Phoolbanu stepped a few paces closer. "What else should you hear? You must hear what's from the heart. Listen, *Ba-jaan's* daughter doesn't want *taka*, she doesn't want any gold or jewelry. She only wishes to honor the man who wins her heart. She likes to see his true might and passion—you follow?"

Motalef nodded—yes, he did follow.

Phoolbanu went on, "But don't do anything foolish, *Mian*—don't sell any of your farmland or holdings. You understand?"

The fact is, Motalef had neither any farmland nor holding that he could sell; however, he did not confess as such to

Phoolbanu. Instead, he assured her, "Fine, just let the few winter monhts pass—I will show you both honor and passion. But, I wonder if *Bibi-jaan* will bear to wait that long?"

Laughing, Phoolbanu replied, "Of course. Don't think I am such an impatient *Bibi*."

Back at the village, Motalef made one more effort at getting a loan. He visited the Mallicks, the Mukhujjes, the Sikdars, the Munshis—all to no avail. The trouble with extending credit to Motalef was that when it came to repaying his loan, he was notoriously slow. The lender would have the worst time collecting his dues from him. Who in his right mind would risk the hassle and aggravation?

Nevertheless, even if he could not get a loan, Motalef managed to get contracts to tap as many as a hundred date palms at the beginning of that winter. The total number of trees had been rising since the preceding winter—this time, the thirty trees in the Chowdhurys' groves represented a significant jump in his tapping assignment. His job was to tap the trees, tie pots, and collect the sap. Half the harvest would go to the landlord, the other half to Motalef. It was no easy job. First, he would have to cut off every last dead branch from each and every tree. Then, he would have to sharpen his drill on a grindstone. Then, drilling holes into the tree, he would have to insert thin half-tubes made by splitting slender sticks of cane. Earthenware pots would have to be tied securely at the ends of the tubes. Then, and only then, would the sap drip, drop by drop, into the pot, all night long. It was a lot of work, a lot of backbreaking toil and care. To extract sap from a tough and dry date palm, you have to sweat and labor intensively first. This was not mother's milk, or cow's milk, for that matter, that it would flow freely simply upon contact with a newborn's lips.

Then, too, hard work alone, or tree-climbing skills alone, will not necessarily yield good results. The workman's hands must have very special qualities. The same drill that causes blood to gush out upon contact with human skin, can induce a date palm to release sweet sap simply by the magic touch of the right hands. This is not like harvesting paddy, or jute, that all you do is sweep your sickle over the base of the crops. This is date palm tapping—you must not only cut and drill, you have to soothingly caress the tree also. You have to be careful that the tree is not hurt, that it comes to no harm. The slightest error, and one is destined to visit a dead tree before the next tapping season comes around. The tree may then be good for making the steps of a *ghat* by the riverbank, or the stairs inside a house, but never again will drops of sap drip from it all night long to fill a clay pot.

It was Razek Mridha who had taught Motalef the art and craft of tapping date palms. It was from him that Motalef had learned all these precepts and caveats. There was not another *gaachhi* nearly as well-known or regarded as Razek. His mere touch would coax the sap out of even trees with seventy-five percent dead branches. Trees that would yield maybe half a pot of sap when drilled by any other tapper, would gladly fill Razek's pot neck-high. With Razek in charge of tapping their date palms, householders could rest assured. Their trees would sustain no damage, and sap would fill their pots. Motalef had been an apprentice under Razek for a few years—he would go with him on tapping assignments, and learn his techniques hands-on. Razek had a few other apprentices—the Sikdars'

Maqbool, the Kazis' Ismail. But none of them became as good or seasoned a hand as Motalef. No one else was able to replace Razek as well as he did.

But then it is not enough to simply tap scores of trees, or haul pot-loads of sap hanging from bamboo poles balanced on shoulders—you need skilled hands to boil the sap down to the much-coveted *khejur-gur*. The menfolk are only good at tapping and collecting the sap; the task of preparing the fire pit, collecting kindling, and then boiling and stirring the sap painstakingly over the pit from dawn till midday until it turns into the perfect *patali* belongs to the women. Mere sap is essentially useless—only when the sap turns into *gur*, and the *gur* into cold hard cash, only then does all the hard work become worthwhile. Sadly, though, such a key person has been lacking within Motalef's home for the last two years. His mother died when he was just a little boy; two years ago, his wife died and left a gaping void in his life.

After dusk, Motalef arrived at Mazu Khatun's shack and stood outside her bolted doorway. "Are you awake or what, Mazu Bibi?"

From within, Mazu Khatun inquired, "Who's that?"

"It's Motalef. Are you lying down, then? If you would trouble yourself and unbolt the door, I would like to talk to you."

Rising, Mazu Khatun opened the door. "Of course I know what you want to say. The sap season is here, and now you think of Mazu Khatun. The sap must be boiled, right? But I tell you, *Mian*, I must have four *annas* for every *seer* of sap this time. I won't do it for less. My body doesn't feel any pleasure working this year."

Motalef sounded sweet and comforting. "Can't blame the body, *Bibi*. The body walks hand-in-hand with the mind. The mind's pleasure is also the body's pleasure."

Mazu Khatun was insistent. "I don't care *what* you say, *Mian*. I won't do it for less than four *annas*."

With a seductive smile, Motalef said, "Why stop at four *annas*, Bibi—would you agree to accept a full sixteen *annas* if I made the offer?"

Charmed by Motalef's alluring smile, Mazu Khatun's heart fluttered for a moment. Maintaining her composure, however, she said, "Keep your fun and *tamasha* to yourself, *Mian*. If you want to talk business, fine, or else I will go back in and lie down."

"Of course you will lie down," Motalef said. "The night is *meant* for lying down and sleeping. But, does simply lying down guarantee sleep, Mazu Bibi? Or can you pass the long winter night staring at the ceiling?"

Forgoing the suggestive talk, Motalef now clearly stated what was on his mind. That he had no intention of taking any undue or unfair advantage. That he would summon a *mullah*, and take Mazu Khatun as his wife only after a proper and formal *nikah*. That he wished to hand over to her the full charge of taking care of the household.

Mazu Khatun was at first quite taken aback by Motalef's proposition. Then she rebuked him mildly. "Couldn't you find someone else to joke around with? Why, is there any lack of young and green things around the country that you would come to *my* door?"

Motalef replied, "Why would there be any lack of those, Mazu Bibi? You can find plenty of those young things. But, after all, they are really nothing more than pots of thin and runny sap."

Mazu Khatun was a little amused by his manner. "Oh, is that right? And how about *me?*"

"You are different. You are what one would describe as toddy for a pick-me-up, *gur* for the sweet tooth. Is there *any* comparing you to them?"

Even after she had seen Motalef off, Mazu Khatun found it difficult to banish his words from her mind. As she lay in the dark on her lonesome bed, reverberations of his words tormented and excited her mind. She had known Motalef for a long time. When Razek was still alive, and Motalef worked as his assistant, he would often visit their home. But there was never any particular depth to that acquaintance. Once in a while they would poke some fun and tease each other, but no one had ever thought of going the next step. Motalef had a wife at home, and Mazu Khatun had her husband. Razek was by nature a little rustic and humourless. His words were generally sharp, tough and terse. In winter they would bring pots of sap to Mazu Khatun's yard by the scores. Boiling the sap down, she would turn them into the much—favored *khejur patali*. She sure had the magic touch. Her *patali* would invariably fetch two *paisas* more per *seer* at the market than the next competitor. Since Razek's death, most of the palm groves in the community have been handed over to Motalef for tapping. Sometimes he politely doles out a pot or two of sap as gratis for her to enjoy, but her yard is no longer crowded with pots of sap like before. Last season, Motalef did let her boil sap for a month or so. They had settled for two *annas* per seer as compensation for her labor. However, a month later, Motalef became suspicious that Mazu Khatun was stealing some of the *gur*, and selling it at the market on the sly through someone else. He realized he was not receiving a hundred percent return on his raw material. As a result, they had a few unpleasant exchanges, and eventually the arrangement had to be voided. However, this time around, Motalef had not arrived at her door to propose that she boil pots of *ras* for him—he had in fact come to take *her* to his home. She had received such proposals earlier from other middle-aged suitors in her vicinity, but had paid scant attention to their advances. When any of the younger set had on occasion gone too far in their perverse pursuit of her, she had dissuaded them by threatening to amputate their ears. Motalef's proposal was quite different. She somehow could not write him off just like that. Even if she tried to brush him off her mind, she could not brush away his words. No one else in the area could speak as well as he did; no one else had either a face as handsome, or a flair for words that matched his looks.

Thereafter, Motalef paid her a couple more visits, and then, decked in a sky-blue *zulahki sari*, arms adorned with multihued glass bangles, Mazu Khatun followed Motalef to his house.

His home had not the slightest order or grace—everything in it was disorganized and covered in dust. Tying her *anchal* around her waist, Mazu Khatun went to work. With repeated applications of her broom, she swept away the trash from the yard. Scrubbing, washing and polishing the floors, she made them look glossy and lustrous.

But Motalef had no time to notice his home or homemaker; his refuge was up in the trees. He had taken charge of a number of new tree-tapping jobs in the area—he now had the contract to tap the Bose and Banrujje orchards as well. He was busy making incisions, hanging the pots, bringing the pots down, and dividing the sap. He had unloaded a stack of jute twigs in the western end of his yard—kindling for Mazu Khatun. Digging a row of pits and lighting the fires, Mazu Khatun boiled the sap in large clay cauldrons from morning till noon. Motalef brings her bundles of dry hay from time to time to replenish her fuel supplies; sometimes he gets her dry branches of date palm. But it is never enough. And so Mazu Khatun sweeps up dry, withered leaves from the jungle and people's gardens, and carries them home in wicker baskets. When evening arrives, she sits by the doorway and cuts twigs and branches into small pieces with a cleaver, stacking them for her fuel reserves. She works non-stop, without any rest, and doesn't feel the least bit weary—after quite a long while, she has found the kind of work she likes, and a man after her heart.

Motalef carries basket-loads of *gur* to the bazaars and farmers' markets, and sells his wares at highly profitable prices. His is the best *gur* in the bazaar. Then, when the daylight begins to fade, he gathers up his possessions, and heads back to the orchards to hang up more pots for sap. Little bamboo cones dangle from the trees. When the pots are full, he hauls them down from the trees, and then ties the cones below the sap incisions. Dirty sap drips out of the incisions all through the day and collects in the cones below. When he returns from the marketplace at the end of the day, he removes the cones, peels off the bark from a part of the tree-trunk, and hangs up his pots again. The dirty sap is not to be thrown out—by boiling it down, you get sticky, low-grade *gur* good for the tobacco pipes. This, too, you can sell at the market for five or six *annas* a seer. Climbing up and down from this many trees twice each morning and afternoon, Motalef becomes greatly overworked. His breath is fast and furious, and streams of perspiration roll down his entire body even in the heightened cold of *Poush*. In the morning sun, the drops of sweat glisten upon his hairy chest. Below his feet, the dewdrops from the night before glisten upon the young blades of grass. Watching him work, the neighbors are filled with amazement. True, Motalef had always been very hardworking; however, he had never before been seen working with such unabated enthusiasm, and with such machine-like intensity and vigour. What was going on? Of course, he had always enjoyed tapping the palm trees, but could it be that this time he also found the woman of his dreams to share his home?

Bearing two pots of the sweetest sap from the best tree in the grove, and about three *seers* of premium *patali gur*, Motalef appeared one day at the home of Elem Sheikh in Charkanda. After offering him a *salaam*, Motalef placed the pots and the *gur* at Elem's feet. Then, extracting five ten-rupee notes from the knot at the end of his *lungi*, he said, "This is an advance for half the payment, Mian Saheb."

Elem asked, "Whatever for?"

Motalef replied, "For your *maiah*—"

He had brought crisp, freshly minted bills. Not a tear in any corner, not a trace of grime from soiled hands. Fifty rupees in cold hard cash. Caressing the notes with his fingers, Elem said, "But what will I do taking advance from you *now*, Mian? I hear you have already married Razek Merdha's widow. Why should my *maiah* go live with a *sateen*? Must she go there and kill herself yelling and screaming, pushing and shoving day and night?"

Smiling demurely, Motalef said, "Why do you worry about that, Mian Saheb? Mazu Khatun will be with me only as long as there is any *ras* left in the trees, and any chill is still felt on the skin. It will all clear out as soon as the southern breeze begins to blow."

Elem Sheikh offered him a footstool, then extended his *hookah* to him. Praising his visitor, he observed, "You have the right stuff in your brain, Mian. You are good to talk to, and work with."

Motalef even wangled from his willing host permission to see Phoolbanu with his own eyes before departing. Now, of course, Phoolbanu was well aware of everything that had gone on from behind the scenes. Yet, facing him, she puckered her lips and complained, "So now who was the impatient one, Mian? Here *I* waited, staring at the road, and *you* went ahead and took someone else home?"

"What else could I do?" Motalef tried to defend himself.

He had to come up with this trick simply driven by the demands of honor and even survival. Without someone home to offer him food and water, how would he survive? Without someone home, who would boil the *ras* and make *gur* for him? Moreover, how else could he preserve his reputation if he did not sell *gur* at the market and bring money home?

Phoolbanu nodded understandingly, and asked, "So maybe you kept your honour and your life, but how do you propose to rid yourself of the odour you picked up from someone else?"

Even if he thought about it, Motalef could not bring himself to tell Phoolbanu that when a person went away, their odour did not really cling to their paramour. If that were so, then surely the same would have happened to Phoolbanu herself. Instead, he put a different twist on the matter. "Why worry about odors, Phool Bibi? I will buy soda and soap from the market. I will sit at the *ghat* with you, dangling my feet from the steps. You can scrub me all over and wash away all bad odors."

Stifling a giggle with her *anchal*, Phoolbanu said, "Is that true?"

"Why, do you think it is false? You can take a whiff then and discover the pleasure of a new-found scent from a new-found man. A magical scent, carried by the southern breeze, wafting from hair and flowers. But you must wait another two months."

Phoolbanu reassured him again, "Don't think of me as *bey-saboor*."

Motalef was a man of his word—Phoolbanu did not have to wait more than two months. As soon as he had sold enough *gur* to collect another fifty rupees, Motalef pronounced *talak* on Mazu Khatun. With great gusto he announced to the neighbors why such a drastic step was necessary—Mazu Khatun was a woman of questionable temper and character. Her flirtatious overtures towards Razek's older brother Wahed Mridha were decidedly offensive.

Mazu Khatun bit her lips and said, "Oh, shame, what a shame! Only your body is *sondar*, Moti Meyan, but your inside is not so *sondar*. Such wickedness, such deceit dwells in your mind? As long as you needed your *gur*, you stuck to me like an ant, and now that you are done with the *gur*, it's *out*, it's *get lost!*"

Motalef, however, did not have the time or the patience to listen to her extended reproach.

The mango trees soon filled up with blossoms; new, copper-hued leaves sprouted on the branches of the *gaab* trees. Spring followed winter, Phoolbanu followed Mazu Khatun. A face pretty as a flower. There was a floral scent in her breath. The neighbours said, "Yes, now *this* is a real match. This time his home has really bloomed."

Unbounded thrills permeate Motalef's mind. All day long he works as apprentice to the farmers. But as soon as evening arrives, he rushes back to Phoolbanu and tugs at her *anchal*. "Let go of your cooking and all that household *gerhastha* stuff. Come sit here with me."

Phoolbanu smiles. "Patience, patience. How did you spend these last months, *Meyan?*"

"With the *khejur* trees, of course." Motalef answers.

Almost suffocating in his arms, Phoolbanu catches her breath and says, "Why don't you go back to your trees. Only a *gaatchh* can bear the embrace of a *gaatchhi*."

Motalef tells her, "But you know that even for a *gaatchhi*, the sap from the *gaatchh* flows only for a few months before drying up. But *Phooljaan*, the sweet sap emanating from you flows round the year."

Mazu Khatun had returned back to Razek's dilapidated old thatch hut. She had hopes that her days would pass like they did before. But now, even if her days would somehow pass, her nights would not. Motalef had ruined her life. Her neighbors walk in constantly and describe in vivid and elaborate detail Motalef and Phoolbanu's life together. Sometimes they seem to rebuke the excessive passion of the couple. "That man is simply obsessed with his wife. It's always something or the other about his pretty wife, no matter where he goes. He's gone crazy; can't talk about anything else."

Mazu Khatun burns up inside. She feels like she will be driven insane. That she will die of a bursting heart.

A few days later, it was Razek's older brother Wahed himself who brought in a proposal to her. Watching her misery had filled him with great compassion. Wahed was a good friend of Nadir Sheikh who lived in Talkanda across the river. Nadir was boatman of one of those ferryboats that transport people in the rainy season. His poor wife had died of cholera about a month ago. She had left behind a brood of minor children. Nadir had fallen into a major crisis with his dependent brood. He does not care for pretty young things. A pretty young thing would likely just sit around doing her makeup; she wouldn't care for the children in the least. Therefore, he would prefer an older, more mature woman like Mazu Khatun with considerable household experience. He could rely on someone like her.

"How old is he?" Mazu Khatun wanted to know.

"Well, he must be like one of us—fifty, may be one and fifty." Wahed replied.

Pleased, Mazu Khatun nodded her head. Yes, this is what she wants, too. She does not trust the young—she has lost her faith in youth.

Then she asked, "I hope he is not a *gaatchhi*? I hope he does not go tapping *khejur* trees in winter?"

Perplexed, Wahed replied, "Why would he tap *khejur* trees?

He knows nothing about tapping. He rows his boat during the rainy season. In winter he works for the farmers, and does odd jobs. Why, *bou*, are you not going to sit in *nikah* with anyone other than a *gaatchhi* or a *ras* trader?"

Mazu Khatun's answer was exactly the opposite. If she were to sit in *nikah* with anyone at all, it would have to be someone who had nothing whatsoever to do with *ras*, who does not go anywhere near the *khejur* grove in winter. She has developed a great revulsion towards the *ras* trade.

Wahed asked her, "Then should I go talk to Nadir? He doesn't want to wait too long."

Mazu Khatun replied, "Why wait? Go right ahead."

It did not take long. Within a week or so, everything was settled. One day Mazu Khatun went on board Nadir's ferryboat. They crossed the river.

Motalef said to his wife, "Good riddance, for sure. All she did was breathe fire on me like a *petni*, and swear and cuss all day. At least now I am finally free from her grip, right, *Phooljaan*?"

Smiling, Phoolbanu asked him, "So are you *really* afraid of *petnis*, Meyan?"

Motalef replied, "No, not anymore. After all, the *petni* just left me. Now all I see when I open my eyes is an angel. It's the angel I now fear."

"Why, what do you have to fear an angel for?"

"And why not? Who knows when she might spread her wings and take flight?"

Phoolbanu answered, "No, Meyan, the angel has no wish to take flight any longer. She has found everything she wanted. All she hopes for is that her man goes on focusing all his attention on her like this."

"As long as he has eyes, his attention will not stray." Motalef reassured her.

Motalef pampers his wife extravagantly night and day. Every day before going to the *haat*, he finds out what particular kind of fish she would prefer that day; then, if he happens to be running low on cash, he borrows from a friend to buy her favourite fish. Likewise, he regularly buys the freshest eggs, vegetables and other produce from the marketplace. And without exception, he brings home from the *haat* his wife's daily *paan*, *supari*, *khayer*, and *masala*.

Phoolbanu objects, "Why do you get so much *paan*? You are not particularly fond of it. All you do is smoke your tobacco pipe, *gurgle, gurgle*."

Motalef tells her, "I get the *paan* for you. You must chew *paan* all day, chew enough to colour your lips scarlet."

Pouting, Mazu Khatun complains, "Why, are my lips not naturally red, that I must chew *paan* to color them? Instead, I say why don't *I* dress *paans* for you, so you can start chewing regularly. Your lips have turned black from tobacco, why not color them with *paan* juice?"

Motalef laughs and tells her, "A man's lips do not turn scarlet only from *paan* juice, *Phooljaan*; they require the touch of another's *paan*-stained lips."

Motalef did not have any tract or arable land of his own. He usually tilled some of the Mallick and Mukhujje holdings as a hired hand. Unfortunately, though, he was not as well known as a farmer as he was as a tapper. Therefore, the size of the land he tilled, and the harvest the landowner reaped were not as impressive as those of some other hired farmers. He would also serve as a farmhand for the Sikdars and the

Munshis—cut, stack, soak and wash their jute harvest, then spread the jute out to dry. It was backbreaking work. His fair complexion darkened from sunburn.

He rarely gets to keep any portion of the harvested jute. The Sikdars and Munshis pay him cash for his work. The only exception to the relatively meagre payment for his toils is the half-share he is allowed to keep of the pre-soaked jute harvested from the four *bighas* or so belonging to the Mallicks and the Mukhujjes. This he loads in the boat and hauls to the bank of the canal. Phoolbanu really gets very excited separating the outer strands of soaked and cleaned jute. Motalef does not approve of her handling the jute. "It'll make you sore, and you will stink all over," he warns her.

Phoolbanu protests. "So what? Here you are, getting darker every day from the sun, and *I* can't handle the jute, *I* will be sore! How can you say such a thing, *Meyan*?"

Their portion of the jute harvest is rather meager; not enough to get a decent quantity of kindling from the stripped jute. Phoolbanu wishes to strip the soaked jute for other households—that way, she would collect a lot more kindling. But Motalef disapproves. He will not let his wife toil and endure so much pain.

Near the end of *Ashwin*, the *aush* paddy ripens and is ready for harvest. Motalef usually crosses the river in someone else's boat to work as a farmhand on someone else's tract. Wading waist-deep in the water, he cuts the paddy. He loads bundle after bundle of paddy into the boat. Unfortunately, though, he cannot run the sickle as quickly as Momin, Karim, Hamid or Aziz. He has a rather slow hand, and he is very uncomfortable in the water. Some days he comes home with eeches stuck to his back and under his arms. Plucking them off, Phoolbanu complains, "Can you not even remove the leeches, *Meyan*, did you not have your arms with you?"

Motalef, replies, "Yes, I had my two paddy-cutting hands with me, but I had left my leech-removing hands home."

Phoolbanu gently applies quicklime to the puncture wounds made by the leeches. Motalef joins five other farmers to beat the paddy stalks; his reward is a fifth of the haul. He brings home his share loaded in cane baskets. Phoolbanu puts the paddy out in the sun, then winnows it on *kula* trays. Sometimes Motalef sympathizes with her, "It's too hard on you, right, *Bou*?"

Phoolbanu tells him, "Oh, sure, it's just killing me, isn't it? Whom are you talking to, *Meyan*? Am I not a *gerhastha* girl, or did you think I fell here straight from the sky?"

Spring passes, then the monsoon, followed by *Ashwin* and *Kartik*. Then, rounding out the cycle of seasons, winter returns. The *ras* season is Motalef's season of the year. This year, though, winter seems to have arrived a little late. It doesn't matter, however; Motalef plans to make up for the delay by taking out contracts to tap more trees than ever before. The number of date palm trees keeps going up every year. Motalef has quite a name in the village in this line of work; in this, he is undoubtedly the best. As expected, the *Banrujjes* extended their contract this year by a score and a half.

It seems like a tapping festival. Motalef has not a moment to spare, or to rest. He has no time to while away in lighthearted banter with Phoolbanu. He has to pay off his yearly debts, and hoard supplies and rations for the coming year by selling *ras* and *gur*. He works like a demon all day, then, with leaden eyes, falls fast asleep the instant he lies down in bed at night. Phoolbanu pushes him with both her hands, wraps her arms around him, but it feels like she is not holding a person, but a tree-trunk. Motalef sleeps like a log. No other limb in his body elicits any response except for his snoring nose. Wrapped inside the thick quilt, Phoolbanu shivers in the chilly night. Without human warmth, how can a quilt alone fend off the icy chills?

Now, it is not enough to bring home the sap; they must also have the fuel to light the fire to boil it. Motalef runs around everywhere trying to fetch dry twigs and straw. He instructs Phoolbanu, "Boil the *ras*—the *gur* should turn out as sweet as your dainty hands. The product must be the best and most desired *gur* at the marketplace."

However, looking at the huge loads of *ras* in vast arrays of pots makes Phoolbanu's heart sink, and a pall of fear clouds her expression. She had boiled down maybe one or two pots of *ras* previously in her father's home, but she had never before *seen* this many pots of sap together, much less boil sap in such enormous quantities.

Noticing her obvious misgivings, Motalef reassures her, "Have no fear—I will be around in case you need any help. If you need instructions, just ask me about it—I will tell you what you need to do. Remember, like the *ras* churns and gurgles in your mind, so too must it inside the pot."

Sitting before the fire from morning till noon, however, it is only the *ras* inside Phoolbanu's mind that begins to dry up, and the fire starts to spend itself out. Yet, the *ras* inside the pot does not seem to bubble with sufficient vigour. As she sits before the fire all afternoon, her face begins to look worn out, and her beauty begins to get charred. Yet, the *gur* does not turn out to be up to the mark. Sometimes it feels soft and soggy; at other times, it becomes burnt and bitter.

Irritated, Motalef complains in a rude voice, "What kind of woman *are* you, pray? I explain everything to you in such detail, and you can't follow a thing! You call this *gur*, huh— you think people will buy *this* for good money?"

Phoolbanu tries on a weak smile, and says, "Why won't they? They *will* buy, if only you know how to sell."

Motalef is not amused. He tells her, "Fine, then *you* go sit there with the *dhama*. You go do the selling. Maybe they'll buy some staring at your pretty face; I'm sure they won't buy *any* if they look at the *gur*."

Now, Phoolbanu was no fool, nor was she lazy or useless. After a few days of sincere coaching and determined trials, she learned how to make *gur* of at least passable quality. The sales improved at the market. But it doesn't fetch quite the same value as last year; the customers are not as pleased with the product.

The old, familiar customers alternately stare at the *gur* and at Motalef's face, as if in disbelief. "What kind of *gur is* this, Miyan? I bought some at last week's *haat*—didn't taste *anything* like last year's. The taste from last year still lingers on my tongue, still hovers around my lips. But not this year's. This year Chhadan Sheikh and Madan Sikdar's *gur* tastes much better."

Motalef burns up inside, he simmers with rage. His *gur* this year does not taste as good as it did last year. Why, it is not like he is working less hard, or toiling with any less intensity. Then why does his *gur* not taste as good, why does it not fetch as good a price, why are people not as pleased, why are they not showering him with compliments? Why is *he* having to listen to such words of disapproval, why indeed?

Lying in bed at night, he related the boiling trick to Phoolbanu one more time. "Check the drops from the ladle to see if the *gur* is ready, if it is time to pour the molten *gur* and let it solidify."

Bored and irked, Phoolbanu tells him, "Oh, sure, I know, I know. Now please stop babbling and let people get some sleep."

Suddenly Motalef remembered Mazu Khatun. How often he had discussed *ras* and *gur* with her in bed at night! She had never, ever, answered him back in this fashion. She had never snapped at him so brusquely, never complained about loss of sleep; in fact, she had always listened to him eagerly, and talked happily till quite late.

The next day, around noon, Motalef came home unexpectedly with a large load of firewood on his head. Dumping the load near the shack of twigs where they boiled the *ras*, he inquired, "How is today's *gur* turning out, *Phooljaan*?"

But no sound came from within the shack. He called her a second time; then, not hearing anything, he peeked inside. Phoolbanu was not there. A strange smell wafted out of the shack—could the *gur* be burning inside the boiling pot? *Ras* was boiling furiously inside five large pots set up in a row. Motalef moved in to take a closer look. It was just as he had feared. The *ras* in the pot at the southernmost end of the row had somehow boiled a little too long, and was beginning to burn and stick. A sharp burning odour emanated from inside it. Motalef felt a searing agony inside his chest, and let out a piercing scream, "Where, where the hell *are* you, bitch?"

Phoolbanu emerged from within the room in a hurry. Having worked till rather late in the day, she had been unable to bathe for two days in a row. To go without bathing in winter makes one's skin feel dry and flaky—she did not like the feeling. Therefore, she had gone to the *ghat* early today, and scrubbed and cleaned herself with soap and soda. After her bath, she had wrapped herself in a sea-blue *sari*. Wringing her hair with a *gamchha*, she was running a comb through it, when, hearing Motalef's angry scream, she rushed right out, comb in hand. Her wet hair fell in a heap over her back. Motalef stared at her for a split second with fiery eyes, then rushed over and grabbed the cascading stack of wet hair in his fist. "Wretched bitch! You wouldn't notice that the *gur* is burning up, would you? You don't give a damn, do you—you would rather go out and while away the time looking like a fairy princess, my sweet *Vidyadhari*, right? This is why my *gur* turns out so bad; why I get heaped with insults; why my reputation is in the gutter across the village! All because of you, witch!"

Phoolbanu protested, "I'm warning you, don't you dare touch my hair, don't you dare lay a hand on me!"

"Ah—so it is *so demeaning* for you to be beaten by bare hands!" Picking up a slender whip from the floor, Motalef began to strike Phoolbanu all over with unrelenting ferocity. "Horsewhipping will not be quite so dishonourable for the *Sheikh's* daughter, will it? The dishonour is in the hands—but there is no dishonor in a *kanchi*, is there?"

Motalef was an ill-tempered man. His rage was as

uncontrolled and irrational as his romantic obsession and possessiveness.

Upon hearing the news, Elem Sheikh arrived from Charkanda. He warned, chided and reprimanded his son-in-law. He did not spare his daughter a few harsh words, either.

Phoolbanu said to him, "Ba-jaan, take me with you. I will not set up house with such a stubborn brute."

Nevertheless, Elem cajoled her patiently, and left her with Motalef. He was afraid that Phoolbanu would ask for a *talak* again at the slightest provocation. But then, was it a good thing for a householder to change homes and partners so often? Would that be good for her honor, or her family's? If she would wait a short while, surely Motalef would soften up again, and they would get along once more. After all, this was a husband-wife spat. Ignites during the daytime, cools off at night. Was that something to worry about!

And cool off it did. Shortly, Motalef himself made a move toward reconciliation. He sweet-talked Phoolbanu to break her resistance. The next day, Phoolbanu once again sat herself in front of the large fires, tending to the boiling *ras*. In the afternoon, Motalef gathered the *gur* in the cane baskets and carried his cargo to the *haat*. On his way to the market, he told her, "If you can only hold on for these two months, *Phooljaan*, your hardship will be over."

Phoolbanu replied, "What hardship?"

It was only a civil and polite exchange; the words did not emanate from their hearts. It was as though they could no longer speak their mind. Words meant sincerely are of a different kind; they even sound different. It was not like they did not know how to recognize such words—they were spoken from, as well as understood within the heart.

Haat after *haat* passed by; the *ras* season ran its course, and before long another arrived. Motalef was unable to regain the reputation he had earned for his *gur*. He would not, however, argue with Phoolbanu about it any longer. Instead, he would only sit quietly in a corner and smoke his *hookah*. Meanwhile, the *ras* would continue to collect, droplet by droplet, inside the pots tied to the date palms. Each morning, Motalef would climb the trees to bring down the large pots of *ras*. Yet, it seemed that he did not have the same zest or passion as in the previous year. This year, too, his body would be covered in sweat from the toil—but his mind would feel dry as kindling, desolate as the afternoon sun. It was as though there was not the slightest *ras* anywhere in his life. His yard was filled with vast pots of *ras*; a nubile woman brimming with *ras* moved about within his home—yet, somehow he felt dissatisfied; somehow the world felt empty.

One day at the *haat* he ran into Nadir Sheikh from across the river.

"Salaam—Meyan Sa'ab."

"Aleikum Aslam."

Motalef inquired, "Everything going well, I hope—the young ones doing fine—?"

He almost brought up Mazu Khatun's name, but could not bring himself to do so. With half a smile, Nadir replied, "Yes Meyan, they are all fine. By Khoda's grace the days are passing off somehow."

With some hesitation Motalef said, "Why not take a seer or two of *gur* for the young ones, Meyan. It's really high grade."

Smiling, Nadir said, "I *know* that, of course. Your *gur* is *always* high grade."

Almost by accident, the words escaped Motalef's lips, "No, Meyan, those days are no more."

Perplexed, Nadir stared at him for a moment. What kind of a merchant was this? Who on earth would come to the *haat* to sell his *gur*, and then berate it before the customer?

"How much are you asking?" Nadir wanted to know.

"You mustn't care about the price. Here's two *seers* of *gur* for your children. Tell them, it's a gift from their *chacha*."

Embarrassed, Nadir protested, "Oh, no, no, how can it be, Meyan—it's your sale item, how can I accept it without a price?"

Motalef reassured him, "Fine, why don't you take it home with you this time—taste it, and maybe pay me at the next *haat*."

As he spoke, Motalef felt choked by his own words. This year, as in the preceding one, he once again had to resort to a deceitful sales tactic like this—bragging about the quality of his *gur* before a customer, even though he was himself convinced that having tried it, the customer would never buy his *gur* at the next *haat*. In fact, there would be hardly anyone lining up in front of his *dhama*.

After much pleading and protesting, Nadir agreed to accept a *seer* of *gur* without payment. For the remaining two *seers*, he forced Motalef to accept payment on the spot.

Back home, Mazu Khatun was incensed to hear everything. "If *you* wish to feed that *gur* to the children, go ahead—but I am telling you, I will not *touch* that infernal thing with my hands. I swear, or I am not the daughter of such a *baap*!"

Another *haat* passed by; Nadir did not get anywhere near Motalef's *gur*. Mazu Khatun had warned him in no uncertain terms, "If you get chummy with that man again, I will leave this house. You will not see me again in the morning."

Deep down, Nadir was very scared of his wife. She was very deft at work, and equally pleasant to talk to; however, if she were to become upset, watch out! There was no telling what she might do.

A few days later, Motalef rose early in the morning, and, collecting two pots of the very best *ras* from two of the very best trees, went to the riverbank and boarded a ferryboat. Later, walking past the bushy plum tree, he arrived at Nadir's front yard. "Meyan, are you home?"

Hookah in hand, Nadir emerged from within. "Who is it? Oh, it's you! Of course, please come on in, please. Now, why have you brought *ras* again, Meyan?"

He received Motalef warmly, no doubt, but within his heart Nadir felt rather worried about Mazu Khatun. Someone is right here at his doorstep the mention of whose very name is intolerable to her. Who knows what scandal might come out of this!

And it turned out to be exactly that. Peeking from behind the bamboo shutters, and noticing Motalef outside, Mazu Khatun summoned Nadir inside, and, speaking in a voice loud enough for Motalef to hear, told him, "Ask him to leave this house right now, ask him to step down. Does he not have the slightest shame? How *dare* he shows up here?"

Nadir tried to hush her up. "Speak softly, Bibi, turn down your voice. He will hear you. Someone has come here on a visit, is this any way to talk about them? People don't chase away even cats and dogs so rudely."

Mazu Khatun replied, "You won't understand, Mian—

there are people worse than cats and dogs out there. People worse than Satan himself. Go ask him, now that he has brought me *ras* to please me and win my sympathy—does he not have *any* apprehension, *any* embarrassment in his devious mind?"

Mazu Khatun did not make any effort to speak in whispers; Motalef heard her every word. Yet amazingly, even language this harsh did not seem to hurt him noticeably; if anything, even her rebuke and reprimand seemed to be mixed with an element of sweetness. Even from within her raspy and jarring voice, there seemed to emerge the hurtful plea of a betrayed and wronged woman. As if drops of *ras* were oozing out of the pierced tree trunk through a tube.

Stepping on the portico, Motalef put down the pots of *ras*, and said, "Will you listen for a second, Meyan Sa'ab?"

Embarrassed, Nadir came out and said, "Pray have a seat, Meyan, have a seat. Here, smoke a little tobacco."

Motalef extended his hand and took the *hookah* from Nadir. However, he did not immediately begin smoking; instead, he looked at Nadir and said, "Would you tell Bibi something for me?"

Nadir replied, "Why don't you say it yourself—there's nothing wrong with that."

Motalef insisted, "No, please, you tell her for me. I no longer have the right to talk to her. Tell her Motalef Meyan did not bring the *ras* to win any points from her—he has at least that much sense."

Before Nadir could say a word in response, Mazu Khatun rejoined from within, "Then why did he bring it, what for?"

Still staring at Nadir, Motalef said, "Tell her he has brought it to have her make two *seers* of *gur* for him from the *ras*. Motalef Mian will carry that *gur* to the *haat* on the top of his head. He will sell that *gur* to his customers. This year he has not sold even a *chhataak*'s worth of premium *gur* at the *haat*. All his tree climbing and back breaking work has been for nothing." His voice began to choke up. Getting his voice back in control, he was about to say something more, when he noticed from between the bamboo shutters two dark eyes on the brink of tears. He stared at those eyes without another word.

Finally, Nadir Sheikh suddenly came to his senses. "What is that, Meyan, you are only holding the *hookah* in your hand—you have not smoked any tobacco at all. Has the fire gone out, or what?"

Placing his mouth over the *hookah*, Motalef simply answered, "No, *Meyan Bhai*, it has not gone out."

Ekti Shatrur Kahini
The Adversary

NARAYAN GANGOPADHYAY

Donalds, the senior padre, is getting old. His hair has turned gray, his beard cottony white. In his better days, he could ride a mule thirty miles almost effortlessly, now he runs out of breath after walking only a few steps. He has already been to the city once to consult the civil surgeon. The doctor has warned him of an elevated blood pressure, and advised him to be cautious.

He must be cautious, that's good advice, but where is the opportunity? This, after all, is the most exasperating, inhospitable place one can imagine. There are no railway lines within a ten-mile radius. The state of the local roads is just as pathetic. The office of the district board is connected by the lone paved roadway about eight miles away from the padre's residence; it may have been constructed in the early days of British rule. It has not been serviced since. The crumbling roadway, riddled with countless potholes and fractures, pounded upon by caravans of bullock carts, now descends into sharp slopes on both embankments. In summertime, pedestrians stumble with every step, and get enveloped by the dust right up to the waistline. The rainy season turns the dust into enormous swamps of mud—an elephant, if trapped, could never be rescued.

Beyond the roadway, nothing but endless fields. Outside of a few thin fertile stretches of green laden with crops, they are mostly arid—no one bothers to plow the *ahalya* soil—the stony earth lies unconscious.

Scattered within the desiccated terrain are slender, muddy filaments—these get so slick with the slightest rain that a single step will instantly guarantee a horizontal state under gravity.

Yet, one must travel along these very roads. This region has no topographical order whatsoever—tiny, fragmentary villages are separated without any proportion. The spaces between them have been made more impenetrable by the rough and bumpy terrain, scattered hillocks, ponds, marshes, dense thickets, and innumerable varieties of venomous snakes.

But, he who has been illuminated within by the cleansing light of knowledge, whose one unwavering mission is to bring unto others the hallowed rays of that light, cannot let himself be dissuaded by these obstacles. Until now, Donalds had never let them. Then, when his close-cropped beard was dark as midnight, his spine straight as an iron rod, his weight in excess of two hundred pounds, his patience unsurpassed by human capacity, his voice uncommonly powerful. Standing in the midst of the village fair, when he would thunder, "Then came the imponderable deluge, the earth was submerged in water, thunderclaps sounded and resounded repeatedly, and it felt like the apocalypse...," the power of his voice would drown out the din of the marketplace. Within moments, a crowd would gather around him, and there would be a stampede of eager buyers elbowing and jostling amongst themselves for a copy of the gospels due to Matthew and Luke at one paise apiece.

But that Donalds is today a thing of the past. Twenty years in this searing land, its scorching winds, and its crimson, rocky terrain has aged him by forty. His heart now begins to race with no more than a few paces—he can no longer muster the will to roam from village to village, fair to fair, drawing non-believers to the Kingdom of the Light. He is constantly wary of the blood pressure threat, finding it impossible to ignore the fatal darts of that invisible foe.

Hence, one day relief appeared at his doorstep in the person of Hans.

He was German. Golden blond hair, deep blue eyes; in height tall even for the purest Aryans, thus appearing slightly stooped. About twenty three or four in age, energetic, agile, enthusiastic. Looked hardly like a padre—one would think a University Blue had been somehow sent off to this snake-filled wilderness in the guise of a padre. That monk's apparel he wore looked like something he would cast off any minute and burst out laughing.

But Donalds was very pleased. He said, "Young man, I believe you can do a lot for me."

Hans replied without any hesitation, "I believe so too."

"Indeed!"—Donalds smiled, "I am glad to hear that. You will see, it is nearly impossible to manage these pagans and heathens. I have tried my best these twenty years, and still failed to make good humans out of them. Now you must carry on the effort."

"Everything will be just fine, don't worry about a thing," Hans answered eagerly.

Most of the vast field is barren, strewn with tons of pebbles and stone chips. The entire field drowns under the monsoon torrents every year; only a spot or two of higher ground, with perhaps a minuscule village riding on it like the back of a tortoise, remain visible. The majority of the inhabitants of this unforgiving, temperamental land are Turis, Mundas, and Santals. Tribes of vagabonds and nomads have made the lifeless land their own—in places tilled the soil, developed farmland, and built humble dwellings. The Christian padres have arrived here with the mission of initiating them to the doctrine of love.

In these twenty years they should all have ascended from darkness to light. But that had not happened. First of all, you cannot expel Satan from all stricken souls; secondly, it is beyond even the Merciful Father to comprehend the whims and mentalities of these utterly disorganized and primitive people. Here today; tomorrow they may simply band together, beat their *madals*, sound their flutes, and disappear. And thirdly, to be baptized today, and to joyfully worship *Bownga* tomorrow does not cause them the slightest moral dilemma. Around them, holy work has no room for rest.

Besides, the soil being dead does not, in any way, hinder the currents of human life. The currents flow relentlessly. If three households chose to fly the coop and vanished out of sight today, you may be sure that five new ones will take their place tomorrow. Should the landowner extend his tax-craving, avaricious hand, someday these, too, will likely disappear, but that will not affect the influx of new residents in the least, nor will it reduce the workload of the missionary. Donalds has found new vistas of work regularly for twenty years, the waves of living humanity in the midst of the stark barrenness of the place have crashed around him every single day. Sometimes he has felt despondent, as though all this added up to nothing more than striking at a steel-armoured battleship—it made some sound, but did not even leave a scratch. In all these years, he has not been able to send more than fifty boys off to their city school—so much for the power of his illuminating sermons. But, missionaries cannot lose faith—be patient, and your efforts will find fruition, this is their fundamental *mantra*.

Unto him that you bestow your standard. Therefore, Hans now had to carry the burden of Donalds' unfinished work upon his shoulders. Then one day, as was customary, Hans set out on his divine mission on a three-legged mule. Leading him went the former Donga Santal, currently *Joseph Immanuel*, Joseph Donga to the people. Joseph Immanuel, of course, does not like the *Donga* appendage to his new title, and because he does not like it, the people simply will not let him forget it. Little kids shout *Donga Sahib* from a distance, and instantly, casting all pretenses of the right cheek—left cheek sermon aside, Joseph chases after them in a fit of rage. He never manages to catch them, though; Joseph eventually grills them with his indignant stare as he retreats, and remembers: *Forgive them, Father, for they know not what they do*.

So Hans mounted the three-legged mule, and with him went Joseph. They headed for the fair at Ram Gopalpur. It was around mid winter. The few fertile stretches in the field were now flowing with abundant golden grains—as though bunches of golden bouquets were radiating the grace of the sun—bright like the warm winter sunlight. Along the barren ridges between the fertile stretches of the field, the mule stumbled along; a languid, uninterrupted motion, somewhere between movement and stillness. Joseph had no difficulty keeping up.

Hans was full of joy as he surveyed the world around him. A new world, a new atmosphere. You see a certain India from her cities, but this was different. This undulating field, this unbroken desolation, the hissing of the chilly winds—somehow they reminded him of the seas in Europe. Happily Hans said, "Mr. Joseph, your country is wonderful."

Joseph was not given to poetic emotions. It was not that the wonder of his country excited him a whole lot, either. Only out of simple courtesy he replied in English, "Yash."

"I have always had a fascination about India, especially from my readings of Max Mueller. I see now that I have not been deluded."

Joseph replied again, "Yash Shar."

But immediately, something caused Joseph to prick up his ears; his face began to grow dark. Over where the searing heat had caused the pond to almost dry up, leaving only a waist-deep muddy puddle and a chunk of slimy matter as residue, where a rowdy bunch of black kids in diapers was creating a noisy racket in search of catfish, he thought he could detect a highly suspicious sound emanate from that end.

Joseph instantly stood at full alert like a hunting dog. Yes—he was absolutely right, he could never make a mistake in this. The shouts were coming loud and clear: *Donga Donga, Thonga Thonga, English Minglish.*

The *thonga* was evidently a meaningless effort at poetic rhyming, and the *English Minglish* a not too subtle reference to the Donga Sahib's proficiency in the English language.

Joseph's facial muscles instantly tightened, a flurry of vicious, foul and very un-Christian-like epithets came out of his mouth.

"What happened, Mr.Joseph?"

"Nothing, Shar!"

"Why are those kids shouting over there?"

"They are a bunch of village hooligans, Shar. Catching fish."

"Catching fish? Oh, that's lovely. Come, let's go take a look."

Joseph recoiled inside even at the thought. Only the fact that the Sahib's Bengali was not particularly well developed, and that he might not be able to decipher any significance inherent in the *Donga* word, gave him some reassurance.

Nevertheless, Donga Sahib made one last effort.

"There's nothing to see, Shar, it's dirty."

"Dirty? Why is it dirty? Never mind, just come with me."

Now, Donga Sahib had figured out from experience that there exists little difference between an obstinate Sahib and an obstinate boar. Yet the shout from the pond end would not abate, *Donga Donga, Thonga Thonga-*.

Well, then it must be settled one way or the other. Getting a hold of his temper with an effort, Joseph said, "OK, Shar, let's go."

But no sooner had they begun to move in their direction, than the boys began to scatter helter skelter.

"What's the matter, Joseph, why did they start running?"

"I don't know, Shar."

"They were probably scared, right?"

"Yash Shar."

"But why? Are we tigers or are we bears? If we must teach

them Christianity, then we better help them conquer their fear, what do you say?"

Joseph answered, "Maybe later, Shar. Now let us get going, otherwise the day will be over before we reach the fair."

"Never mind," said Hans, and then abruptly descending from the mule, began to sprint at high speed after the boys.

"What are you doing, Shar?"

Hans had no time to speak. By then he was running right through the middle of the field. The boys raised a cacophony of terror as they scooted hither and thither, and Hans was behind them, unrelenting. Holding the mule by the reins, a completely startled Joseph began to witness the whole spectacle.

More than six feet tall, with proportionately long legs; on top of that, a Leipzig University Blue—it was impossible to outrun him. In a matter of minutes, the Sahib held two screaming boys in his two arms.

Hans reassured them, "Why are you afraid? I am a white man, I've come from Europe. I am not from the Philippines, I am not a cannibal."

The boys did not understand his language, but they could read his eyes. In only a few minutes, everything had changed. Eventually, most of the boys had gathered around Hans.

Joseph could not believe his eyes. It was not a believable situation. Not that it was anything unusual for missionaries to associate with the natives of this country; in fact, it was quite natural and reasonable. However, no one could be prepared for such excesses, and Joseph was no exception.

Hans had removed his white surplice, then his shoes and socks. Rolling his trousers up to his knees, he had excitedly stepped into the muddy puddle to fish with the boys. His clothes were filthy beyond description, he was covered all over with slime, mud was splattered even on his face. Yet he seemed totally oblivious of his appearance—he was absorbed in an unearthly thrill.

Donga Sahib stood frozen with the reins in his hand. Was *this* the right behavior for a Reverend! Was there to be nothing honorable any more, would people respect the padres or the missionaries at this rate? If this went on, surely the Sahibs would be dragged to the same level as any old puffed rice, rock candy, Rama or Shyama!

When the Sahib walked back along the field, it was dark already. Behind him the boys shouted, "O Sahib, will you come again tomorrow?"

Eagerly the Sahib replied, "Of course, I will."

Finally, his voice grave with disapproval, Joseph spoke: "It's dark now—we can't go today."

"I am truly very sorry," said Hans regretfully. "I just could not resist the temptation. At the University, we too had played rugby in mud. Then, when I joined the bishops, I had to abandon all that. Seeing them brought back those old memories for me—"

"Yash Shar—," said Joseph in the same somber tone, "Please mount your horse now, it's getting late. The roads are terribly bad, there are snakes about."

"Snakes? Oh, lovely. I am very fond of Indian snakes—" Gesticulating and muttering to himself in his native Santali, Donga Sahib said, "Let them bite once, you'll see how *lovely*."

Donalds only smiled a little after Joseph had described everything to him.

"He's still young, so—"

"Yash Shar, but you don't understand—these are riffraff, black pagans-"

Donalds' smile broadened, his gaze fell on Joseph; a dense black varnish on a tan skin, thick lips, curly negroid hair. Poorly delivered English on a thick and sluggish tongue. Yet what an amazing transformation in Joseph within two years! His own great distance from the "black pagans" has become eminently clear to him, he has learned to despise the riffraff. Christianity sure works wonders—one cannot have the slightest doubt about that.

"Very well, I'll explain that to him."

"Yash Shar. He is new, does not know anything—"

"Very well."

Joseph went out; Donald continued to sit quietly. Hans' exuberance did not make him anxious or even worried. Mentally, he had attained an amazing tranquillity. On certain peaceful evenings, as he sits and reads the Bible, that empty, far-flung field stretching to the horizon magically engrosses his mind. The horizon gradually melts in the darkness, the tall and short hills in the distance, and the scattered jungle all begin to fade away. Among their shadows, one sees a few misty silhouettes—the tribals returning to their homes at the end of the day.

That's when it occurs to him. It occurs to him that along precisely such thorny paths infested with doubts and misgivings that the Son of Man walks in silent footsteps. With him walk thirteen others, his disciples, of whom Judas Iscariot is one. They have no weapons, no trumpets of victory. Only the malevolent and vengeful Yehudi eyes follow him, looking for any opportunity to strike at him like a reptile. But the light of Truth has wiped away all doubts from his mind, destroyed even the last trace of any fear. He moves forward, guided by the bright star twinkling above Bethlehem.

Donalds feels this preaching mission is meaningless, there is not an ounce of value in roaming from place to place carrying this sack of gospels. The One who had first preached these mantras, he had no trumpets, drums and gongs, he had no roving bands of padres. The Sun which had arisen inside his heart, had shone forth on its own; every drop of blood in his thorn-ravaged body had proclaimed his deathless message. Those people, walking stealthily like silhouettes in the dark— some day He will awaken in the midst of those mute, impoverished souls of his own accord. Who could tell whence among these unknown, uncared-for villages will arise the Bethlehem of tomorrow? The One will arrive out of his own need, why then must one—

Fortunately, the above attitude does not last long. Sometimes Donalds rebukes himself strongly. This kind of thinking is wrong, downright sinful. Could it be that the soil and water of India were instilling weakness in his bloodstream too? Making him lethargic, unmotivated and fatalistic like the rest of the infidels of this land? No, he cannot sit around quietly—unless he prepared the field right, how would the resurrection of the Son of God happen, how would the prophecy of the millennium be realized?

"Good evening, Father."

"Good evening-" Donalds turned his head. "Come in."
Hans quietly walked in and sat in the adjoining chair.

"How do you like it here?"

"Wonderful. It's an amazing country."

"It does seem that way at first," Donalds replied politely.
"But gradually your mind will change."

"I do not think so-" came Hans' emphatic response.

"Very well indeed, if that happens." Donalds did not wish
to prolong the discussion. He went on, "There's a lot to be
done, we have been unable to do much so far. You must take
your tasks seriously."

"That I will, but—" Hans paused abruptly.

"What is it?"

"Please forgive me Father, I just remembered something."

"Well?"

Hans paused to think for a while before speaking. He
started to nibble on the small finger of his left hand absent-
mindedly.

"Is any of this really necessary?"

"Any of what?"

"The preaching?"

Donalds' countenance took on an alarmed expression.

"Why do you say this all of a sudden?"

"Seems to me-" Hans said after a pause, "Seems to me,
we cannot make anyone good or bad, no matter how hard we
try. Every person can become good in his or her own
individual way, and that is the best possible way."

With a sharp, quizzical look, Donalds said, "I don't quite
follow you."

"I was saying-" Hans bit his finger nervously, "We cannot

enhance the prestige of Christianity by manufacturing creatures like Joseph Immanuel. Their humanity will best develop if left to their own natural instruments."

"What nonsense are you talking about?" Donalds moaned, "*This is our work!* It is we who must show the path of light to those who dwell in the darkness. Are you saying that these idol-worshipping heathens should remain prey to Satan forever?"

"I don't really understand—"

Hans abruptly stood up, as if he wished to end the discussion. Somewhere a sense of uneasiness was tormenting him deeply. He stepped out on the nearly dark field in front, and began to pace up and down.

Knotting his eyebrows together, Donalds stared for a few seconds. The young man is new here, still has a bit of philanthropy left. Donalds smiled a little: Surely this won't last for long. The romance will slowly wear out—the way it wore off for Donalds himself years ago.

But there is an uncontrollable sprightliness in the German, an implicit, restless life-force. Unlike the British, his life does not revolve around the unperturbed tranquillity of a conservative lifestyle. Perhaps this is a good quality, a sign of a full life. But for him who must shout himself hoarse in godforsaken boonies for the good of simple creatures, tooting the Bible and explaining the book of John, it is not only an inconvenient characteristic, but a rather dangerous one as well.

Hence, Donalds felt a great sense of anxiety and his mind was in turmoil.

Soon, reports began to reach Donalds inflated at least thirty-six times the magnitude of the event. Of all the reporters, Joseph Immanuel was by far the most agitated. He was convinced that the arrival of this new padre had endangered the glory of Christianity.

It is true they go from market to market, but what transpires may be interpreted as anything but sermonizing. On any given day, Hans will perhaps tether his three-legged mule, and eagerly join the riffraff to eat the local *jalebis* and other finger foods in the roadside food-stalls. And then, with genuine delight, declare, "O, how nice these Indian sweets!"

Meanwhile, conscious of his higher station, Donga Sahib stands at a distance and grinds his teeth. A fierce, violent rage burns inside him. What madness is this—is *this* any way to preach! The kind of honour and prestige they had hitherto enjoyed as the royal race, Hans was heaping dishonour and humiliation upon it, dragging it to the filth and the dirt of the street. This was far too excessive, in fact, quite intolerable.

But it is no use—complaining will not yield any result. Donga Sahib wishes to wipe out his Indian root; that identity is a source of extreme embarrassment and shame to him. Yet— to his utter chagrin and consternation, a feeling of indulgent affection and love for that very same India seems to be developing in this white Sahib's heart. He appears to have fallen in love with this condemned land—her bumpy, rocky fields, her illiterate, barbaric people—he has fallen for this Bharatvarsha. This surely is a sign of either senility or craziness.

Complaining to Donalds had not helped. Somehow the old padre, too, was not the same as before. These days he says very little, only nods his head slowly. Then, finally, he only says, he's too young, he'll be all right before long.

oving his thick lips in his customary manner, Joseph makes

a sound like a muffled echo and says, "Yash Shar." To himself, however, he mutters, "All right my foot."

Sometimes his muttering becomes a little loud. Cupping a hand behind his ear, Donalds asks, "I beg your pardon?"

"Nothing Shar—."

Still, there is a limit to a person's patience.

A desolate path, shaded by the blossoming *bakula* trees. Whispering a prayer to himself, Joseph walks along like a good Christian. Only every now and then he glances at his shiny, polished shoes in disgust, noticing how the dust of filthy India is discoloring them. No, enough is enough—he decides, no longer in this country. He *must* flatter the senior padre well enough to make sure of his passage to Europe, his motherland. Bharatvarsha is continually wounding and contaminating his delicate and civilized sensibilities.

"Donga Donga, Thonga Thonga—"

As though the words were carried by the airwaves! However, the reaction occurred in less than one one-hundredth of a second. The words from the Holy Bible evaporated from his lips, as Joseph Sahib stiffened his body and stood straight as a rod. The veins in his hands became taut in anticipation of striking out at some invisible foe.

But *where* is the foe? The path is completely deserted, without even the trace of a single soul. Can this be something supernatural?

"Donga Donga, Thonga Thonga—"

And then it was like Columbus discovering America! After all, the Donga Santal did not merely graze like cattle in the field to turn into Joseph Sahib. He possesses a fair amount of gray matter in his brain, too! His glance moved skyward.

Yes, indeed, it was just like he had imagined. Up in the higher branches, a bunch of black kids—a pack of dirty pagans!

"Nasty imps!"

Once again, the profound principle of the left and right cheeks simply vanished like black magic. Likewise vanished Joseph Immanuel's sense of aristocracy. Suddenly, there emerged the original, unadulterated Donga Santal, who removed his prized shoes, and swiftly began climbing up the tree.

But the boys are smarter. Instantly, they have jumped from the tree to the ground, and, before Immanuel can even run after them, they have all disappeared. From far away, one can still detect a faint sound, "English Minglish..."

After chasing the boys haphazardly for a while, Joseph returned, panting heavily. Then he noticed that his shoes have disappeared from under the tree.

"Damned be those Devil's children—"

Seething in anger and barefoot, Joseph had walked some distance, when suddenly he was startled by something unexpected. Not far from him, with hands resting on his waist, stood the junior padre Hans. There seemed to be a faint smile on his face, and a mischievous twinkle in his eyes.

"What's the matter, why were you running like that?"

Immediately, Joseph's mind became clouded by a deep suspicion. There was a hint of something mysterious in Hans' expression. Could he be somehow connected with the whole sordid business of the hooligan kids? It wouldn't be impossible!

Nevertheless, he could only mutter his usual, "Yash Shar—nothing Shar."

"I really enjoyed watching you. Your running is very interesting, Mr. Thonga."

"Thonga!" Then there can be no doubt whatsoever. Suddenly, a murderous impulse surged inside Joseph's head, a homicidal desire sparkled in his eyes. But only for an instant. Thereafter, without uttering another word, he walked away with brisk and determined steps.

The situation began to take such a sinister turn from one day to the next that in the end even the placid and inoffensive old padre himself began to lose his patience.

Besides, it *was* true that nothing was getting done. Not through Joseph alone, but through several other sources Donalds was learning that this whimsical young German was carrying things too far. These days it would take a great deal of prodding to get him to go on the preaching rounds. Things had come to such a pass that old Donalds himself had to go out again to preach every so often. Again, he had to stand under the banyan tree and shout, "Come hither, come to the Light. Our Father, our Shepherd in Heaven, shall carry His flock to His Heavenly abode." However, with his croaking voice, the sermons do not carry any punch—Donalds realizes quite well that all his efforts are in vain.

So, little wonder that Donalds is irritated. If he will not be of the slightest use, then why bother sending that kid all the way here? He will not even remain indoors quietly for a while. No one knows whereabouts he roams and loiters all day. Smokes tobacco in one house, munches a bowl of *muri* in another, wades into the muddy shallows with a bunch of boys and gets dirty all over. Then, returning after dusk, declares, "India is a beauty. I like India—I *love* India."

It maybe that padres love the world, but to stomach this much love for the world is difficult even for them.

One evening Donalds was down with a touch of fever. This was the one sure gain Donalds had made in the course of his mission in India—this malaria. After countless doses of quinine, and many injections, he had found little relief. Every few days the fever came back. The veins would pound inside his aching temple, and inside his head, he would feel the disquieting rush of blood. At such moments, a strange metamorphosis would completely alter the otherwise calm and inoffensive personality of the old padre. An irritable, almost ugly feeling of revulsion for India would envelope his entire consciousness. The blue waters of the English Channel, the graceful trails of poplars, the hills and arcades, the radiant health and beauty of England—all would come back to him like a distant dream. This life would seem to him like a horrid exile—an intolerable, unintentional exile. And, of course, it is these Indians who are to blame for his situation, these dirty idolators!

Covering himself right up to the neck with a blanket, Donalds lay quietly on his deck-chair. Joseph Immanuel sat alongside. His black face was blacker than tar this day.

In other words, a new poem has made its way to his ears. After refining the native language somewhat, it read as follows:

That old padre's a loony breed
Thonga Sahib is a goat indeed.

After hearing the couplet, Donalds simply said, "Hum!"

Joseph complained, "I have told you many times, Shar, this is all the younger Sahib's fault. These kids have been terribly pampered by him. If one of your own should thus become your worst enemy, Shar, then why bother trying anything good? It's better to go straight to Jerusalem instead."

Donalds only said, "Hum."

Time passed silently for a while. It felt as though an oppressive heat wave started to circulate in the windless air. The foamy music of the English Channel gurgling inside Donalds's ears was being continually interrupted by the blighted drone of the Indian mosquitoes. And, staring at Joseph's face, Donalds felt an intense burning inside with a revolting disgust. He felt like dispatching that dirty nigger like a dog to a faraway dump with one swift kick.

It was dark. A brisk sound of boots, accompanied by a joyful whistling tune came from the street outside. Hans was coming home. Joseph sat up with a shuffle.

With an ebullient voice, Hans inquired, "What's the matter, Father, why is everything so quiet?"

There was no answer.

Hans continued, "Father, look what a fine fowl I have brought. The Indian hens are lovely.—"

Donalds took a look at the hen. "Where did you find it?"

"They were worshipping something—this was the sacrifice. They presented it to me. Really, I love—"

"Damned idolatry!" Losing any pretense of self-control, Donalds suddenly let out a violent scream: "Hans, I am sorry, but there is no need for you to stay here any longer, you will go back tomorrow."

His eyes bulging with astonishment, Hans asked, "What happened?"

"Nothing," Donalds replied bitterly, "The Church is not for you. You try yourself elsewhere!"

Joseph sat quietly rocking his knees, as if a completely disinterested third party. Taking a glance at him, Hans said, "I know. It must be this Donga chap—"

Donga chap! Instantly an electrical charge passed through Joseph's body. He stood up straight as an arrow: "I warn you, Shar—I am no Donga."

Hans laughed loudly—the rippling waves of his deep, clear laughter made the darkness sing.

"Of course a Donga! Not only a Donga, in fact, Thonga, Thonga—"

What happened next occurred before one could bat an eyelid. Like a blood-thirsty wild beast, Joseph snarled and pounced upon Hans. But the Leipzig University Blue dodged him like an alert reptile. Then, like a solid slab of iron, a powerful straight-cut landed squarely on Joseph's chin. Instantly, he was deflected to a wall, from where he collapsed to the ground like a pumpkin.

Infuriated, agitated by the fever, Donalds became livid and almost maniacal. With the voice of a madman, he screamed, "Get out of here, both of you! This is a Church, not a brawlers' alley!"

"You really want me to go, Father?"

"This instant. Christianity disowns you. Get out of my sight—"

Donalds' head suddenly began to swim from the excitement of his own vocal exertions. Trembling, and covering his face with his hands, he sat down on his chair— he felt as though the swelling tide of high-pressure blood was boiling in his veins. When things had finally returned to a semblance of normalcy, opening his eyes, he noticed that Joseph was sitting by his feet like a pet dog; blood was streaming from his thick lips, and on his bloodied face was a confounding smile. Only an Indian could possibly smile under such circumstances!

And what about Hans? There was no sign of him. Only the impenetrable darkness of a new moon night pervaded the heart of Bharatvarsha. In that darkness there could be no vision.

Six months later, it was the big village fair and open market.

A huge crowd had gathered around in the shade under the old banyan tree with the tangled secondary roots. One could hardly bear the deafening din of the gongs and drums. They were observing Shiva's *gajan*.

> *"Old Shiva's caught the dance frenzy*
> *The dance frenzy of old Bholanath—"*

With the rhythmic drumbeats, there was Bholanath himself, dancing like one possessed. The matted locks of coiled jute on his head matched wonderfully with his red hair. The painted tiger skin around his waist looked exquisitely beautiful on Shiva's chiseled, athletic body. Keeping pace with the blissful dance of the tall, fair and luminous Shiva was the joyous orchestra of the gongs and drums.

> *"We haven't any rice to eat, O Shiva,*
> *No paddy in our barns,*
> *With what shall we save, O Shiva*

The lives of our young ones?
Have mercy on us, old Shiva—"

Tears came to Shiva's eyes as he danced. They had no rice to eat, no paddy in their barns—there was not the slightest exaggeration in that—in the past six months he had seen it vividly with his own eyes. He had longed to see India, to know her. What he actually saw would have been better not to have seen at all. Shiva began to wonder—there was a connection between this great want and penury, and the old padre Donalds, a connection with holy Christianity. The connection was fine and subtle, but its effect—

O Shiva, you missed a beat!

Embarrassed, Shiva resumed his dance. But inside his ears, he only heard the plaintive drone. No rice to eat, no paddy in the barns. It is far better not to want to see Bharatvarsha. It is much easier to disinfect your conscience with the Doctrine of Love, to blindfold common humanity—

Suddenly, Shiva awoke from his trance. The music had stopped, and a terrified murmur had replaced it. Above the noise, one could hear the voice of Donga Sahib: There, Shar, just look at the spectacle. The man's gone berserk! An absolute lunatic! Shame, Shame, Shame—"

Joseph's eyes had not betrayed him even in the dark. After all, who else knew the ins and outs of this area better than him? He had not wasted any time finding the District Magistrate and his troopers, and bringing them to the spot.

The white District Magistrate's face went livid with anger and consternation. Behind him, frozen like a statue, stood Donalds. The magistrate turned around to look at the padre.

Donalds turned his face away in disgust—he spat on the ground loudly. He only muttered to himself: Blasted infidel! A new Judas to Christianity!"

"Infidel—Judas!" The magistrate echoed the words. Then he jammed a revolver against Shiva's chest and growled, "You are under arrest."

Amazing! Had Hans not even read a newspaper in these six months? Or had he become a one-hundred percent barbarian dancing like Shiva with the Indians! Even Joseph became curious. With large, innocent eyes, Hans inquired, "My crime? *Infidel?*"

Fire pouring from his mouth, the magistrate said, "Disgraceful! Have you no shame at all? You have dragged the honor of Europe and Christianity to the dirt. You should have been hanged for that alone, but the law is too liberal!" Still pointing the revolver, the magistrate went on, "But that is not why you are being arrested. You are the enemy."

"Enemy? Whose enemy? This Donga's?"—Hans began to laugh.

"No, India's! India is now at war with Germany. Come, let's go."

"*I* am an enemy of Bharatvarsha! How lovely!" Hans smiled sadly: "Thank you. Let's go—"

Hans climbed inside the car in his Shiva costume. Turning his face away in contempt, Donalds spat out, while a curious, slimy smile played upon Joseph's thick, black lips.

A starved and impoverished India watched the car as it disappeared in the distance—her sight became blurred from the welling tears of mute anguish.

The man must have gone completely crazy. Why else would someone do something like that along the way!

The problem was that the car had stopped somewhere briefly. A festive Kali worship was going on there. The magistrate himself climbed out of the car and, walking over to the *puja mandap*, stood there respectfully.

Bewildered, Hans asked, "What is this?"

The armed *gurkha* accompanying him explained to him that the Kalipuja was being conducted in the hope of winning the war. The government itself had provided the funds—the magistrate himself was one of its chief organizers.

"Is *that* so? Lovely!" Hans's blue eyes suddenly began to sparkle: "Would you please give me your water bottle, I feel very thirsty."

The unsuspecting gurkha handed Hans his flask. But Hans did not drink—instead, he did something scandalous. The flask flew out of his hand—it went straight to the bull's eye. The Kali image's head blew up and fell to the ground with a terrible sound, and an ugly pandemonium ensued.

Instantly, Hans burst out of the car like a meteor, and started to dance Shiva's *gajan*: "Now I am a true enemy *and* a true European. Am I not?"

Glossary

abhagi	:	a name which literally means *one born to misfortune*.
abhagya	:	misfortune.
adaav	:	a Muslim greeting.
adda	:	a favourite Bengali pastime; friendly chat or conversation from the most mundane to the most sophisticated.
Adra, Asansol	:	towns in West Bengal, India.
aghori, chattaraj,	:	tribal communities in rural Bengal near the bottom of, or outside the Hindu caste structure.
Agni	:	the Vedic fire god.
Ahalya	:	a legendary woman of ancient India, turned into stone by a curse; rescued by the divine Rama, hero of the *Ramayana*.
Alamgir	:	title assumed by Aurangzeb, youngest son of Mughal emperor Shah Jahan, who had deposed his father and ruthlessly assassinated his brothers to ascend to the coveted throne in Delhi.
aleikum aslam	:	a Muslim greeting implying a salutation.
bey-saboor	:	a Hindi/Urdu expression meaning impatient.
Bibi-jaan	:	a respectful Muslim address for a woman, often a married woman.
alpana	:	an artistic floor decoration rendered by hand using typically a rice flour paste.

Aratidamana	:	a feudal landlord's title; literally, a demon-slayer.
alta	:	a deep red paint used by Indian women to decorate the borders of their feet.
aman	:	a fragrant variety of rice grown in Bengal.
amani	:	a cool drink or potion for countering hangovers.
ambubachi	:	a one-week observance by Hindu widows during which they subsist only on fruits and select, uncooked vegetarian food. Mangoes are an essential component of the diet.
amchur	:	powdered green mangoes.
amlaki	:	a tart, pale green, translucent berry.
amra	:	a fruit similar to the olive.
amsattva	:	dried mango pulp.
anantamul	:	a tropical tree; literally, one with an infinite root.
anchal	:	the loose end of a *sari* which falls over the shoulder.
anjali	:	an offering of flowers and/or prayers made with joined palms during a worship ceremony.
anna	:	an Indian currency in colonial times equivalent to one-sixteenth of a rupee.
arandhan	:	a ritual in which nothing is cooked on a given day.
Arya Samaj	:	a Hindu reformist society founded by Swami Dayanand Saraswati.
Asharh	:	a Bengali month, approximately June and July, covering the peak rainy season.
ashirvad	:	a Hindu act of blessing in which an elder touches the head of a younger person and expresses words of beneficence; also a ritual blessing ceremony for the formal confirmation of a wedding agreement.

ash	:	*sheora*-a large tropical tree; also known to be occasionally haunted.
Ashwin	:	a month on the Bengali calendar; approximately September-October.
aush	:	a rice crop less fragrant than *aman*.
baap	:	a derisive (in this case) appellation for *father*; also a colloquial address for father.
babla	:	a tropical tree.
babu	:	a honorific title for a gentleman.
Babuji	:	a Hindi mode of address for a gentleman.
Babumashay	:	venerable master.
Baddhaman	:	a corruption of Burdwan or Bardhaman- a city and district in West Bengal.
Badshah	:	an Urdu/Arabic word for an emperor or king.
bagdis, dules	:	low-caste members of Hindu society, such as fishermen and palanquin bearers.
bagh, baghini	:	literally, a tiger and a tigress respectively. Here denoting the last name of a man and that of his wife by association.
Ba	:	*jaan*-a respectful Muslim address for Father.
bakula	:	a fragrant Indian flower.
bamoon	:	a colloquial corruption of *Brahmin*.
bania	:	a Hindi word for merchants and traders.
Bankim, Navin Prabhat Kumar	:	the renowned nineteenth century authors Bankim Chandra Chatterjee, Navin Chandra Sen and Prabhat Kumar Mukhopadhyay.
Bankura	:	a small town in West Bengal, India.
banyan	:	also called *vata vriksha*, a large tropical tree known for its secondary roots reaching back to the ground from the branches.
baran	:	an auspicious welcoming.
Bardhaman	:	a city in West Bengal, India.
basar	:	a gathering of revelers in a large hall following a marriage ceremony.

bashi biye : follow-up ceremony the day after the actual marriage. Literally, a stale marriage.

baul : an order of ascetic, wandering singers and composers of Bengal.

Bauri : a tribal community of Bengal.

Begum : an Urdu/Arabic word for an empress or queen; also commonly used to signify a lady of a household.

begunis, phuluris, : fried delicacies eaten during the Rath
papad bhaja (Jagannath or *Juggernaut*) Carnival.

behai : the father of a son or daughter-in-law.

bel : the fruit of the stone apple tree. Considered holy by Vaishnavas and members of other sects in India. Here the reference is to the Bengali idiom *Bel Pakle Kaker Ki*, which states that it makes little difference to the crow when the *bel* fruit ripens, since it does not have the ability to break the hard shell of the fruit to get at the flesh.

bemmhachari : a corruption of Brahmachari, i.e., one who has assumed an austere and celibate life for meditation and realization of Brahman.

Bhagavadgita : a profoundly philosophical poem on the nature of phenomenal existence and Man's relationship to the divine which appears within the Indian epic poem Mahabharata. Also called simply the Gita.

bhai : address for a brother, usually younger.

bhang : an intoxicating drink made from a hemp-based concoction.

Bhattacharya : a Brahmin surname chiefly associated with priesthood.

Bhil : one of several tribal people from north-eastern India.

bigha	:	a parcel of land smaller than an acre.
bhoot	:	the ghost or spirit of a man trapped in the world.
bioscope	:	an early (now almost defunct) word used to describe a motion picture.
bou/bouma	:	a daughter-in-law; also, a sister-in-law to a husband's older sister.
bou	:	a (usually younger) brother's wife.
boudi	:	a (usually older) brother's wife.
Bownga	:	tribal deity.
brahmin	:	the highest Hindu caste, ideally scholars and priests.
buddha ghora	:	a non-flattering epithet; literally, old and decrepit horse.
burqa	:	a veil used by a Muslim woman to cover her face.
chacha	:	Hindi/Urdu for uncle.
chachchari	:	a spicy vegetable medley, made primarily of stems and greens.
chadar	:	a wrap worn like a shawl.
Chaitra	:	a month on the Bengali calendar; approximately February-March.
Chandimandap	:	a permanent dais found outside traditional village homes (typically zamindari mansions) in Bengal, usually intended for the various *pujas* and other celebrations.
chatak	:	a mythical bird known to be under a curse whereby it suffers endless and unquenchable thirst.
chinre	:	a flattened and dried form of boiled rice.
chokh	:	*udan*-a tropical tree.
compounder	:	a physician's assistant in India who typically fills out orders by making a compound mixture out of several prescribed liquid medicines.

cowrie	:	a small, hard, conch-like shell used in earlier times as legal financial tender.
daktar	:	a colloquial corruption of doctor.
dal	:	Indian soup made of lentils and other legumes.
daro mat	:	a colloquial Hindi usage implying *fear not*.
darwan	:	a guard or doorkeeper.
datura	:	a tree and a flower thereof, from which narcotics such as *ganja* can be extracted.
dehi padapallava mudarang-	:	a *sloka* or poetic phrase which appears in the divine/devotional poem *Gita-Govinda*. Literally, *Place thy feet, soft as the petals of a flower, upon mine head.*
dempo	:	a slang for a smart aleck boy.
dhama	:	a large cane basket.
dhangar	:	a toilet cleaner.
dhaora	:	a tribal word for a home or shelter.
Dharmapala	:	a feudal landlord's title; literally, keeper of *dharma* or righteousness.
Dharmaraj	:	another name for the enforcer of the natural order, i.e., the Lord of Death, Yama.
dholak / dhak	:	a double-ended drum usually suspended from the neck for playing; a large, barrel shaped drum which is placed on the floor for playing.
dhoti	:	a long piece of cloth worn by Hindu men around their waist.
dhulo-pa	:	a ceremony in which a newlywed couple revisits the bride's home a few days after the marriage. Literally, dusty-feet.
dhurrie	:	a lightweight, colorful Indian rug.
didi	:	older sister.
donga	:	a canoe-type wooden boat.
doyel	:	a songbird of Bengal.
dule	:	a low-caste Hindu denomination; by profession, *palki* or palanquin bearers.

Durbar / durbar	:	a ruler in his court; the court itself.
Durga	:	one of the most powerful of Vedic goddesses; the consort of Shiva, the third member of the Hindu trinity.
Durvasa	:	a sage known for his irascibility who appears in Kalidasa's famous play *Shakuntala*; Durvasa's curse causes King Dushyanta to forget that Shakuntala was his wife.
Dwijendralal	:	Dwijendralal Roy, a renowned Bengali playwright from the nineteenth century.
Foujdar	:	a law-enforcement official; a commissioner of police.
gaab	:	a tropical tree; also known to be occasionally haunted.
gaatchhi	:	a tree tapper.
gaddi	:	a merchant's cushion, typical of traders from north-western India. Sometimes used to signify a seat of *power*.
gajan	:	a type of folk songs and dances associated with Shiva; induced by ganja or hemp.
gamchha	:	a *Madras*-printed cotton cloth commonly used as a traditional bath towel in India.
gangajal	:	literally, water from the Ganges. Here used as a metaphor for someone playing too pure or innocent.
Garuda	:	a legendary bird of Indian mythology; the cosmic vehicle of Vishnu.
gerhastha	:	a colloquial corruption of *grihastha*, a householder.
ghat	:	a series of steps at a riverbank or the edge of a tank or lake leading to the water.
ghee	:	clarified butter used in Hindu ceremonies and cooking.

ghoraneem	:	a tropical tree.
gobarjal	:	a mixture of Ganges water and cowdung considered to have purifying powerswhen smeared over any place rendered impure by touch or association.
go-hata	:	a village marketplace where cattle are bought and sold.
gokhura	:	the Indian cobra.
gomasta	:	an accounts-keeper in a zamindari estate.
gur	:	jaggery or molasses.
Gurkha	:	a Nepalese soldier, known for courage and tenacity.
gymkhana	:	a word from British India for a club or retreat with facilities for physical activities and other recreation.
haat	:	an extended farmer's market with fruits, vegetables and handicrafts.
hanri	:	a covered cooking pot made of clay, aluminium, brass or stainless steel.
hanria	:	an alcoholic drink.
lathi	:	a baton or stick used by a gendarme or policeman.
Hardwar	:	a city in Northwest India considered one of India's holiest.
Hari	:	another name for Vishnu; Hindu funerals are usually accompanied by chants of Hari or Rama, both associated with Vishnu, the Lord of Salvation. Literally, One who steals away sins and transgressions.
Haribol	:	a chant of the name of Hari (popular in Bengal).
Hetampur	:	a town in West Bengal, India.
Hindustani	:	in Bengal, denoting a person from the Hindi-speaking region of India.

hookah	:	a classical smoking pipe.
Huzoor	:	a mode of address for a person of rank; similar to Sir.
Indira	:	title of a novel by Bankim Chandra Chatterjee; its heroine by that name.
Itu	:	the sun-god, associated with a golden harvest; the corresponding celebration on a Sunday.
Jaishtha	:	a month on the Bengali calendar; approximately May-June.
jalebi	:	an Indian sweet pretzel.
jamai	:	a son-in-law.
jamun	:	a deeply purple and sweet berry which has a stone inside, about an inch in length.
Jatayu	:	name of a legendary bird from the epic *Ramayana*, who had attempted to rescue Sita from the demon-king Ravana and was killed as a result.
jyotsna	:	the silvery light of a full moon night.
kaath champa	:	a fragrant flower of the *champa* family.
Kabhi Nahi	:	a colloquial Hindi implying *Never, Ever*.
kadam/kadamba	:	a golden yellow, spherical-shaped fragrant flower, associated with Krishna.
kahan	:	a measure for a bale or stack of hay.
kaishore vivaha	:	youthful marriage.
kalabou	:	a mythical banana-plant which represents a bride for the elephant-headed god Ganesha; used as an auspicious symbol in puja, marriage and other ceremines.
kaka	:	a paternal uncle, also an address of respect.
kalmegh	:	a tropical tree.
kana bhains	:	a non-flattering epithet; literally, a half-blind buffalo.
kancha kala	:	an unripened banana.

kanchi	:	a slender piece of stick; a cane.
Kangali	:	a name which literally means *one born as a destitute*.
kantha	:	a patchwork quilt.
Kartik	:	a month on the Bengali calendar, approximately October-November.
kash	:	a tall grass with exquisite, long, silky white flowers which bloom in autumn around the time of the Durga Puja festival.
katchhari	:	a zamindari office complex.
katha	:	a parcel of land smaller than a *bigha*.
katla	:	a sweet-water fish similar to the *rohu* or carp.
kaviraj	:	a practitioner of herbal medicine.
kayet	:	a colloquial corruption of Kayastha, a caste denomination second only to a Brahmin.
khal	:	a broad canal, usually man-made.
khayer	:	a deep burgundy-colored flavoring used in stuffing *paan* or betel leaves.
khejur	:	dates; the date palm.
khoka	:	an endearing word for a little boy.
kheer	:	thick, sweet condensed milk with the consistency of cheese.
Khoda	:	another word for *Allah* or God.
khonra hans	:	a non-flattering epithet; literally, a lame duck.
Kobrej	:	a colloquial corruption of Kaviraj.
kojagari purnima	:	a special full moon following the end of the Durga Puja festival during which the goddess Lakshmi is worshipped.
kokila	:	the Indian cuckoo bird.
kshatriya	:	the second highest Hindu caste; warriors, administrators, and rulers.
kula	:	a winnowing tray made of wicker.
kumbhakar	:	a low-caste; potters.

Kumbha Karna	:	mythical brother of Ravana, the demon king of the Ramayana, known for voracious appetite, and capacity to sleep for months at a stretch.
Kurmi	:	one of several tribal people from north-eastern India.
kurta	:	a traditional, loose-fitting coat worn by Indian men on festive occasions.
lagna	:	an auspicious hour for a ceremony determined from the Hindu almanac.
Lakshmi	:	the Hindu goddess of wealth and good fortune.
lomfo	:	a corruption of the medical degree L.M.F., which is at a level somewhat lower than an M.B.B.S.
loth	:	a corruption of *noth*- a nose ornament.
lungi	:	a striped and colored *dhoti* worn around the waist by men in the Indian subcontinent.
madal	:	a percussion instrument, sometimes used by tribals.
Magh	:	the coldest winter month on the Bengali calendar; approximately January-February.
Mahabharata	:	the larger of the two ancient epic poems of India. Source of the Bhagavadgita.
Mahadeva	:	another name for Shiva; literally, the great god.
Mahakavi	:	literally, a great poet.
mahapurusha	:	a title used to describe a great man.
Mahashay	:	an address for a venerable person.
maiya	:	a colloquial Bengali word for a girl or daughter.
majhi	:	a boatman.
mandal	:	a union or assembly of working people.
masala	:	a mixture of spices
maya	:	the Hindu view that the manifested world is an illusory veil which covers reality.
mehendi	:	a henna-like dye for hands and feet.

meherbani	:	with kindness and grace.
Mian	:	an address for a Muslim man.
mlechha	:	a derogatory word for a non-Hindu; somewhat similar to infidel.
Mukhopadhyay	:	the (original) Indian version of the anglicized surname Mukherjee.
Mukhujje	:	a colloquial corruption of Mukherjee.
mungeri	:	a type of firearm with origin traceable to the city of Munger or Monghyr.
muri	:	puffed rice.
Mussalman	:	a word for a Muslim person.
nabanna	:	a harvest ceremony.
nandai, nanadini:		the husband of one's husband's sister; one's husband's sister.
Narapala	:	a feudal landlord's title; literally, ruler of the people.
Narasimha	:	one of the ten *avatars* or incarnations of Vishnu, in which a man-lion form is assumed.
nari-ratna	:	an adjective for an exceptional woman; literally, a jewel among women.
narugopal	:	an metaphor used to describe an innocent-type; literally, the name ascribed to a child Krishna who is often depicted with a large molasses-and-puffed-rice candy ball in hand.
nikah	:	a Muslim marriage.
nilkuthi	:	indigo zamindari estates.
nullah	:	a narrow, man-made canal.
paan	:	a *betel* leaf which is stuffed with quicklime, nuts and spices, then chewed like tobacco.
palash	:	a flowering tree.
palki	:	a palanquin.
paisa	:	the lowest monetary denomination in British and modern India. One-hundredth of a *rupee*.

pakshi-raj	:	a word commonly associated with a mythical winged horse; literally, a bird-king.
pakur	:	a large, tropical tree; one of several sometimes considered haunted.
pariah	:	a Hindi word for someone who is shunned and isolated by society. Equivalent to the Bengali *ekghare*.
patali	:	a slab of date palm jaggery.
pathshala	:	a country school.
patisapta	:	a Bengali crepe stuffed with kheer or caramelized shredded coconut.
payesh, jhol-puli	:	festive desserts.
pennam	:	a corruption of *pranam*.
pentool	:	a corruption of pantaloon.
petni	:	the evil spirit or ghost of a woman trapped in the world.
Phalgun	:	month on the Bengali calendar, approximately between February and March.
phanimanasa	:	a tropical bush.
phoolsajya	:	a flower bedecked bed which is festively decorated for a newlywed couple on their first night after marriage.
pice	:	Plural of a paise, a now defunct unit of currency, the equivalent of oneninety-sixth of a rupee.
piran	:	a loose shirt worn by Indian men on festive occasions.
pishimani	:	a paternal aunt.
pishi	:	a paternal aunt, here addressed out of respect.
pitali	:	a tropical tree.
pithe	:	generic name for a variety of rice and wheat-based festive sweets.
pitralaya	:	one's father's home.
planchette	:	an occult/seance session in which a small group

		of participants attempts to invoke a departed spirit back to a verifiable manifestation via a person who serves as a "medium."
pochi	:	a corruption of *paschima*- a word for the rain-carrying westerly winds.
Pous/Poush	:	Bengali month, approximating December.
prachittir	:	a colloquial corruption of the Sanskrit *prayashchitta*, which is an act of penance and contrition usually ordained as atonement for a heretical or sinful act.
pranam	:	A Hindu act of veneration in which a younger person touches the feet of an elder in order to be blessed by the propitious dust. Sometimes also the simple act of folding one's palms before a deity or someone else.
prasad	:	food consecrated to a deity, then distributed to the worshippers as holy.
pretayoni	:	a spirit or apparition.
priyatama	:	dearest of my heart.
puin	:	an edible vine with large, fleshy, deep green leaves.
puja	:	one of many Hindu worship ceremonies.
puja tattva	:	gifts sent to in-laws by girl's parents during puja.
pugree	:	any of several headdresses worn by Indian men belonging to different communities.
punya	:	spiritual merit acquired through kind and charitable acts, as well as from visits to places of pilgrimage.
purusha dharma	:	the nature or principle of manhood.
pushpanjali	:	flower offerings made along with prayers during a worship ceremony.
Rajput	:	a martial clan originating from Rajputana

(modern Rajasthan), known for valor and courage.

rakshasas	:	cannibals/demons.
Ramlila	:	an autumn festival celebrating the life of Rama, hero of the *Ramayana*.
Serestadar	:	a treasurer in an estate or principality.
shula	:	a sharp metal spike implanted in the ground; used to impale convicts in the middle ages.
Ranigunj	:	a town in West Bengal, India.
ras	:	the sap of a date and other palm trees suitable for tapping.
rathayatra	:	a carnival of the chariot of Jagannath, another name of Sri Krishna, commemorating Krishna, his older brother Balarama and their sister Subhadra's return to their kingdom's capital city of Dwarka.
rosogolla	:	a spherical confection made of riccota cheese and drenched in rose-flavored syrup.
Sachiv	:	a secretary of an estate or principality.
sadhana	:	an Indian concept of undivided attention and efforts towards a higher goal.
sal	:	a large tropical tree known for the hardness of its timber.
salsa	:	a fragrant tropical bush.
sankha, bala	:	a bangle made from conch shell, and a metal such as iron, gold or silver, respectively; traditionally worn by married women in India.
sankranti	:	an auspicious day in Hinduism which falls at the junction of the end of one lunar phase and the beginning of another.
sansara	:	the phenomenal world subject to the illusory effects of Maya.
Saraswati	:	the Hindu goddess of learning.

sari	:	the traditional dress of Indian women.
sateen	:	the relationship between the wives of a polygamous man.
Sati, Lakshmi	:	two divine figures of ideal Hindu womanhood; *Sati* is the consort of Shiva, and *Lakshmi*, a goddess associated with wealth and prosperity, is the consort of Vishnu.
seer	:	a weight measure, approximately (37/40) of a kilogram.
shakchunni	:	a member of a large family of female ghosts which includes the *petni*.
shala	:	here used as a pejorative word implying a bastard or a scoundrel. Literally, a wife's brother.
shaluk	:	a water lily.
Shanra Shashthi	:	an aspect of the goddess of fertility, associated with a vine.
shehnai	:	A musical instrument belonging to the wind instrument family.
Sheora, Vanbhant	:	tall trees with dense foliage.
shiuli	:	an exquisitely fragrant flower which blooms profusely around the Durga Puja festival.
shraddh	:	a Hindu feast, normally dedicated to Brahmin guests, to honor a departed soul, and usher it on the path to salvation.
shubha drishti	:	an auspicious moment in a Hindu marriage in which the bride and groom behold each other for the first time.
shukla	:	the lunar phase from new to full moon.
shyalak	:	a wife's brother.
Sondar	:	colloquial corruption of Sundar, meaning beautiful or handsome.
srotriya	:	a family with lineage not very high in the caste hierarchy.

supari	:	a betel nut, used in small pieces to stuff a *paan*.
swasurbari	:	a father-in-law's home.
taal	:	a type of palm tree with a round, fleshy fruit.
taka	:	a currency unit used in Bengal, equivalent generally to the *rupee*.
talak	:	a civilian Muslim divorce whereby the pronouncement for nullifying a marriage is made typically by the husband.
tamarind	:	a long, bean-shaped sour fruit with hard stones inside.
tamasha	:	a show; a spectacle; a public entertainment.
Taraka	:	a mythical demoness who appears in the *Ramayana*.
Tehsildar	:	inspector of a *tehsil* or agrarian territory.
Thakur	:	honorific title given to a person of prestige and learning.
thakurjhi	:	husband's younger sister.
thana	:	a local or regional police station.
Than	:	*didi*-term of endearment for a grandmotherly old lady.
Tilottama	:	a woman in Hindu mythology supposedly created in bits the size of a sesame seed to ensure that she was flawlessly beautiful.
tirtha	:	a place of pilgrimage.
tonga	:	a kind of horse carriage popular in northern India.
topor	:	a conical pith crown worn by bridegrooms.
Tribhuvanapati	:	a feudal landlord's title; literally, lord of the three worlds.
uchchhugge	:	a colloquial corruption of *utsarga*, to give as an offering.
upavita	:	a sacred thread worn by a Brahmin man upon initiation to Brahminical

Vaishakh : the first month on the Bengali calendar; approximately April-May.

vanabasa : an exile into forest life; the reference here is to the exile of Prince Rama in the *Ramayana*.

Varna Parichay : an introductory book of Bengali alphabets and grammar authored by Ishwar Chandra Vidyasagar.

Vidyasagar : a venerable address for Ishwar Chandra Vidyasagar, extraordinary *Mahashay* scholar, reformer and philanthropist of nineteenth century Bengal.

Vidyadhari : someone with many talents, here used pejoratively.

vilaiti : anything foreign, especially English or European.

yuga : a measure of time equivalent to twelve years.

zamindar : A feudal landlord.

zarda : a strong and dizzying flavored condiment used in stuffing *paan* by some chewers.

Biographical Notes on Authors

Sarat Chandra Chattopadhyay

Born September 15, 1876 in Devanandapur, Hooghly District, Bengal. Commenced writing stories at age 17. In 1902 received the Kuntalin Prize for the story *Mandir*. Also wrote several articles and stories under the pseudonym Anila Devi. Author of numerous widely acclaimed short stories and novels. Received the Jagattarini Gold Medal from the University of Calcutta in 1923. Died January 16, 1938 in Calcutta.

Bibhuti Bhushan Bandyopadhyay

Born September 9, 1894 in Muratipur, 24 Parganas District, Bengal. First published story was *Upekshita*, which appeared in the magazine Prabasi in 1922. In a literary career of 21 years, he wrote novels, short stories, travelogues and children's stories. Was awarded the Rabindra Puraskar posthumously in 1951 for the novel *Ichhamati*. Died November1, 1950 in Ghatshila.

Tarashankar Bandyopadhyay

Born August 23, 1898 in Lovepur, Birbhum District, Bengal. Wrote several books under the pseudonym Kamandak. Many writings first appeared as stories, and later were re-written as novels or plays. Credited with numerous acclaimed stories. *Tarini Majhi* was first published in the 1935 Sharadiya Anandabazaar. Awarded the Sahitya Academy Award and the Rabindra Puraskar for *Arogya Niketan* in 1955 and 1956 respectively. Won the prestigious Jnanapith Award for *Ganadevata* in 1966. Died September 14, 1971 in Calcutta.

Saradindu Bandyopadhyay

Born March 30, 1899 in Purnia District, Bihar. In 1923, renounced his law practice to concentrate on a literary career. Wrote screenplays for films in Bombay for many years. His detective character Byomkesh remains an exceptional creation in Bengali literature. Wrote prolific works of fiction, historic novels, and suspense. Awarded the Rabindra Puraskar for *Tungabhadrar Tirey* in 1967. Died September 22, 1970 in Calcutta.

Bonophool

Born July 19, 1899 in Manihari, Purnia District, Bihar. The first of his over 100 books was *Trinakhanda*. Creator of the "micro-story" genre in Bengali literature. Received the Rabindra Puraskar in 1962 for *Hatey Bazaarey*. Also awarded the Jagattarini Gold Medal. Died February 9, 1979 in Calcutta.

Manik Bandopadhyay

Born May 29, 1908 in Dumka, Bihar. The third of the
"Bandyopadhyay triumvirate." His first story *Atasi Mami* was
published in Vichitra in 1928, and was an immediate
sensation. At age 21 wrote his acclaimed novel *Divaratrir
Kavya*. Worked professionally for a living only for 2 or 3 years.
Despite extreme penury, chose literature as his work and his
source for wages. Died December 3, 1956 in Calcutta.

Subodh Ghosh

Born September 14, 1909 in Hazaribagh, Bihar. First
published stories *Ajantrik* and *Fossil* in 1940 brought him
instant recognition. His acclaimed books include *Fossil*,
Parashuramer Kuthar, and *Manikarnika*. Received the Ananda
Puraskar and the Jagattarini Gold Medal. Was a journalist by
profession. Died March 9, 1980 in Calcutta.

Narendranath Mitra

Born January 30, 1917 in Sadardih, Faridpur District,
Bangladesh. First published story was *Mrityu O Jivan* in 1936.
First anthology of stories, *Asamatal,* was published in 1945.
First novel was *Dwippunja*. Wrote almost fifty books. Was a
journalist by profession. Received the Ananda Puraskar in
1961. Died September 14, 1975 in Calcutta.

Narayan Gangopadhyay

Born in Baliadangi, Dinajpur, in 1918. His first novel, *Upanivesh*, published serially in Bharatvarsha brought him immediate recognition as a leading author in Bengali. First published anthology of stories was *Bitangsha*. Wrote well over 100 books, including several for young readers. Received the Ananda Puraskar. Died November 8, 1970 in Calcutta.

Bimal Kar

Born September 19, 1921 near Taki, 24 Parganas District, Bengal. First published story was *Baraf Saheber Meye* in Desh in 1952. Prolific writer of highly acclaimed novels and short stories. Recipient of numerous awards, including the Sahitya Academy Awrad for the novel *Ashamay* in 1975, Ananda Puraskar in 1967, Sarat Chandra Chattopadhyay Puraskar of the University of Calcutta in 1981, and the Narasimha Das Puraskar of the University of Delhi in 1982.